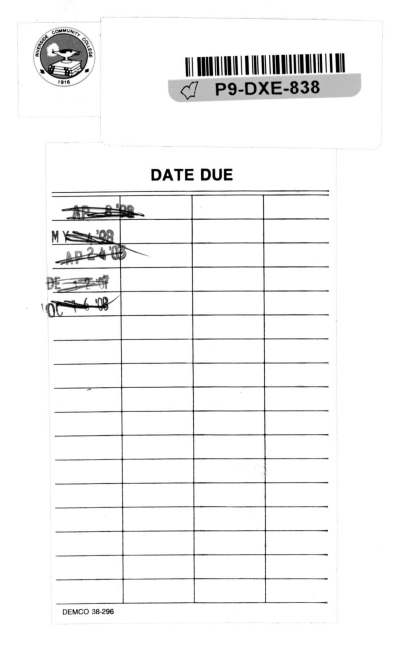

DATE DUE

THE STREET

Other Volumes in the Black Women Writers Series
Series Editor: Deborah E. McDowell

Marita Bonner/*Frye Street and Environs*
Octavia E. Butler/*Kindred*
Alice Childress/*Like One of the Family*
Frances E. W. Harper/*Iola Leroy*
Gayl Jones/*Corregidora; Eva's Man*
Ann Petry/*Miss Muriel and Other Stories; The Narrows*
Carlene Hatcher Polite/*The Flagellants*

Ann Petry

THE STREET

Beacon Press   Boston

                                                    lin" by Frances
.... .y.........y........g... ....wledgment is
hereby made to the Duo Publishing Corporation.

The characters in this book are fictitious, and any resemblance
to actual persons is accidental and unintentional.

Beacon Press
25 Beacon Street
Boston, Massachusetts 02108

Beacon Press books are published under the auspices of the
Unitarian Universalist Association of Congregations in
North America.

First published as a Beacon paperback in 1985 by arrangement
with Houghton Mifflin Company

Printed in the United States of America

92   91   8   7

Library of Congress Cataloging in Publication Data

Petry, Ann Lane, 1911–
   The street.

   Reprint. Originally published: Boston: Houghton
Mifflin, 1946.
   I. Title.
PS3531.E933S75   1985   813'.54   85-47522
ISBN 0-8070-6357-6 (pbk.)

To My Mother

BERTHA JAMES LANE

THE STREET

Chapter 1

THERE was a cold November wind blowing through 116th Street. It rattled the tops of garbage cans, sucked window shades out through the top of opened windows and set them flapping back against the windows; and it drove most of the people off the street in the block between Seventh and Eighth Avenues except for a few hurried pedestrians who bent double in an effort to offer the least possible exposed surface to its violent assault.

It found every scrap of paper along the street — theater throwaways, announcements of dances and lodge meetings, the heavy waxed paper that loaves of bread had been wrapped in, the thinner waxed paper that had enclosed sandwiches, old envelopes, newspapers. Fingering its way along the curb, the wind set the bits of paper to dancing high in the air, so that a barrage of paper swirled into the faces of the people on the street. It even took time to rush into doorways and areaways and find chicken bones and pork-chop bones and pushed them along the curb.

It did everything it could to discourage the people walking along the street. It found all the dirt and dust and grime on the sidewalk and lifted it up so that the dirt got into their noses, making it difficult to breathe; the dust got into their eyes and blinded them; and the grit stung their skins. It wrapped newspaper around their feet entangling them until the people cursed deep in their throats, stamped their feet, kicked at the paper. The wind blew it back again and again until they were forced to stoop and dislodge the paper with their hands. And then the wind grabbed their hats, pried their scarves from around their necks, stuck its fingers inside their coat collars, blew their coats away from their bodies.

The wind lifted Lutie Johnson's hair away from the back of her neck so that she felt suddenly naked and bald, for her hair had been resting softly and warmly against her skin. She shivered as the cold fingers of the wind touched the back of her neck, explored the sides of her head. It even blew her eyelashes away from her eyes so that her eyeballs were bathed in a rush of coldness and she had to blink in order to read the words on the sign swaying back and forth over her head.

Each time she thought she had the sign in focus, the wind pushed it away from her so that she wasn't certain whether it said three rooms or two rooms. If it was three, why, she would go in and ask to see it, but if it said two — why, there wasn't any point. Even with the wind twisting the sign away from her, she could see that it had been there for a long time because its original coat of white paint was streaked with rust where years of rain and snow had finally eaten the paint off down to the metal and the metal had slowly rusted, making a dark red stain like blood.

It was three rooms. The wind held it still for an instant in front of her and then swooped it away until it was standing at an impossible angle on the rod that suspended it from the building. She read it rapidly. Three rooms, steam heat, parquet floors, respectable tenants. Reasonable.

She looked at the outside of the building. Parquet floors here meant that the wood was so old and so discolored no amount of varnish or shellac would conceal the scars and the old scraped places, the years of dragging furniture across the floors, the hammer blows of time and children and drunks and dirty, slovenly women. Steam heat meant a rattling, clanging noise in radiators early in the morning and then a hissing that went on all day.

Respectable tenants in these houses where colored people were allowed to live included anyone who could pay the rent, so some of them would be drunk and loud-mouthed and quarrelsome; given to fits of depression when they would curse and cry violently, given to fits of equally violent elation. And, she thought, because the walls would be flimsy, why, the good people, the bad people, the children, the dogs, and the godawful smells would all be wrapped up together in one big package — the package that was called respectable tenants.

The Street

The wind pried at the red skullcap on her head, and as though angered because it couldn't tear it loose from its firm anchorage of bobby pins, the wind blew a great cloud of dust and ashes and bits of paper into her face, her eyes, her nose. It smacked against her ears as though it were giving her a final, exasperated blow as proof of its displeasure in not being able to make her move on.

Lutie braced her body against the wind's attack determined to finish thinking about the apartment before she went in to look at it. Reasonable — now that could mean almost anything. On Eighth Avenue it meant tenements — ghastly places not fit for humans. On St. Nicholas Avenue it meant high rents for small apartments; and on Seventh Avenue it meant great big apartments where you had to take in roomers in order to pay the rent. On this street it could mean almost anything.

She turned and faced the wind in order to estimate the street. The buildings were old with small slit-like windows, which meant the rooms were small and dark. In a street running in this direction there wouldn't be any sunlight in the apartments. Not ever. It would be hot as hell in summer and cold in winter. 'Reasonable' here in this dark, crowded street ought to be about twenty-eight dollars, provided it was on a top floor.

The hallways here would be dark and narrow. Then she shrugged her shoulders, for getting an apartment where she and Bub would be alone was more important than dark hallways. The thing that really mattered was getting away from Pop and his raddled women, and anything was better than that.

Dark hallways, dirty stairs, even roaches on the walls. Anything. Anything. Anything.

Anything? Well, almost anything. So she turned toward the entrance of the building and as she turned, she heard someone clear his or her throat. It was so distinct — done as it was on two notes, the first one high and then the grunting expiration of breath on a lower note — that it came to her ears quite clearly under the sound of the wind rattling the garbage cans and slapping at the curtains. It was as though someone had said 'hello,' and she looked up at the window over her head.

There was a faint light somewhere in the room she was looking into and the enormous bulk of a woman was silhouetted against the light. She half-closed her eyes in order to see better. The woman was very black, she had a bandanna knotted tightly around her head, and Lutie saw, with some surprise, that the window was open. She began to wonder how the woman could sit by an open window on a cold, windy night like this one. And she didn't have on a coat, but a kind of loose-looking cotton dress — or at least it must be cotton, she thought, for it had a clumsy look — bulky and wrinkled.

'Nice little place, dearie. Just ring the Super's bell and he'll show it to you.'

The woman's voice was rich. Pleasant. Yet the longer Lutie looked at her, the less she liked her. It wasn't that the woman had been sitting there all along staring at her, reading her thoughts, pushing her way into her very mind, for that was merely annoying. But it was understandable. She probably didn't have anything else to do; perhaps she was sick and the only pleasure she got out of life was in watching what went on in the street outside her window. It wasn't that. It was the woman's eyes. They were as still and as malignant as the eyes of a snake. She could see them quite plainly — flat eyes that stared at her — wandering over her body, inspecting and appraising her from head to foot.

'Just ring the Super's bell, dearie,' the woman repeated.

Lutie turned toward the entrance of the building without answering, thinking about the woman's eyes. She pushed the door open and walked inside and stood there nodding her head. The hall was dark. The low-wattage bulb in the ceiling shed just enough light so that you wouldn't actually fall over — well, a piano that someone had carelessly left at the foot of the stairs; so that you could see the outlines of — oh, possibly an elephant if it were dragged in from the street by some enterprising tenant.

However, if you dropped a penny, she thought, you'd have to get down on your hands and knees and scrabble around on the cracked tile floor before you could ever hope to find it. And she was wrong about being able to see an elephant or a piano because the hallway really wasn't wide enough to admit either one. The stairs went up steeply — dark high narrow steps. She stared at them fascinated. Going up stairs like those you ought to find a newer and more intricate — a much-involved and perfected kind of hell at the top — the very top.

She leaned over to look at the names on the mail boxes. Henry Lincoln Johnson lived here, too, just as he did in all the other houses she'd looked at.

Either he or his blood brother. The Johnsons and the Jacksons were mighty prolific. Then she grinned, thinking who am I to talk, for I, too, belong to that great tribe, that mighty mighty tribe of Johnsons. The bells revealed that the Johnsons had roomers — Smith, Roach, Anderson — holy smoke! even Rosenberg. Most of the names were inked in over the mail boxes in scrawling handwriting — the letters were big and bold on some of them. Others were written in pencil; some printed in uneven scraggling letters where names had been scratched out and other names substituted.

There were only two apartments on the first floor. And if the Super didn't live in the basement, why, he would live on the first floor. There it was printed over One A. One A must be the darkest apartment, the smallest, most unrentable apartment, and the landlord would feel mighty proud that he'd given the Super a first-floor apartment.

She stood there thinking that it was really a pity they couldn't somehow manage to rent the halls, too. Single beds. No. Old army cots would do. It would bring in so much more money. If she were a landlord, she'd rent out the hallways. It would make it so much more entertaining for the tenants. Mr. Jones and wife could have cots number one and two; Jackson and girl friend could occupy number three. And Rinaldi, who drove a cab nights, could sublet the one occupied by Jackson and girl friend.

She would fill up all the cots — row after row of them. And when the tenants who had apartments came in late at night, they would have the added pleasure of checking up on the occupants. Jackson

7

not home yet but girl friend lying in the cot alone —
all curled up. A second look, because the lack of
light wouldn't show all the details, would reveal —
ye gods, why, what's Rinaldi doing home at night!
Doggone if he ain't tucked up cozily in Jackson's cot
with Jackson's girl friend. No wonder she looked
contented. And the tenants who had apartments
would sit on the stairs just as though the hall were a
theater and the performance about to start — they'd
sit there waiting until Jackson came home to see
what he'd do when he found Rinaldi tucked into his
cot with his girl friend. Rinaldi might explain that
he thought the cot was his for sleeping and if the cot
had blankets on it did not he, too, sleep under blankets; and if the cot had girl friend on it, why should
not he, too, sleep with girl friend?

Instead of laughing, she found herself sighing.
Then it occurred to her that if there were only two
apartments on the first floor and the Super occupied
one of them, then the occupant of the other apartment would be the lady with the snake's eyes. She
looked at the names on the mail boxes. Yes. A Mrs.
Hedges lived in One B. The name was printed on the
card — a very professional-looking card. Obviously
an extraordinary woman with her bandanna on her
head and her sweet, sweet voice. Perhaps she was a
snake charmer and she sat in her window in order to
charm away at the snakes, the wolves, the foxes, the
bears that prowled and loped and crawled on their
bellies through the jungle of 116th Street.

Lutie reached out and rang the Super's bell. It
made a shrill sound that echoed and re-echoed inside
the apartment and came back out into the hall. Im-

mediately a dog started a furious barking that came closer and closer as he ran toward the door of the apartment. Then the weight of his body landed against the door and she drew back as he threw himself against the door. Again and again until the door began to shiver from the impact of his weight. There was the horrid sound of his nose snuffing up air, trying to get her scent. And then his weight hurled against the door again. She retreated toward the street door, pausing there with her hand on the knob. Then she heard heavy footsteps, the sound of a man's voice threatening the dog, and she walked back toward the apartment.

She knew instantly by his faded blue overalls that the man who opened the door was the Super. The hot fetid air from the apartment in back of him came out into the hall. She could hear the faint sound of steam hissing in the radiators. Then the dog tried to plunge past the man and the man kicked the dog back into the apartment. Kicked him in the side until the dog cringed away from him with its tail between its legs. She heard the dog whine deep in its throat and then the murmur of a woman's voice — a whispering voice talking to the dog.

'I came to see about the apartment — the three-room apartment that's vacant,' she said.

'It's on the top floor. You wanta look at it?'

The light in the hall was dim. Dim like that light in Mrs. Hedges' apartment. She pulled her coat around her a little tighter. It's this bad light, she thought. Somehow the man's eyes were worse than the eyes of the woman sitting in the window. And she told herself that it was because she was so tired; that was the reason she was seeing things, building up pretty pictures in people's eyes.

He was a tall, gaunt man and he towered in the doorway, looking at her. It isn't the bad light, she thought. It isn't my imagination. For after his first quick furtive glance, his eyes had filled with a hunger so urgent that she was instantly afraid of him and afraid to show her fear.

But the apartment — did she want the apartment? Not in this house where he was super; not in this house where Mrs. Hedges lived. No. She didn't want to see the apartment — the dark, dirty three rooms called an apartment. Then she thought of where she lived now. Those seven rooms where Pop lived with Lil, his girl friend. A place filled with roomers. A place spilling over with Lil.

There seemed to be no part of it that wasn't full of Lil. She was always swallowing coffee in the kitchen; trailing through all seven rooms in housecoats that didn't quite meet across her lush, loose bosom; drinking beer in tall glasses and leaving the glasses in the kitchen sink so the foam dried in a crust around the rim — the dark red of her lipstick like an accent mark on the crust; lounging on the wide bed she shared with Pop and only God knows who else; drinking gin with the roomers until late at night.

And what was far more terrifying giving Bub a drink on the sly; getting Bub to light her cigarettes for her. Bub at eight with smoke curling out of his mouth.

Only last night Lutie slapped him so hard that Lil cringed away from her dismayed; her housecoat slipping even farther away from the fat curve of her breasts. 'Jesus!' she said. 'That's enough to make him deaf. What's the matter with you?'

But did she want to look at the apartment? Night after night she'd come home from work and gone out right after supper to peer up at the signs in front of the apartment houses in the neighborhood, looking for a place just big enough for her and Bub. A place where the rent was low enough so that she wouldn't come home from work some night to find a long sheet of white paper stuck under the door: 'These premises must be vacated by ——' better known as an eviction notice. Get out in five days or be tossed out. Stand by and watch your furniture pile up on the sidewalk. If you could call those broken beds, worn-out springs, old chairs with the stuffing crawling out from under, chipped porcelain-topped kitchen table, flimsy kitchen chairs with broken rungs — if you could call those things furniture. That was an important point — now could you call fire-cracked china from the five-and-dime, and red-handled knives and forks and spoons that were bent and coming apart, could you really call those things furniture?

'Yes,' she said firmly. 'I want to look at the apartment.'

'I'll get a flashlight,' he said and went back into his apartment, closing the door behind him so that it made a soft, sucking sound. He said something, but she couldn't hear what it was. The whispering voice inside the apartment stopped and the dog was suddenly quiet.

Then he was back at the door, closing it behind him so it made the same soft, sucking sound. He had a long black flashlight in his hand. And she went up

the stairs ahead of him thinking that the rod of its
length was almost as black as his hands. The flashlight was a shiny black — smooth and gleaming
faintly as the light lay along its length. Whereas
the hand that held it was flesh — dull, scarred, worn
flesh — no smoothness there. The knuckles were
knobs that stood out under the skin, pulled out from
hauling ashes, shoveling coal.

But not apparently from using a mop or a broom,
for, as she went up and up the steep flight of stairs,
she saw that they were filthy, with wastepaper, cigarette butts, the discarded wrappings from packages
of snuff, pink ticket stubs from the movie houses. On
the landings there were empty gin and whiskey bottles.

She stopped looking at the stairs, stopped peering
into the corners of the long hallways, for it was cold,
and she began walking faster trying to keep warm.
As they completed a flight of stairs and turned to walk
up another hall, and then started climbing another
flight of stairs, she was aware that the cold increased.
The farther up they went, the colder it got. And in
summer she supposed it would get hotter and hotter
as you went up until when you reached the top floor
your breath would be cut off completely.

The halls were so narrow that she could reach out
and touch them on either side without having to
stretch her arms any distance. When they reached
the fourth floor, she thought, instead of her reaching
out for the walls, the walls were reaching out for her
— bending and swaying toward her in an effort to
envelop her. The Super's footsteps behind her were
slow, even, steady. She walked a little faster and
apparently without hurrying, without even increas-

ing his pace, he was exactly the same distance behind her. In fact his heavy footsteps were a little nearer than before.

She began to wonder how it was that she had gone up the stairs first, why was she leading the way? It was all wrong. He was the one who knew the place, the one who lived here. He should have gone up first. How had he got her to go up the stairs in front of him? She wanted to turn around and see the expression on his face, but she knew if she turned on the stairs like this, her face would be on a level with his; and she wouldn't want to be that close to him.

She didn't need to turn around, anyway; he was staring at her back, her legs, her thighs. She could feel his eyes traveling over her — estimating her, summing her up, wondering about her. As she climbed up the last flight of stairs, she was aware that the skin on her back was crawling with fear. Fear of what? she asked herself. Fear of him, fear of the dark, of the smells in the halls, the high steep stairs, of yourself? She didn't know, and even as she admitted that she didn't know, she felt sweat start pouring from her armpits, dampening her forehead, breaking out in beads on her nose.

The apartment was in the back of the house. The Super fished another flashlight from his pocket which he handed to her before he bent over to unlock the door very quietly. And she thought, everything he does, he does quietly.

She played the beam of the flashlight on the walls. The rooms were small. There was no window in the bedroom. At least she supposed it was the bedroom. She walked over to look at it, and then went inside for a better look. There wasn't a window — just an air shaft and a narrow one at that. She looked around the room, thinking that by the time there was a bed and a chest of drawers in it there'd be barely space enough to walk around in. At that she'd probably bump her knees every time she went past the corner of the bed. She tried to visualize how the room would look and began to wonder why she had already decided to take this room for herself.

It might be better to give it to Bub, let him have a real bedroom to himself for once. No, that wouldn't do. He would swelter in this room in summer. It would be better to have him sleep on the couch in the living room, at least he'd get some air, for there was a window out there, though it wasn't a very big one. She looked out into the living room, trying again to see the window, to see just how much air would come through, how much light there would be for Bub to study by when he came home from school, to determine, too, the amount of air that would reach into the room at night when the window was open, and he was sleeping curled up on the studio couch.

The Super was standing in the middle of the living room. Waiting for her. It wasn't anything that she had to wonder about or figure out. It wasn't by any stretch of the imagination something she had conjured up out of thin air. It was a simple fact. He was waiting for her. She knew it just as she knew she was standing there in that small room. He was holding his flashlight so the beam fell down at his feet. It turned him into a figure of never-ending tallness. And his silent waiting and his appearance of incredible height appalled her.

With the light at his feet like that, he looked as though his head must end somewhere in the ceiling. He simply went up and up into darkness. And he radiated such desire for her that she could feel it. She told herself she was a fool, an idiot, drunk on fear, on fatigue and gnawing worry. Even while she thought it, the hot, choking awfulness of his desire for her pinioned her there so that she couldn't move. It was an aching yearning that filled the apartment, pushed against the walls, plucked at her arms.

She forced herself to start walking toward the kitchen. As she went past him, it seemed to her that he actually did reach one long arm out toward her, his body swaying so that its exaggerated length almost brushed against her. She really couldn't be certain of it, she decided, and resolutely turned the beam of her flashlight on the kitchen walls.

It isn't possible to read people's minds, she argued. Now the Super was probably not even thinking about her when he was standing there like that. He probably wanted to get back downstairs to read his paper. Don't kid yourself, she thought, he probably can't read, or if he can, he probably doesn't spend any time at it. Well — listen to the radio. That was it, he probably wanted to hear his favorite program and she had thought he was filled with the desire to leap upon her. She was as bad as Granny. Which just went on to prove you couldn't be brought up by someone like Granny without absorbing a lot of nonsense that would spring at you out of nowhere, so to speak, and when you least expected it. All those tales about things that people sensed before they actually happened. Tales that had been handed down and down

and down until, if you tried to trace them back, you'd
end up God knows where — probably Africa. And
Granny had them all at the tip of her tongue.

Yet would wanting to hear a radio program make a
man look quite like that? Impatiently she forced
herself to inspect the kitchen; holding the light on
first one wall, then another. It was no better and no
worse than she had anticipated. The sink was battered; and the gas stove was a little rusted. The faint
smell of gas that hovered about it suggested a slow, in-
curable leak somewhere in its connections.

Peering into the bathroom, she saw that the fixtures
were old-fashioned and deeply chipped. She thought
Methuselah himself might well have taken baths in
the tub. Certainly it looked ancient enough, though
he'd have had to stick his beard out in the hall while
he washed himself, for the place was far too small for
a man with a full-grown beard to turn around in.
She presumed because there was no window that the
vent pipe would serve as a source of nice, fresh, clean
air.

One thing about it the rent wouldn't be very much.
It couldn't be for a place like this. Tiny hall. Bathroom on the right, kitchen straight ahead; living
room to the left of the hall and you had to go through
the living room to get to the bedroom. The whole
apartment would fit very neatly into just one good-
sized room.

She was conscious that all the little rooms smelt
exactly alike. It was a mixture that contained the
faint persistent odor of gas, of old walls, dusty plaster,
and over it all the heavy, sour smell of garbage — a
smell that seeped through the dumb-waiter shaft.

She started humming under her breath, not realizing she was doing it. It was an old song that Granny used to sing. 'Ain't no restin' place for a sinner like me. Like me. Like me.' It had a nice recurrent rhythm. 'Like me. Like me.' The humming increased in volume as she stood there thinking about the apartment.

There was a queer, muffled sound from the Super in the living room. It startled her so she nearly dropped the flashlight. 'What was that?' she said sharply, thinking, My God, suppose I'd dropped it, suppose I'd been left standing here in the dark of this little room, and he'd turned out his light. Suppose he'd started walking toward me, nearer and nearer in the dark. And I could only hear his footsteps, couldn't see him, but could hear him coming closer until I started reaching out in the dark trying to keep him away from me, trying to keep him from touching me — and then — then my hands found him right in front of me —— At the thought she gripped the flashlight so tightly that the long beam of light from it started wavering and dancing over the walls so that the shadows moved — shadow from the light fixture overhead, shadow from the tub, shadow from the very doorway itself — shifting, moving back and forth.

'I cleared my throat,' the Super said. His voice had a choked, unnatural sound as though something had gone wrong with his breathing.

She walked out into the hall, not looking at him; opened the door of the apartment and stepping over the threshold, still not looking at him, said, 'I've finished looking.'

He came out and turned the key in the lock. He kept his back turned toward her so that she couldn't have seen the expression on his face even if she'd looked at him. The lock clicked into place, smoothly. Quietly. She stood there not moving, waiting for him to start down the hall toward the stairs, thinking, Never, so help me, will he walk down those stairs in back of me.

When he didn't move, she said, 'You go first.' Then he made a slight motion toward the stairs with his flashlight indicating that she was to precede him. She shook her head very firmly.

'Think you'll take it?' he asked.

'I don't know yet. I'll think about it going down.'

When he finally started down the hall, it seemed to her that he had stood there beside her for days, weeks, months, willing her to go down the stairs first. She followed him, thinking, It wasn't my imagination when I got that feeling at the sight of him standing there in the living room; otherwise, why did he have to go through all that rigamarole of my going down the stairs ahead of him? Like going through the motions of a dance; you first; no, you first; but you see, you'll spoil the pattern if you don't go first; but I won't go first, you go first; but no, it'll spoil the ——

She was aware that they'd come up the stairs much faster than they were going down. Was she going to take the apartment? The price wouldn't be too high from the looks of it and by being careful she and Bub could manage — by being very, very careful. White paint would fix the inside of it up; not exactly

fix it up, but keep it from being too gloomy, shove the
darkness back a little.

Then she thought, Layers and layers of paint won't
fix that apartment. It would always smell; finger
marks and old stains would come through the paint;
the very smell of the wood itself would eventually
win out over the paint. Scrubbing wouldn't help
any. Then there were these dark, narrow halls, the
long flights of stairs, the Super himself, that woman
on the first floor.

Or she could go on living with Pop. And Lil.
Bub would learn to like the taste of gin, would learn
to smoke, would learn in fact a lot of other things
that Lil could teach him — things that Lil would
think it amusing to teach him. Bub at eight could
get a liberal education from Lil, for she was home all
day and Bub got home from school a little after three.

You've got a choice a yard wide and ten miles long.
You can sit down and twiddle your thumbs while
your kid gets a free education from your father's
blowsy girl friend. Or you can take this apartment.
The tall gentleman who is the superintendent is supposed to rent apartments, fire the furnace, sweep the
halls, and that's as far as he's supposed to go. If he
tries to include making love to the female tenants,
why, this is New York City in the year 1944, and as
yet there's no grass growing in the streets and the
police force still functions. Certainly you can holler
loud enough so that if the gentleman has some kind
of dark designs on you and tries to carry them out, a
cop will eventually rescue you. That's that.

As for the lady with the snake eyes, you're supposed
to be renting the top-floor apartment and if she went

with the apartment the sign out in front would say
so. Three rooms and snake charmer for respectable
tenant. No extra charge for the snake charmer
Seeing as the sign didn't say so, it stood to reason if
the snake charmer tried to move in, she could take
steps — whatever the hell that meant.

Her high-heeled shoes made a clicking noise as she
went down the stairs, and she thought, Yes, take
steps like these. It was all very well to reason light-
heartedly like that; to kid herself along — there was
no explaining away the instinctive, immediate fear
she had felt when she first saw the Super. Granny
would have said, 'Nothin' but evil, child. Some
folks so full of it you can feel it comin' at you —
oozin' right out of their skins.'

She didn't believe things like that and yet, looking
at his tall, gaunt figure going down that last flight of
stairs ahead of her, she half-expected to see horns
sprouting from behind his ears; she wouldn't have
been greatly surprised if, in place of one of the heavy
work shoes on his feet, there had been a cloven hoof
that twitched and jumped as he walked so slowly
down the stairs.

Outside the door of his apartment, he stopped and
turned toward her.

'What's the rent?' she asked, not looking at him,
but looking past him at the One A printed on the
door of his apartment. The gold letters were filled
with tiny cracks, and she thought that in a few more
years they wouldn't be distinguishable from the dark
brown of the door itself. She hoped the rent would
be so high she couldn't possibly take it.

'Twenty-nine fifty.'

He wants me to take it, she thought. He wants it so badly that he's bursting with it. She didn't have to look at him to know it; she could feel him willing it. What difference does it make to him? Yet it was of such obvious importance that if she hesitated just a little longer, he'd be trembling. No, she decided, not that apartment. Then she thought Bub would look cute learning to drink gin at eight.

'I'll take it,' she said grimly.

'You wanta leave a deposit?' he asked.

She nodded, and he opened his door, standing aside to let her go past him. There was a dim light burning in the small hall inside and she saw that the hall led into a living room. She didn't wait for an invitation, but walked on into the living room. The dog had been lying near the radio that stood under a window at the far side of the room. He got up when he saw her, walking toward her with his head down, his tail between his legs; walking as though he were drawn toward her irresistibly, even though he knew that at any moment he would be forced to stop. Though he was a police dog, his hair had such a worn, rusty look that he resembled a wolf more than a dog. She saw that he was so thin, his great haunches and the small bones of his ribs were sharply outlined against his skin. As he got nearer to her, he got excited and she could hear his breathing.

'Lie down,' the Super said.

The dog moved back to the window, shrinking and walking in such a way that she thought if he were human he'd walk backward in order to see and be able to dodge any unexpected blow. He lay down calmly enough and looked at her, but he couldn't control the twitching of his nose; he looked, too, at the Super as though he were wondering if he could possibly cross the room and get over to her without being seen.

The Super sat down in front of an old office desk, found a receipt pad, picked up a fountain pen and, carefully placing a blotter in front of him, turned toward her. 'Name?' he asked.

She swallowed an impulse to laugh. There was something so solemn about the way he'd seated himself, grasping the pen firmly, moving the pad in front of him to exactly the right angle, opening a big ledger book whose pages were filled with line after line of heavily inked writing that she thought he's acting like a big businessman about to transact a major deal.

'Mrs. Lutie Johnson. Present address 2370 Seventh Avenue.' Opening her pocketbook she took out a ten-dollar bill and handed it to him. Ten whole dollars that it had taken a good many weeks to save. By the time she had moved in here and paid the balance which would be due on the rent, her savings would have disappeared. But it would be worth it to be living in a place of her own.

He wrote with a painful slowness, concentrating on each letter, having difficulty with the numbers twenty-three seventy. He crossed it out and bit his lip. 'What was that number?' he asked.

'Twenty-three seventy,' she repeated, thinking perhaps it would be simpler to write it down for him. At the rate he was going, it would take him all of fifteen minutes to write ten dollars and then figure out the difference between ten dollars and twenty-nine dollars which would in this case constitute that innocuous looking phrase, 'the balance due.' She shouldn't be making fun of him, very likely he had taught himself to read and write after spending a couple of years in grammar school where he undoubtedly didn't learn anything. He looked to be in his fifties, but it was hard to tell.

It irritated her to stand there and watch him go through the slow, painful process of forming the letters. She wanted to get out of the place, to get back to Pop's house, plan the packing, get hold of a moving man. She looked around the room idly. The floor was uncarpeted — a terrible-looking floor. Rough and splintered. There was a sofa against the long wall; its upholstery marked by a greasy line along the back. All the people who had sat on it from the time it was new until the time it had passed through so many hands it finally ended up here must have ground their heads along the back of it.

Next to the sofa there was an overstuffed chair and she drew her breath in sharply as she looked at it, for there was a woman sitting in it, and she had thought that she and the dog and the Super were the only occupants of the room. How could anyone sit in a chair and melt into it like that? As she looked, the shapeless small dark woman in the chair got up and bowed to her without speaking.

Lutie nodded her head in acknowledgment of the bow, thinking, That must be the woman I heard whispering. The woman sat down in the chair again. Melting into it. Because the dark brown dress she wore was almost the exact shade of the dark brown of the upholstery and because the overstuffed chair swallowed her up until she was scarcely distinguishable from the chair itself. Because, too, of a shrinking withdrawal in her way of sitting as though she were trying to take up the least possible amount of space. So that after bowing to her Lutie completely forgot the woman was in the room, while she went on studying its furnishings.

No pictures, no rugs, no newspapers, no magazines, nothing to suggest anyone had ever tried to make it look homelike. Not quite true, for there was a canary huddled in an ornate birdcage in the corner. Looking at it, she thought, Everything in the room shrinks: the dog, the woman, even the canary, for it had only one eye open as it perched on one leg. Opposite the sofa an overornate table shone with varnish. It was a very large table with intricately carved claw feet and looking at it she thought, That's the kind of big ugly furniture white women love to give to their maids. She turned to look at the shapeless little woman because she was almost certain the table was hers.

The woman must have been looking at her, for when Lutie turned the woman smiled; a toothless smile that lingered while she looked from Lutie to the table.

'When you want to move in?' the Super asked, holding out the receipt.

'This is Tuesday — do you think you could have the place ready by Friday?'

'Easy,' he said. 'Some special color you want it painted?'

'White. Make all the rooms white,' she said, studying the receipt. Yes, he had it figured out correctly — balance due, nineteen fifty. He had crossed out his first attempt at the figures. Evidently nines were hard for him to make. And his name was William Jones. A perfectly ordinary name. A highly suitable name for a superintendent. Nice and normal. Easy to remember. Easy to spell. Only the name didn't fit him. For he was obviously unusual, extraordinary, abnormal. Everything about him was the exact opposite of his name. He was standing up now looking at her, eating her up with his eyes.

She took a final look around the room. The whispering woman seemed to be holding her breath; the dog was dying with the desire to growl or whine, for his throat was working. The canary, too, ought to be animated with some desperate emotion, she thought, but he had gone quietly to sleep. Then she forced herself to look directly at the Super. A long hard look, malignant, steady, continued. Thinking, That'll fix you, Mister William Jones, but, of course, if it was only my imagination upstairs, it isn't fair to look at you like this. But just in case some dark leftover instinct warned me of what was on your mind — just in case it made me know you were snuffing on my trail, slathering, slobbering after me like some dark hound of hell seeking me out, tonguing along in back of me, this look, my fine feathered friend, should give you much food for thought.

She closed her pocketbook with a sharp, clicking final sound that made the Super's eyes shift suddenly to the ceiling as though seeking out some pattern in the cracked plaster. The dog's ears straightened into sharp points; the canary opened one eye and the whispering woman almost showed her gums again, for her mouth curved as though she were about to smile.

Lutie walked quickly out of the apartment, pushed the street door open and shivered as the cold air touched her. It had been hot in the Super's apartment, and she paused a second to push her coat collar tight around her neck in an effort to make a barrier against the wind howling in the street outside. Now that she had this apartment, she was just one step farther up on the ladder of success. With the apartment Bub would be standing a better chance, for he'd be away from Lil.

Inside the building the dog let out a high shrill yelp. Immediately she headed for the street, thinking he must have kicked it again. She paused for a moment at the corner of the building, bracing herself for the full blast of the wind that would hit her head-on when she turned the corner.

'Get fixed up, dearie?' Mrs. Hedges' rich voice asked from the street-floor window.

She nodded at the bandannaed head in the window and flung herself into the wind, welcoming its attack, aware as she walked along that the woman's hard flat eyes were measuring her progress up the street.

Chapter 2

A CROWD OF PEOPLE surged in to the Eighth Avenue express at 59th Street. By elbowing other passengers in the back, by pushing and heaving, they forced their bodies into the coaches, making room for themselves where no room had existed before. As the train gathered speed for the long run to 125th Street, the passengers settled down into small private worlds, thus creating the illusion of space between them and their fellow passengers. The worlds were built up behind newspapers and magazines, behind closed eyes or while staring at the varicolored show cards that bordered the coaches.

Lutie Johnson tightened her clutch on an overhead strap, her tall long-legged body swaying back and forth as the train rocked forward toward its destination. Like some of the other passengers, she was staring at the advertisement directly in front of her and as she stared at it she became absorbed in her own thoughts. So that she, too, entered a small private world which shut out the people tightly packed around her.

For the advertisement she was looking at pictured a girl with incredible blond hair. The girl leaned close to a dark-haired, smiling man in a navy uniform. They were standing in front of a kitchen sink — a sink whose white porcelain surface gleamed under the train lights. The faucets looked like silver. The linoleum floor of the kitchen was a crisp black-and-white pattern that pointed up the sparkle of the room. Casement windows. Red geraniums in yellow pots.

It was, she thought, a miracle of a kitchen. Completely different from the kitchen of the 116th Street apartment she had moved into just two weeks ago. But almost exactly like the one she had worked in in Connecticut.

So like it that it might have been the same kitchen where she had washed dishes, scrubbed the linoleum floor and waxed it afterward. Then gone to sit on the small porch outside the kitchen, waiting for the floor to dry and wondering how much longer she would have to stay there. At the time it was the only job she could get. She had thought of it as a purely temporary one, but she had ended up by staying two years — thus earning the money for Jim and Bub to live on.

Every month when she got paid she walked to the postoffice and mailed the money to Jim. Seventy dollars. Jim and Bub could eat on that and pay the interest on the mortgage. On her first trip to the postoffice, she realized she had never seen a street like that main street in Lyme. A wide street lined with old elm trees whose branches met high overhead in the center of the street. In summer the sun could just filter through the leaves, so that by the time its rays reached the street, it made a pattern like the lace on expensive nightgowns. It was the most beautiful street she had ever seen, and finally she got so she would walk to the little postoffice hating the street, wishing that she could get back to Jamaica, back to Jim and Bub and the small frame house.

In winter the bare branches of the trees made a pattern against the sky that was equally beautiful in snow or rain or cold, clear sunlight. Sometimes she took Little Henry Chandler to the postoffice with her and she couldn't help thinking that it wasn't right. He didn't need her and Bub did. But Bub had to do without her.

And because Little Henry Chandler's father manufactured paper towels and paper napkins and paper handkerchiefs, why, even when times were hard, he could afford to hire a Lutie Johnson so his wife could play bridge in the afternoon while Lutie Johnson looked after Little Henry. Because as Little Henry's father used to say, 'Even when times are hard, thank God, people have got to blow their noses and wipe their hands and faces and wipe their mouths. Not quite so many as before, but enough so that I don't have to worry.'

Her grip on the subway strap tightened until the hard enameled surface cut into her hand and she relaxed her hand and then tightened it. Because that kitchen sink in the advertisement or one just like it was what had wrecked her and Jim. The sink had belonged to someone else — she'd been washing someone else's dishes when she should have been home with Jim and Bub. Instead she'd cleaned another woman's house and looked after another woman's child while her own marriage went to pot; breaking up into so many little pieces it couldn't be put back together again, couldn't even be patched into a vague resemblance of its former self.

Yet what else could she have done? It was her fault, really, that they lost their one source of income. And Jim couldn't get a job, though he hunted for one — desperately, eagerly, anxiously. Walking from one employment agency to another; spending long hours in the musty agency waiting-rooms, reading old newspapers. Waiting, waiting, waiting to be called up for a job. He would come home shivering from the cold, saying, 'God damn white people anyway. I don't want favors. All I want is a job. Just a job. Don't they know if I knew how I'd change the color of my skin?'

There was the interest to be paid on the mortgage. It didn't amount to much, but they didn't have anything to pay it with. So she answered an advertisement she saw in the paper. The ad said it was a job for an unusual young woman because it was in the country and most help wouldn't stay. 'Seventy-five dollars a month. Modern house. Own room and bath. Small child.'

She sat down and wrote a letter the instant she saw it; not telling Jim, hoping against hope that she would get it. It didn't say 'white only,' so she started off by saying that she was colored. And an excellent cook, because it was true — anyone who could fix good meals on practically no money at all was an excellent cook. An efficient housekeeper — because it was easy to keep their house shining, so she shouldn't have any trouble with a 'modern' one. It was a good letter, she thought, holding it in her hand a little way off from her as she studied it — nice neat writing, no misspelled words, careful margins, pretty good English. She was suddenly grateful to Pop. He'd known what he was doing when he insisted on her finishing high school. She addressed the envelope, folded the letter, and put it inside the envelope.

She was about to seal it when she remembered that she didn't have any references. She couldn't get a job without them, and as she'd never really had a job, why, she didn't have any way of getting a reference. Somehow she had been so sure she could have got the job in the ad. Seventy-five dollars a month would have meant they could have saved the house; Jim would have got over that awful desperate feeling, that bitterness that was eating him up; and there wouldn't have been any need to apply for relief.

Mrs. Pizzini. That was it. She'd go to Mrs. Pizzini where they bought their vegetables. They owed her a bill, and when she explained that this job would mean the bill would be paid, why, Mrs. Pizzini would write her out a reference.

Business was slow and Mrs. Pizzini had plenty of time to listen to Lutie's story, to study the advertisement in the paper, to follow the writing on Lutie's letter to Mrs. Henry Chandler, line by line, almost tracing the words on the page with her stubby fingers.

'Very good,' she said when she finished reading it. 'Nice job.' She handed the letter and the newspaper to Lutie. 'Me and Joe don't write so good. But my daughter that teaches school, she'll write for me. You can have tomorrow.'

And the next day Mrs. Pizzini stopped weighing potatoes for a customer long enough to go in the back of the vegetable store and bring the letter out carefully wrapped up in brown paper to keep it clean. Lutie peeled off the brown paper and read the letter through quickly. It was a fine letter, praising her for being hard-working and honest and intelligent; it said that the writer hated to lose Lutie, for she'd worked for her for two years. It was signed 'Isabel Pizzini.'

The handwriting was positively elegant, she thought, written with a fine pen and black ink on nice thick white paper. She looked at the address printed on the top and then turned to stare at Mrs. Pizzini in astonishment, because that part of Jamaica was the section where the houses were big and there was lawn around them and evergreen trees grew in thick clusters around the houses.

Mrs. Pizzini nodded her head. 'My daughter is a very smart woman.'

And then Lutie remembered the letter in her hand. 'I can't ever thank you,' she said.

Mrs. Pizzini's lean face relaxed in a smile, 'It's all right. You're a nice girl. Always known it.' She walked toward her waiting customer and then, hesitating for the barest fraction of a second, turned back to Lutie. 'Listen,' she said. 'It's best that the man do the work when the babies are young. And when the man is young. Not good for the woman to work when she's young. Not good for the man.'

Curiously enough, though she only half-heard what Mrs. Pizzini was saying, she remembered it. Off and on for the past six years she had remembered it. At the time, she hurried home from the vegetable store to put the precious reference in the letter to Mrs. Henry Chandler and mail it.

After she had dropped it in the mail box on the corner, she got to thinking about the Pizzinis. Who would have thought that the old Italian couple who ran the vegetable store would be living in a fine house in a fine neighborhood? How had they managed to do that on the nickels and dimes they took in selling lettuce and grapefruit? She wanted to tell Jim about it, but she couldn't without revealing how she knew where they lived. They had a fine house and they had sent their daughter to college, and yet Mrs. Pizzini had admitted she herself 'couldn't write so good.' She couldn't read so good either, Lutie thought. If she could find out how the Pizzinis had managed, it might help her and Jim.

Then she forgot about them, for Mrs. Chandler wrote to her sending the train fare to Lyme, telling her what train to take. When she showed Jim the letter, she was bursting with pride, filled with a jubilance she hadn't felt in months because now they could keep the house. And she need no longer feel guilty about having been responsible for losing the

State children that had been their only source of income.

'How'm I going to look after Bub and him only
two?' he asked, frowning, handing the letter back to
her, not looking at her.

Even on the day she was to leave he was sullen.
Not talking. Frowning. Staring off into space. He
came into the bedroom where she was putting carefully ironed clothes into her suitcase. He stood in
front of the window and looked out at the street, his
back turned to her, his hands in his pockets as he told
her he wouldn't be going to the station with her.

'We can't afford that extra dime for carfare,' he
explained briefly.

So she went by herself. And feeling the suitcase
bump against her legs when she walked down the
long ramp at Grand Central to get on the train, she
wished that Jim had been along to carry it. So that
she could have kissed him good-bye there in the train
shed and thus carried the memory of his lips right
onto the train with her — so that it could have
stayed with her those first few days in Lyme, helping
her to remember why she had taken the job. If he'd
come to the train with her, he would have lost that
pretended indifference; the sight of her actually getting on the train would have broken down the wall
of reserve he had built around himself. Instead of
that quick hard peck at her forehead, he would have
put his arms around her and really kissed her. Instead of holding his body rigid, keeping his arms
hanging limp and relaxed at his sides, he would have
squeezed her close to him.

As the train left the city, she stopped thinking

about him, not forgetting him, but thrusting him far back in her mind because she was going to a new strange place and she didn't want to get off the train wrapped in gloom, and that's exactly what would happen if she kept on thinking about Jim. It was important that Mrs. Henry Chandler should like her at sight, so Lutie carefully examined the country-side as the train went along, concentrating on it to shut out the picture of Jim's tall figure.

There was low, marshy land on each side of the train tracks. Where the land was like that, there were very few houses. She noticed that near the cities the houses were small and mean-looking, for they were built close to the railroad tracks. In Bridgeport the houses were blackened with soot and smoke from the factories. Then the train stopped in New Haven and stayed there for all of ten minutes. She looked at the timetable and saw that it was a scheduled stop for that length of time. Saybrook was the next stop. That's where she was to get off. And she began to worry. How would Mrs. Chandler recognize her? How would she recognize Mrs. Chandler? Suppose they missed each other. What would she do stranded in some little jerk-water town? Mrs. Chandler had said in her letter that she lived in Lyme, and Lutie began to wonder how she could get to Lyme if Mrs. Chandler didn't meet her or missed her at the station.

But almost the instant she stepped on the platform at Saybrook, a young blond woman came toward her smiling and saying, 'Hello, there. I'm Mrs. Chandler. You must be Lutie Johnson.'

Lutie looked around the platform. Very few people had got off the train, and then she wanted to laugh. She needn't have worried about Mrs. Chandler recognizing her; there wasn't another colored person in sight.

'The car's over there.' Mrs. Chandler waved in the direction of a station wagon parked in the dirt road near the platform.

Walking toward the car, Lutie studied Mrs. Chandler covertly and thought, What she's got on makes everything I'm wearing look cheap. This black coat fits too tightly and the velvet collar is all wrong, just like these high-heeled shoes and thin stockings and this wide-brimmed hat. For Mrs. Chandler wore ribbed stockings made of very fine cotton and flat-heeled moccasins of a red-brown leather that caught the light. She had on a loose-fitting tweed coat and no hat. Lutie, looking at the earrings in her ears, decided that they were real pearls and thought, Everything she has on cost a lot of money, yet she isn't very much older than I am — not more than a year or so.

Lutie didn't say anything on the ride to Lyme, for she was thinking too hard. Mrs. Chandler pointed out places as they rode along. 'The Connecticut River,' she said with a wave of her hand toward the water under the bridge they crossed. They turned off the road shortly after they crossed the river, to go for almost a mile on a country road where the trees grew so thickly Lutie began to wonder if the Chandlers lived in a forest.

Then they entered a smaller road where there were big gates and a sign that said 'private road.' The road turned and twisted through thick woods until finally they reached a large open space where there was a house. Lutie stared at it, catching her lip between her teeth; it wasn't that it was so big; there were houses in certain parts of Jamaica that were just as big as this one, but there weren't any so beautiful. She never quite got over that first glimpse of the outside of the house — so gracious with such long low lines, its white paint almost sparkling in the sun and the river very blue behind the house.

'Would you like to sort of go through the inside of the house before I show you your room?' Mrs. Chandler asked.

'Yes, ma'am,' Lutie said quietly. And wondered how she had been able to say 'yes, ma'am' so neatly and so patly. Some part of her mind must have had it already, must have already mapped out the way she was to go about keeping this job for as long as was necessary by being the perfect maid. Patient and good-tempered and hard-working and more than usually bright.

Later she was to learn that Mrs. Chandler's mother and father regarded this house as being very small. 'The children's house.' The very way they said it told her they were used to enormous places ten times the size of this and that they thought this doll-house affair cute and just right for children for a few years. Mr. Chandler's father never commented on it one way or the other. So it was impossible for Lutie to tell what he thought about it when he came to stay for an occasional week-end.

But to Lutie the house was a miracle, what with the four big bedrooms, each one with its own bath; the nursery that was as big as the bedrooms, and

under the nursery a room and bath that belonged to
her. On top of that there was a living room, a dining
room, a library, a laundry. Taken all together it was
like something in the movies, what with the size of
the rooms and the big windows that brought the river
and the surrounding woods almost into the house.
She had never seen anything like it before.

That first day when she walked into Mrs. Chandler's bedroom her breath had come out in an in-
voluntary 'Oh!'

'You like it?' Mrs. Chandler asked, smiling.

Lutie nodded and then remembered and said, 'Yes,
ma'am.' She looked at the room, thinking there
wasn't any way she could say what this bedroom
looked like to her when all her life she had slept on
couches in living rooms, in cubicles that were little
more than entrances to and exits from other rooms
that were rented out to roomers; when the first real
bedroom she ever had was that small one in Jamaica,
where if you weren't careful you would bump your
head on the low-hanging ceiling, for the dormer
window only raised the ceiling right where the window was.

No, she decided, there wasn't any way to explain
what this room looked like to her. It ran across one
whole end of the house so that windows looked out
on the river, out on the gardens in front, out on the
woods at the side. It was covered from wall to wall
with thick red carpet and right near the fourposter
bed was a round white rug — a rug with pile so deep
it looked like fur. Muted chintz draperies gleamed
softly at the windows, formed the petticoat on the
bed, covered the chaise longue in front of the win-

dows that faced the river and the pair of chairs drawn up near the fireplace.

The rest of the house was just as perfect as Mrs. Chandler's bedroom. Even her room — the maid's room with its maple furniture and vivid draperies — that, too, was perfect. Little Henry Chandler, who was two years older than Bub, was also perfect — that is, he wasn't spoiled or anything. Just a nice, happy kid, liking her at once, always wanting to be with her. The Chandlers called him Little Henry because his father's name was Henry. She thought it funny at first, because colored people always called their children 'Junior' or 'Sonnie' when the kid's name was the same as his father's. But she had to admit that calling a kid Little Henry gave him a certain dignity and a status all his own, while it prevented confusion, for there was no mistaking whom you were talking about.

Yes. The whole thing was perfect. Mr. Chandler was young and attractive and obviously made plenty of money. Yet after six months of living there she was uneasily conscious that there was something wrong. She wasn't too sure that Mrs. Chandler was overfond of Little Henry; she never held him on her lap or picked him up and cuddled him the way mothers do their children. She was always pushing him away from her.

Mr. Chandler drank too much. Most people wouldn't have noticed it, but having lived with Pop who had an unquenchable thirst it was easy for her to recognize all the signs of a hard drinker. Mr. Chandler's hands were shaking when he came down for breakfast and he had to have a pick-up before he could even face a cup of coffee. When he came in the house at night, the first thing he did was to get himself a good-sized drink. It was almost impossible for her to keep full bottles in the liquor cabinet, their contents disappeared in no time at all.

'Guess Lutie forgot to put a new supply in the bar,' Mr. Chandler would say when she came in in answer to his ring.

'Yes, sir,' she would say quietly and go to get more bottles.

The funny thing about it was that Mrs. Chandler never noticed. After a while Lutie discovered that Mrs. Chandler never noticed anything about Mr. Chandler anyway. Yet she was awfully nice; she was always laughing; she had a great many young friends who dressed just like she did — some of them even had small children about the age of Little Henry.

But she didn't like Mrs. Chandler's friends much. They came to the house to luncheon parties or to bridge parties in the afternoon. Either they ate like horses or they didn't eat at all, because they were afraid they would get too fat. And she never could decide which irritated her the most, to see them gulp down the beautiful food she had fixed, eating it so fast they really didn't taste it, or to see them toy with it, pushing it around on their plates.

Whenever she entered a room where they were, they stared at her with a queer, speculative look. Sometimes she caught snatches of their conversation about her. 'Sure, she's a wonderful cook. But I wouldn't have any good-looking colored wench in my house. Not with John. You know they're al-

ways making passes at men. Especially white men.'
And then, 'Now I wonder —— '

After that she continued to wait on them quietly,
efficiently, but she wouldn't look at them — she
looked all around them. It didn't make her angry
at first. Just contemptuous. They didn't know she
had a big handsome husband of her own; that she
didn't want any of their thin unhappy husbands.
But she wondered why they all had the idea that
colored girls were whores.

It was, she discovered slowly, a very strange world
that she had entered. With an entirely different set
of values. It made her feel that she was looking
through a hole in a wall at some enchanted garden.
She could see, she could hear, she spoke the language
of the people in the garden, but she couldn't get past
the wall. The figures on the other side of it loomed up
life-size and they could see her, but there was this
wall in between which prevented them from mingling
on an equal footing. The people on the other side of
the wall knew less about her than she knew about
them.

She decided it wasn't just because she was a maid;
it was because she was colored. No one assumed
that the young girl from the village who came in to
help when they had big dinner parties would eagerly
welcome any advances made toward her by the male
guests. Even the man who mowed the lawn and
washed the windows and weeded the garden didn't
move behind a wall that effectively and automatically placed him in some previously prepared classi-
fication. One day when he was going to New Haven,
Mrs. Chandler drove him to the railroad station in

Saybrook, and when he got out of the car Lutie saw her shake hands with him just as though he had been an old friend or one of her departing week-end guests.

When she was in high school she had believed that white people wanted their children to be president of the United States; that most of them worked hard with that goal in mind. And if not president — well, perhaps a cabinet member. Even the Pizzinis' daughter had got to be a school-teacher, showing that they, too, had wanted more learning and knowledge in the family.

But these people were different. Apparently a college education was all right, and seemed to have become a necessity even in the business world they talked about all the time. But not important. Mr. Chandler and his friends had gone through Yale and Harvard and Princeton, casually, matter-of-factly, and because they had to. But once these men went into business they didn't read anything but trade magazines and newspapers.

She had watched Mr. Chandler reading the morning newspaper while he ate his breakfast. He riffled through the front pages where the news was, and then almost immediately turned to the financial section. He spent quite a while reading that, and then, if he had time, he would look at the sports pages. And he was through. She could tell by looking at him that the effort of reading had left him a little tired just like Pop or Mrs. Pizzini. Mr. Chandler's father did the same thing. So did the young men who came up from New York to spend the week-end.

No. They didn't want their children to be president or diplomats or anything like that. What they wanted was to be rich — 'filthy' rich, as Mr. Chandler called it.

When she brought the coffee into the living room after dinner, the conversation was always the same.

'Richest damn country in the world ——'

'Always be new markets. If not here in South America, Africa, India —— Everywhere and anywhere ——'

'Hell! Make it while you're young. Anyone can do it ——'

'Outsmart the next guy. Think up something before anyone else does. Retire at forty ——'

It was a world of strange values where the price of something called Tell and Tell and American Nickel and United States Steel had a direct effect on emotions. When the price went up everybody's spirits soared; if it went down they were plunged in gloom.

After a year of listening to their talk, she absorbed some of the same spirit. The belief that anybody could be rich if he wanted to and worked hard enough and figured it out carefully enough. Apparently that's what the Pizzinis had done. She and Jim could do the same thing, and she thought she saw what had been wrong with them before — they hadn't tried hard enough, worked long enough, saved enough. There hadn't been any one thing they wanted above and beyond everything else. These people had wanted only one thing — more and more money — and so they got it. Some of this new philosophy crept into her letters to Jim.

When she first went to work for the Chandlers,

Mrs. Chandler had suggested that, instead of her taking one day off a week, it would be a good idea if she took four days off right together all at once at the end of a month; pointing out that that way Lutie could go home to Jamaica and not have to turn right around and come back. As Lutie listened to the conversations in the Chandlers' house, she came more and more under the influence of their philosophy. As a result she began going home only once in two months, pointing out to Jim how she could save the money she would have spent for train fare.

She soon discovered that the Chandlers didn't spend very much time at home in spite of their big perfect house. They always went out in the evening unless they had guests of their own. After she had been there a year and a half, she discovered, too, that Mrs. Chandler paid a lot more attention to other women's husbands than she did to her own. After a dinner party, Mrs. Chandler would walk through the garden with someone else's husband, showing him the river view, talking to him with an animation she never showed when talking to Mr. Chandler. And, Lutie observed from the kitchen window, leaning much too close to him.

Once, when Lutie went into the living room, Mrs. Chandler was sitting on the window-seat with one of the dinner guests and his arms were tight around her and he was kissing her. Mr. Chandler came right in behind Lutie, so that he saw the same thing. The expression on his face didn't change — only his lips went into a straight thin line.

Two weeks before Christmas, Mrs. Chandler's mother came for a visit. A tall, thin woman with cold gray eyes and hair almost exactly the same color as her eyes. She took one look at Lutie and hardly let her get out of the door before she was leaning across the dining-room table to say in a clipped voice that carried right out into the kitchen: 'Now I wonder if you're being wise, dear. That girl is unusually attractive and men are weak. Besides, she's colored and you know how they are ——'

Lutie moved away from the swinging door to stand way over by the stove so she couldn't hear the rest of it. Queer how that was always cropping up. Here she was highly respectable, married, mother of a small boy, and, in spite of all that, knowing all that, these people took one look at her and immediately got that now-I-wonder look. Apparently it was an automatic reaction of white people — if a girl was colored and fairly young, why, it stood to reason she had to be a prostitute. If not that — at least sleeping with her would be just a simple matter, for all one had to do was make the request. In fact, white men wouldn't even have to do the asking because the girl would ask them on sight.

She grew angrier as she thought about it. Of course, none of them could know about your grandmother who had brought you up, she said to herself. And ever since you were big enough to remember the things that people said to you, had said over and over, just like a clock ticking, 'Lutie, baby, don't you never let no white man put his hands on you. They ain't never willin' to let a black woman alone. Seems like they all got a itch and a urge to sleep with 'em. Don't you never let any of 'em touch you.'

Something that was said so often and with such

gravity it had become a part of you, just like breathing, and you would have preferred crawling in bed with a rattlesnake to getting in bed with a white man. Mrs. Chandler's friends and her mother couldn't possibly know that, couldn't possibly imagine that you might have a distrust and a dislike of white men far deeper than the distrust these white women had of you. Or know that, after hearing their estimation of you, nothing in the world could ever force you to be even friendly with a white man.

And again she thought of the barrier between her and these people. The funny part of it was she was willing to trust them and their motives without questioning, but the instant they saw the color of her skin they knew what she must be like; they were so confident about what she must be like they didn't need to know her personally in order to verify their estimate.

The night before Christmas Mr. Chandler's brother arrived — a tall, sardonic-looking man. His name was Jonathan, and Mrs. Chandler smiled at him with a warmth Lutie had never seen on her face before. Mr. Chandler didn't have much to say to him and Mrs. Chandler's mother pointedly ignored him.

Lutie heard them arguing in the living room long after she had gone to bed. An argument that grew more and more violent, with Mrs. Chandler screaming and Mr. Chandler shouting and Mrs. Chandler's mother bellowing any time the other voices stopped. She drifted off to sleep, thinking that it was nice to know white people had loud common fights just like colored people.

Right after breakfast, everybody went into the

living room to see the Christmas tree and open their presents. Lutie went along, too, with Little Henry by the hand. It was a big tree, and even though Lutie had helped Mrs. Chandler's mother decorate it the day before, she couldn't get over how it looked standing there in front of the river windows, going up and up, all covered with tinsel and stars and brilliantly colored baubles.

Everybody got down on the floor near the tree to sort out and open the presents. Lutie happened to look up because Jonathan Chandler had moved away from the tree, and she wondered if he was looking for an ash tray because there was one right on the small table near the tree and he didn't need to go all the way across the room to find one. So she saw him reach into the drawer in the secretary. Reach in and get Mr. Chandler's revolver and stand there a moment fingering it. He walked back toward the tree, and she couldn't figure out whether he had put the gun back or not. Because he had closed the drawer quickly. She couldn't see his hand because he had it held a little in back of him.

Mrs. Chandler was holding out a package to Lutie and she looked at her to see why she didn't take it and then followed the direction of Lutie's eyes. So that she, too, became aware that Jonathan Chandler was walking right toward the Christmas tree and saw him stop just a little way away from it.

Lutie knew suddenly what he was going to do and she started to get up from the floor to try and stop him. But she was too late. He drew the gun out quickly and fired it. Held it under his ear and pulled the trigger.

After that there was so much confusion that Lutie only remembered a few things here and there. Mrs. Chandler started screaming and went on and on and on until Mr. Chandler said roughly, 'Shut up, God damn you!'

She stopped then. But it was worse after she stopped because she just sat there on the floor staring into space.

Mrs. Chandler's mother kept saying: 'The nerve of him. The nerve of him. Deliberately embarrassing us. And on Christmas morning, too.'

Mr. Chandler poured drink after drink of straight whiskey and then, impatiently shoving the small glass aside, raised the bottle to his lips letting its contents literally run down his throat. Lutie watched him, wondering why none of them said a word about it's being a shame; thinking they acted worse and sounded worse than any people she had ever seen before.

Then she forgot about them, for she happened to look down at Little Henry crouching on the floor, his small face so white, so frightened, that she very nearly cried. None of them had given him a thought; they had deserted him as neatly as though they had deposited him on the doorstep of a foundling hospital. She picked him up and held him close to her, letting him get the feel of her arms around him; telling him through her arms that his world had not suddenly collapsed about him, that the strong arms holding him so close were a solid, safe place where he belonged, where he was safe. She made small, comforting noises under her breath until some of the whiteness left his face. Then she carried him out into the kitchen and held him on her lap and rocked him back and forth in her arms until the fright went out of his eyes.

After Mr. Chandler's brother killed himself in the living room, she didn't lose her belief in the desirability of having money, though she saw that mere possession of it wouldn't necessarily guarantee happiness. What was more important, she learned that when one had money there were certain unpleasant things one could avoid — even things like a suicide in the family.

She never found out what had prompted Jonathan Chandler to kill himself. She wasn't too interested. But she was interested in the way in which money transformed a suicide she had seen committed from start to finish in front of her very eyes into 'an accident with a gun.' It was done very neatly, too. Mrs. Chandler's mother simply called Mrs. Chandler's father in Washington. Lutie overheard the tail-end of the conversation, 'Now you get it fixed up. Oh, yes, you can. He was cleaning a gun.'

And Mr. Chandler talked very quietly but firmly to the local doctor and to the coroner. It took several rye highballs and some of the expensive imported cigars, and Lutie could only conjecture what else, but it ended up as an accident with a gun on the death certificate. Everybody was sympathetic — so tragic to have it happen on Christmas morning right in the Chandlers' living room.

However, after the accident both Mr. and Mrs. Chandler started drinking far too much. And Mrs. Chandler's mother arrived more and more often to stay two and three weeks at a time. There were

three cars in the garage now instead of two. And
Mrs. Chandler had a personal maid and there was
talk of getting a bigger house. But Mrs. Chandler
seemed to care less and less about everything and
anything — even the bridge games and parties.

She kept buying new clothes. Dresses and coats
and suits. And after wearing them a few times, she
would give them to Lutie because she was tired of
looking at them. And Lutie accepted them gravely,
properly grateful. The clothes would have fitted her
perfectly, but some obstinacy in her that she couldn't
overcome prevented her from ever wearing them.
She mailed them to Pop's current girl friend, taking
an ironic pleasure in the thought that Mrs. Chandler's
beautiful clothes Designed For Country Living would
be showing up nightly in the gin mill at the corner of
Seventh Avenue and 110th Street.

For in those two years with the Chandlers she had
learned all about Country Living. She learned about
it from the pages of the fat sleek magazines Mrs.
Chandler subscribed for and never read. *Vogue*,
Town and Country, *Harper's Bazaar*, *House and Garden*,
House Beautiful. Mrs. Chandler didn't even bother
to take them out of their wrappings when they came
in the mail, but handed them to Lutie, saying, 'Here,
Lutie. Maybe you'd like to look at this.'

A bookstore in New York kept Mrs. Chandler
supplied with all the newest books, but she never
read them. Handed them to Lutie still in their
wrappings just like the magazines. And Lutie decided that it was almost like getting a college education free of charge. Besides, Mrs. Chandler was
really very nice to her. The wall between them

wasn't quite so high. Only it was still there, of course.

Sometimes, when she was going to Jamaica, Mrs. Chandler would go to New York. And they would take the same train. On the ride down they would talk — about some story being played up in the newspapers, about clothes or some moving picture.

But when the train pulled into Grand Central, the wall was suddenly there. Just as they got off the train, just as the porter was reaching for Mrs. Chandler's pigskin luggage, the wall suddenly loomed up. It was Mrs. Chandler's voice that erected it. Her voice high, clipped, carrying, as she said, 'I'll see you on Monday, Lutie.'

There was a firm note of dismissal in her voice so that the other passengers pouring off the train turned to watch the rich young woman and her colored maid; a tone of voice that made people stop to hear just when it was the maid was to report back for work. Because the voice unmistakably established the relation between the blond young woman and the brown young woman.

And it never failed to stir resentment in Lutie. She argued with herself about it. Of course, she was a maid. She had no illusions about that. But would it hurt Mrs. Chandler just once to talk at that moment of parting as though, however incredible it might seem to anyone who was listening, they were friends? Just two people who knew each other and to whom it was only incidental that one of them was white and the other black?

Even while she argued with herself, she was answering in a noncommittal voice, 'Yes, ma'am.'

And took her battered suitcase up the ramp herself, hastening, walking faster and faster, hurrying toward home and Jim and Bub. To spend four days cleaning house and holding Bub close to her and trying to hold Jim close to her, too, in spite of the gap that seemed to have grown a little wider each time she came home.

She had been at the Chandlers exactly two years on the day she got the letter from Pop. She held it in her hand before she opened it. There was something terribly wrong if Pop had gone to all the trouble of writing a letter. If the baby was sick, he would have phoned. Jim couldn't be sick, because Pop would have phoned about that, too. Because he had the number of the Chandlers' telephone. She had given it to him when she first came here to work. Reluctantly she opened the envelope. It was a very short note: *Dear Lutie: You better come home. Jim's carrying on with another woman. Pop.*

It was like having the earth suddenly open up so that it turned everything familiar into a crazy upside down position, so that she could no longer find any of the things that had once been hers. And she was filled with fear because she might not ever be able to find them again. She looked at the letter for a third, a fourth, a fifth time, and it still said the same thing. That Jim had fallen for some other woman. And it must be something pretty serious if it so alarmed Pop that he actually wrote her a letter about it. She thought Pop can't suddenly have turned moral — Pop who had lived with so many Mamies and Lauras and Mollies that he must have long since forgotten some of them himself. So it must be that Jim had admitted some kind of permanent attachment for this woman whoever she was.

She thrust the thought away from her and went to tell Mrs. Chandler that she had to go home that very day because the baby was seriously ill. She couldn't bring herself to tell her what the real trouble was because, if Mrs. Chandler was anything like her mother, she took it for granted that all colored people were immoral and Lutie saw no reason for providing further evidence.

On the train she kept remembering Mrs. Pizzini's words: 'Not good for the woman to work when she's young. Not good for the man.' Queer. Though she hadn't paid too much attention at the time, just remembering the words made her see the whole inside of the vegetable store again. The pale yellow color of the grapefruit, dark green of mustard greens and spinach. The patient brown color of the potatoes. The delicate green of the heads of lettuce. She could see Mrs. Pizzini's dark weather-beaten skin and remembered how Mrs. Pizzini had hesitated and then turned back to say: 'It's best that the man do the work when the babies are young.'

She forgot that Jim wasn't expecting her as she hurried to the little frame house in Jamaica, not thinking about anything except the need to get there quickly, quickly, before every familiar thing she knew had been destroyed.

Still hurrying, she opened the front door and walked in. Walked into her own house to find there was another woman living there with Jim. A slender, dark brown girl whose eyes shifted crazily when she saw her. The girl was cooking supper and Jim was sitting at the kitchen table watching her.

If he hadn't held her arms, she would have killed the other girl. Even now she could feel rage rise inside her at the very thought. There she had been sending practically all her wages, month after month, keeping only a little for herself; skimping on her visits because of the carfare and because she was trying to save enough money to form a backlog for them when she quit her job. Month after month and that black bitch had been eating the food she bought, sleeping in her bed, making love to Jim.

He forced her into a chair and held her there while the girl packed and got out. When Lutie finally cooled off enough to be able to talk coherently, he only laughed at her. Even when he saw that she was getting into a red rage at the sight of his laughter.

'What did you expect?' he asked. 'Maybe you can go on day after day with nothing to do but just cook meals for yourself and a kid. With just enough money to be able to eat and have a roof over your head. But I can't. And I don't intend to.'

'Why didn't you say so?' she asked fiercely. 'Why did you let me go on working for those white people and not tell me ——'

He only shrugged and laughed. That was all she could get out of him — laughter. What's the use — what's the point — who cares? If even once he had put his arms around her and said he was sorry and asked her to forgive him, she would have stayed. But he didn't. So she called a moving man and had him take all the furniture that was hers. Everything that belonged to her: the scarred bedroom set, the radio, the congoleum rug, a battered studio couch, an easy-chair — and Bub. She wasn't going to leave him behind for Jim to abuse or ignore as he saw fit.

She and Bub went to live with Pop in that crowded, musty flat on Seventh Avenue. She hunted for a job with a grim persistence that was finally rewarded, for two weeks later she went to work as a hand presser in a steam laundry. It was hot. The steam was unbearable. But she forced herself to go to night school — studying shorthand and typing and filing. Every time it seemed as though she couldn't possibly summon the energy to go on with the course, she would remind herself of all the people who had got somewhere in spite of the odds against them. She would think of the Chandlers and their young friends — 'It's the richest damn country in the world.'

Mrs. Chandler wrote her a long letter and Jim forwarded it to her from Jamaica. '*Lutie dear: We haven't had a decent thing to eat since you left. And Little Henry misses you so much he's almost sick* ——' She didn't answer it. She had more problems than Mrs. Chandler and Little Henry had and they could always find somebody to solve theirs if they paid enough.

It took a year and a half before she mastered the typing, because at night she was so tired when she went to the business school on 125th Street she couldn't seem to concentrate on what she was doing. Her back ached and her arms felt as though they had been pulled out of their sockets. But she finally acquired enough speed so that she could take a civil service examination. For she had made up her mind that she wasn't going to wash dishes or work in a laundry in order to earn a living for herself and Bub.

Another year dragged by. A year in which she

passed four or five exams each time way down on the list. A year that she spent waiting and waiting for an appointment and taking other exams. Four years of the steam laundry and then she got an appointment as a file clerk.

That kitchen in Connecticut had changed her whole life — that kitchen all tricks and white enamel like this one in the advertisement. The train roared into 125th Street and she began pushing her way toward the doors, turning to take one last look at the advertisement as she left the car.

On the platform she hurried toward the downtown side and elbowed her way toward the waiting local. Only a few minutes and she would be at 116th Street. She didn't have any illusions about 116th Street as a place to live, but at the moment it represented a small victory — one of a series which were the result of her careful planning. First the white-collar job, then an apartment of her own where she and Bub would be by themselves away from Pop's boisterous friends, away from Lil with her dyed hair and strident voice, away from the riff-raff roomers who made it possible for Pop to pay his rent. Even after living on 116th Street for two weeks, the very fact of being there was still a victory.

As for the street, she thought, getting up at the approaching station signs, she wasn't afraid of its influence, for she would fight against it. Streets like 116th Street or being colored, or a combination of both with all it implied, had turned Pop into a sly old man who drank too much; had killed Mom off when she was in her prime.

In that very apartment house in which she was

now living, the same combination of circumstances had evidently made the Mrs. Hedges who sat in the street-floor window turn to running a fairly well-kept whorehouse — but unmistakably a whorehouse; and the superintendent of the building — well, the street had pushed him into basements away from light and air until he was being eaten up by some horrible obsession; and still other streets had turned Min, the woman who lived with him, into a drab drudge so spineless and so limp she was like a soggy dishrag. None of those things would happen to her, Lutie decided, because she would fight back and never stop fighting back.

She got off the train, thinking that she never felt really human until she reached Harlem and thus got away from the hostility in the eyes of the white women who stared at her on the downtown streets and in the subway. Escaped from the openly appraising looks of the white men whose eyes seemed to go through her clothing to her long brown legs. On the trains their eyes came at her furtively from behind newspapers, or half-concealed under hatbrims or partly shielded by their hands. And there was a warm, moist look about their eyes that made her want to run.

These other folks feel the same way, she thought — that once they are freed from the contempt in the eyes of the downtown world, they instantly become individuals. Up here they are no longer creatures labeled simply 'colored' and therefore all alike. She noticed that once the crowd walked the length of the platform and started up the stairs toward the street it expanded in size. The same people who had made themselves small on the train, even on the platform, suddenly grew so large they could hardlv get up the stairs to the street together. She reached the street at the very end of the crowd and stood watching them as they scattered in all directions, laughing and talk-ing to each other.

Chapter 3

AFTER she came out of the subway, Lutie walked slowly up the street, thinking that having solved one problem there was always a new one cropping up to take its place. Now that she and Bub were living alone, there was no one to look out for him after school. She had thought he could eat lunch at school, for it didn't cost very much — only fifty cents a week.

But after three days of school lunches, Bub protested, 'I can't eat that stuff. They give us soup every day. And I hate it.'

As soon as she could afford to, she would take an afternoon off from work and visit the school so that she could find out for herself what the menus were like. But until then, Bub would have to eat lunch at home, and that wasn't anything to worry about. It was what happened to him after school that made her frown as she walked along, for he was either in the apartment by himself or playing in the street.

She didn't know which was worse — his being alone in those dreary little rooms or his playing in the street where the least of the dangers confronting him came from the stream of traffic which roared through 116th Street: crosstown buses, postoffice trucks, and newspaper delivery cars that swooped up and down the street turning into the avenues without warning. The traffic was an obvious threat to his safety that he could see and dodge. He was too young to recognize and avoid other dangers in the street. There were, for instance, gangs of young boys who were always on the lookout for small fry Bub's age, because they found young kids useful in getting in through narrow fire-escape windows, in distracting a storekeeper's attention while the gang light-heartedly helped itself to his stock.

Then, in spite of the small, drab apartment and the dent that moving into it had made in her week's pay and the worry about Bub that crept into her thoughts, she started humming under her breath as she went along, increasing her stride so that she was walking faster and faster because the air was crisp and clear and her long legs felt strong and just the motion of walking sent blood bubbling all through her body so that she could feel it. She came to an abrupt halt in the middle of the block because she suddenly remembered that she had completely forgotten to shop for dinner.

The butcher shop that she entered on Eighth

Avenue was crowded with customers, so that she had ample time to study the meat in the case in front of her before she was waited on. There wasn't, she saw, very much choice — ham hocks, lamb culls, bright-red beef. Someone had told Granny once that the butchers in Harlem used embalming fluid on the beef they sold in order to give it a nice fresh color. Lutie didn't believe it, but like a lot of things she didn't believe, it cropped up suddenly out of nowhere to leave her wondering and staring at the brilliant scarlet color of the meat. It made her examine the contents of the case with care in order to determine whether there was something else that would do for dinner. No, she decided. Hamburger would be the best thing to get. It cooked quickly, and a half-pound of it mixed with breadcrumbs would go a long way.

The butcher, a fat red-faced man with a filthy apron tied around his enormous stomach, joked with the women lined up at the counter while he waited on them. A yellow cat sitting high on a shelf in back of him blinked down at the customers. One of his paws almost touched the edge of a sign that said 'No Credit.' The sign was fly-specked and dusty; its edges curling back from heat.

'Kitty had her meat today?' a thin black woman asked as she smiled up at the cat.

'Sure thing,' and the butcher roared with laughter, and the women laughed with him until the butcher shop was so full of merriment it sounded as though it were packed with happy, carefree people.

It wasn't even funny, Lutie thought. Yet the women rocked and roared with laughter as though they had heard some tremendous joke, went on laughing until finally there were only low chuckles and an occasional half-suppressed snort of laughter left in them. For all they knew, she thought resentfully, the yellow cat might yet end up in the meat-grinder to emerge as hamburger. Or perhaps during the cold winter months the butcher might round up all the lean, hungry cats that prowled through the streets; herding them into his back room to skin them and grind them up to make more and more hamburger that would be sold way over the ceiling price.

'A half-pound of hamburger,' was all she said when the butcher indicated it was her turn to be waited on. A half-pound would take care of tonight's dinner and Bub could have a sandwich of it when he came home for lunch.

She watched the butcher slap the hamburger on a piece of waxed paper; fold the paper twice, and slip the package into a brown paper bag. Handing him a dollar bill, she tucked the paper bag under her arm and held her pocketbook in the other hand so that he would have to put the change down on the counter. She never accepted change out of his hand, and watching him put it on the counter, she wondered why. Because she didn't want to touch his chapped roughened hands? Because he was white and forcing him to make the small extra effort of putting the change on the counter gave her a feeling of power?

Holding the change loosely in her hand, she walked out of the shop and turned toward the grocery store next door, where she paused for a moment in the doorway to look back at 116th Street. The sun was going down in a blaze of brilliant color that

bathed the street in a glow of light. It looked, she
thought, like any other New York City street in a
poor neighborhood. Perhaps a little more down-at-
the-heels. The windows of the houses were dustier
and there were more small stores on it than on streets
in other parts of the city. There were also more
children playing in the street and more people walking about aimlessly.

She stepped inside the grocery store, thinking that
her apartment would do for the time being, but the
next step she should take would be to move into a
better neighborhood. As she had been able to get
this far without help from anyone, why, all she had
to do was plan each step and she could get wherever
she wanted to go. A wave of self-confidence swept
over her and she thought, I'm young and strong,
there isn't anything I can't do.

Her arms were full of small packages when she left
Eighth Avenue — the hamburger, a pound of potatoes, a can of peas, a piece of butter. Besides six
hard rolls that she bought instead of bread — big
rolls with brown crusty outsides. They were good
with coffee in the morning and Bub could have one
for his lunch tomorrow with the hamburger left
over from dinner.

She walked slowly, avoiding the moment when she
must enter the apartment and start fixing dinner.
She shifted the packages into a more comfortable
position and feeling the hard roundness of the rolls
through the paper bag, she thought immediately of
Ben Franklin and his loaf of bread. And grinned
thinking, You and Ben Franklin. You ought to take
one out and start eating it as you walk along 116th

Street. Only you ought to remember while you eat that you're in Harlem and he was in Philadelphia a pretty long number of years ago. Yet she couldn't get rid of the feeling of self-confidence and she went on thinking that if Ben Franklin could live on a little bit of money and could prosper, then so could she. In spite of the cost of moving the furniture, if she and Bub were very careful they would have more than enough to last until her next pay-day; there might even be a couple of dollars over. If they were very careful.

The glow from the sunset was making the street radiant. The street is nice in this light, she thought. It was swarming with children who were playing ball and darting back and forth across the sidewalk in complicated games of tag. Girls were skipping double dutch rope, going tirelessly through the exact center of a pair of ropes, jumping first on one foot and then the other. All the way from the corner she could hear groups of children chanting, 'Down in Mississippi and a bo-bo push! Down in Mississippi and a bo-bo push!' She stopped to watch them, and she wanted to put her packages down on the sidewalk and jump with them; she found her foot was patting the sidewalk in the exact rhythm of their jumping and her hands were ready to push the jumper out of the rope at the word 'push.'

You'd better get your dinner started, Ben Franklin, she said to herself and walked on past the children who were jumping rope. All up and down the street kids were shining shoes. 'Shine, Miss? Shine, Miss?' the eager question greeted her on all sides.

She ignored the shoeshine boys. The weather had

changed, she thought. Just last week it was freezing cold and now there was a mildness in the air that suggested early spring and the good weather had brought a lot of people out on the street. Most of the women had been marketing, for they carried bulging shopping bags. She noticed how heavily they walked on feet that obviously hurt despite the wide, cracked shoes they wore. They've been out all day working in the white folks' kitchens, she thought, then they come home and cook and clean for their own families half the night. And again she remembered Mrs. Pizzini's words, 'Not good for the woman to work when she's young. Not good for the man.' Obviously she had been right, for here on this street the women trudged along overburdened, overworked, their own homes neglected while they looked after someone else's while the men on the street swung along empty-handed, well dressed, and carefree. Or they lounged against the sides of the buildings, their hands in their pockets while they stared at the women who walked past, probably deciding which woman they should select to replace the wife who was out working all day.

And yet, she thought, what else is a woman to do when her man can't get a job? What else had there been for her to do that time Jim couldn't get a job? She didn't know, and she lingered in the sunlight watching a group of kids who were gathered around a boy fishing through a grating in the street. She looked down through the grating, curious to see what odds and ends had floated down under the sidewalk. And again she heard that eager question, 'Shine, Miss? Shine, Miss?'

She walked on, thinking, That's another thing. These kids should have some better way of earning money than by shining shoes. It was all wrong. It was like conditioning them beforehand for the rôle they were supposed to play. If they start out young like this shining shoes, they'll take it for granted they've got to sweep floors and mop stairs the rest of their lives.

Just before she reached her own door, she heard the question again, 'Shine, Miss?' And then a giggle. 'Gosh, Mom, you didn't even know me.'

She turned around quickly and she was so startled she had to look twice to be sure. Yes. It was Bub. He was sitting astride a shoeshine box, his round head silhouetted against the brick wall of the apartment house behind him. He was smiling at her, utterly delighted that he had succeeded in surprising her. His head was thrown back and she could see all his even, firm teeth.

In the brief moment it took her to shift all the small packages under her left arm, she saw all the details of the shoeshine box. There was a worn piece of red carpet tacked on the seat of the box. The brassy thumbtacks that held it in place picked up the glow from the sunset so that they sparkled. Ten-cent bottles of shoe polish, a worn shoe brush and a dauber, were neatly lined up on a little shelf under the seat. He had decorated the sides of the box with part of his collection of book matches.

Then she slapped him sharply across the face. His look of utter astonishment made her strike him again — this time more violently, and she hated herself for doing it, even as she lifted her hand for another blow.

'But Mom ——' he protested, raising his arm to protect his face.

'You get in the house,' she ordered and yanked him to his feet. He leaned over to pick up the shoeshine box and she struck him again. 'Leave that thing there,' she said sharply, and shook him when he tried to struggle out of her grasp.

Her voice grew thick with rage. 'I'm working to look after you and you out here in the street shining shoes just like the rest of these little niggers.' And she thought, You know that isn't all there is involved. It's also that Little Henry Chandler is the same age as Bub, and you know Little Henry is wearing gray flannel suits and dark blue caps and long blue socks and fine dark brown leather shoes. He's doing his home work in that big warm library in front of the fireplace. And your kid is out in the street with a shoeshine box. He's wearing his after-school clothes, which don't look too different from the ones he wears to school — shabby knickers and stockings with holes in the heels, because no matter how much you darn and mend he comes right out of his stockings.

It's also that you're afraid that if he's shining shoes at eight, he will be washing windows at sixteen and running an elevator at twenty-one, and go on doing that for the rest of his life. And you're afraid that this street will keep him from finishing high school; that it may do worse than that and get him into some kind of trouble that will land him in reform school because you can't be home to look out for him because you have to work.

'Go on,' she said, and pushed him ahead of her toward the door of the apartment house. She was aware that Mrs. Hedges was, as usual, looking out of the window. She shoved Bub harder to make him go faster so they would get out of the way of Mrs. Hedges' eager-eyed stare as fast as possible. But Mrs. Hedges watched their progress all the way into the hall, for she leaned her head so far out of the window her red bandanna looked as though it were suspended in midair.

Going up the stairs with Bub just ahead of her Lutie thought living here is like living in a tent with everything that goes on inside it open to the world because the flap won't close. And the flap couldn't close because Mrs. Hedges sat at her street-floor window firmly holding it open in order to see what went on inside.

As they climbed up the dark, narrow stairs, darker than ever after the curious brilliance the setting sun had cast over the street, she became aware that Bub was crying. Not really crying. Sobbing. He must have spent a long time making that shoeshine box. Where had he got the money for the polish and the brush? Maybe running errands for the Super, because Bub had made friends with the Super very quickly. She didn't exactly approve of this sudden friendship because the Super was — well, the kindest way to think of him was to call him peculiar.

She remembered quite clearly that she had told him she wanted all the rooms in the apartment painted white. He must have forgotten it, for when she moved in she found that the rooms had been painted blue and rose color and green and yellow. Each room was a different color. The colors made the rooms look even smaller, and she had said instantly,

'What awful colors!' The look of utter disappointment on his face had made her feel obligated to find something that she could praise and in seeking for it she saw that the windows had been washed. Which was unusual because one of the first things you had to do when you moved in a place was to scrape the splashes of paint from the windows and then wash them.

So she said quickly, 'Oh, the windows have been washed.' And when the Super heard the pleased note in her voice, he had looked like a hungry dog that had suddenly been given a bone.

She hurried up the last flight of stairs, fumbling for her keys, pausing in the middle of the hallway to peer inside her pocketbook, so that Bub reached their door before she did. She pushed him away and unlocked the door and the can of peas slipped out from under her arm to roll clumsily along the hall in its brown-paper wrapping. While Bub scrambled after it, she opened the door.

Once inside the apartment he turned and faced her squarely. She wanted to put her arm around him and hug him, for he still had tears in his eyes, but he had obviously been screwing his courage up to the point where he could tell her whatever it was he had on his mind, even though he wasn't certain what her reaction would be. So she turned toward him and instead of hugging him listened to him gravely, trying to tell him by her manner that whatever he had to say was important and she would give it all her attention.

'You said we had to have money. You kept saying it. I was only trying to earn some money by shining shoes,' he gulped. Then the words tumbled out, 'What's wrong with that?'

She fumbled for an answer, thinking of all the times she had told him no, no candy, for we can't afford it. Or yes, it's only twenty-five cents for the movies, but that twenty-five cents will help pay for the new soles on your shoes. She was always telling him how important it was that people make money and save money — those things she had learned from the Chandlers. Then when he tried to earn some of his own she berated him, slapped him. So that suddenly and with no warning it was all wrong for him to do the very thing that she had continually told him was important and necessary.

She started choosing her words carefully. 'It's the way you were trying to earn money that made me mad,' she began. Then she leaned down until her face was on a level with his, still talking slowly, still picking her words thoughtfully. 'You see, colored people have been shining shoes and washing clothes and scrubbing floors for years and years. White people seem to think that's the only kind of work they're fit to do. The hard work. The dirty work. The work that pays the least.' She thought about this small dark apartment they were living in, about 116th Street which was filled to overflowing with people who lived in just such apartments as this, about the white people on the downtown streets who stared at her with open hostility in their eyes, and she started talking swiftly, forgetting to choose her words.

'I'm not going to let you begin at eight doing what white folks figure all eight-year-old colored boys ought to do. For if you're shining shoes at eight, you'll probably be doing the same thing when you're eighty. And I'm not going to have it.'

He listened to her with his eyes fixed on her face, not saying anything, concentrating on her words. His expression was so serious that she began to wonder if she should have said that part about white folks. He was awfully young to be told a thing like that, and she wasn't sure she had made her meaning quite clear. She couldn't think of any way to soften it, so she patted him on the shoulder and straightened up and began taking off her hat and coat.

She selected four potatoes from the package she had put on the kitchen table, washed them, found a paring knife, and seating herself at the table began peeling them.

Bub came to stand close beside her, almost but not quite leaning against her as though he was getting strength and protection from his closeness to her. 'Mom,' he said, 'why do white people want colored people shining shoes?'

She turned toward him, completely at a loss as to what to say, for she had never been able to figure it out for herself. She looked down at her hands. They were brown and strong, the fingers were long and well-shaped. Perhaps because she was born with skin that color, she couldn't see anything wrong with it. She was used to it. Perhaps it was a shock just to look at skins that were dark if you were born with a skin that was white. Yet dark skins were smooth to the touch; they were warm from the blood that ran through the veins under the skin; they covered bodies that were just as well put together as the bodies that

were covered with white skins. Even if it were a
shock to look at people whose skins were dark, she
had never been able to figure out why people with
white skins hated people who had dark skins. It
must be hate that made them wrap all Negroes up in
a neat package labeled 'colored'; a package that
called for certain kinds of jobs and a special kind of
treatment. But she really didn't know what it was.

'I don't know, Bub,' she said finally. 'But it's for
the same reason we can't live anywhere else but in
places like this' — she indicated the cracked ceiling,
the worn top of the set tub, and the narrow window,
with a wave of the paring knife in her hand.

She looked at him, wondering what he was thinking. He moved away from her to lean on the edge of
the kitchen table, poking at a potato peeling with an
aimless finger. Then he walked over to the window
and stood there looking out, his chin resting on his
hands. His legs were wide apart and she thought,
He's got nice strong legs. She was suddenly proud
of him, glad that he was hers and filled with a strong
determination to do a good job of bringing him up.
The wave of self-confidence she had felt on the street
came back again. She could do it, too — bring him
up so that he would be a fine, strong man.

The thought made her move about swiftly, cutting
the potatoes into tiny pieces so they would cook
quickly, forming the ground meat into small flat
cakes, heating the peas, setting the table, pouring a
glass of milk for Bub. She put two of the hard
crusty rolls on a plate and smiled, remembering how
she had compared herself to Ben Franklin.

Then she went to the window and put her arm

around Bub. 'What are you looking at?' she asked.

'The dogs down there,' he said, pointing. 'I call one of 'em Mother Dog and the other Father Dog. There are some children dogs over yonder.'

She looked down in the direction in which he was pointing. Shattered fences divided the space in back of the houses into what had once been back yards. But as she looked, she thought it had become one yard, for the rusted tin cans, the piles of ashes, the pieces of metal from discarded automobiles, had disregarded the fences. The rubbish had crept through the broken places in the fences until all of it mingled in a disorderly pattern that looked from their top-floor window like a huge junkpile instead of a series of small back yards. She leaned farther out the window to see the dogs Bub had mentioned. They were sleeping in curled-up positions, and it was only by the occasional twitching of an ear or the infrequent moving of a tail that she could tell they were alive.

Bub was explaining the details of the game he played with them. It had something to do with which one moved first. She only half-heard him as she stared at the piled-up rubbish and the sluggish dogs. All through Harlem there were apartments just like this one, she thought, and they're nothing but traps. Dirty, dark, filthy traps. Upstairs. Downstairs. In my lady's chamber. Click goes the trap when you pay the first month's rent. Walk right in. It's a free country. Dark little hallways. Stinking toilets.

She had wanted an apartment to herself and she got it. And now looking down at the accumulation of rubbish, she was suddenly appalled, for she didn't know what the next step would be. She hadn't thought any further than the apartment. Would they have to go on living here year after year? With just enough money to pay the rent, just enough money to buy food and clothes and to see an occasional movie? What happened next?

She didn't know, and she put her arm around Bub and hugged him close to her. She didn't know what happened next, but they'd never catch her in their dirty trap. She'd fight her way out. She and Bub would fight their way out together. She was holding him so tightly that he turned away from his game with the dogs to look up in her face.

'You're pretty,' he said, pressing his face close to hers. 'Supe says you're pretty. And he's right.'

She kissed his forehead, thinking what's the Super saying things like that to Bub for? And she was conscious of a stabbing fear that made her tighten her arm around Bub's shoulder. 'Let's eat,' she said.

All through the meal she kept thinking about the Super. He was so tall and so silent he was like some figure of doom. She rarely went in or out of the building that she didn't meet him in the hallways or just coming out of his apartment, and she wondered if he watched for her. She had noticed that the other tenants rarely talked to him, merely nodding when they saw him.

He usually had his dog with him when he stood outside on the street leaning against the building. The dog would open his mouth, fairly quivering with the urge to run down the street. She imagined that if he ever satisfied the urge to run, he would plunge

madly through the block biting people as he went
He would look up at the Super with something half-
adoring, half-fearful in his expression, drawing a
little away from him, edging along slowly a half-
inch at a time, wanting to run. Then the Super
would say, 'Buddy!' and the dog would come back
to lie down close beside the man.

She couldn't decide which was worse: the half-
starved, cringing dog, the gaunt man or the shapeless
whispering woman who lived with him. Mrs.
Hedges, who knew everything that went on in this
house and most of the other houses on the street, had
informed her confidentially that the Super's wife
wasn't really his wife, that she just stayed there with
him. 'They comes and they goes,' Mrs. Hedges had
added softly, her hard black eyes full of malice.

Bub took a big swallow of milk and choked on it.
'Sorry,' he murmured.

Lutie smiled at him and said, 'Don't drink it so
fast.' And her thoughts returned to the Super. She
had to figure out some way of keeping Bub away from
him. There were those long hours from the time
Bub got out of school until she came home from work.
She couldn't get over Bub's saying so innocently,
'Supe thinks you're pretty.' It wouldn't do to tell
Bub point-blank not to have anything to do with
him. For after that business with the shoeshine box,
he would begin to believe there wasn't much of anything he could do after school that would meet with
her approval. But she would figure out something.

Again she thought that every time she turned
around there was a new problem to be solved. There
ought to be someone she could talk to, someone she

could ask for advice. During those years she had worked in the laundry and gone to school at night, she had lost track of all her friends. And Pop didn't believe in discussing problems — 'Just goin' out of your way to look for trouble,' was his answer to anything that looked like a serious question. Granny could have told her what to do if she had lived. She had never forgotten some of the things Granny had told her and the things she had told Pop. Mostly she had been right. She used to sit in her rocking chair. Wrinkled. Wise. Rocking back and forth, talking in the rhythm of the rocker. Granny had even foreseen men like this Super. She had told Pop, 'Let her get married, Grant. Lookin' like she do men goin' to chase her till they catches up. Better she get married.'

And she had. At seventeen when she finished high school. Only the marriage had busted up, cracking wide open like a cheap record. Come to think about it, an awful lot of colored marriages ended like that.

Mrs. Hedges had implied the same thing shortly after they moved in. Lutie was coming home from work, and Mrs. Hedges having greeted her cordially from the window said, 'You married, dearie?'

Her spine had stiffened until it felt rigid. Did the woman think that Bub was some nameless bastard she had obtained in a dark hallway? 'We're separated,' she said sharply.

Mrs. Hedges nodded. 'Thought so. Most of the ladies on the street is separated.'

Some day she would ask Mrs. Hedges why most of the ladies on this street were separated from their husbands. Certainly Mrs. Hedges should be able to explain it, because she knew this block between

The Street

Eighth Avenue and Seventh Avenue better than most people know their own homes, and she should be able to tell her whether the women were separated before they came there to live or whether it was something that the street had done to them. If what Mrs. Hedges said was true, then this street was full of broken homes, and she thought the men must have been like Jim — unable to stand the day after day of drab living with nothing to look forward to but just enough to eat and a shelter overhead. And the women working as she had worked and the men getting fed up and getting other women.

She made an impatient movement and pushed her plate away from her. Bub was playing with a piece of meat ball, using his fork to slide it from one side of his plate to another, then arranging a neat circle of peas around it.

'How about you going to a movie?' she asked.

'Tonight?' he said, and when she nodded his face lit up. Then he frowned. 'Can we afford it?'

'Sure,' she said. 'Hurry up and finish eating.' The peas and the hamburger disappeared from his plate like magic. He was still chewing when he got up from the table to help count out the money for his ticket.

'Listen,' she said. 'You can't get in alone at night ——'

'Sure I can. All I have to do is go up to some old lady and ask her to let me go along in with her. I'll show her my money, so she'll know I can pay my own way. It always works,' he said confidently.

Then he was gone, slamming the door behind him, running swiftly down the stairs. She could hear his footsteps going down the stairs. She turned the radio on in the living room and stood listening to the dance music that filled the room, thinking that she would like to go somewhere where there was music like that and dancing and young people laughing.

In the kitchen she sighed deeply before she began washing the dishes. Bub shouldn't be going to the movies alone at night. How had he known how to get in despite the fact kids weren't allowed in the movies alone at night? Probably learned it from the kids in the street or at school. It wasn't right, though. She should have told him to go Saturday morning or in the afternoon after school.

There must be something he could do after school, some place he could go where he would have some fun and be safe, too. Leaning out of a kitchen window to play some kind of game with those dogs down there in the rubbish wasn't exactly wholesome play for an eight-year-old boy. She would have to move into a street where there wasn't a playground or a park for blocks around! He had been so happy about going to the movies. A simple little thing like that and he got all excited. She hoped he knew it was a peace offering for having lost her temper and slapped him out there in the street.

She found she was rattling the dishes noisily to cover up the quiet in the apartment. The radio was on full blast, but under it there was a stillness that crept through all the rooms. It's these ratty little rooms, she thought. Yet she found she kept looking over her shoulder, half-expecting to find someone had stolen up in back of her under cover of the quiet.

Yes, she thought. The trouble is that these rooms

are so small. After she had been in them just a few minutes, the walls seemed to come in toward her, to push against her. Now that she had this apartment, perhaps the next thing she ought to do was to find another one with bigger rooms. But she couldn't pay any more rent than she was paying now and moving to another street would simply mean getting a new address, for the narrow dark rooms would be the same. Everything would be the same — the toilets that didn't work efficiently, the hallways dank with the smell of urine, the small inadequate windows. No matter where she moved, if twenty-nine dollars was all the rent she could pay, why, she would simply be changing her address, for the place she moved into would be exactly like the one she moved out of.

She hung the dishtowels on the rack over the sink, straightening them so that the edges were even and stood looking at them without really seeing them. There wasn't any point in getting a more expensive apartment, for the rent on this one was all she could manage. She wondered if landlords knew what it was like to be haunted by the fear of not being able to pay the rent. After a while the word 'rent' grew so big it loomed up in all your thinking.

Some people took so much a week out of their pay envelopes and stuck it in books or tucked it in kitchen cupboards in cups or teapots or sugar bowls, so that by the end of the month it would be there in a lump sum all ready to hand over to the agent or the super or whoever collected. But someone would get a toothache or lose a job or a roomer wouldn't pay, and at the end of the month the rent money would come up short. So the landlord took to asking for it every two weeks, sometimes every week if he was especially doubtful about his tenants.

As she remembered, Pop preferred to pay weekly, for on Saturday nights he did a brisk business selling the bootleg liquor that he manufactured, so that on Sunday morning he had the week's rent money ready to turn over to the agent.

From the time her mother died when she was seven until she turned seventeen and married Jim, Saturday nights were always the same. Shortly after she got in bed there would be a furtive knock at the door. Pop would pad up the hall and hold a whispered conversation at the door. Then he would go back down the hall and a few minutes later return to the door. There would be the clink of silver and the door would close quietly. Granny would snort so loud you could hear her all through the apartment because she knew Pop had sold another bottle and she didn't approve of it, even though each knock meant they were that much closer to having the rent money ready.

Pop would further aggravate Granny by announcing loudly as he clinked the silver in his pocket, 'That's all right. It's guaranteed to put hair on a dog's back and new life in an old man.'

Sometimes Pop would try to get a regular steady job and would return home after a few hours to spend the rest of the day, saying wrathfully, 'White folks just ain't no damn good.' Then he would start mixing a new batch of his buckjuice as he called it, muttering, 'Can't get no job. White folks got 'em all.'

Granny would look at him coldly and her lips

would curl back as she rocked and frowned, saying, 'Men like him don't get nowhere, Lutie. Think folks owe 'em a livin'. And mebbe they do, but not nowhere near the way he thinks.'

Lutie found herself wondering if Pop would have been different if he had lived in a different part of town and if he had been able to find a decent job that would have forced him to use all of his energy and latent ability. There wasn't anything stupid about Pop. Life just seemed to have reacted on him until he turned sly and a little dishonest. Perhaps that was one way of fighting back.

Even the succession of girl friends that started shortly after her mother died could have been the result of his frustration — a way he had of proving to himself that there was one area of achievement in which he was the equal of any man — white or black. Though his public explanation of them was simply that he didn't intend to marry again. 'It don't work out after the first time. And I gotta keep my freedom.'

Granny had observed the procession of buxom lady friends with unconcealed disapproval, which she expressed by folding her lips into a thin straight line and rocking faster and faster. Eventually Granny's baleful eye would discourage even the boldest of them, but a few weeks later some other fat woman would show up to share Pop's bed and board.

Again she was aware of the silence under the sound of the radio. And she went into the living room and sat down close to it, so that the dance music would shut out the silence. She had been so dead set on moving away from Pop and Lil, getting this apartment for herself and Bub, that she hadn't stopped to figure out what was to happen next. Listening to the music she thought she couldn't possibly go on living here with nothing to look forward to. As she sat there, it seemed to her that time stretched away in front of her so far that it couldn't be measured; it couldn't be encompassed or even visualized if it meant living in this place for years and years.

What else was there? She couldn't hope to get a raise in pay without taking another civil service examination, for more pay depended on a higher rating, and it might be two years, ten years, even twenty years before it came through. The only other way of getting out was to find a man who had a good job and who wanted to marry her. The chances of that were pretty slim, for once they found out she didn't have a divorce they lost interest in marriage and offered to share their apartments with her.

It would be more years than she cared to think about before she would be able to get a divorce because it was an expensive business. She would either have to move to some other state and establish residence there and on top of that have enough money to pay for the divorce, or she would have to get sufficient evidence to prove that Jim was living with some other woman and on top of that hire a lawyer. Either way it was done, it would cost two or three hundred dollars and it would take her years and years to save up that much money.

She got up from the chair, thinking, I can't stay here in this little place for another minute. I'll go for a walk. As she changed her clothes, she thought,

The Street

This is the same thing that happened to Jim. He couldn't stand being shut up in the little house in Jamaica just like I can't stand being shut up in this apartment. Only I have a job that takes me out of here every day and I ought to be able to stand it better. But I can't. It seems like life is going past me so fast that I'll never catch up with it, and it wouldn't matter particularly, but I can't see anything ahead of me except these walls that push in against me.

She didn't intend to go anywhere except for a walk, but she found herself dressing as slowly and as carefully as though she had a special date, putting on a plain black dress and fastening a gold-colored chain around her neck. She reached in her closet for her best coat, which was perfectly plain, too, except that it hung from the shoulders so that it flared loose and full in the back. It was a coat that she had made herself, saving up the money to buy the material, cutting it out on her bed in Pop's apartment, stitching it up on Lil's sewing machine. She only wore it when she was going somewhere special at night or when she went for a walk with Bub on Sunday afternoons.

Tonight wasn't anything special. When she put the coat on, it was with the thought that wearing it would give her the feeling that she was on her way to a place where she could forget for a little while about the gas bill and the rent bill and the light bill. It would be a place where there was a lot of room and the walls didn't continually walk at you — crowding you.

She reached in a drawer for a pair of white gloves

and even as she pulled them on she knew where she was going.

'A glass of beer,' she said softly. 'I'll get a glass of beer at the Junto on the corner.' It would take the edge off the loneliness.

Outside on the street, she felt mildly triumphant, for just once she had managed to walk past Mrs. Hedges' window without being seen. Just once. But no ——

'Dearie, I been thinkin' ——' Mrs. Hedges' voice halted her.

Mrs. Hedges studied her from head to foot with a calculating eye. 'If you ever want to make a little extra money, why, you let me know. A nice white gentleman I met lately ——'

Lutie walked up the street without answering. Mrs. Hedges' voice followed her, 'Just let me know, dearie.'

Sure, Lutie thought, as she walked on, if you live on this damn street you're supposed to want to earn a little extra money sleeping around nights. With nice white gentlemen.

By the time she reached the Junto Bar and Grill on the corner, she was walking so fast she almost passed it.

Chapter 4

J ONES, THE SUPER, came out of his apartment just in time to catch a glimpse of Lutie striding up the street toward the Junto. She was walking so fast her coat flared out above her straight slim skirt.

As his eyes followed her swift progress up the street, he wished she hadn't worn such a full coat so that he could have had a better view of her well-shaped hips as she hurried toward the corner. Ever since the night she had first rung his bell to ask about the apartment, he hadn't been able to get her out of his mind. She was so tall and brown and young. She made him more aware of the deadly loneliness that ate into him day and night. It was a loneliness born of years of living in basements and sleeping on mattresses in boiler rooms.

The first jobs he had had been on ships and he stayed

on them until sometimes it seemed to him he had been buried alive in the hold. He took to talking to himself and dreaming of women — brown women that he would hold in his arms when he got ashore. He used to plan the detail of his love-making until when the dream became a reality and he was actually ashore, he went half-mad with a frenzied kind of hunger that drove the women away from him. When he was younger, he didn't have any trouble getting women — young, well-built women. It didn't worry him that they left him after a few days because he could always find others to take their places.

After he left the sea, he had a succession of jobs as a night watchman. And he was alone again. It was worse than the ships. Because he had to sit in the basements and the hallways of vast, empty buildings that were filled with shadows, and the only sound that came to his ears was that made by some occasional passer-by whose footsteps echoed and re-echoed in his eardrums. Until finally he couldn't stand it any more and got a job as super in a building in Harlem because that way there would be people around him all the time.

He had been on 116th Street for five years. He knew the cellars and the basements in this street better than he knew the outside of streets just a few blocks away. He had fired furnaces and cleaned stairways and put washers in faucets and grown gaunter and lonelier as the years crept past him. He had gone from a mattress by a furnace to basement rooms until finally here in this house he had three rooms to himself — rent free.

But now that he had an apartment of his own, he had grown so much older he found it more and more difficult to get a woman to stay with him. Even women who wanted a refuge and who couldn't hope to find one anywhere else stayed only three months or so and then were gone. He had thought he would see more people as super of a building, but he was still surrounded by silence. For the tenants didn't like him and the only time they had anything to do with him was when a roof leaked or a windowpane came out or something went wrong with the plumbing. And so he had developed the habit of spending his spare time outside the buildings in which he worked; looking at the women who went past, estimating them, wanting them.

It was all of three years since he had had a really young woman. The last young round one left after three days of his violent love-making. She had stood in the door and screamed at him, her voice high and shrill with rage. 'You old goat!' she said. 'You think I'm goin' to stay in this stinkin' apartment with you slobberin' over me day after day?'

After her the succession of drab, beaten, middle-aged women started again. As a result he wanted this young one — this Lutie Johnson — worse than he had ever wanted anything in his life. He had watched her ever since she moved in. She was crazy about her kid. So he had gone out of his way to be friends with him.

'Hey, kid, go get me a pack of smokes,' and he would give the kid a nickel for going. Or, 'Run around the corner and get a paper for me,' giving him a couple of pennies when he came back with the paper.

They planned the shoeshine box together and made it in the basement. He brought a hammer and a saw down, fished a piece of old carpet out of the rubbish, got the nails to tack it on with, and showed the kid how to hold the hammer.

'Gee, Mom'll be proud of me,' Bub had said. He was sweating and he leaned back on his knees to grin up at the Super.

The man shifted his weight uneasily. He had been standing close to the furnace at the time and he remembered how difficult it was to keep from frowning, for standing there looking down at the kid like that he saw the roundness of his head, how sturdily his body was built, the beginnings of what would be a powerful chest, the straightness of his legs, how his hair curled over his forehead.

And he suddenly hated the child with a depth of emotion that set him trembling. He looks like whoever the black bastard was that used to screw her, he thought, and his mind fastened on the details. He could fairly see Lutie, brown and long-legged, pressed tight against the body of that other man, a man with curly hair and a broad chest and straight back and legs.

'Damn him,' he muttered.

'Whatsamatter, Supe?' Bub asked. 'Hey, you look sick.'

'Go away,' the man motioned violently as the boy stood up. He had felt that if the child should touch him he would try to kill him. Because the child was an exact replica of his father — that unknown man who had held Lutie in his arms, caressed her breasts, felt her body tremble against him. He watched the child back away from him, saw that his eyes were wide with fear, and by a prodigious effort he controlled himself. Don't scare the kid, he told himself. And again, Don't scare the kid. You'll scare off the mother if you do and she's what you want — what you gotta have.

'I got a headache,' he muttered. 'Come on and let's tack the carpet on the seat.'

He forced himself to kneel down beside him and to hold the carpet taut while the kid nailed it in place. The kid lifted the hammer and began swinging it with a regular rhythm, up and down, down and up. Watching him he had thought, When he grows up he's going to be strong and big like his father. The thought made him draw away from the nearness of the boy who was so like the father — that man who had Lutie when she was a virgin. He couldn't look at the child again after thinking that, so he stared at the dust and the accumulation of grime on the furnace pipes that ran overhead.

Now standing here on the street watching Lutie walk toward the corner, he was aware that Mrs. Hedges was looking at him from her window. He was filled with a vast uneasiness, for he was certain that she could read his thoughts. Sometimes standing out on the street like this, he forgot she was there, and he would stare hungry-eyed at the women who went past. Some movement she made would attract his attention and he would look toward the window to find that she was sitting there blandly observing him.

When Lutie disappeared around the corner, he looked up and Mrs. Hedges leaned toward him, smiling.

'Ain't no point in you lickin' your chops, dearie,' she said. 'There's others who are interested.'

He frowned up at her. 'What you talkin' about?'

'Mis' Johnson, of course. Who you think I'm talkin' about?' She leaned farther out of the window. 'I'm just tellin' you for your own good, dearie. There ain't no point in you gettin' het up over her. She's marked down for somebody else.'

She was still smiling, but her eyes were so unfriendly that he looked away, thinking, She ain't never been able to mind her own business. If he could he would have had her locked up long ago. She oughtta be in jail, anyway, running the kind of place she did.

He had hated her ever since he had dropped a hint to her one afternoon, after months of looking at the round young girls who lived with her. He had said, 'Kin I come in some night?' He had made his voice soft and tried to say it in such a way that she would know instantly what it was he wanted.

'You got anything you want to talk about, you kin say it at the window, dearie. I'm always a-settin' right here where folks kin see me.' She said it coldly, and loud enough so that anyone passing on the street could hear her.

He was so furious and frustrated that he made up his mind to find some way of getting even with her. There must be, he finally decided, some kind of complaint he could make to the police. He asked the super next door about it.

'Sure,' the man said. 'Runnin' a disorderly house. Go down to the precinct and tell 'em.'

The cop he talked to at the station house was

young, and Jones thought he acted real pleased when he heard what he had come for. He began filling out a long printed form. Everything was all right until a lieutenant came in and looked over the cop's shoulder as he wrote.

'What's the woman's name?' he asked sharply, though he was looking right at it where the cop had written it on the paper.

'Mis' Hedges,' the Super said eagerly, and thought, Maybe there's something else against her and she'll get locked up for a long time. Perhaps she would spend the rest of her life sticking her fat head out between jail bars. That red bandanna of hers would look real good in a jail-house yard.

The lieutenant frowned at him and pursed up his lips. 'How do you know this is true?'

'I'm the super of the building,' he explained.

'Ever hear any noise? Do the neighbors complain? People in the house complain?'

'No,' he said slowly. 'But I see them girls she's got there. And men go in and out.'

'The girls room there? Or do they come in from the street?'

'They rooms there,' he said.

The lieutenant reached out and took the paper away from the cop and the cop's pen sort of slid across it because he was still writing on it. The lieutenant tore it up into little fine pieces and the pieces drifted slowly out of his hands into a wastebasket near the desk. The cop's face turned redder and redder as he watched the pieces fall into the basket.

The lieutenant said, 'That isn't enough evidence

for a complaint,' and turned on his heel and walked out.

Jones and the cop stared at each other. When Jones started toward the door, he could hear the cop swearing softly under his breath. He went back and stood outside the building. He couldn't figure it out. Everything had been all right until the lieutenant came in. The cop was taking it all down and then suddenly, 'Not enough evidence.'

He asked the super next door what that meant. 'You gotta get people to complain about her. And then take 'em down to the station with you,' the man explained.

Jones tried out the people in the house. He talked to some of the women first, keeping his voice casual. 'That Mis' Hedges is runnin' a bad place downstairs. She hadn't oughta live here.'

All he got were indignant looks. 'Mis' Hedges' girls come up here and looked after me when I was sick.' Or, 'Mis' Hedges keeps her eye on Johnnie after school.'

'Them girls she's got in there ain't no good,' he argued.

'Good's most of the folks round here. And they minds they own business. You leave Mis' Hedges alone' — and the door would slam in his face.

The men roared with laughter. 'Wotsa matter, Poppa? Won't she let you buy nothin' in there?' Or, 'Go on, man, them gals is the sweetest things on the block.' 'Hell, she's got a refined place in there. What you kickin' about?'

And so there was nothing he could do about Mrs. Hedges. He had resigned himself to just looking at the young girls who lived in her apartment and the

sight of them further whetted his appetite for a
young woman of his own. In a sense Mrs. Hedges
even spoiled his daily airings on the street, for he
became convinced that she could read his mind. His
eyes no sooner fastened on some likely looking girl
than he became aware of Mrs. Hedges looming larger
than life itself in the window — looking at him,
saying nothing, just looking, and, he was certain,
reading his mind.

He was certain about her being able to read his
mind because shortly after he tried to have her locked
up the white agent who collected the rents from him
said to him, 'I'd advise you to leave Mrs. Hedges
alone.'

'I ain't done nothin' to her,' he said sullenly.

'You tried to get her locked up, didn't you?'

He had stared at the man in astonishment. How
could he know that? He hadn't said anything to
the tenants about having her put in jail. Thus he
began to believe that she could sit in her window
and look at him and know exactly what he was
thinking. It frightened him so that he didn't enjoy
his visits to the street. He could only stand there for
a little while at a time, for whenever he looked up at
her she was looking at him with a derisive smile
playing about her mouth.

'She's always sittin' in the window,' he had said
defensively to the white agent.

The man threw his head back and roared. 'You
want her locked up for just sitting in the window?
You're crazy.' He suddenly stopped laughing and
a sharp note came in his voice. 'Just remember that
you're to leave her alone.'

The Street

They were all on her side, he thought. And then he remembered that he was still standing on the street and she was looking at him. He wished he could think of a cutting reply to make to her, but he couldn't, so he whistled to the dog and went in the house stifling an impulse to shake his fist at her.

He turned on the radio in the living room and slumped down in the shabby chair near it. He didn't turn his head at the sound of a key being timidly turned in the lock. He knew it was Min, the shapeless woman who lived with him. He had got to know her when she stopped at his door every two weeks to pay her rent. He was living alone at the time, for the last shabby woman who stayed with him had been gone for nearly two months.

Min used to sit and talk to him while he wrote out her rent receipt, and linger in the doorway afterward talking, talking, talking. One day when she came down to his door, the keys of her apartment were dangling loose from her hand. Usually she held them tightly clutched in her palm as though they represented something precious. 'I gotta move,' she said simply.

Jones held out his hand for the keys, thinking that it was lonesome in his apartment, especially at night when he couldn't see anything if he stood outside on the street and therefore stayed inside the house by himself. Standing up outside like that his feet got tired, too. If he had a window where he could look out and see the street like Mrs. Hedges, it would be different, but the only windows in his place were in the back, facing the yard which was piled high with rusting tin cans, old newspapers, and other rubbish.

94

'You could stay here' — he indicated his apartment
with a backward jerk of his head. The sound of her
talking would drive away his loneliness and she
might stay a long time because her husband had deserted her. He had heard one of the tenants telling
Mrs. Hedges about it. He watched a warm look of
pleasure lighten her face, and he thought, Why, she
musta fell for me. She musta fell for me.

She moved in with him that same day. She didn't
have very much furniture, so it wasn't any problem to
fit it into his rooms. A bed, a bureau, a kitchen table,
some chairs, and a long console table with ornate
carved feet. 'One of my madams gave me that,' she
explained, and told him to be careful with it on the
stairs.

They got along all right until Lutie Johnson moved
in. Then he began to feel like he couldn't bear the
sight of Min any more. Her shapeless body in bed
beside him became in his mind a barrier between him
and Lutie. Min wore felt slippers in the house and
they flapped against the dark paleness of her heels
when she walked. There was a swish-swish noise
when she moved from the stove to the sink as she was
doing now. Whenever he heard the sound, he
thought of Lutie's high-heeled shoes and the clicking
noise her heels made when she walked. The swish of
Min's slippers shut the other sound out and her dark
knotted legs superimposed themselves on his dreams
of Lutie's long brown legs.

As he sat listening to Min slop back and forth in
the kitchen, he realized that he hated her. He wanted
to hurt her, make her cringe away from him until she
was as unhappy as he was.

'Supper's ready,' she said in her soft sing-song voice.

He didn't move out of his chair. He wasn't going to eat with her any more. It was a sudden decision made while he sat listening to the soft clop of her slippers as she went to and fro in the kitchen.

She came to stand in the doorway. 'You ain't eatin'?'

He shook his head and waited for her to ask him why, so he could shout at her and threaten her with violence. But she went back into the kitchen without saying anything, and he felt cheated. He listened to the sounds of her eating. The clink of the fork against the plate, a cup of tea being stirred, the loud sucking noise she made when she drank the tea, a knife clattering against the plate. She poured a second cup of tea from the teapot sitting on the stove and he heard the scuffing of the slippers as she walked back to the table.

And he got up abruptly and walked out of the apartment. He couldn't bear to stay in there with her for another moment. He would go down and put coal on the furnace and sit in the furnace room awhile. When he came back up, he would eat, and then go stand outside on the street where he might get a glimpse of Lutie when she came home.

As he stepped out into the hall, the street door opened. Bub bounded in, his face still glowing with the memory of the movies he had seen. He paused when he saw Jones. 'Hi, Supe,' he said.

The Super nodded, thinking, She ain't home. Wonder what he does up there by himself when she ain't home.

'Mom didn't like that shoeshine box,' he said. 'She got awful mad.'

Jones stared at the boy, not saying anything.

'You goin' to fix the fire?' Bub asked.

'Yeah,' he said, and walked quickly toward the cellar door under the stairs. He hooked the door behind him, thinking that he couldn't stand the sight of the kid tonight. Not the way he was feeling.

He put shovel after shovel of coal on the furnace. Then he stared into the fire, watching the blue flame lick up over the fresh coal, and studying the deep redness that glowed deep under it.

His thoughts turned almost immediately to Lutie and he stood there leaning on the shovel oblivious to the intense heat that surged out of the open door. So she hadn't liked the shoeshine box. Too bad. He had thought she'd be so pleased and that she would come down and ring his bell and stand there smiling at him. Tall and slim and young. Her breasts pointing up at him. Mebbe she would have got so she rang his bell often.

'Just to say hello to you,' she would say.

'That's mighty nice of you, Mis' Johnson,' and he would pat her arm or mebbe hold her hand for a moment.

He wouldn't do anything to scare her. He would just be friendly and give her little presents at first. 'Saw this in a store. Thought you'd like it, Mis' Johnson.' Perhaps a pair of stockings. Yes, that would be it — stockings. Some of those long, mesh ones. Mis' Greene who lived on the third floor worked downtown — she'd get them for him.

'Oh, you shouldn't have, Mr. Jones,' Lutie would

say, and put her hand on his shoulder.

'How about me seein' if they fit?' That was it. Playfully. Not doing anything that would scare her.

He leaned harder on the shovel imagining what it would be like. Seeing her there in his apartment with one of her long legs thrust forward — a bare, brown leg with red stuff on the toenails. And he would shake out the long stocking and pull it slowly over her foot. The soft brown skin would show through the meshes as he pulled the stocking up, up over the smooth flesh. He would lean nearer and nearer, as the stocking reached the rounded part of her leg where the fatness of the curve came, until he was pressing his mouth hot and close against that curve. Closer and closer so that he could nibble at it with his mouth, nibble the curve of her leg, and her skin would be sweet from soap and cool against the hotness of his mouth.

He had to stop thinking about it. And as he stood there, he could see all those other women who had lived with him. Of the whole lot only one had been young and she had left at the end of three days. The rest of them had been bony women past fifty, toothless women past fifty, big ones and little ones — all past fifty. At that, none of them stayed very long. Three months, six months, and then they were gone.

All except Min. Min had stayed two years. Talking, talking, talking. At first he had thought it was kind of cheerful to have her around. She kept the place from getting so deadly quiet. Now the sound of her voice shut Lutie's voice out and he could never remember what it sounded like. Min's voice would thrust it away from him the minute he started trying to remember.

The thing for him to do was get rid of her. Min was probably the reason Lutie never even looked at him. Only sort of nodded when she went past. He should have thrown Min out that first night he saw Lutie. He remembered how her long legs had looked going up the stairs ahead of him. Just watching her like that he had wanted her so badly it was like a pain in his chest. Those long legs walking up and up in front of him, her rump moving from side to side as she walked. He remembered how his hand had cupped into a curve — unconsciously, uncontrollably, as he walked in back of her.

And in the living room of the apartment he had stood there the light from the flashlight down at his feet so she couldn't see the expression on his face as he fought with himself to keep from springing on her as she stood in the bedroom playing her light on the walls. She went into the kitchen and the bathroom and he made himself stand still. For he knew if he followed her in there, he would force her down on the floor, down against the worn floor boards. He had tried to imagine what it would be like to feel her body under his — soft and warm and moving with him. And he made a choking, strangled noise in his throat.

'What's that?' she had said. And he had seen the light from her flashlight waver from the trembling of her hand.

He had scared her. He tried to speak softly so that the sound of his voice would reassure her, but his throat was working so violently that he couldn't make any words come. Finally he said, 'I cleared my throat, ma'am,' and even to his own ears his voice had sounded strange.

After he had given her a receipt for the deposit she left on the apartment, he tried to figure out something he could do for her. Something special that would make her like him. He decided to do a special paint job in her apartment — not just that plain white paint she had ordered. So he put green in the living room, yellow in the kitchen, deep rose color in the bedroom, and dark blue in the bathroom. When it was finished, he was very proud of it, for it was the best paint job he'd ever done. He did something else, too. He scraped the paint from the windows, those long-dried spatters from his brush and then he washed them. The agent nearly caught him at it. Fortunately he had locked the door, but the man pounded on it and shouted for quite a while. 'Hey, Jones! Jones! Where the devil is he?' He had stayed quiet inside holding the window cloth in his hand until the man went away.

When Lutie came to get the keys, he got his first good look at her in daylight. Her eyes were big and dark and her mouth was rosy with lipstick. She had a small turned-up nose that made her face look very young and her skin was so smooth and so brown that he couldn't stop looking at her.

'You might have trouble with the door,' he had said. 'I'll show you how it works.' He couldn't wait to see her face when she found out what a wonderful job he had done on the apartment. This way, too, he would again walk up the stairs in back of her. But she said, 'You lead the way,' and stood and waited until he had to start up ahead of her.

In the apartment she looked at the rooms, and at first she didn't say anything until after she had looked in the bathroom, and then she said, 'What awful colors!' He couldn't help looking disappointed, but then she added with surprise in her voice, 'Why, the windows have been washed. That's wonderful.' And he had begun to feel better.

Tonight she wasn't home and the kid was upstairs by himself. Where could she have gone? Out with some man, he supposed. Some big-chested man like the kid's father. Probably now at this moment they were alone together somewhere. Sweat broke out on his forehead and for the first time he became conscious of the heat from the furnace door. He put the shovel down and shut the door and walked away from the furnace. He had a sudden desire to see what the apartment looked like now that she had been living in it. It would be all right, he decided. She might even come home while he was up there and she would be glad he had stayed with Bub. That was it. He would go up and keep Bub company while she was out. And he would see how the place looked. He would see her bedroom.

He walked up the stairs slowly, deliberately making himself go slow when what he wanted to do was to run up them. He stopped outside the door. There was a thin thread of light reaching out from under the door and the radio was going. Maybe she had come home while he was down in the cellar. In that case he would explain that he just came up to see if Bub was all right, he had thought Bub was up here alone ——

Bub opened the door a cautious crack in answer to his ring. When he saw Jones he opened it wide 'Hi, Supe,' he said and grinned broadly.

'Thought I'd come up and see if you was all right.'

'Come on in.'

He walked into the living room and looked around. It smelt sweet with some faint fragrance that came from the bedroom. He looked toward it eagerly. That was the room he wanted to see most of all.

'Your ma ain't home yet?'

Bub shook his head. 'I been to the movies,' he said. 'You shoulda seen it. This guy came out to the West and was going to be a lawyer. And he set up in business and a rich man who got his land crooked ——'

The boy's voice went on and on and Jones forgot he was there. He was imagining that Lutie was curled up on the couch where the boy sat. He wouldn't sit by her; he would stay where he was and talk to her. He wouldn't scare her. He would be very careful about that — not make any sudden moves toward her.

'Everything all right?' he'd ask.

'Just fine.'

'Brought you a little present,' and he would reach in his pocket and bring out some earrings — some long gold-colored hoops.

'You want to fasten 'em on?'

'I'm kinda clumsy,' he would say playfully. And then he would be beside her on the couch. Right beside her on the couch. He could pull her close to him, very close. So close she would be leaning against him. He looked down at his overalls. They had been blue once, but they had faded to a grayish-white from much washing. At least they're clean, he thought defensively. But the next time he came up, he would wear his good black suit and a white shirt. He would get Min to starch the collar.

And then he remembered that he was going to get rid of Min. That would be easy. He would fix her so that she'd light out in a hurry and she wouldn't come back. She and her carpet slippers and her whispering voice. He moved his shoulders distastefully. Why would he have to think about her here in Lutie's apartment? He frowned.

'You mad about somep'n?' the boy asked.

Jones shifted uneasily in the chair, made an effort to erase the frown. Now what the hell had the kid been talking about — oh, yes, the movies he had seen. 'Naw, I ain't mad. Just thinkin',' he said, and thought, I gotta keep him talking. Keep him busy talking. He took out a cigarette and lit it. 'You only see one pitcher?' he asked.

'Nope. Two of 'em.'

'What's the other one about? That fust one sounded good.'

'Gangsters,' the boy said eagerly. 'A man who arrested 'em. He pretended to be one, only he was really a cop. They had tommy guns and sawed off shotguns and ——'

That'll hold him for a while, he thought. There must be some way he could get to look around in the apartment. He stood up abruptly. 'Want a glass of water,' he explained, and started walking toward the kitchen before the kid could get up from the couch. But the kid got the water for him so fast that he didn't get much chance to look around. He saw there were three empty beer bottles and a couple of Pepsi-Cola bottles under the kitchen sink. Even while drinking the water, his mind kept peering into the bedroom. What kind of bed did she sleep on? Perhaps he could open the closet door and just touch her clothes hanging there. They would be soft and sweet-smelling.

Back in the living room the boy went on with his endless telling of the movie, and Jones thought there must be some way he could get to look in the bedroom.

'Your ma need any extra shelves in her closet?' he asked suddenly.

Bub stopped talking to look at the Super. What did he keep interrupting him for? He shook his head, 'Naw,' he said indifferently. Then he picked up the thread of the story, 'This guy that was really a cop ——'

Jones lit another cigarette. The ash tray was slowly filling up with butts. His throat and mouth were hot from the smoke. It seemed to him they must be raw inside and the rawness was beginning to go all the way down inside him.

'Let's you and me play some cards,' he said abruptly. 'You kin get some matches for the stakes,' he suggested.

He watched the kid go into the kitchen and he got up quickly and tiptoed toward the bedroom. He was almost inside the door when he heard Bub start toward the living room. He cursed the boy inside his head while he stood in the center of the room pretending to be stretching.

'Pull your chair up, Supe,' Bub said. 'We can play on top of this table.' He moved a bowl of artificial flowers that were on top of the blue-glass-topped coffee table in front of the couch.

'Pull your chair up, Supe,' he repeated when the man didn't move.

Jones was staring at a lipstick that was on the table-top. It had been lying close to the bowl of flowers so that he hadn't noticed it. The case was ivory-colored and there was a thin line of scarlet that went all the way around the bottom of it. He kept staring at the lipstick and almost involuntarily he reached out without moving his chair and picked it up. He pulled the top off and looked at the red stick inside. It was rounded from use and the smooth-ness of the red had a grainy look from being rubbed over her mouth.

He wanted to put it against his lips. That's the way her mouth would smell and it would feel like this stuff, only warm. Holding it in his hand he got the smell from it very clearly — it was sweet like the soap that round girl had used. The one who stayed three days and then left. He raised the lip-stick toward his mouth and the boy suddenly reached out and took it out of his hand, putting it in his pants pocket. It was a swift, instinctive, protective gesture.

'Mom thought she'd lost it,' he said, almost apologetically.

Jones glared at the boy. He had been so wrapped up in his own thoughts he had forgotten he was there. And he had been holding the lipstick so loosely that the boy took it away from him without any effort. He hadn't even seen him reach out for it. And he thought again of Bub's father and that the boy had known there was something wrong about his lifting the lipstick toward his mouth. He was conscious of the loud ticking of a small clock that stood on a table near the couch. He could hear it going tick-tock, tick-tock, over the sound of the radio. He leaned forward aware that he had been silent too long.

'Let's get the game started,' he said roughly.

He showed the boy how to play black jack. Bub learned the game quickly and started playing with a conservative kind of daring that made the pile of matches in front of him increase steadily. Jones studied him in the blue-glass table-top. There ought to be some way of getting that lipstick away from him. It would be good to hold it in his hands at night before he went to sleep so that the sweet smell would saturate his nostrils. He could carry it in his pocket where he could touch it during the day and take it out and fondle it down in the furnace room.

When he stood outside on the street, he wouldn't have to touch it, but he would know it was there lying deep in his pocket. He could almost feel it there now — warm against him. Mrs. Hedges could stare at him till she dropped dead and she wouldn't know about it. The thought of her made him wish desperately that he could just once get his hands on her. Wished that just once she would come out on the street and stand near him. 'She's marked for somebody else.' Grinning like an ape when she said it and her eyes cold and unfriendly like the eyes of a snake. No expression in them, but you knew you weren't safe. 'Ain't no point in you lickin' your chops, dearie.' And her eyes boring into him, going through him, threatening him. Mrs. Hedges or nobody else was going to get Lutie away from him. He'd seen her first. Yes, sir. And he was going to have her.

He lit another cigarette and, when he inhaled, he was aware that the dry hotness in his mouth and throat had gone all the way down him. He laid the cards he was holding down on the table. He had to have a drink of beer. Had to have it bad.

'Hey, kid, go get me some beer and a pack of smokes' — he reached in his pocket and laid thirty-five cents on the table. 'You kin keep the change.'

As the boy slammed the door behind him, he wondered why he hadn't thought of it before. He was alone in the place as easily as that — just by sending the kid on an errand. He listened to the boy running down the stairs and then got up quietly and walked into the bedroom.

He stood inside the room without moving The sweet smell was stronger in here. It came from the side of the room. He fumbled for the light and hit his knee against a chest of drawers. And stood there for a moment rubbing the place and cursing. Then he turned on the light. The bed was covered with a flowered pink spread and the same kind of stuff was at the air shaft. Everything was so close together that he could look all around the room without moving.

The sweet smell came from a can of talcum on the bureau. He picked it up and looked at it. She sprinkled this under her arms and between her legs — that's how she would smell when he got close to her. Just like this. He opened the top of the can and sprinkled some of the powder in his hand. It lay there dead-white against the dark paleness of his palm. He rubbed his hands together and the sweet smell grew stronger in the room.

He turned away abruptly. He mustn't stay in here too long, the kid would soon be coming back. The way he ran down the stairs it wouldn't take him any time to get to the store. Probably ran all the way to the corner. He wished that Lutie would come home while he was there. But the kid ought to come back now, he thought fretfully. She might not like it if she came home and found he had sent the kid out on an errand at night. What was keeping him so long? She'd probably be home any minute, now. Why hadn't he told him to get two bottles of beer? Given him enough money for two bottles and then she and him could have sat out in the living room on the couch drinking beer.

He opened the closet door. It seemed to him that the clothes bent toward him as he looked inside — a blue dress, the coat she wore to work, a plaid skirt, some blouses. He looked closely at the blouses. Yes, there was the thin, white one he had seen one day when she came down the stairs with her coat open. It had a low round neck and the fullness of the cloth in the front made a nest for her breasts to sit in. He took it out and looked at it. It smelt like the talcum and he crushed it violently between his hands squeezing the soft thin material tighter and tighter until it was a small ball in his hands except the part where the metal hanger was near the top.

Then he tried to straighten it out, patting it and

smoothing and thinking that he must go quickly.
Now. At once. Before the kid came back, so that no
one would see the look on his face. He thrust the
blouse back into the closet, closed the door, reached
up and turned out the light.

He hurried out into the living room intent on
leaving before the kid came back. He paused in front
of the open bathroom door. It wouldn't hurt to look
inside, to see how that blue color looked. There were
white towels hung on a rack over the tub. He walked
all the way into the small room trying to imagine
how Lutie would look with water from the shower
running down over her. Or lying there in the tub,
her warm brownness sharply outlined against the
white of the tub. The room would be hot from the
steam of the water and sweet with the smell of soap.
He would just be able to see her through the steami-
ness. Perhaps he could hold her next to him while
he patted her body dry with one of those white
towels.

Why didn't the kid hurry? He felt a sharp anger
against him. She would be coming home at any
minute now. She wouldn't like it if the kid was out.
He forced himself to look away from the tub and he
was conscious that the thirst in him had become red-
hot. He sat down on the toilet seat and buried his
head in his hands. Instantly his nose was filled with
the smell of the talc he had rubbed between his
palms.

He began thinking of Min. He would throw her
out tonight. He had to get rid of her tonight. He
wouldn't be able to stand the sight of her any more
after being close to Lutie like this. He heard the kid

tearing up the stairs and he reached up and jerked out the light. He was standing in the living room when the kid opened the door.

'Get me a opener,' he ordered, and reached for the brown-paper bag Bub was carrying. He followed the boy into the kitchen and stood in the middle of the room under the glaring, unshaded kitchen light while he lifted the bottle to his mouth. He didn't even wait to take it out of the bag, but drank in long swallows — faster and faster. He sighed when he put the bottle down empty. 'Thanks, kid,' he said. 'That's what I needed.' He started for the door.

'You goin' now?'

'Yeah. I'll be seein' you tomorrow.'

He walked heavily down the stairs. He was tired. And he thought, It's got to be soon. He had to have her soon. He couldn't go on just looking at her. He'd crack wide open if he did. There musta been some way he could have got that lipstick away from the little bastard. He thought derisively of Mrs. Hedges. 'There's others interested.' Yeah. But not as interested as him.

He opened the door of his apartment, thinking that he was going to throw Min out so hard she would walk on the other side of the street when she passed this house. He set the stage for it by letting the door bang behind him so that the sound went up and up through the flimsy walls of the house until it became only a mild clapping noise when it reached the top floor.

Just inside of the door he stood still because all the rooms were dark. Buddy, the police dog, came toward him whining deep in his throat. Jones fumbled for the light in the foyer, pushing the dog away from him with his foot.

Min wasn't in the kitchen, the bedroom, or the bathroom. A look in each room had merely confirmed what he had already known when he found the apartment dark. Amazing as it seemed, she had gone out. She never went anywhere at night. She always came home from work and stayed in the house until she went back to work the next day. It occurred to him that she might have left him like all the others had. Even though he had come downstairs with the intention of putting her out, the thought of her leaving him was unbearable.

In the bedroom he pulled the closet door open in a kind of frenzy. Her few clothes still hung there — shapeless house dresses and the frayed coat she wore every day. The run-over felt slippers were on the closet floor, the raised places along the sides mute testimony to the size of the bunions on her feet. But her best hat and coat were gone; and the ugly black oxfords she wore on her occasional trips to church.

Could she have gone off and left him like the others? It was impossible to tell from the contents of the closet — these limp house dresses weren't important to her. She could always buy some others. And the felt slippers, though easy on her feet, were practically worn out. She didn't own a suitcase, so he couldn't tell whether she would be back.

If she had really left him, it didn't look so good for his chances with Lutie. For the first time he felt doubtful about Lutie's having him. Up to now he had been confident that it was only a matter of time and he would have her. This way he couldn't be sure, because if a creature like Min didn't want him there was no reason for him to believe that Lutie would have him.

Yet he still didn't know for sure. He reached in toward the clothes, pushing them into a corner with a wide violent gesture of his arm as if by threatening them they would reveal whether Min had walked out on him. Abruptly he turned toward the living room, for it occurred to him that he could tell very easily whether she had gone for good. Just one glance would be enough to tell him. No. He nodded his head with satisfaction. She hadn't walked out. She'd be coming back. For the big shiny table with the claw feet was still there against the living-room wall. She would never go away and leave that behind her. All he had to do was sit down and wait for her. Because he was going to put her out tonight and the shiny table could go right along with her.

He dozed in the chair by the radio, waiting to hear Min's key click in the lock, wondering where she had gone. This was the first time he had ever known her to go out again after she came home from work. For she did the shopping on her way from work and then cooked and cleaned and soaked her feet for the rest of the evening. She didn't have any friends that she visited. He grew angrier as he waited because he wanted to think about Lutie and instead he found himself wondering uneasily where Min had gone.

Chapter 5

ARLIER IN THE EVENING, when Min was in the kitchen enjoying her supper, she was quite certain that Jones was planning some devilment while he sat in the living room. Even though he didn't answer when she told him supper was ready, the thought of him sitting there by himself, probably hungry but being stubborn about it, finally brought her to the door to ask, 'You ain't eatin'?'

He shook his head and she went back to the kitchen to pour herself another cup of tea and spread butter thickly on a third slice of bread, thinking, He don't know me. He thinks I don't know what's the matter with him.

She had seen him look at that young Mrs. Johnson

the night she paid the deposit on the top-floor apartment. He had almost eaten her up looking at her,
overwhelmed by her being so tall, by the way her
body fairly brimmed over with being young and
healthy. Three different times since then she had
opened the hall door just a crack and seen him standing out there watching young Mrs. Johnson as she
went up the stairs.

'He thinks I don't know what's on his mind,' she
said to herself.

She knew all right, and she also knew what she
was going to do about it. Though she had to find
out first from Mrs. Hedges the right place to go. She
felt certain Mrs. Hedges would know and would be
only too glad to tell her because she was always ready
to help folks out. Though Jones didn't think so,
because he didn't like Mrs. Hedges. He didn't know
that she knew that either. But she had seen him roll
his eyes up at Mrs. Hedges' window; his face had been
so full of hate he looked like Satan — black and
evil.

Jones went out of the apartment and Min got up
from the kitchen table, walked softly to the door
and looked out into the hall. He was talking to Mrs.
Johnson's boy — a right healthy-looking boy he
was, too. Maybe she ought to sort of hint to Mrs.
Johnson that it wasn't a good idea to let him hang
around Jones. Not that there was anything wrong
with Jones; it was just that he had lived in basements such a long time he was kind of queer, got
notions in his head about things.

She stayed there at the door until she saw Jones
open the cellar door and heard his footsteps go heavily

down the stairs. He would be down there long
enough for her to get dressed and consult with Mrs.
Hedges.

She hastily washed the dishes, thinking that
whether he came up out of the cellar before she got
back from where she was going would make a bit of
difference. She dressed hurriedly, putting on her
good dress and her best black coat, even the newish
pair of oxfords. She hesitated about a hat. The
triangular scarf she tied over her head for going back
and forth from work was much more comfortable,
but a hat was more dignified. So she pinned a high-
crowned black felt hat on top of her head with long
hatpins, thus anchoring it against the wind that
sometimes blew through the street with such speed
and force.

She looked out into the living room with a cautious
movement, just to make sure Jones hadn't come in
while she was dressing. Sometimes he got into the
house so quiet she didn't hear him, but turning
around would find he was sitting in the chair by the
radio or standing almost behind her in the kitchen.
Just like a ghost.

Just to make certain she was by herself, she looked
into the kitchen and the bathroom. Then she walked
over to the big table in the living room and squatting
down carefully so that the coat wouldn't touch the
floor she reached way up under the table. When she
straightened up, she was holding a thin roll of bills in
her hand. It was the money she had been saving for
her false teeth. She looked at it, trying to decide
whether she should take all of it with her. Yes, she
thought, tucking it in her pocketbook, because she

had no way of knowing how much she would need.

Before she left the room she patted the table gently. It was the best place to keep money she had ever found. She loved its smooth shiny surface and the way the curves of the claw feet gleamed when the light struck them, but the important thing about it was that secret drawer it contained. Until she got the table she had never been able to save any money. For her husbands could find her money, even if it was only a dollar bill or some silver, no matter where she put it. Almost as though they could smell it out whether it was put in coffee pots, under plates, in the icebox, under mattresses, between the sheets or under rugs.

Big Boy, her last husband before Jones, would snatch and tear it from her stocking, reach hard clutching hands inside her dresses in his eagerness to get at it. But with this table, Big Boy had been frustrated. That was really why he had left her. And she hadn't cared at all about his leaving because he was always drunk and broke and hungry and trying to feed him was like trying to fill up a bottomless pit.

So when Jones invited her to move in with him, she had accepted readily. Because she didn't have any place in particular to go to. Besides, she had the table, and if he turned out to be like the others it wouldn't matter, because the table would protect her money and one of these days she would have enough to buy a set of false teeth. But Jones wasn't like the others. He never asked her for money. That and the fact that he had invited her to come and live with him gave her a secure, happy feeling. He had wanted her just for herself, not for any money he might be able to get from her.

So when she came home from work, she cleaned the apartment and cooked for him and ironed his clothes. She bought a canary bird and a large ornate cage to put him in because she felt she ought to pretty the place up a little bit to show how grateful she was. What with not having to pay any rent, she was saving money so fast she would soon have her false teeth besides all the little things she saw and bought in the stores along Eighth Avenue.

She didn't mind Jones being kind of quiet and his spells of sullenness — those spells he had when both she and the dog had to keep out of his way. In his own silent, gloomy way he was fond of her and he really needed her. She didn't know when she had ever been so happy. It kind of bubbled up in her so that she talked and talked and talked to him and to the dog. And when he and the dog went to stand outside the building, she talked to herself, but quietly so that folks wouldn't hear her and think she was queer.

Everything was fine until that young Mrs. Johnson moved in. Then Jones changed so that he stayed mean and sullen all the time. Kicking at Buddy, snarling at her, slapping her. Only last night when she leaned over to take some beans out of the oven, he kicked her just like she was the dog. She had managed to hold on to the pan of beans, not saying anything, swallowing the hurt cry that rose in her throat, because she knew what was the matter with him. He had been comparing the way she looked

from behind with the way young Mrs. Johnson would
look if she should stoop over.

So the false teeth would just have to wait awhile
longer, because she was going to spend her teeth
money in order to stay in this apartment. She closed
the door behind her gently. 'Bless that table,' she
said aloud, and went outside to stand under Mrs.
Hedges' window.

'Mis' Hedges,' she said timidly.

'Hello, Min,' Mrs. Hedges said immediately and
settled her arms comfortably on the window sill in
preparation for a long talk.

'I wonder if I could come in for a minute,' Min
said. 'I got something important to talk over with
you.'

'Sure, dearie. Just walk right in the door. It's
always open. You better ring a coupla times first so
the girls won't think you're a customer.'

Min rang the bell twice and opened the door,
thinking now, If she don't help me I don't know
what I'll do. She can tell me if she wants to, but
sometimes folks won't do things out of pure meanness. But not Mis' Hedges, she thought hopefully.
Surely not Mis' Hedges.

She had never seen the inside of Mrs. Hedges'
apartment before and she stopped to look around,
surprised to see how comfortable it was. The hall
door led into the kitchen and there was bright linoleum on the floor, the kitchen curtains were freshly
done up, and the pots and pans hanging over the
sink had been scrubbed until they were shiny. There
were potted plants growing in a stand under the
window and she would have liked to examine them

more closely, but she didn't want Mrs. Hedges to think she was being nosy, so she went on through the kitchen to the next room where Mrs. Hedges was sitting by the window.

'Pull up a chair, Min,' Mrs. Hedges said. She verified the fact that Min was wearing her good coat and hat and then said, 'What's on your mind, dearie?'

'It's Jones,' Min said, and stopped, not knowing how to go on. The doorbell tinkled and she started to get up, thinking that it might be Jones, that he had seen her come in and followed her, wanting to know what she was doing there.

'It's all right' — Mrs. Hedges waved her hand indicating Min was to sit down again. 'Just a customer for one of the girls. Saw him go past the window.' She paused, waiting for Min to go on, and when Min said nothing, simply sat staring at her with miserable unhappy eyes, Mrs. Hedges said, 'What about Jones, dearie?'

Once Min started talking, she couldn't seem to stop. 'He's got his eye on that young Mis' Johnson. Ever since she moved in he's been hungerin' after her till it's made him so mean he ain't fit to live with no more.' She leaned toward Mrs. Hedges in an effort to convey the urgency of the situation. 'I ain't never had nothing of my own before. No money to spend like I wanted to. And now I'm living with him where they ain't no rent to pay, why, I can get things that I see. And it was all right until that Mis' Johnson come here to live. He'll be putting me out pretty soon. I can tell by the way he acts. And Mis' Hedges, I ain't goin' back to having nothing. Just paying rent. Jones don't ask for no money from me and he wasn't never this mean until that young Mis Johnson come here. And I ain't goin' to be put out'

She paused for breath, and then continued: 'I come to you because I thought mebbe you could tell me where I can find a root doctor who could help me. Because I ain't going to be put out,' she repeated firmly. Opening her pocketbook she took out the thin roll of bills. 'I can pay for it,' she said. 'This was the money I was saving for my false teeth,' she added simply.

Mrs. Hedges glanced at the roll of bills and began to rock, turning her head occasionally to look out on the street. 'Listen, dearie,' she said finally. 'I don't know nothing about root doctors. Don't hold with 'em myself, because I always figured that as far as my own business is concerned I was well able to do anything any root doctor could do.'

Min's face clouded with disappointment and Mrs. Hedges added hastily: 'But the girls tell me the best one in town is up on Eighth Avenue right off 140th Street. Supposed to be able to fix anything from ornery husbands to a body sickness. Name's David. That's all it says on the sign — just David, the Prophet. And if I was you, dearie, I wouldn't let him see them bills all at one time. Root doctor or not, he's probably jest as hungry as you and me.'

Min got up from the chair so eager to be on her way to the root doctor that she almost forgot to thank Mrs. Hedges. She was halfway out of the room when she remembered and she turned back to say, 'Oh, Mis' Hedges, I can't ever thank you.' She opened her purse and took out a bill. 'I'll just leave this,' she said, putting it down on a table.

'That's all right, dearie,' Mrs. Hedges said. Her eyes stayed for a long moment on the bill and it was with a visible effort that she looked away from it. 'Put it back in your pocketbook,' she said finally.

Min hesitated and then picked it up. When she looked back into the room, Mrs. Hedges was staring out of the window, brooding over the street like she thought, if she stopped looking at it for as much as a minute, the whole thing would collapse.

Before Min stepped out into the hall, she cracked the door of Mrs. Hedges' apartment and peered out to make sure she wouldn't run head-on into Jones. She stood there listening to make certain that he wasn't coming up the cellar stairs, and she heard heavy footsteps going up and up the stairs, from the second floor to the third. It sounded like Jones. And listening more and more intently, she knew that it was Jones. What was he going upstairs for? She opened the door wider in order to hear better. The footsteps kept going up and up, getting fainter as he kept climbing. He was going to the top floor.

'You're letting all the cold air in, dearie,' Mrs. Hedges called out.

Min hastily closed the door and scuttled out into the street. She waved a hasty salute toward Mrs. Hedges' window and almost ran toward the bus stop at the corner. What was he doing going up to that Mis' Johnson's apartment? She shivered. The air wasn't cold, but it seemed to come right through her coat in spite of her going along so fast. It was always colder on this street than anywhere else, she thought irritably, and Jones kept the apartment so hot she felt the cold go right through her when she first went

out. And the thought of him set her to walking
faster. His going up to Mrs. Johnson's apartment
tonight meant Mrs. Hedges had told her about the
Prophet David just in time.

The Eighth Avenue bus was so crowded that she
had to stand to 140th Street, hanging on to a strap as
best she could, for her arms were short and she had to
reach to get hold of the strap. The bus no sooner got
under way than her feet began to hurt, rebelling
against the unaccustomed oxfords. For the stiff
leather encased her bunions so tightly that they
burned and throbbed with pain until she was forced
to shift her weight from one foot to the other in an
effort to ease them.

They could keep right on hurting, she thought
grimly, because no matter what she had to go through,
no matter how much money it cost, she wasn't going
to let Jones put her out. She swayed back and forth
as the bus lurched, trying to wipe out the thought of
the pain in her feet by determinedly repeating, 'And
I ain't a-goin' to be put out.'

It was nice of Mrs. Hedges to tell her where to find
a root doctor, she thought. Yet now that she was
actually on her way to consult him, she felt a little
guilty. The preacher at the church she went to would
certainly disapprove, because in his eyes her dealing
with a root doctor was as good as saying that the
powers of darkness were stronger than the powers
of the church. Though she went to church infre-
quently, because she usually had to work on Sundays,
the thought of the preacher disturbed her. But he
didn't need to know anything about her going, she
decided. Besides, even the preacher must know

there were some things the church couldn't handle, had no resources for handling. And this was one of them — a situation where prayer couldn't possibly help.

She climbed awkwardly out of the bus at 140th Street, putting her weight on her feet gingerly to cushion them against the quick stab of pain any sudden, careless movement would bring. Before she was quite off the steps, she was already looking for the root doctor's sign, so that she collided with the passengers waiting to get on. Someone stepped on her feet and instantly hot fingers of pain clawed at her bunions, reached up her legs and thighs, making her draw her breath in sharply.

Then she saw the sign and she forgot about the pain. It was right near the corner as Mrs. Hedges had said — a big sign that winked and blinked off and on in the dark so that she thought the words 'David, the Prophet' were like a warm, friendly hand beckoning to her to come in out of the cold. She looked at it so long her eyes started to blink open and shut just like the sign. So he really was a prophet. She had thought perhaps Mrs. Hedges had made up that part about his being a prophet. That was fine, for he would be able to tell her what the future looked like for her.

It wasn't a very big place she discovered when she got right in front of it, though it did have a large window that was sparkling clean. She stopped to look at the objects displayed in the window. Some of them were familiar, but most of them she had never seen before and could only conjecture about the way in which they were used. There were colored candles, incense burners, strangely twisted roots, fine powders in small boxes, dream books, lucky-number books, medallions, small figures of monkeys and elephants, a number of rabbits' feet, monkey's fur, and candlesticks of all sizes and shapes. The window also contained a great many statues of the Madonna. They were illuminated with red lights, and there were so many of the statues and thus so many of the lights that they sent a rose-colored glow out onto the sidewalk.

She tried to see what the shop looked like inside, but the curtain at the window and another at the door effectively blocked her gaze. Remembering Mrs. Hedges' warning, she took part of the bills from her pocketbook, and opening her coat pushed them deep inside her dress. Then she opened the door.

The air inside was heavy with the smell of incense and she saw that it came from an incense burner on the counter that ran along one side of the small shop. Her first confused impression was that the place was full of people, but a second, careful look revealed five or six women seated on the chairs that lined the long wall opposite the counter. Three women were standing in front of the counter and she walked toward it keenly disappointed that the Prophet wasn't right there behind the counter instead of the young girl who was waiting on the customers. The girl looked up at her approach and said, 'Yes?' very quietly.

Min noticed that the girl's eyes were almond-shaped and then she looked down at the counter. There was a thick book on one side of it. The rest of the top was covered with trays that held brilliantly colored glistening powders — bright orange, green, purple, yellow, scarlet. She stared at them fascinated, noting how finely ground they were, wondering what they were used for and which one the Prophet would recommend to her. She forgot about the girl behind the counter.

'Yes?' the girl repeated.

Min held on to the counter at a loss for words, suddenly frightened at having actually come to the place. Her fright confused her so that for a moment she couldn't remember why she had come. Jones. It had to do with Jones and she let go the counter. 'I come to see the Prophet David,' she said in her sing-song voice, the words coming out half-muffled so that she sounded as though she were whispering.

'Won't you sit down?' The girl nodded toward the line of chairs across the room. 'Those ladies are waiting to see him, too. He takes everybody in turn.'

Min sat down next to a light-complexioned woman whose face was covered with freckles, and glancing at the woman she thought, It's better to have a dark skin; lots of times these light-skinned women have freckles all over them till they look like they've been marked by the Devil's fingertips. The woman kept turning her pocketbook over and over between her hands with a nervous gesture that finally had the eyes of all the women near her following the constant restless motion of her hands. She had a big awkwardly wrapped package on her lap and in order to keep turning the pocketbook between her hands she had to reach over and around the package.

Wonder why she doesn't set the package on a chair

instead of holding it, Min thought. And tried to conjecture what was in it — whatever it was bulged here and there, and she couldn't think of anything that would look quite like that after it was wrapped up, so she stopped thinking about it. She moved impatiently in the straight-backed chair, thinking that sitting like this just waiting was enough to drive anybody crazy. The thought that had frightened her when she was standing at the counter returned suddenly. How had she dared to come here?

It was the first defiant gesture she had ever made. Up to now she had always accepted whatever happened to her without making any effort to avoid a situation or to change one. During the years she had spent doing part-time domestic work she had never raised any objections to the actions of cruelly indifferent employers. She had permitted herself to be saddled with whole family washes when the agency that had sent her on the job had specified just 'personal pieces.' When the madam added sheets, towels, pillowcases, shirts, bedspreads, curtains — she simply allowed herself to be buried under the great mounds of dirty clothes and it took days to work her way out from under them, getting no extra pay for the extra time involved.

On other jobs the care of innumerable children had been added when the original agreement was for her to do the cooking and a little cleaning. The little cleaning would increase and increase until it included washing windows and walls and waxing floors. Some of her madams had been openly contemptuous women who laughed at her to her face even as they piled on more work; acting as though she were a deaf, dumb, blind thing completely devoid of understanding, but able to work, work, work. Years and years like that.

Never once had she protested. Never once, she thought with pride, had she left a job, no matter how much work there was or how badly the people treated her. As long as they paid her, she stayed on in spite of their reneging on her days off, in spite of having to work on Sundays so she couldn't get to church, though when she first started work it was always with the understanding she wouldn't be in on Sundays. Day after day she'd go back until the people moved away or got somebody else. She was never the one to make the change.

It was the same thing with the various husbands she had had. They had taken her money and abused her and given her nothing in return, but she was never the one who left.

And here she was sitting waiting to see the Prophet David — committing an open act of defiance for the first time in her life. And thinking about it that way, she was frightened by her own audacity. For in coming here like this, in trying to prevent Jones from putting her out, she was actually making an effort to change a situation. No. It was better to think of it as being an effort to keep a situation the way it had been before. That is, she was trying to stay there in his house because there she was free from the yoke of that one word: rent. That word that meant padlocked doors with foul-mouthed landladies standing in front of them or sealed keyholes with marshals waving long white papers in their hands. Then she thought if Jones ever found out she had come here,

he would try to kill her because he was dead set on
having that young Mrs. Johnson.

As she waited, she became aware that the women
standing at the counter were spending a long time
going through the thick book that was placed so
handily right on top of the counter. They turned the
pages and talked to the girl behind the counter before
they finally put in an order.

When they told her what they wanted, their voices
had a firm sound with an underlying note of triumph.
'Fifteen cents worth of 492.' The girl would take it
down from the shelf in back of her or scoop it up from
a tray on the counter and then weigh the fine powders
on the scales. 'Fifty cents of 215'; or, 'I guess a
dime's worth of 319 will fix it.'

Listening to them, Min was filled with envy. She
watched them turn away from the counter with the
small packages safely tucked away in pocketbooks or
thrust deeply into their coat pockets, and she saw
such a glow of satisfaction on their faces that she
thought if she only knew what to get she'd buy it the
same way and go on home without waiting for the
Prophet. But she wouldn't know how to use any of
the powders after she got them. Some, she knew,
were for sprinkling around the house, some for putting in coffee or tea, others were intended to be burnt
in incense burners like those in the shop window,
but she didn't know one from the other. There
wouldn't be any point in her looking through the
thick pages of the book on the counter, because the
very sight of so much print would only bewilder
her.

Then she forgot about the book, because a woman

emerged from behind the white curtains that hung at the back of the store. All the women sitting on the chairs moved slightly at the sight of the man who followed the woman from behind the curtains. He was tall and he wore a white turban on his head. The whiteness of the turban accentuated the darkness of his skin. He beckoned toward the row of chairs and the woman sitting nearest the back of the shop got up and disappeared behind the curtains with him. The curtains fell back in place with a graceful movement.

Like the others, Min moved in her chair when she saw him — shifting her feet, leaning forward away from the chair and then leaning back against it. That musta been the Prophet, she thought. Though she listened intently, she could hear no sound from behind the curtains. No murmur of conversation. Nothing. The quiet in back of the curtains disturbed her so that she wished uneasily she hadn't come. Then, remembering that she was dead set on not being put out, dead set on keeping Jones away from young Mrs. Johnson, she folded her hands over her pocketbook, content to wait her turn; determined to finish this action she had begun.

But her tranquillity was disturbed by the freckled woman who sat next to her. The woman kept turning her pocketbook over and over, first one side then the other, until the constant restless motion was unbearable.

In desperation Min turned toward the woman. 'You been here before?' she asked, and saw with relief that the pocketbook stayed still in the woman's lap.

'Sure,' the woman said. 'I come about once a week.'

'Oh' — Min tried to conceal her chagrin, tried to keep it from showing in her face. 'I thought if you come once he could fix whatever was wrong on the one trip.' She couldn't come every week. It was out of the question, for she never went anywhere at night, and Jones would get suspicious and probably act nastier than ever if she started going out regularly when she'd never done it before.

'Depends on what it is,' the woman said. 'Some things ain't easy. I ain't got a easy case. Prophet's helped a lot, but it ain't all fixed yet.'

'No?' Min hoped if she acted interested but not too interested the woman would tell her about it. Then she could get some idea about her and Jones — whether she'd have to pay weekly visits to the Prophet or whether this one time would be enough.

'No,' the woman lowered her voice slightly. 'You see Zeke, that's my husband, has got a way of not styin' in bed nights. He just disappears. Goes to bed like anybody else and then all of a sudden he's gone. I've stayed awake all night and I ain't never seen him go. Next day he's there for breakfast and don't know nothing about not being in bed all night. Says he don't know where he's been or nothing.'

Min frowned as she listened to her. Sounded to her like the woman's husband was fooling her. Probably with some other woman. 'Prophet don't know how to fix it?' she asked and waited impatiently for the answer, beginning to doubt the Prophet's power, beginning even to question his honesty, for it looked like to her anybody ought to

130

be able to see the woman's husband was fooling her.

'Oh, yes, he don't disappear quite so often. Prophet's cut him down a lot,' the woman said eagerly. 'But he say Zeke ain't co-operatin'.' She indicated the bulky package on her lap. 'Prophet's goin' to sprinkle his shoes tonight. He put off doing it, but he says ain't nothing else to do now seein's Zeke ain't co-operatin'.'

Min wanted to ask more questions, but at that moment the Prophet appeared from behind the curtain and beckoned to the woman. She watched her walk toward the white curtains, thinking that perhaps Mrs. Hedges had been right not to put any faith in root doctors, for surely that woman with the freckles didn't need to come here every week. She was glad she had talked to her, though, for if after the first few minutes of talking to the Prophet she decided he was just stringing her along like he was obviously doing with this woman, why, she wouldn't give him any money — she would just leave and look up another root doctor that was honest.

Sprinkling the shoes evidently didn't take very long, Min thought, for when she looked up again the freckled woman was coming out from behind the curtains. Her face was lit up by such a luminous, radiant smile that Min couldn't help but stare at her, thinking, Well, whatever else he might be able to do the Prophet deserved some credit for making that fidgety woman look so happy. The Prophet beckoned toward the row of chairs.

'It's your turn,' said the fat woman sitting next to her.

Min walked toward the curtains in the back, and

the nearer she got to them, the more she wished that she hadn't come or that while she was sitting waiting outside she had got up and gone home. Her heart started jumping so that she began to breathe heavily. Then the curtains swished together behind her and she was standing in a small room. The Prophet was already sitting behind a desk looking at her.

'Will you close the door, please?' he said.

She turned to close it, thinking, That's why there wasn't any sound outside. Because there was a solid wall in back of the curtains, a wall that went right up to the ceiling and effectively separated the room from the shop. With the door shut no sound could get outside.

After she sat down across from him, she found she couldn't bring herself to look right at him so she looked at his turban. It was like Mrs. Hedges and that bandanna she wore all the time, you couldn't tell what kind or color of hair headgears like that concealed. And staring at the Prophet's turban she got the sudden jolting thought that perhaps Mrs. Hedges wore that bandanna all the time because she was bald. There must be some reason why nobody who lived in the house had ever seen her without it.

'You're in trouble?' asked the Prophet David.

This was worse than when she had tried to get started on telling Mrs. Hedges about it. She shrank into the chair, wondering why she had thought she could tell a strange man about Jones and Mis' Johnson and herself. The more she thought about it, the more bewildered she became until finally, in the confusion of her thinking, her eyes shifted from his turban and she was looking directly at him.

'Tell me about it,' he urged. And when she didn't say anything he added, 'Is it your husband?'

'Yes,' she said eagerly, and then stopped speaking. Her husband. Jones wasn't her husband any more than any of those others she had lived with in between. She hadn't seen her husband in twenty-five years. She had stayed with the others because a woman by herself didn't stand much chance; and because it was too lonely living by herself in a rented room. With a man attached to her she could have an apartment — a real home.

'Tell me about it,' the Prophet said again.

If he's a prophet he ought to know without my telling him, she thought resentfully. Then the resentment left her because his eyes were deep-set and they didn't contain the derisive look she was accustomed to seeing in people's eyes. He sat looking at her and his manner was so calm and so patient that without further thinking about it she started talking. It was suddenly quite easy to tell him about how she'd never really had anything before and about Jones and young Mis' Johnson.

'And I ain't a-goin' to be put out,' she ended defiantly. Then she added, 'Leastways that's why I come to you. So you could give me something to fix it so I won't be put out.'

'Which is more important? Your not being put out or Jones forgetting about the young lady?'

Min looked at him, thinking hard. 'Both,' she said finally. 'Because if he loses his taste for young Mis' Johnson, he ain't goin' to put me out.'

'One depends on the other. Is that it?'

'Yes.'

'Most of these things do.' The Prophet folded the tips of his fingers against the palms of his hands and stared at them.

Min following the direction of his eyes saw that his hands were long, the fingers flexible. The skin on his hands was as smooth as that on his face. Once or twice he looked at her intently and then went back to studying his hands.

'I can fix things so you won't be put out,' he said finally. 'I'll see what I can do about taking Jones's mind off the young lady, but I won't promise results on that.'

He got up to open the wooden doors of a cupboard which stood directly behind the desk. Its shelves were laden with vials and bottles and small packages.

'Does he drink coffee for breakfast?' he asked over his shoulder.

'Yes.'

He filled a tiny glass vial with a bright red liquid. The vial was so small that he used a medicine dropper to fill it with. Next he put a bright green powder in a square cardboard box and Min watching him was a little disappointed, for this powder was dull, not shiny like those on the counter outside. He put two squat white candles on the desk and then, reaching far back in the cabinet, brought out a cross which he held carefully in his hands for a moment and then placed beside the candles.

Seating himself behind the desk he said: 'These things and the consultation will cost you ten dollars. I make no guarantee about the young lady. However, I can guarantee that you won't be put out. Is that all right?'

The Street

Min opened her purse, took out two limp five-dollar bills and placed them on the desk. The Prophet folded them together and stuck them in his vest pocket.

'Now listen carefully. Every morning put one drop of this red liquid in his coffee. Just one drop. No more.' When Min indicated that she understood, he went on: 'Every night at ten o'clock burn these candles for five minutes. You must clean the apartment every day. Clean it until there isn't a speck of dirt anywhere. In the corners. On the cupboard shelves. The window sills.'

Min thought of the dust in the corners of the closet floor — the unfinished splintery boards in there seemed to attract it. Then there was the grease she'd let accumulate in the oven. Soot on the window sills. She'd get after all of it as soon as she got home.

He pointed at the cross with one of his long fingers. 'This,' he said, 'will keep you safe at night. Hang it right over your bed. As for the powder' — he leaned toward her and talked more slowly — 'it's very powerful. You only need a little of it at a time. Always carry some of it with you because if Jones should try to put you out this powder will stop him. Sprinkle a little of it on the floor if he gets violent and he won't dare touch you.'

The cross, the candles, and the small vial of red liquid made a very neat package, for he put them all into a cardboard box and then wrapped them in white paper. He handed her the box of powder. 'Put it in your coat pocket,' he directed, 'for you might need it tonight. If you'll stop at the counter on your way out, the girl will give you a medicine dropper.'

'Oh, I thank you,' she said. 'You don't know what you done for me.'

Then he shook hands with her and she thought talking to him had been the most satisfying experience she had ever known. True, he hadn't said very much except toward the last when he was telling her how to use the things. The satisfaction she felt was from the quiet way he had listened to her, giving her all of his attention. No one had ever done that before. The doctors she saw from time to time at the clinic were brusque, hurried, impatient. Even while they asked questions — is the pain here, is it often, do your shoes fit — their minds weren't really on her as a person. They were looking at her feet, but not as though they belonged to her and were therefore different, individual, because they were hers. All they saw were a pair of feet with swollen, painful bunions on them — nigger feet. The words were in the expressions in their faces. Even with the colored doctors she felt humble, apologetic.

Even Jones when he was in a good mood never listened to her. She might as well not have been there. All the time she was talking, his mind was on something else, something that set him to frowning and biting his lips. And her madams. And her madams — short ones, fat ones, harried ones, calm ones, drunken ones — none of them had ever listened when she talked. They issued orders to some point over her head until sometimes she was tempted to look up to see if there was another head on top of her own — a head she had grown without knowing it. And the minute she started answering, they turned away. The few times she had a chance to talk to the preacher at the church, he interrupted her with, 'We all got our troubles, Sister. We all got our troubles.' And he, too, turned away.

But this man had listened and been interested, and all the time she had talked he had never shifted his gaze, so that when she came out from behind the white curtains the satisfaction from his attentive listening, the triumph of actually possessing the means of controlling Jones, made her face glow. The women waiting in the chairs outside stared at her and she walked past them, not caring, for she had got what she came after. And it had been simple and easy and not as expensive as she had expected.

Riding toward 116th Street on the bus, she decided that every time she heard about some poor woman in trouble she would send her to the Prophet David. He was so easy to talk to, his eyes were so kind, and he knew his business. Seeing as Mrs. Hedges had been responsible for her finding him, she really ought to do something in return. As she clung to the bus strap she wondered what she could do. She thought about it so hard that she rode past 116th Street and the bus was at 112th Street before she realized it.

She walked up Eighth Avenue, still thinking about Mrs. Hedges. She stopped to look in the window of a florist shop and then went inside.

'How much are them cactuses in the gray dishes in the window?' she asked.

'Dollar and a quarter.'

'Wrap one up,' she ordered, and when the clerk reached in to the window for one of the plants she took the remainder of the flat roll of bills from her bosom. Peeling off two dollars she saw there wasn't much left over, but what she'd got in return for spending it was worth far more than she had paid for it.

There was a dim light in Mrs. Hedges' living room, and as Min turned the corner of the building Mrs. Hedges' voice came from the window, 'Get fixed up, dearie?' she asked.

'I sure did,' Min said. Her voice was so full of life and confidence that Mrs. Hedges stared at her amazed. 'I saw you liked plants,' she went on. 'So I brought you a little present.' She handed the package up to Mrs. Hedges.

'Sure was sweet of you, dearie.' Mrs. Hedges leaned forward holding the plant and waiting to hear about the Prophet David. But Min walked swiftly toward the apartment house door. There was such energy and firmness about the way she walked that Mrs. Hedges' eyebrows lifted as she craned her neck for a further look.

Jones, dozing in the chair by the radio, heard Min's key go in the lock. It was the sound he had been waiting for, and he got up out of the chair to stand in the middle of the floor stretching to get himself thoroughly awake. The dog got up, too, cocking his ears at the click of the lock.

It was the sound he had been waiting to hear, but it came to his ears with an offensive, decisive loudness. Normally Min's key was inserted in the lock timidly, with a vague groping movement, and when the lock finally clicked back, she stood there for a second as though overwhelmed by the sound it made. This key was being thrust in with assurance, and the door was pushed open immediately afterward. He frowned as he listened because on top of that she slammed the door. Let it go out of her hand with a bang that echoed through the apartment and in the hall outside, could even be heard going faintly up the stairs.

Her unaccustomed actions surprised him so greatly that when she came into the living room, instead of starting immediately to throw her out and her table along with her, he found himself saying, 'Where you been?'

'Out,' she said, and walked into the bedroom.

And he sat down again, appalled at the thought that she might have taken up with some other man. He slowly clenched his fist and then relaxed his fingers until his hand lay limp along the arm of the chair. Here he was thinking about her again when what he wanted was Lutie. And Lutie wouldn't even look at him while Min stayed here. He saw Lutie again in his mind's eye — her long brown legs, the way her pointed breasts pushed against the fabric of her clothing. The thought sent him striding toward the bedroom, his hands itching to do violence to Min. Even his foot was itching, he thought, for he was going to plant his foot squarely in her wide shapeless bottom.

Min was unpinning her high-crowned hat, looking at herself in the mirror over the bureau as she withdrew the long pins. There was something so smug and satisfied about her and her bland, flat face reflected in the mirror was so ugly that the sight of her standing there contentedly surveying herself sent a wave of fury through him.

He took a hasty step toward her and he saw her eyes shift in the mirror. He turned his head to see what she was staring at, it was something that must be near the bed and he followed the direction of her glance. When he saw the great gold cross hanging over the headboard, he stood still. It was like an accusing finger pointing at him.

Almost immediately he started backing away from the sight of it, retreating toward the living room where he wouldn't be able to see it. Though he didn't believe in religion and never went to church, though he only had contempt for the people who slobbered about their sins and spent Sundays pleading for forgiveness, he had never been able to rid himself of a haunting fear of the retribution which he had heard described in his early childhood. The retribution which, for example, awaited men who lusted after women — men like himself.

Hence to him a cross was an alarming and unpleasant object, for it was a symbol of power. It was mixed up in his mind with the evil spirits and the powers of darkness it could invoke against those who outraged the laws of the church. It was fear of the evil the cross could conjure up that forced him out of the bedroom, made him sit down in the chair in the living room.

He covered his eyes with his hands, for it seemed to him the great gold-colored cross was hanging directly in front of him instead of over the headboard of the bed where he had last seen it. He muttered under his breath and got up once to kick savagely at the dog and then sat down again.

In the bedroom Min smiled as she bent forward to light the fat white candles she had placed on each side of the bureau.

Chapter 6

THERE WAS ALWAYS A CROWD in front of the Junto Bar and Grill on 116th Street. For in winter the street was cold. The wind blew the snow into great drifts that stayed along the curb for weeks, gradually blackening with soot until it was no longer recognizable as snow, but appeared to be some dark eruption from the street itself.

As one cold day followed swiftly on the heels of another, the surface of the frozen piles became encrusted with bags of garbage, old shoes, newspapers, corset lacings. The frozen débris and the icy wind made the street a desolate place in winter and the people found a certain measure of escape from it by standing in front of the Junto where the light streaming from the windows and the music from its jukebox created an oasis of warmth.

The Street

In summer the street was hot and dusty, for no trees shaded it, and the sun beat straight down on the concrete sidewalks and the brick buildings. The inside of the houses fairly steamed; the dark hallways were like ovens. Even the railings on the high steep stairways were warm to the touch.

As the thermometer crawled higher and higher, the people who lived on the street moved outdoors because the inside of the buildings was unbearable. The grown-ups lounging in chairs in front of the houses, the half-naked children playing along the curb, transformed the street into an outdoor living room. And because the people took to sleeping on rooftops and fire escapes and park benches, the street also became a great outdoor bedroom.

The same people who found warmth by standing in front of the Junto in winter continued to stand there in summer. In fact, the number of people in front of the Junto increased in summer, for the whirr of its electric fans and the sound of ice clinking in tall glasses reached out to the street and created an illusion of coolness.

Thus, in winter and in summer people stood in front of the Junto from the time its doors opened early in the morning until they were firmly shut behind the last drunk the following morning.

The men who didn't work at all — the ones who never had and never would — stood in front of it in the morning. As the day slid toward afternoon, they were joined by numbers runners and men who worked nights in factories and warehouses. And at night the sidewalk spilled over with the men who ran elevators and cleaned buildings and swept out subways.

The Street

All of them — the idle ones and the ones tired from their day's labor — found surcease and refreshment either inside or outside the Junto's doors. It served as social club and meeting place. By standing outside it a man could pick up all the day's news: the baseball scores, the number that came out, the latest neighborhood gossip. Those who were interested in women could get an accurate evaluation of the girls who switched past in short tight skirts. A drinking man who was dead broke knew that if he stood there long enough a friend with funds would stroll by and offer to buy him a drink. And a man who was lonely and not interested in drinking or in women could absorb some of the warmth and laughter that seeped out to the street from the long bar.

The inside of the Junto was always crowded, too, because the white bartenders in their immaculate coats greeted the customers graciously. Their courteous friendliness was a heart-warming thing that helped rebuild egos battered and bruised during the course of the day's work.

The Junto represented something entirely different to the women on the street and what it meant to them depended in large measure on their age. Old women plodding past scowled ferociously and jerked the heavy shopping bags they carried until the stalks of celery and the mustard greens within seemed to tremble with rage at the sight of the Junto's doors. Some of the old women paused to mutter their hatred of it, to shake their fists in a sudden access of passion against it, and the men standing on the sidewalk moved closer to each other, forming a protective island with their shoulders, talking louder, laughing harder so as to shut out the sound and the sight of the old women.

Young women coming home from work — dirty, tired, depressed — looked forward to the moment when they would change their clothes and head toward the gracious spaciousness of the Junto. They dressed hurriedly in their small dark hall bedrooms, so impatient for the soft lights and the music and the fun that awaited them that they fumbled in their haste.

For the young women had an urgent hunger for companionship and the Junto offered men of all sizes and descriptions: sleek, well-dressed men who earned their living as numbers runners; even better-dressed and better-looking men who earned a fatter living supplying women to an eager market; huge, grimy longshoremen who were given to sudden bursts of generosity; Pullman porters in on overnight runs from Washington, Chicago, Boston; and around the first of the month the sailors and soldiers flush with crisp pay-day money.

On the other hand, some of the young women went to the Junto only because they were hungry for the sight and sound of other young people and because the creeping silence that could be heard under the blaring radios, under the drunken quarrels in the hall bedrooms, was no longer bearable.

Lutie Johnson was one of these. For she wasn't going to the Junto to pick up a man or to quench a consuming, constant thirst. She was going there so that she could for a moment capture the illusion of having some of the things that she lacked.

As she hurried toward the Junto, she acknowledged

the fact that she couldn't afford a glass of beer there. It would be cheaper to buy a bottle at the delicatessen and take it home and drink it if beer was what she wanted. The beer was incidental and unimportant. It was the other things that the Junto offered that she sought: the sound of laughter, the hum of talk, the sight of people and brilliant lights, the sparkle of the big mirror, the rhythmic music from the juke-box.

Once inside, she hesitated, trying to decide whether she should stand at the crowded bar or sit alone at one of the small tables in the center of the room or in one of the booths at the side. She turned abruptly to the long bar, thinking that she needed people around her tonight, even all these people who were jammed against each other at the bar.

They were here for the same reason that she was — because they couldn't bear to spend an evening alone in some small dark room; because they couldn't bear to look what they could see of the future smack in the face while listening to radios or trying to read an evening paper.

'Beer, please,' she said to the bartender.

There were rows of bottles on the shelves on each side of the big mirror in back of the bar. They were reflected in the mirror, and looking at the reflection Lutie saw that they were magnified in size, shining so that they had the appearance of being filled with liquid, molten gold.

She examined herself and the people standing at the bar to see what changes the mirror wrought in them. There was a pleasant gaiety and charm about all of them. She found that she herself looked young, very young and happy in the mirror.

The Street

Her eyes wandered over the whole room. It sparkled in the mirror. The people had a kind of buoyancy about them. All except Old Man Junto, who was sitting alone at the table near the back.

She looked at him again and again, for his reflection in the mirror fascinated her. Somehow even at this distance his squat figure managed to dominate the whole room. It was, she decided, due to the bulk of his shoulders which were completely out of proportion to the rest of him.

Whenever she had been in here, he had been sitting at that same table, his hand cupped behind his ear as though he were listening to the sound of the cash register; sitting there alone watching everything — the customers, the bartenders, the waiters. For the barest fraction of a second, his eyes met hers in the mirror and then he looked away.

Then she forgot about him, for the juke-box in the far corner of the room started playing 'Swing It, Sister.' She hummed as she listened to it, not really aware that she was humming or why, knowing only that she felt free here where there was so much space.

The big mirror in front of her made the Junto an enormous room. It pushed the walls back and back into space. It reflected the lights from the ceiling and the concealed lighting that glowed in the corners of the room. It added a rosy radiance to the men and women standing at the bar; it pushed the world of other people's kitchen sinks back where it belonged and destroyed the existence of dirty streets and small shadowed rooms.

She finished the beer in one long gulp. Its pleasant

bitter taste was still in her mouth when the bartender handed her a check for the drink.

'I'll have another one,' she said softly.

No matter what it cost them, people had to come to places like the Junto, she thought. They had to replace the haunting silences of rented rooms and little apartments with the murmur of voices, the sound of laughter; they had to empty two or three small glasses of liquid gold so they could believe in themselves again.

She frowned. Two beers and the movies for Bub and the budget she had planned so carefully was ruined. If she did this very often, there wouldn't be much point in having a budget — for she couldn't budget what she didn't have.

For a brief moment she tried to look into the future. She still couldn't see anything — couldn't see anything at all but 116th Street and a job that paid barely enough for food and rent and a handful of clothes. Year after year like that. She tried to recapture the feeling of self-confidence she had had earlier in the evening, but it refused to return, for she rebelled at the thought of day after day of work and night after night caged in that apartment that no amount of scrubbing would ever get really clean.

She moved the beer glass on the bar. It left a wet ring and she moved it again in an effort to superimpose the rings on each other. It was warm in the Junto, the lights were soft, and the music coming from the juke-box was sweet. She listened intently to the record. It was 'Darlin',' and when the voice on the record stopped she started singing: 'There's no sun, Darlin'. There's no fun, Darlin'.'

The Street

The men and women crowded at the bar stopped drinking to look at her. Her voice had a thin thread of sadness running through it that made the song important, that made it tell a story that wasn't in the words — a story of despair, of loneliness, of frustration. It was a story that all of them knew by heart and had always known because they had learned it soon after they were born and would go on adding to it until the day they died.

Just before the record ended, her voice stopped on a note so low and so long sustained that it was impossible to tell where it left off. There was a moment's silence around the bar, and then glasses were raised, the bartenders started making change, and opening long-necked bottles, conversations were resumed.

The bartender handed her another check. She picked it up mechanically and then placed it on top of the first one, held both of them loosely in her hand. That made two glasses and she'd better go before she weakened and bought another one. She put her gloves on slowly, transferring the checks from one hand to the other, wanting to linger here in this big high-ceilinged room where there were no shadowed silences, no dark corners; thinking that she should have made the beer last a long time by careful sipping instead of the greedy gulping that had made it disappear so quickly.

A man's hand closed over hers, gently extracted the two checks. 'Let me take 'em,' said a voice in her ear.

She looked down at the hand. The nails were clean, filed short. There was a thin coating of colorless polish on them. The skin was smooth. It was the hand of a man who earned his living in some way that didn't call for any wear and tear on his hands. She looked in the mirror and saw that the man who had reached for the checks was directly in back of her.

He was wearing a brown overcoat. It was unfastened so that she caught a glimpse of a brown suit, of a tan-colored shirt. His eyes met hers in the mirror and he said, 'Do you sing for a living?'

She was aware that Old Man Junto was studying her in the mirror and she shifted her gaze back to the man standing behind her. He was waiting to find out whether she was going to ignore him or whether she was going to answer him. It would be so simple and so easy if she could say point-blank that all she wanted was a little companionship, someone to laugh with, someone to talk to, someone who would take her to places like the Junto and to the movies without her having to think about how much it cost — just that and no more; and then to explain all at once and quickly that she couldn't get married because she didn't have a divorce, that there wasn't any inducement he could offer that would make her sleep with him.

It was out of the question to say any of those things. There wasn't any point even in talking to him, for when he found out, which he would eventually, that she wasn't going to sleep with him, he would disappear. It might take a week or a month, but that was how it would end.

No. There wasn't any point in answering him. What she should do was to take the checks out of his hand without replying and go on home. Go home to wash out a pair of stockings for herself, a pair of socks and a shirt for Bub. There had been night after night like that, and as far as she knew the same thing lay ahead in the future. There would be the three rooms with the silence and the walls pressing in ——

'No, I don't,' she said, and turned around and faced him. 'I've never thought of trying.' And knew as she said it that the walls had beaten her or she had beaten the walls. Whichever way she cared to look at it.

'You could, you know,' he said. 'How about another drink?'

'Make it beer, please.' She hesitated, and then said, 'Do you mean that you think I could earn my living singing?'

'Sure. You got the kind of voice that would go over big.' He elbowed space for himself beside her at the bar. 'Beer for the lady,' he said to the bartender. 'The usual for me.' He leaned nearer to Lutie, 'I know what I'm talkin' about. My band plays at the Casino.'

'Oh,' she said. 'You're ——'

'Boots Smith.' He said it before she could finish her sentence. And his eyes on her face were so knowing, so hard, that she thought instantly of the robins she had seen on the Chandlers' lawn in Lyme, and the cat, lean, stretched out full length, drawing itself along on its belly, intent on its prey. The image flashed across her mind and was gone, for he said, 'You want to try out with the band tomorrow night?'

'You mean sing at a dance? Without rehearsing?'

'Come up around ten o'clock and we'll run over some stuff. See how it goes.'

She was holding the beer glass so tightly that she could feel the impression of the glass on her fingers and she let go of it for fear it would snap in two. She couldn't seem to stop the excitement that bubbled up in her; couldn't stop the flow of planning that ran through her mind. A singing job would mean she and Bub could leave 116th Street. She could get an apartment some place where there were trees and the streets were clean and the rooms would be full of sunlight. There wouldn't be any more worry about rent and gas bills and she could be home when Bub came from school.

He was standing so close to her, watching her so intently, that again she thought of a cat slinking through grass, waiting, going slowly, barely making the grass move, but always getting nearer and nearer.

The only difference in the technique was that he had placed a piece of bait in front of her — succulent, tantalizing bait. He was waiting, watching to see whether she would nibble at it or whether he would have to use a different bait.

She tried to think about it dispassionately. Her voice wasn't any better or any worse than that of the women who sang with the dance bands over the radio. It was just an average good voice and with some coaching it might well be better than average. He had probably tossed out this sudden offer with the hope that she just might nibble at it.

Only she wasn't going to nibble. She was going to swallow it whole and come back for more until she ended up as vocalist with his band. She turned to look at him, to estimate him, to add up her chances.

His face was tough, hard-boiled, unscrupulous. There was a long, thin scar on his left cheek. It was a dark line that stood out sharply against the dark brown of his skin. And she thought that at some time someone had found his lack of scruple unbearable and had in desperation tried to do something about it. His body was lean, broad-shouldered, and as he lounged there, his arm on the bar, his muscles relaxed, she thought again of a cat slinking quietly after its prey.

There was no expression in his eyes, no softness, nothing, to indicate that he would ever bother to lift a finger to help anyone but himself. It wouldn't be easy to use him. But what she wanted she wanted so badly that she decided to gamble to get it.

'Come on. Let's get out of here,' he suggested. He shoved a crisp ten-dollar bill toward the barkeep and smiled at her while he waited for his change, quite obviously satisfied with whatever he had read in her face. She noticed that, though his mouth curved upward when he smiled, his eyes stayed expressionless, and she thought that he had completely lost the knack of really smiling.

He guided her toward the street, his hand under her elbow. 'Want to go for a ride?' he asked. 'I've got about three hours to kill before I go to work.'

'I'd love to,' she said.

Eighth Avenue was lined with small stores. And as they walked toward 117th Street, Lutie looked at each store, closely reacting to it as violently as though she had never seen it before. All of them provided a sudden shocking contrast to the big softly lit interior of the Junto.

The windows of the butcher shops were piled high with pigs' feet, hog maw, neck bones, chitterlings, ox tails, tripe — all the parts that didn't cost much because they didn't have much solid meat on them, she thought. The notion stores were a jumble of dark red stockings, imitation leather pocketbooks, gaudy rayon underwear edged with coarse yellow lace, sleazy blouses — most of it good for one wearing and no more, for the underwear would fade and ravel after the first washing and the pocketbooks would begin to disintegrate after they had been opened and closed a few times.

Withered oranges and sweet potatoes, wilting kale and okra, were stacked up on the vegetable stands — the culls, the windfalls, all the bruised rotten fruit and vegetables were here. She stole a side glance at Boots striding along cat-footed, silent beside her.

It was a good thing that she had walked past these mean little stores with Boots Smith because the sight of them stiffened her determination to leave streets like this behind her — dark streets filled with shadowy figures that carried with them the horror of the places they lived in, places like her own apartment. Otherwise she might have been afraid of him.

She thought about the stores again. All of them — the butcher shops, the notion stores, the vegetable stands — all of them sold the leavings, the sweepings, the impossible unsalable merchandise, the dregs and dross that were reserved especially for Harlem.

Yet the people went on living and reproducing in spite of the bad food. Most of the children had straight bones, strong white teeth. But it couldn't go on like that. Even the strongest heritage would one day run out. Bub was healthy, sturdy, strong, but he couldn't remain that way living here.

'I ain't seen you in Junto's before, baby,' said Boots Smith.

'I don't go there very often,' she said. There was something faintly contemptuous about the way he said 'baby.' He made it sound like 'bebe,' and it slipped casually, easily, out of his mouth as though it were his own handy, one-word index of women.

Then, because she was still thinking about the stores and their contents, she said, 'When you look at the meat in these windows it's a wonder people in Harlem go on living.'

'They don't have to eat it,' he said indifferently.

'What are they going to do — stop eating?'

'If they make enough money they don't have to buy that stuff.'

'But that's just it. Most of them don't make enough to buy anything else.'

'There's plenty of money to be made in Harlem if you know how.'

'Sure,' she said. 'It's on the trees and bushes. All you have to do is shake 'em.'

'Look, baby,' he said. 'I ain't interested in how they eat or what they eat. Only thing I'm interested in right now is you.'

They were silent after that. So there's plenty of money to be made in Harlem. She supposed there was if people were willing to earn it by doing something that kept them just two jumps ahead of the law. Otherwise they eked out a miserable existence.

They turned down 117th Street, and she wondered whether a ride with him meant a taxi or a car of his own. If there was plenty of money floating through the town, then she assumed he must have a car of his own. So when he opened the door of a car drawn in close to the curb, she wasn't oversurprised at its length, its shiny, expensive look. It was about what she had expected from the red leather upholstery to the white-walled tires and the top that could be thrown back when the weather was warm.

She got in, thinking, This is the kind of car you see in the movies, the kind that swings insolently past you on Park Avenue, the kind that pulls up in front of the snooty stores on Fifth Avenue where a doorman all braid and brass buttons opens the door for you. The girls that got out of cars like this had mink coats swung carelessly from their shoulders, wore sable scarves tossed over slim wool suits.

This world was one of great contrasts, she thought, and if the richest part of it was to be fenced off so that people like herself could only look at it with no expectation of ever being able to get inside it, then it would be better to have been born blind so you couldn't see it, born deaf so you couldn't hear it, born with no sense of touch so you couldn't feel it. Better still, born with no brain so that you would be completely unaware of anything, so that you would never know there were places that were filled with sunlight and good food and where children were safe.

Boots started the car and for a moment he leaned so close to her that she could smell the after-shaving lotion that he used and the faint, fruity smell of the bourbon he had been drinking. She didn't draw

155

away from him; she simply stared at him with a cold kind of surprise that made him start fumbling with the clutch. Then the car drew away from the curb.

He headed it uptown. 'We got time to get up the Hudson a ways. Okay?'

'Swell. It's been years since I've been up that way.'

'Lived in New York long, baby?'

'I was born here.' And next he would ask if she was married. She didn't know what her answer would be.

Because this time she wanted something and it made a difference. Ordinarily she knew exactly how it would go — like a pattern repeated over and over or the beginning of a meal. The table set with knife, fork, and spoons, napkin to the left of the fork and a glass filled with water at the tip end of the knife. Only sometimes the glass was a thin, delicate one and the napkin, instead of being paper, was thick linen still shining because a hot iron had been used on it when it was wet; and the knife and fork, instead of being red-handled steel from the five-and-ten, was silver.

He had said there was plenty of money in Harlem, so evidently this was one of the thin glass, thick napkin, thin china, polished silver affairs. But the pattern was just the same. The soup plate would be removed and the main course brought on. She always ducked before the main course was served, but this time she had to figure out how to dawdle with the main course, appear to welcome it, and yet not actually partake of it, and continue trifling and toy-ing with it until she was successfully launched as a singer.

They had left Harlem before she noticed that there was a full moon — pale and remote despite its size. As they went steadily uptown, through the commercial business streets, and then swiftly out of Manhattan, she thought that the streets had a cold, deserted look. The buildings they passed were without lights. Whenever she caught a glimpse of the sky, it was over the tops of the buildings, so that it, too, had a faraway look. The buildings loomed darkly against it.

Then they were on a four-ply concrete road that wound ahead gray-white in the moonlight. They were going faster and faster. And she got the feeling that Boots Smith's relationship to this swiftly moving car was no ordinary one. He wasn't just a black man driving a car at a pell-mell pace. He had lost all sense of time and space as the car plunged forward into the cold, white night.

The act of driving the car made him feel he was a powerful being who could conquer the world. Up over hills, fast down on the other side. It was like playing god and commanding everything within hearing to awaken and listen to him. The people sleeping in the white farmhouses were at the mercy of the sound of his engine roaring past in the night. It brought them half-awake — disturbed, uneasy. The cattle in the barns moved in protest, the chickens stirred on their roosts and before any of them could analyze the sound that had alarmed them, he was gone — on and on into the night.

And she knew, too, that this was the reason white people turned scornfully to look at Negroes who swooped past them on the highways. 'Crazy niggers with autos' in the way they looked. Because they sensed that the black men had to roar past them, had for a brief moment to feel equal, feel superior; had to take reckless chances going around curves, passing on hills, so that they would be better able to face a world that took pains to make them feel that they didn't belong, that they were inferior.

Because in that one moment of passing a white man in a car they could feel good and the good feeling would last long enough so that they could hold their heads up the next day and the day after that. And the white people in the cars hated it because — and her mind stumbled over the thought and then went on — because possibly they, too, needed to go on feeling superior. Because if they didn't, it upset the delicate balance of the world they moved in when they could see for themselves that a black man in a ratclap car could overtake and pass them on a hill. Because if there was nothing left for them but that business of feeling superior to black people, and that was taken away even for the split second of one car going ahead of another, it left them with nothing.

She stopped staring at the road ahead to look at Boots. He was leaning over the steering wheel, his hands cupped close on the sides of it. Yes, she thought, at this moment he has forgotten he's black. At this moment and in the act of sending this car hurtling through the night, he is making up for a lot of the things that have happened to him to make him what he is. He is proving all kinds of things to himself.

'Are you married, baby?' he asked. His voice was

loud above the sound of the engine. He didn't look at her. His eyes were on the road. After he asked the question, he sent the car forward at a faster pace.

'I'm separated from my husband,' she said. It was strange when he asked the question, the answer was on the tip of her tongue. It was true and it was the right answer. It put up no barriers to the next step — the removal of the soup plates and the bringing-on of the main course. Neither did it hurry the process.

'I thought you musta been married,' he said. 'Never saw a good-looking chick yet who didn't belong to somebody.'

She saw no point in telling him that she didn't belong to anybody; that she and Jim were as sharply separated as though they had been divorced, and that the separation wasn't the result of some sudden quarrel but a clean-cut break of years standing. She had deliberately omitted all mention of Bub because Boots Smith obviously wasn't the kind of man who would maintain even a passing interest in a woman who was the mother of an eight-year-old child. She felt as though she had pushed Bub out of her life, disowned him, by not telling Boots about him.

He slowed the car down when they went through Poughkeepsie, stopping just long enough to pay the guard at the entrance to the Mid-Hudson Bridge. Once across the river, she became aware of the closeness of the hills, for the moon etched them clearly against the sky. They seemed to go up and up over her head.

'I don't like mountains,' she said.

Why?'

'I get the feeling they're closing in on me. Just a crazy notion,' she added hastily, because she was reluctant to have him get the slightest inkling of the trapped feeling she got when there wasn't a lot of unfilled space around her.

'Probably why you sing so well,' he said. 'You feel things stronger than other folks.' And then, 'What songs do you know?'

'All the usual ones. Night and Day. Darlin'. Hurry Up, Sammy, and Let's Go Home.'

'Have any trouble learnin' 'em?'

'No. I've never really tried to learn them. Just picked them up from hearing them on the radio.'

'You'll have to learn some new ones,' — he steered the car to the side of the road and parked it where there was an unobstructed view of the river.

The river was very wide at this point and she moved closer to him to get a better look at it. It made no sound, though she could see the direction of its flow between the great hills on either side. It had been flowing quietly along like this for years, she thought. It would go on forever — silent, strong, knowing where it was going and not stopping for storms or bridges or factories. That was what had been wrong with her these last few weeks — she hadn't known where she was going. As a matter of fact, she had probably never known. But if she could sing — work hard at it, study, really get somewhere, it would give direction to her life — she would know where she was going.

'I don't know your name, baby,' Boots said softly.

'Lutie Johnson,' she said.

'Mrs. Lutie Johnson,' he said slowly. 'Very nice. Very, very nice.'

The soft, satisfied way he said the words made her sharply aware that there wasn't a house in sight, there wasn't a car passing along the road and hadn't been since they parked. She hadn't walked into this situation. She had run headlong into it, snatching greedily at the bait he had dangled in front of her. Because she had reached such a state of despair that she would have clutched at a straw if it appeared to offer the means by which she could get Bub and herself out of that street.

As his tough, unscrupulous face came closer and closer to hers, she reminded herself that all she knew about him was that he had a dance band, that he drove a high-priced car, and that he believed there was plenty of money in Harlem. And she had gone leaping and running into his car, emitting little cries of joy as she went. It hadn't occurred to her until this moment that from his viewpoint she was a pick-up girl.

When he turned her face toward his, she could feel the hardness of his hands under the suede gloves he wore. He looked at her for a long moment. 'Very, very nice,' he repeated, and bent forward and kissed her.

Her mind sought some plausible way of frustrating him without offending him. She couldn't think of anything. He was holding her so tightly and his mouth was so insistent, so brutal, that she twisted out of his arms, not caring what he thought, intent only on escaping from his ruthless hands and mouth.

The Street

The dashboard clock said nine-thirty. She wanted to pat it in gratitude.

'You're going to be late,' she said, pointing at the clock.

'Damn!' he muttered, and reached for the ignition switch.

Chapter 7

THEY CAME BACK over the Storm King Highway. 'It's the quickest way,' he explained. 'But you better hold on tight, baby.' The road kept turning back on itself, going in and out and around until she was dizzy. They went through the abrupt curves so fast that she had to hold on to the door with both hands to keep from being thrown against Boots.

He seemed to have forgotten she was sitting beside him. She decided that he was playing a game, a dangerous, daring game — trying to see how fast he could go around the sudden, sickening curves without turning the car over. He kept his eyes on the road as it wound in and out ahead of them. He was half-smiling as though he was amused by the risks he was taking. As the lurching and swaying of the car increased, she began to believe that it was only staying on the road because he was forcing it to.

The headlights picked up the signs that bordered the road: 'Winding Road Slow Down'; 'Watch For Fallen Rock.' She lost interest in whatever defiance Boots was hurling at the high hills above and the river below. If they should plunge over into the river, Bub would never know what had happened to her. No one would know. The car would go down, down, down into the river. The river would silently swallow it and quietly continue toward the sea. Or these craggy hills might suddenly spew mountains of rock down on them and crush them beneath it.

She thought of the apartment where she lived with a sudden access of warmth, for it was better to be there alive than buried under this silent river or pinioned beneath masses of rock on the highway.

And then they were down. As the road straightened out into a broad expanse of concrete highway, she relaxed against the seat. There was very little traffic. They passed an occasional car, a lumbering heavy-laden truck and that was all.

'How do you get gas?' she asked.

'Pay more for it. There's plenty of it around if you know where to go.'

Yes, he would know where to go to get gas and anything else he wanted. He would know where and how to get the money to pay for it with. Money made all the difference in the things you could have and the things that were denied to you — even rationed gas. But there were some things —— 'How come you're not in the army?' she asked.

'Who — me?' He threw his head back, and for the first time laughed out loud — a soft, sardonic sound that filled the car. The thought amused him so that he kept chuckling so that for a moment he couldn't talk. 'You don't think I'd get mixed up in that mess.'

'But why weren't you drafted?' she persisted.

He turned toward her and frowned. The long scar on his cheek was more distinct than she remembered it. 'Something wrong with one ear,' he said, and his voice was so unpleasant that she said nothing more about it.

As they approached the upper reaches of the Bronx, he slowed the car down. But he didn't slow it down quite enough. There was the shrill sound of a whistle from somewhere in back of them.

A cop on a motorcycle roared alongside, waved them to the curb. 'Goin' to a fire?' he demanded.

He peered into the car and Lutie saw a slight stiffening of his face. That meant he had seen they were colored. She waited for his next words with a wincing feeling, thinking it was like having an old wound that had never healed and you could see someone about to knock against it and it was too late to get out of the way, and there was that horrible tiny split second of time when you waited for the contact, anticipating the pain and quivering away from it before it actually started.

The cop's mouth twisted into an ugly line. 'You ——'

'Sorry, Officer,' Boots interrupted. 'My band's playin' at the Casino tonight. I'm late and I was steppin' on it. Should have been there a half-hour ago.' He pulled a wallet from an inside pocket, handed the cop a card and his driver's license.

The cop's expression softened. When he handed the license and the card back to Boots, he almost but not quite smiled. Lutie saw that he was holding something else in his hand. It was a bill, but she couldn't see the denomination.

The cop looked at her. 'Don't know that I blame you for being late, Mack,' he said suggestively. 'Well, so long.'

And he was gone. Even with cops money makes a difference, she thought. Even if you're colored, it makes a difference — not as much, but enough to make having it important. Money could change suicide into an accident with a gun; it could apparently keep Boots out of the army, because she didn't believe that business about there being something wrong with one of his ears. He had acted too strangely when he said it.

Money could make a white cop almost smile when he caught a black man speeding. It was the only thing that could get her and Bub out of that street. And the lack of it would keep them there forever. She reaffirmed her intention of using Boots Smith. Somehow she would manage to dodge away from his hard, seeking hands without offending him until she signed a contract to sing with his band. After the contract was signed, she would tell him pointedly that she wasn't even faintly interested in knowing him any better.

She contemplated this goal with satisfaction and the old feeling of self-confidence soared in her. She could do it and she would.

Boots started the car. 'I'm so late I'll have to dump you at 135th Street in front of the Casino.' He was silent for a moment and then said, 'Where do you live, baby?'

'On 116th Street. It isn't far from the Junto.'

They were silent the rest of the way downtown. Boots took advantage of every opening in the traffic, barely waiting for a light to change to green, soaring past them as they turned to red at intersections.

He parked the car between the no parking signs in front of the Casino. 'I'll look for you tomorrow night, baby,' he said. 'Come by about ten and you can go over some stuff with the band.'

'Okay.' She got out of the car without waiting for him to open the door.

'Wear a long dress, huh?' he said. He came to stand beside her on the sidewalk.

When he started to put his arm around her, she smiled at him and walked away. 'Good night,' she said over her shoulder.

He watched her until she reached the corner of the street. 'Very, very nice,' he said softly, and then turned into the Casino.

Lutie crossed Seventh Avenue, thinking that by this time tomorrow night she would know whether she was going to leave 116th Street or whether she was to go on living there. Doubt assailed her. She had never sung with an orchestra before, she knew nothing about the technique of singing over a mike — suppose she couldn't do it.

A Fifth Avenue bus lumbered to a stop at the corner. She climbed the narrow stairs to the top deck arguing with herself. Spending a dime for car fare was sheer extravagance. But it didn't matter too much, because Boots had paid for the beer she drank at the Junto, so she hadn't dented her budget as much as she had anticipated. But the Eighth Avenue bus only cost a nickel. Yes, and she would have had to stand up all the way home; besides, five cents saved didn't make that much difference.

The bus started down the street with a grinding of gears and a rumbling and groaning that she immediately contrasted with the swift, silent motion of Boots' car. He could spend money carelessly. He never had to stop and weigh the difference in price between two modes of transportation.

She began to compare him with Jim. There was a streak of cruelty in Boots that showed up plain in his face. Jim's face had been open, honest, young. Come to think of it, when she and Jim got married it looked as though it should have been a happy, successful marriage. They were young enough and enough in love to have made a go of it. It always came back to the same thing. Jim couldn't find a job.

So day by day, month by month, big broad-shouldered Jim Johnson went to pieces because there wasn't any work for him and he couldn't earn anything at all. He got used to facing the fact that he couldn't support his wife and child. It ate into him. Slowly, bit by bit, it undermined his belief in himself until he could no longer bear it. And he got himself a woman so that in those moments when he clutched her close to him in bed he could prove that he was still needed, wanted. His self-respect was momentarily restored through the woman's desire for him.

The Street

Thus, too, he escaped from the dreary monotony of his existence.

She examined this train of thought with care, a little surprised to realize that somehow during the last few years she had stopped hating him, and finally reached the point where she could think about him objectively. What had happened to them was, she supposed, partly her fault. And yet was it? They had managed to live on the income from having State children there in the house in Jamaica and it had been her fault that they lost them.

She began to go over the whole thing step by step. Jim's mother died when Bub was not quite two. There was a mortgage on the house and the mortgage money had to be paid.

'We don't have to worry about a thing, Lutie,' Jim had said. 'Mom left a thousand dollars insurance money.'

So he didn't put too much effort into looking for a job. Somehow the thousand dollars melted away — interest on the mortgage, and taxes and gas and light bills nibbled at it. Mom's funeral took three hundred and fifty dollars of it. They had to have clothes and food.

Six months after the funeral there wasn't any money left in the bank. She found the bank book on the kitchen table. Its pages were neatly perforated with the words 'Account Closed.' The last entry left a nice row of zeros where the balance would normally have been. Jim started hunting for a job in dead earnest and couldn't find one.

Finally they went into Harlem to consult Pop. It was on a Sunday — a warm spring day. Irene,

Pop's girl friend at the moment, gave them beer and they sat around the kitchen table drinking it.

'You got the house,' Pop offered. He spoke slowly as though he were thinking hard. 'Tell you what you do. You get some of these State chillern. They pay about five dollars a week apiece for 'em. You get four or five of 'em and you can all live on the money.'

Lutie sipped the beer and thought about the house. There was an unfinished room in the attic and three small bedrooms on the second floor. Put two kids in each room and they could take six of them — six times five would mean thirty dollars a week.

'He's right, Jim,' she said. 'It would be about thirty bucks a week.' She took a big swallow of beer. 'We could manage on that.'

There were papers to be filled out and investigators to be satisfied, but finally the children arrived. Lutie was surprised at how easy it was. Surprised and a little chagrined because theirs wasn't a completely honest setup. For they had said Jim worked in Harlem and a friend had verified the fact when inquiries were made. So the State people didn't know that the children were their only source of income. It made her uneasy, for it didn't seem quite right that two grown people and another child should be living on the money that was supposed to be used exclusively for the State children.

She had to work very hard to make ends meet. She tried to make all the meals good, appetizing ones and that meant spending most of her time hunting bargains in the markets and preparing dishes that required long, careful cooking. It was during that period that she learned about soups and stews and baked beans and casserole dishes. She invented new recipes for macaroni and spaghetti and noodles.

It had been nothing but work, work, work — morning, noon, and night — making bread, washing clothes and ironing them, looking after the children, and cleaning the house. The investigator used to compliment her, 'Mrs. Johnson, you do a wonderful job. This house and the children fairly shine.'

She had to bite her lips to keep from saying that that wasn't half the story. She knew she was doing a fine job. She was feeding eight people on the money for five and squeezing out what amounted to rent money in the bargain. It got so at night she couldn't go to sleep without seeing figures dancing before her eyes, and mornings when she got up, she was so tired she would have given anything just to lie still in bed instead of getting up to cook quantities of oatmeal because it was cheap and filling, to walk twelve blocks to get co-operative milk because it cost less.

She could hear the word 'cheap,' 'cheap,' 'cheap,' whether she was asleep or awake. It dominated all her thinking. Cheap cuts of meat, cheap yellow laundry soap, yeast in bulk because it was cheap, white potatoes because they were cheap and filling, tomato juice instead of orange juice because it was cheaper; even unironed sheets because they saved electricity. They went to bed early because it kept the light bill down. Jim smoked a pipe because cigarettes were a luxury they couldn't afford. It seemed to her their whole lives revolved around the price of things and as each week crawled by she grew a little more nervous, a little more impatient and irritable.

Jim finally stopped looking for work entirely. Though to be fair about it he did help around the house — washing clothes, going to the market, cleaning. But when there wasn't anything for him to do, he would read day-old newspapers and play the radio or sit by the kitchen stove smoking his pipe until she felt, if she had to walk around his long legs just one more time, get just one more whiff of the rank, strong smell of his pipe, she would go mad.

Then Pop almost got caught selling the liquor he concocted in his apartment. So he stopped making it. He couldn't get a job either, so he couldn't pay the rent on his apartment and he came home one night to find one of those long white eviction notices under his door.

He came all the way to Jamaica to tell her about it.

'You can come stay with us till things look up if you don't mind sleeping in the living room,' she offered.

'You'll never regret it, Lutie darlin',' he said fondly. 'I'll make it up to you.' His lips brushed against her cheek and she caught the strong smell of the raw whiskey he had been drinking.

She stood on the little glass-enclosed front porch and watched him walk down the path. He didn't seem to grow any older, no stoop in his shoulders; his step was firm. As a matter of fact he held himself more stiffly erect with each passing year. She sighed as she watched him cross the street heading toward the bus stop. He might hold himself up straighter and straighter as the years slipped by, but he drank more and more as he grew older.

That night after dinner she told Jim. 'Pop's been put out of his apartment. He's coming here to stay with us.'

'He can't stay here,' Jim protested. 'He drinks and carries on. He can't stay here with these kids.'

She remembered that she had been washing dishes at the kitchen sink and the dishwater slopped over on her legs from the sudden abrupt movement she made. She never wore stockings in the house because it was cheaper not to and the dishwater was lukewarm and slimy on her bare legs, so that she made a face and thought again of the word 'cheap.' She was tired and irritable and the least little thing upset her.

She couldn't stop herself from answering him and she was too exhausted to be persuasive about it, too incensed by the criticism of Pop to let the whole thing drop and bring it up again later, leading around to it, not arguing but gently showing how she really couldn't do anything else.

'He's my father and he hasn't any other place to go. He's going to stay here with us.' Her voice was insistent and she threw the words at him bluntly, using no tact.

Jim got up from the chair where he'd been sitting and stood over her, newspaper in hand. 'You're crazy!' he shouted.

Then they were both shouting. The small room vibrated with the sound of their anger. They had lived on the edge of nothing for so long that they had finally reached the point where neither of them could brook opposition in the other, could not or would not tolerate even the suggestion of being in the wrong.

It ended almost as swiftly as it began. Because she said, 'All right, I'm crazy.' Her voice was tight with rage. 'But either he comes or I go.'

So Pop came. At first he was apologetic about being there and so self-effacing that she was only aware of him as a quiet, gray-haired figure doing the marketing, wiping the dishes, playing gently with the children. And she thought it was working out beautifully. Jim was wrong as usual.

After the first couple of weeks, Pop started drinking openly. She would meet him at the door with a brown-paper package in his hand. He would come downstairs from the bathroom holding himself very straight and eat supper in a genial expansive mood smelling to high heaven of raw whiskey.

He urged her and Jim to go out at night. 'You're nothin' but kids,' he said, loftily waving his hands to give his words emphasis and managing to get into the gesture a sense of the freedom and joyousness that belonged to the young. 'Shouldn't be shut up in the house all day. Go out and have yourselves a time. I'll look after the kids.'

Somehow he always managed to have a little money and he would take two or three limp dollar bills from his pocket and shove them into her reluctant hands. When she protested, his invariable answer was, 'Oh, call it room rent if you gotta be formal about it.'

They would head straight for Harlem. The trip rarely included anything more than an evening spent drinking beer in someone's living room and dancing to a radio. But it was like being let out of jail to be able to forget about the houseful of kids, forget about not having any money. Sometimes they would stop at Junto's Bar and Grill, not so much to drink the beer as to listen to the juke-box and the warm, rich flow of talk and laughter that rippled through the place. The gay, swirling sounds inside the Junto made both of them believe that one of these days they would be inside a world like that to stay for keeps.

Going home on the subway, Jim would put his arm around her and say, 'I'll make it all up to you some day, Lutie. You just wait and see. I'm going to give you everything you ever wanted.'

Just being close to him like that, knowing that they were both thinking much the same thing, shut out the roar and rush of the train, blotted out the other passengers. She would ride home dreaming of the time when she and Jim and Bub would be together — safe and secure and alone.

They were always very late coming home. And walking through the quiet little street they lived on, past the small houses that seemed to nudge against each other in the darkness, she used to imagine that the world at that hour belonged to her and Jim. Just the two of them alone traveling through a world that slept. It was easy to believe it, for there was no sound except that of their own footsteps on the side-walk.

They would tiptoe into the house so as not to wake Pop and the kids. The living room always smelt strongly of whiskey.

'The place smells like a gin mill,' she would say, and giggle as they went up the stairs toward their bedroom. Because somehow the fact of having been away for a while, the lateness of the hour, the stealth with which they had come into the house, made her feel young and carefree.

As they went up the stairs, Jim would put his arm around her waist. His silence, the bulky feel of his shoulders in the darkness, turned their relationship into something mysterious and exciting, and she wanted to put off the moment when she would undress and get in bed beside him, wanted to defer it at the same time that she wanted to hurry it.

It got so they went to Harlem two or three times a week. They wanted to go, anyway, and Pop made it very easy, for he insisted that they go and he invariably proffered a crumpled bill or two with which to finance the trip.

And then all the fun went out of it. Mrs. Griffin, who lived next door, banged on the kitchen door early one morning. She was filled with an indignation that thrust her mouth forward in such an angry pout that Lutie was prepared for something unpleasant.

'There's so much noise over here nights 'at my husband and me can't sleep,' she said bluntly.

'Noise?' Lutie stared at her, not certain that she had heard correctly. 'What kind of noise?'

'I dunno,' she said. 'But it's got to stop. Sounds like wild parties to me. Las' night it kept up till all hours. An' my husband say if somep'n ain't done about it he's going to complain.'

'I'm sorry. I'll see that it doesn't happen any more.' She said it quickly because she knew what it was. Pop had been having parties on the nights they went to Harlem.

As soon as Mrs. Griffin left the kitchen, slamming the door behind her, Lutie asked Pop about it.

'Parties?' he said innocently. His forehead wrinkled as though he were trying to figure out what she was talking about. 'I ain't had no parties. Some of my friends come out a coupla times. But I ain't had no parties.' His voice sounded hurt.

'You must have made a lot of noise,' she said, ignoring his denial of having had any parties. 'We gotta be careful, Pop. The neighbors might complain to the State people.'

She tried to eliminate the trips to Harlem after that. But Jim was unaccountably and violently suspicious of the headaches that came on suddenly just before they were to leave, of the other thin excuses that she found for not going with him. She couldn't bring herself to tell him that she was scared to go off and leave Pop in the house alone.

'You think I'm too shabby to go out with,' Jim had said. And then later, 'Or have you got yourself another boy friend?'

She wouldn't swallow her pride and tell him about Pop, so they continued going to Harlem two or three times a week. Besides, every time Jim said something about her having a boy friend his face turned resentful, sullen, and she couldn't bear to see him like that, so she stopped making excuses and pretended an anticipation and an enthusiasm for the trips that she didn't feel.

Now when she came home she was filled with a fear that made her walk faster and faster, hastening toward their street in her eagerness to ascertain that the house was dark and quiet. Once in bed, she twisted and turned the rest of the night, impatiently waiting for morning to come when the neighbors would soon inform her if anything had happened while they were gone.

She could remember so vividly the night they returned to find the house blazing with light. She got a sick feeling deep in her stomach, for there was an uproar coming from it that could be heard way up the street. As she got closer, she saw there were two police cars pulled up in front of the door.

They walked into the living room and a cop sneered, 'Little late, ain't you? The party's over.'

'We live here,' Jim explained.

'Christ!' The cop spat in the direction of the floor. 'No wonder they won't let you all live near decent people.'

Pop was very drunk. He got up from the sofa where he had been sitting and he was rocking back and forth, though he stood very tall and straight once he finally got his balance. The dignity of his reproachful remarks to the cop was ruined by the fact that the fat woman who had been lolling against him kept reaching both hands out toward him. She was so drunk that she was half-laughing and half-crying at the same time. Her words came out in a blur, 'Um's my daddy. Um's my daddy. Um's my daddy.'

'Ain't got no right to talk like that to a American citizen,' Pop said, swaying out of the reach of the woman's clutching hands.

Lutie looked away from Pop. The living room was filled with strange people, with noise and confusion and empty whiskey bottles. The kids were crying upstairs.

The Street

It took Jim nearly a half-hour to persuade the cops not to lock everybody up, a half-hour in which she could see his pride and self-respect ooze slowly away while he pleaded, pretending not to hear the gruff asides about 'drunken niggers.'

Before the cops left, one of them turned to Jim. 'Okay,' he said. 'But let me tell you this, boy. It all goes on the report.'

All Jim said to her that night was, 'You wanted that whiskey-soaked old bum here. Now you've got him, I hope you're satisfied.'

The next afternoon a disapproving white woman arrived and took the children away with her. 'They can't stay in a place where there's any such goings-on as there is here,' she said.

Lutie pleaded with her, promised her that everything would be different; it couldn't possibly happen again if she would just let the children stay.

The woman was unmoved. 'These children belong to your own race, and if you had any feelings at all you wouldn't want them to stay here,' she said, going out the door. In less than half an hour she had the youngsters packed and was putting them into a station wagon. She moved competently with no waste motion.

Lutie watched her from the front porch. Damn white people, she thought. Damn them. And then — but it isn't that woman's fault. It's your fault. That's right, but the reason Pop came here to live was because he couldn't get a job and we had to have the State children because Jim couldn't get a job. Damn white people, she repeated.

The house was very quiet and empty with the

children gone. Pop fidgeted around for a while, then put his hat and coat on. 'Got some business in Harlem,' he explained, not looking at her.

As the day dragged along, she kept thinking with dread of what Jim would say when he came home. He had left the house early to hunt for a job. She hoped that this time he would return swaggering with triumph because he had been successful. She kept remembering how he had pleaded with the cops the night before. Getting a job would make him forget about it. He might not notice the absence of the children.

She fed Bub and bathed him and put him to bed a little earlier than usual. It was something tangible to do. She kept listening for Jim's key in the lock. When she heard a slight sound at the front door, it was after nine and she hurried into the small hall. But it was Pop looking shamefaced and apologetic at the sight of her.

'Pop,' she said, 'now that the kids are gone, you might as well sleep in one of the bedrooms.'

'Okay,' he said humbly.

She undressed and went to bed, but she couldn't go to sleep. She remembered how she had kept getting out of bed to look up the street, glancing at the clock, listening to footsteps. When Jim finally came at eleven o'clock, she didn't hear him until he opened the front door. He came straight up the stairs and she turned the light on so he would know she was awake.

He stopped in the tiny upstairs hall and opened the bedroom doors — both of them. She strained her ears to get some clue to his reaction when he saw that

Bub was in one of the rooms and Pop was in the other. But there was only silence.

Then he was standing in the door. He was still wearing his hat and overcoat and the sight angered her. He came over to the bed and the room was filled with the smell of cheap gin. And, she thought, he reeks of it. That's the way he looks for a job — in bars and drinking joints and taverns.

'Where are the kids?' he demanded.

'Did you have any supper?' she asked.

'What the hell — you heard me. Where are the kids?'

'They're gone. The State woman came and got them this morning.'

'I suppose you figured if those little bastards were taken away, I'd have to find a job. That I'd go out and make one. Buy one, mebbe.'

'Oh, Jim, don't ——' she protested.

'You knew what would happen when you brought that old booze hound here to live.'

Perhaps if she kept quiet, and let him go on raving without answering him, he would get tired and stop. She bit her lip, looked away from him, and the words came out in spite of her, 'Don't you talk about my father like that.'

'A saint, ain't he?' he sneered. 'He and those old bitches he sleeps with. I suppose I'm not good enough to talk about him.'

'Oh, shut up,' she said wearily.

'Mebbe it runs in the family. Mebbe that's why you had him come here. Because you figured with him here you'd be able to get rid of the kids. And that would give you more time to sleep with some

Harlem nigger you've got your eye on. That's it, ain't it?'

'Shut up!' This time she shouted. And she saw Pop go quietly down the hall, his worn old traveling bag in his hand. The sight shocked her. He didn't have any place to go, yet he was leaving because of the way she and Jim were carrying on. 'Oh, Jim,' she said. 'Don't let's fight. It's all over and done with. There isn't any point in quarreling like this.'

'Oh, yeah? That's what you think.' He leaned over the bed. His eyes were bloodshot, angry. 'I oughtta beat you up and down the block.' He slapped her across the face.

She was out of bed in a flash. She picked up a chair, the one chair in the bedroom — a straight-backed wooden one. She had painted it with bright yellow enamel shortly after they were married. And she had said, 'Jim, look. It makes sunlight walk right into the room.'

He had looked at her squatting on the floor, paint-brush in hand, her face glowing as she smiled up at him. He had leaned over and kissed her forehead, saying, 'Honey, you're all the sunlight I'll ever need.'

It was the same chair. And she aimed it at his head as she shouted, 'You come near me and so help me I'll kill you.'

It had been a loud, bitter, common fight. It woke Bub up and set him to crying. And it was more than a week afterward before they were able to patch it up. In the meantime the mortgage money was due and, though Jim didn't say so, she felt that if they lost the house by not being able to pay the interest, it would be her fault.

The Street

The Fifth Avenue bus lurched to a stop at 116th Street. She climbed down the steep stairs from the top deck, thinking that if they hadn't been so damn poor she and Jim might have stayed married. It was like a circle. No matter at what point she started, she always ended up at the same place. She had taken the job in Connecticut so they could keep the house. While she was gone, Jim got himself a slim dark girl whose thighs made him believe in himself again and momentarily released him from his humdrum life.

She had never seen him since the day she had gone to the house in Jamaica and found that other woman there. The only time she had heard from him was when he had forwarded the letter from Mrs. Chandler — and then all he had done was put Pop's address on the envelope. There had been no messages, no letters — nothing for all these years.

Once Pop had said to her, 'Hear Jim's left town. Nobody knows where he went.'

And she was so completely indifferent to anything concerning Jim that she had made no comment. She watched the bus until it disappeared out of sight where Seventh Avenue joins 110th Street. This clear understanding she had of what caused Jim to acquire that other woman was because the same thing was happening to her. She was incapable of enduring a bleak and lonely life encompassed by those three dark rooms.

She wondered uneasily if she was fooling herself in believing that she could sing her way out of the street. Suppose it didn't work and she had to stay there. What would the street do to her? She thought of Mrs. Hedges, the Super, Min, Mrs. Hedges' little girls. Which one would she be like, say five years from now? What would Bub be like? She shivered as she headed toward home.

Chapter 8

I T WAS A COLD, CHEERLESS NIGHT. But in
spite of the cold, the street was full of people.
They stood on the corners talking, lounged half
in and half out of hallways and on the stoops of the
houses, looking at the street and talking. Some of
them were coming home from work, from church
meetings, from lodge meetings, and some of them
were not coming from anywhere or going anywhere,
they were merely deferring the moment when they
would have to enter their small crowded rooms for
the night.

In the middle of the block there was a sudden thrust
of raw, brilliant light where the unshaded bulbs in
the big poolroom reached out and pushed back the
darkness. A group of men stood outside its windows

watching the games going on inside. Their heads were silhouetted against the light.

Lutie, walking quickly through the block, glanced at them and then at the women coming toward her from Eighth Avenue. The women moved slowly. Their shoulders sagged from the weight of the heavy shopping bags they carried. And she thought, That's what's wrong. We don't have time enough or money enough to live like other people because the women have to work until they become drudges and the men stand by idle.

She made an impatient movement of her shoulders. She had no way of knowing that at fifty she wouldn't be misshapen, walking on the sides of her shoes because her feet hurt so badly; getting dressed up for church on Sunday and spending the rest of the week slaving in somebody's kitchen.

It could happen. Only she was going to stake out a piece of life for herself. She had come this far poor and black and shut out as though a door had been slammed in her face. Well, she would shove it open; she would beat and bang on it and push against it and use a chisel in order to get it open.

When she opened the street door of the apartment house, she was instantly aware of the silence that filled the hall. Mrs. Hedges had been quiet, too, for if she was sitting in her window she had given no indication of her presence.

There was no sound except for the steam hissing in the radiator. The silence and the dimly lit hallway and the smell of stale air depressed her. It was like a dead weight landing on her chest. She told herself that she mustn't put too much expectation in getting the singing job. Almost anything might happen to prevent it. Boots might change his mind.

She went up the stairs, thinking, But he can't. She wouldn't let him. It meant too much to her. It was a way out — the only way out of here and she and Bub had to get out.

On the third-floor landing she stopped. A man was standing in the hall. His back was turned toward her. She hesitated. It wasn't very late, but it was dark in the hall and she was alone.

He turned then and she saw that he had his arms wound tightly around a girl and he was pressed so close to her and was bending so far over her that they had given the effect of one figure. He wore a sailor's uniform and the collar of his jacket was turned high around his neck, for it was cold in the hall.

The girl looked to be about nineteen or twenty. She was very thin. Her black hair, thick with grease, gleamed in the dim light. There was an artificial white rose stuck in the center of the pompadour that mounted high above her small, dark face.

Lutie recognized her. It was Mary, one of the little girls who lived with Mrs. Hedges. The sailor gave Lutie a quick, appraising look and then turned back to the girl, blotting her out. The girl's thin arms went back around his neck.

'Mary,' Lutie said, and stopped right behind the sailor.

The girl's face appeared over the top of the sailor's shoulder.

'Hello,' she said sullenly.

'It's so cold out here,' Lutie said. 'Why don't you go inside?'

'Mis' Hedges won't let him come in no more,'
Mary said. 'He's spent all his money. And she says
she ain't in business for her health.'

'Can't you talk to him somewhere else? Isn't
there a friend's house you could go to?'

'No, ma'am. Besides, it ain't no use, anyway.
He's got to go back to his ship tonight.'

Lutie climbed the rest of the stairs fuming against
Mrs. Hedges. The sailor would return to his ship
carrying with him the memory of this dark narrow
hallway and Mrs. Hedges and the thin resigned little
girl. The street was full of young thin girls like this
one with a note of resignation in their voices, with
faces that contained no hope, no life. She shivered.
She couldn't let Bub grow up in a place like this.

She put her key in the door quietly, trying to avoid
the loud click of the lock being drawn back. She
pushed the door open, mentally visualizing the trip
across the living room to her bedroom. Once inside
her room, she would close the door and put the light
on and Bub wouldn't wake up. Then she saw that
the lamp in the living room was lit and she shut the
door noisily. He should have been asleep at least
two hours ago, she thought, and walked toward the
studio couch, her heels clicking on the congoleum rug.

Bub sat up and rubbed his eyes. For a moment she
saw something frightened and fearful in his expression, but it disappeared when he looked at her.

'How come you're not in bed?' she demanded.

'I fell asleep.'

'With your clothes on?' she said, and then added:
'With the light on, too? You must be trying to make
the bill bigger ——' and she stopped abruptly. She

was always talking to him about money. It wasn't good. He would be thinking about nothing else pretty soon. 'How was the movie?' she asked.

'It was swell,' he said eagerly. 'There was one guy who caught gangsters ——'

'Skip it,' she interrupted. 'You get in bed in a hurry, Mister. I still don't know what you're doing up ——' Her eyes fell on the ash tray on the blue-glass coffee table. It was filled with cigarette butts. That's funny. She had emptied all the trays when she washed the dinner dishes. She knew that she had. She looked closer at the cigarette ends. They were moist. Whoever had smoked them had held them, not between their lips, but far inside the mouth so that the paper got wet and the tobacco inside had stained and discolored it. She turned toward Bub.

'Supe was up.' Bub's eyes had followed hers. 'We played cards.'

'You mean he was in here?' she said sharply. And thought, Of course, dope, he didn't stand outside and throw his cigarette butts into the ash tray through a closed door.

'We played cards,' Bub said again.

'Let's get this straight once and for all.' She put her hands on his shoulders. 'When I'm not home, you're not to let anyone in here. Anyone. Understand?'

He nodded. 'Does that mean Supe, too?'

'Of course. Now you get in bed fast so you can get to school on time.'

While Bub undressed, she took the cover off the studio couch, smoothed the thin blanket and the sheets, pulled a pillowslip over one of the cushions. He seemed to be taking an awfully long time in the bathroom. 'Hey,' she said finally. 'Step on it. You can't get to heaven that way.'

She heard him giggle and smiled at the sound. Then her face sobered. She looked around the living room. One of these days he was going to have a real bedroom to himself instead of this shabby, sunless room. The plaid pattern of the blue congoleum rug was wearing off in front of the studio couch. It was scuffed down to the paper base at the door that led to the small hall. Everything in the room was worn and old — the lumpy studio couch, the overstuffed chair, the card table that served as desk, the bookcase filled with second-hand textbooks and old magazines. The blue-glass top on the coffee table was scratched and chipped. The small radio was scarred with cigarette burns. The first thing she would do would be to move and then she would get some decent furniture.

Bub got into bed, pulled the covers up under his chin. 'Good night, Mom,' he said.

He was almost asleep when she leaned over and kissed him on the forehead. She turned the light on in her bedroom, came back and switched the light off in the living room.

'Sleep tight!' she said. His only reply was a drowsy murmur — half laugh, half sigh.

She undressed, thinking of the Super sitting in the living room, of the time when she had come to look at the apartment and he had stood there in that room where Bub was now sleeping and how he had held the flashlight so that the beam of light from it was

down at his feet. Now he had been back in there —
sitting down, playing cards with Bub — making
himself at home.

What had he talked to Bub about? The thought of
his being friendly with Bub was frightening. Yet
what could she do about it other than tell Bub not to
let him into the apartment again? There was no telling
what went on in the mind of a man like that — a man
who had lived in basements and cellars, a man who
had forever to stay within hailing distance of whatever building he was responsible for.

The last thing she thought before she finally went
to sleep was that the Super was something less than
human. He had been chained to buildings until he
was like an animal.

She dreamed about him and woke up terrified, not
certain that it was a dream and heard the wind sighing in the airshaft. And went back to sleep and
dreamed about him again.

He and the dog had become one. He was still tall,
gaunt, silent. The same man, but with the dog's
wolfish mouth and the dog's teeth — white, sharp,
pointed, in the redness of his mouth. His throat
worked like the dog's throat. He made a whining
noise deep inside it. He panted and strained to get
free and run through the block, but the building was
chained to his shoulders like an enormous doll's
house made of brick. She could see the people moving around inside the building, drearily climbing the
tiny stairs, sidling through the narrow halls. Mrs.
Hedges sat on the first floor smiling at a cage full of
young girls.

The building was so heavy he could hardly walk

with it on his shoulders. It was a painful, slow, horrible crawl of a walk — hesitant, slowing down, now stopping completely and then starting again. He fawned on the people in the street, dragged himself close to them, stood in front of them, pointing to the building and to the chains. 'Unloose me! Unloose me!' he begged. His voice was cracked and hollow.

Min walked beside him repeating the same words. 'Unloose him! Unloose him!' and straining to reach up toward the lock that held the chains.

He thought she, Lutie, had the key. And he followed her through the street, whining in his throat, nuzzling in back of her with his sharp, pointed dog's face. She tried to walk faster and faster, but the shambling, slow, painful sound of his footsteps was always just behind her, the sound of his whining stayed close to her like someone talking in her ear.

She looked down at her hand and the key to the padlock that held the chains was there. She stopped, and there was a whole chorus of clamoring voices: 'Shame! Shame! She won't unloose him and she's got the key!'

Mrs. Hedges' window was suddenly in front of her. Mrs. Hedges nodded, 'If I was you, dearie, I'd unloose him. It's so easy, dearie. It's so easy, dearie. Easy — easy — easy ——'

She reached out her hand toward the padlock and the long white fangs closed on her hand. Her hand and part of her arm were swallowed up inside his wolfish mouth. She watched in horror as more and more of her arm disappeared until there was only the shoulder left and then his jaws closed and she felt the sharp teeth sink in and in through her shoulder. The arm was gone and blood poured out.

She screamed and screamed and windows opened and the people poured out of the buildings — thousands of them, millions of them. She saw that they had turned to rats. The street was so full of them that she could hardly walk. They swarmed around her, jumping up and down. Each one had a building chained to its back, and they were all crying, 'Unloose me! Unloose me!'

She woke up and got out of bed. She couldn't shake loose the terror of the dream. She felt of her arm. It was still there and whole. Her mouth was wide open as though she had been screaming. It felt dry inside. She must have dreamed she was screaming, for Bub was still asleep — apparently she had made no sound. Yet she was so filled with fright from the nightmare memory of the dream that she stood motionless by the bed, unable to move for a long moment.

The air was cold. Finally she picked up the flannel robe at the foot of the bed and pulled it on. She sat down on the bed and tucked her feet under her, then carefully pulled the robe down over her feet, afraid to go back to sleep for fear of a recurrence of the dream.

The room was dark. Where the airshaft broke the wall there was a lighter quality to the darkness — a suggestion of dark blue space. Even in the dark like this her knowledge of the position of each piece of furniture made her aware of the smallness of the room. If she should get up quickly, she knew she would bump against the small chest and moving past it she might collide with the bureau.

The Street

Huddled there on the bed, her mind still clouded with the memory of the dream, her body chilled from the cold, she thought of the room, not with hatred, not with contempt, but with dread. In the darkness it seemed to close in on her until it became the sum total of all the things she was afraid of and she drew back nearer the wall because the room grew smaller and the pieces of furniture larger until she felt as though she were suffocating.

Suppose she got used to it, took it for granted, became resigned to it and all the things it represented. The thought set her to murmuring aloud, 'I mustn't get used to it. Not ever. I've got to keep on fighting to get away from here.

All the responsibility for Bub was hers. It was up to her to keep him safe, to get him out of here so he would have a chance to grow up fine and strong. Because this street and the other streets just like it would, if he stayed in them long enough, do something terrible to him. Sooner or later they would do something equally as terrible to her. And as she sat there in the dark, she began to think about the things that she had seen on such streets as this one she lived in.

There was the afternoon last spring when she had got off the subway on Lenox Avenue. It was late afternoon. The spring sunlight was sharp and clear. The street was full of people taking advantage of the soft warm air after a winter of being shut away from the sun. They had peeled off their winter coats and sweaters and mufflers.

Kids on roller skates and kids precariously perched on home-made scooters whizzed unexpectedly through the groups of people clustered on the sidewalk. The sun was warm. It beamed on the boys and girls walking past arm in arm. It made their faces very soft and young and relaxed.

She had walked along slowly, thinking that the sun transformed everything it shone on. So that the people standing talking in front of the buildings, the pushcart men in the side streets, the peanut vendor, the sweet potato man, all had an unexpected graciousness in their faces and their postures. Even the drab brick of the buildings was altered to a deep rosy pinkness.

Thus she had come on the crowd suddenly, quite unaware that it was a crowd. She had walked past some of the people before she sensed some common impulse that had made this mass of people stand motionless and withdrawn in the middle of the block. She stopped, too. And she became sharply aware of a somber silence, a curious stillness that was all around her. She edged her way to the front of the crowd, squeezing past people, forcing her way toward whatever it was that held them in this strangely arrested silence.

There was a cleared space near the buildings and a handful of policemen and cameramen and reporters with pink cards stuck in their hatbands were standing in it looking down at something. She got as close to the cleared space as she could — so close that she was almost touching the policeman in front of her.

And she saw what they were looking at. Lying flat on the sidewalk was a man — thin, shabby, tall from the amount of sidewalk that his body occupied. There was blood on the sidewalk, and she saw that it was coming from somewhere under him. Part of his body and his face were covered with what looked to be a piece of white canvas.

But the thing she had never been able to forget were his shoes. Only the uppers were intact. They had once been black, but they were now a dark dull gray from long wear. The soles were worn out. They were mere flaps attached to the uppers. She could see the layers of wear. The first outer layer of leather was left near the edges, and then the great gaping holes in the center where the leather had worn out entirely, so that for weeks he must have walked practically barefooted on the pavement.

She had stared at the shoes, trying to figure out what it must have been like to walk barefooted on the city's concrete sidewalks. She wondered if he ever went downtown, and if he did, what did he think about when he passed store windows filled with sleek furs and fabulous food and clothing made of materials so fine you could tell by looking at them they would feel like sea foam under your hand?

How did he feel when the great long cars snorted past him as he waited for the lights to change or when he looked into a taxi and saw a delicate, soft, beautiful woman lifting her face toward an opulently dressed man? The woman's hair would gleam and shine, her mouth would be knowingly shaped with lip rouge. And the concrete would have been rough under this man's feet.

The people standing in back of her weren't moving. They weren't talking. They were simply standing there looking. She watched a cop touch one of the man's broken, grayish shoes with his foot. And she got a sick feeling because the cop's shoes were glossy with polish and the warm spring sunlight glinted on them.

One of the photographers and a newspaperman elbowed through the crowd. They had a thin, dark young girl by the arm. They walked her over to a man in a gray business suit. 'She thinks it's her brother,' the reporter said.

The man stared at the girl. 'What makes you think so?'

'He went out to get bread and he ain't home yet.'

'Look like his clothes?' He nodded toward the figure on the sidewalk.

'Yes.'

One of the cops reached down and rolled the canvas back from the man's face.

Lutie didn't look at the man's face. Instead, she looked at the girl and she saw something — some emotion that she couldn't name — flicker in the girl's face. It was as though for a fraction of a second something — hate or sorrow or surprise — had moved inside her and been reflected on her face. As quickly as it came, it was gone and it was replaced by a look of resignation, of complete acceptance. It was an expression that said the girl hoped for no more than this from life because other things that had happened to her had paved the way so that she had lost the ability to protest against anything — even death suddenly like this in the spring.

'I always thought it'd happen,' she said in a flat voice.

Why doesn't she scream? Lutie had thought angrily. Why does she stand there looking like that? Why doesn't she find out how it happened and yell her head off and hit out at people? The longer she looked at that still, resigned expression on the girl's face, the angrier she became.

Finally she had pushed her way to the back of the crowd. 'What happened to him?' she asked in a hard voice.

A woman with a bundle of newspapers under her arm answered her. She shifted the papers from one arm to the other. 'White man in the baker shop killed him with a bread knife.'

There was a silence, and then another voice added: 'He had the bread knife in him and he walked to the corner. The cops brought him back here and he died there where he's layin' now.'

'White man in the store claims he tried to hold him up.'

'If that bastard white man puts one foot out here, we'll kill him. Cops or no cops.'

She went home remembering, not the threat of violence in that silent, waiting crowd, but instead the man's ragged soleless shoes and the resigned look on the girl's face. She had never been able to forget either of them. The boy was so thin — painfully thin — and she kept thinking about his walking through the city barefooted. Both he and his sister were so young.

The next day's papers said that a 'burly Negro' had failed in his effort to hold up a bakery shop, for the proprietor had surprised him by resisting and stabbed him with a bread knife. She held the paper in her hand for a long time, trying to follow the reasoning by which that thin ragged boy had become in the eyes of a reporter a 'burly Negro.' And she decided that it all depended on where you sat how these things looked. If you looked at them from inside the framework of a fat weekly salary, and you thought of colored people as naturally criminal, then you didn't really see what any Negro looked like. You couldn't, because the Negro was never an individual. He was a threat, or an animal, or a curse, or a blight, or a joke.

It was like the Chandlers and their friends in Connecticut, who looked at her and didn't see her, but saw instead a wench with no morals who would be easy to come by. The reporter saw a dead Negro who had attempted to hold up a store, and so he couldn't really see what the man lying on the sidewalk looked like. He couldn't see the ragged shoes, the thin, starved body. He saw, instead, the picture he already had in his mind: a huge, brawny, blustering, ignorant, criminally disposed black man who had run amok with a knife on a spring afternoon in Harlem and who had in turn been knifed.

She had gone past the bakery shop again the next afternoon. The windows had been smashed, the front door had apparently been broken in, because it was boarded up. There were messages chalked on the sidewalk in front of the store. They all said the same thing: 'White man, don't come back.' She was surprised to see that there were men still standing around, on the nearest corners, across the street. Their faces were turned toward the store. They weren't talking. They were just standing with their hands in their pockets — waiting.

Two police cars with their engines running were

drawn up in front of the store. There were two cops right in front of the door, swinging nightsticks. She walked past, thinking that it was like a war that hadn't got off to a start yet, though both sides were piling up ammunition and reserves and were now waiting for anything, any little excuse, a gesture, a word, a sudden loud noise — and pouf! it would start.

Lutie moved uneasily on the bed. She pulled the robe more tightly around her. All of these streets were filled with violence, she thought. You turned a corner, walked through a block, and you came on it suddenly, unexpectedly.

For it was later in the spring that she took Bub to Roundtree Hospital. There was a cold, driving rain and she had hesitated about going out in it. But Bub had fallen on the sidewalk and cut his knee. She had come home from work to find him sitting disconsolately in Pop's kitchen. It was a deep, nasty cut, so she took him to the emergency room at Roundtree in order to find out just how bad it was.

She and Bub sat on the long bench in the center of the waiting room. There were two people ahead of them, and she waited impatiently because she should have been at home fixing dinner and getting Bub's clothes ready for school the next day.

Each time the big doors that led to the street swung open, a rush of wet damp air flushed through the room. She took to watching the people who came in, wondering about them. A policeman came in with a tired-looking, old man. The man's suit was shabby, but it was neatly pressed. He was wearing a stiff white collar.

The policeman guided him toward the bench. 'Sit

here,' he said. The man gave no indication that he had heard. 'Sit here,' the policemen repeated. Naw,' as the old man started to move away. 'Just sit down here, Pop.' Finally the old man sat down.

She had watched him out of the corner of her eyes. He stared at the white hospital wall with a curious lack of interest. Nurses walked past him, white-coated internes strode by. There was a bustle and flurry when a stocky, gray-haired man with pince-nez glasses emerged from the elevator. 'How are you, Doctor?' 'Nice to see you back, Doctor.'

The old man remained completely oblivious to the movement around him. The focus of his eyes never shifted from the expanse of wall in front of him.

Bub moved closer to her. 'Hey, Mom,' he whispered, 'what's the matter with him?'

'I don't know,' she said softly. 'Maybe he's just tired.'

Right across from where they were sitting was a small room filled with volunteer ambulance drivers. They were lounging in the chairs, their shirt collars open, smoking cigarettes. The blue haze of the smoke drifted out into the waiting room. The cop went into the room to use the telephone.

She heard him quite clearly. 'I dunno. Picked him up on Eighth Avenue. Woman at the candy store said he'd been sittin' there all day. Naw. On the steps. Yeah. Psychopathic, I guess.'

The old man didn't move, apparently didn't hear. She found him strangely disturbing, because there was in his lack-luster staring the same quality of resignation that she had seen in the face of the girl on Lenox Avenue earlier in the spring. She remembered how she had tried to tie the two together and reach a conclusion about them and couldn't because the man was old. She kept thinking that if he had lived that long, he should have been able to develop some inner strength that would have fought against whatever it was that had brought him to this aimless staring.

The telephone in the room across from them rang and she forgot about the old man. The woman who answered it said, 'Okay. Right away.' She turned to one of the drivers, gave him an address on Morningside Avenue, and said, 'Hustle! They say it's bad.'

Lutie had hoped that she would be able to get Bub into the emergency room before the ambulance came back, so that he wouldn't be sitting round-eyed with fear when he saw whatever it was they brought back that was 'bad.' She kept telling herself she shouldn't have brought him here, but the fee was so low that it was almost like free treatment.

The big street doors opened suddenly and the stretcher came through. The men carrying it moved quickly and with such precision that the stretcher was practically on top of them before Lutie realized it. The room was full of a low, terrible moaning, and the young girl on the stretcher was trying to sit up and blood was streaming out of the center of her body.

A gray-haired woman walked beside the stretcher. She kept saying, 'Cut to ribbons! Cut to ribbons! Cut to ribbons!' — over and over in a monotonous voice. It was raining so hard that even in getting from the street to the waiting room the woman had been soaked and water dripped from her coat, from her hatbrim.

The Street

There was a long, awful moment while they maneuvered the stretcher past the bench and the girl moaned and tried to talk, and every once in a while she screamed — a sharp, thin, disembodied sound. The policeman looked at the girl in astonishment, but the old man never turned his head.

Lutie had grabbed Bub and covered his face with her face so that he couldn't see. He tried to squirm out of her arms and she held him closer and tighter. When she lifted her head, the stretcher was gone.

Bub stood up and looked around. 'What was the matter with her?' he asked.

'She got hurt.'

'How did she get hurt?'

'I don't know. It was an accident, I guess.'

'Somebody cut her, didn't they?' And when she didn't answer, he repeated, 'Didn't they?'

'I guess so, but I really don't know.'

'One of the kids at school got cut up like that,' he said, and then, 'Why wouldn't you let me look, Mom?'

'Because I didn't think it was good for you to look. And when people are hurt badly like that, it doesn't help them to have someone stare at them.'

While the interne dressed Bub's knee, she thought about the girl on the stretcher. Just a kid. Not much over sixteen, and she had that same awful look of resignation, of not expecting anything better than that of life. She was like the girl on Lenox Avenue who had looked down at her brother lying on the sidewalk to say, 'I always thought it'd happen.'

Lutie sat motionless staring into the dark She

was cold and yet she didn't move. She thought of
the old man, the young girls. What reason did she
have to believe that she and Bub wouldn't become
so accustomed to the sight and sound of violence and
of death that they wouldn't protest against it —
they would become resigned to it; or that Bub finally
wouldn't end up on a sidewalk with a knife in his
back?

She felt she knew the steps by which that girl
landed on the stretcher in the hospital. She could
trace them easily. It could be that Bub might follow
the same path.

The girl probably went to high school for a few
months and then got tired of it. She had no place to
study at night because the house was full of roomers,
and she had no incentive, anyway, because she didn't
have a real home. The mother was out to work all
day and the father was long gone. She found out
that boys liked her and she started bringing them to
the apartment. The mother wasn't there to know
what was going on.

They didn't have real homes, no base, no family
life. So at sixteen or seventeen the girl was fooling
around with two or three different boys. One of
them found out about the others. Like all the rest
of them, he had only a curious supersensitive kind of
pride that kept him going, so he had to have revenge
and knives are cheap.

It happened again and again all through Harlem.
And she saw in her mind's eye the curious procession
of people she had met coming out of 121st Street.
They were walking toward Eighth Avenue.

She had been to the day-old bakery on Eighth

Avenue and she stopped on the corner for the stop
light. Down the length of the block she saw this
group of people. They formed at first glance what
appeared to be a procession, for they were walking
slowly, stiffly. There was a goodish space between
each one of them as though they didn't want to be
too close to each other and yet were held together in
a group by shock. They were young — sixteen,
seventeen, eighteen, nineteen — and they were moving like sleepwalkers.

Then she saw that they had set their pace to that
of the girl walking in the very front. Someone was
leading her by the arm, and she was walking slowly,
her body was limp, her shoulders sagged.

She had cringed away from the sight of the girl's
face. She couldn't collect her thoughts for a· moment, and then almost automatically the toneless
reiterated words of the gray-haired woman in Roundtree Hospital came back to her: 'Cut to ribbons!
Cut to ribbons!'

She couldn't really see the girl's face, because blood
poured over it, starting at her forehead. It was oozing down over her eyes, her nose, over her cheeks,
dripped even from her mouth. The bright red blood
turned what had been her face into a gaudy mask with
patches of brown here and there where her skin
showed through.

Lutie got that same jolting sense of shock and then
of rage, because these people, all of them — the girl,
the crowd in back of her — showed no horror, no
surprise, no dismay. They had expected this. They
were used to it. And they had become resigned to it.

Yes, she thought, she and Bub had to get out of

116th Street. It was a bad street. And then she thought about the other streets. It wasn't just this street that she was afraid of or that was bad. It was any street where people were · packed together like sardines in a can.

And it wasn't just this city. It was any city where they set up a line and say black folks stay on this side and white folks on this side, so that the black folks were crammed on top of each other — jammed and packed and forced into the smallest possible space until they were completely cut off from light and air.

It was any place where the women had to work to support the families because the men couldn't get jobs and the men got bored and pulled out and the kids were left without proper homes because there was nobody around to put a heart into it. Yes. It was any place where people were so damn poor they didn't have time to do anything but work, and their bodies were the only source of relief from the pressure under which they lived; and where the crowding to- gether made the young girls wise beyond their years.

It all added up to the same thing, she decided — white people. She hated them. She would always hate them. She forced herself to stop that train of thought. It led nowhere. It was unpleasant.

She slipped out of the wool robe and got back into bed and lay there trying to convince herself that she didn't have to stay on this street or any other street like it if she fought hard enough. Bub didn't have to end up stretched out on a sidewalk with a knife through his back. She was going to sleep, and she wasn't going to dream about supers who were transformed into wolfish dogs with buildings chained on their backs.

She searched her mind for a pleasant thought to drift off to sleep on. And she started building a picture of herself standing before a microphone in a long taffeta dress that whispered sweetly as she moved; of a room full of dancers who paused in their dancing to listen as she sang. Their faces were expectant, worshiping, as they looked up at her.

It was early when she woke up the next morning and she yawned and stretched and tried to remember what it was that had given her this feeling of anticipation. She burrowed her head deep into her pillow after she looked at the small clock on the bureau, because she could stay in bed for a few more minutes.

And then she remembered. Tonight was the night that she was going to sing at the Casino. Perhaps after tonight was over she could leave this street and these dark, narrow rooms and these walls that pressed in against her. It would be like discarding a worn-out dress, a dress that was shiny from wear and faded from washing and whose seams were forever giving way. The thought made her fling her arms out from under the covers. She pulled the covers close around her neck, for the room was cold and the steam was as yet only a rattling in the radiator.

Immediately she began planning the things she had to do. When she got home from work, she would wash her hair and curl it, then press the long black taffeta skirt which with a plain white blouse would have to serve as evening gown. She wouldn't wear her winter coat, even though it was cold out, for the little short black coat would look better.

The hands of the battered clock moved toward seven and she jumped out of bed, shivered in the cold air, and slammed the airshaft shut.

Pulling her bathrobe around her, she went into the living room. Bub was still sleeping and she tucked the covers tight under his chin, thinking that sometime soon he would wake up in a bedroom of his own. It would have maple furniture and the bedspread and draperies would have ships and boats on them. There would be plenty of windows in the room and it would look out over a park.

In the kitchen she poured water into a saucepan, lit the gas stove, and stood waiting for the water to boil. While she stirred oatmeal into the boiling water, she began to wonder if perhaps she shouldn't wear that thin white summer blouse instead of one of the plain long-sleeved ones. The summer blouse had a low, round neck. It would look a lot more dressed-up. She turned the flame low under the oatmeal, set the table, filled small glasses with tomato juice, thinking that Bub could sleep about fifteen more minutes. She would have just time enough to take a bath.

But first she would look at the blouse to see if it needed pressing. She went into the bedroom and opened the closet door quietly. The blouse was rammed in between her one suit and her heavy winter coat. She reached her hand toward it, thinking, That's just plain careless of me. It must be terribly wrinkled from having been put in there like that.

She took the blouse out and held it up in front of her, staring at it in amazement. Why, it's all crushed.

and there's dirt on it, she thought — great smudges of dirt and tight, small wrinkles as though it had been squeezed together. What on earth had Bub been doing with it?

She shook him awake. 'What were you doing in my closet?' she demanded.

'Closet?' He looked up at her his eyes still full of sleep. 'I ain't been in your closet.'

'Will you stop saying "ain't"?' she said. 'Were you playing with my blouse?' She held it in front of him.

He was wide awake now, and he looked up at her with such obvious astonishment that she knew he was telling the truth. 'Honest, Mom,' he protested, 'I ain't had it.'

Unconsciously she thrust the blouse a little farther away from her, holding it by the metal hanger and thinking, Well, then who had done this? She knew that she hadn't hung it up wrinkled and dirty. Then she remembered that Jones, the Super, had been in the apartment last night playing cards with Bub. But he couldn't, she thought — what would he be doing with her blouse and when had he done it?

'Bub,' she said sharply, 'did you go out while the Super was here?'

He nodded. 'I got him some beer.'

She turned away and went into the kitchen so that Bub wouldn't see the expression on her face, because she was afraid and angry and at the same time she felt sickened. She could picture him, hungry-eyed, gaunt, standing there in her room crushing the blouse between his hands.

She opened the set tubs, dumped soapflakes in —

great handfuls of them — and ran hot water on the flakes until the suds foamed up high. She almost let the water run over the top of the tub, because she stood in front of it, not moving, thinking, He's crazy. He's absolutely crazy.

Finally she shut the faucet off and poked the blouse deep into the hot, soapy water. She couldn't wear it again — not for a long time. Certainly she wouldn't wear it tonight.

Chapter 9

BUB STOOD IN THE DOORWAY of Lutie's bedroom, watching her dress. It was nine-thirty, and he kept thinking, If she's going out so late it will be a long time before she gets back home. He didn't want her to know that he was afraid to stay in the house alone. He wished there was some way he could keep her with him without telling her he was scared.

It would be like last night all over again. He hadn't fallen asleep with the light on as he'd told her. After Supe left, he sat on the couch and finally lay down on it, but he wouldn't turn the light out because even with his eyes held tight shut he could somehow see the dark all around him. The furniture changed in the dark — each piece assumed a strange and menacing shape that transformed the whole room.

He leaned against the door jamb, standing first on one foot and then the other in an effort to see how long he could remain on one foot without losing his balance or getting tired. Lutie picked up a lipstick and he watched her intently as she made her mouth a rosy red color. She frowned a little as she looked at herself in the mirror.

'You look awful pretty,' he said. She had on a long black skirt that made a soft noise when she walked and a white blouse and a red scarf tied around her waist. 'Where you going, Mom?'

'To a dance at the Casino. I'm going to sing there tonight.'

He accepted the fact that she was going to sing with a nod of approval, because he loved to hear her sing or to hum, and he took it for granted that other people would, too. But if she was going to a dance, she wouldn't be home until late. The floor would creak and the wind would rattle the windows like something outside trying to get in at him, and he would be in the house alone. When she was here, he never heard noises like that — footsteps in the hall outside and doors that banged with a loud, clapping noise. He never woke up frightened and not knowing why he was frightened like last night. The dark didn't bother him when she was with him, for he knew all he had to do was call out and she would come to him.

'Will you be gone very long?' he asked.

'Not very long. I'll tuck you in bed before I go.' She turned away from the mirror. 'You start getting undressed now, so I can turn the light out when I go out.'

The Street

He lingered in the door, watching her fasten the straps on her high-heeled red shoes, wanting to ask her not to turn the light out when she left and remembering that the bill got bigger and bigger the longer the light burned.

'Could I read some before I go to sleep?'

'I should say not. You go right to sleep.' And when he still stood there, holding one foot up in back of him, she walked over and patted his shoulder. 'Hurry up, honey. I haven't got much time.'

He went toward the bathroom reluctantly and spent a long time putting on his pajamas. He examined his shoes and socks with great care as though he had never seen them before and was puzzled as to what they could be used for. He ran water in the bathroom sink and stirred it with a lackadaisical finger, watching the little ripples that formed as his finger moved back and forth, and wishing that he had come right out and told her he was afraid to stay by himself. Perhaps she would have asked him if he wanted Supe to come up and stay until she got back. Supe would come, too. Only she didn't seem to like Supe very much. He washed his face and hands, picked up his clothes, and went into the living room.

Lutie was turning back the covers on his bed and he stood in the middle of the room looking at the way the long skirt sort of flowed around her as she moved. It looked as though the bottom of it bowed up at her, and as she leaned over and then straightened up, the ends of the red sash moved briskly as though the red sash were dancing. He watched it with delight.

'Okay,' she said. 'I'll put my coat on while you're getting in bed.'

He lay down in the middle of the couch and looked up at the ceiling, trying to think of something that would delay her going out. When she wasn't there, he was filled with a sense of loss. It wasn't just the darkness, for the same thing happened in the daylight when he came home from school. The instant he opened the door, he was filled with a sense of desolation, for the house was empty and quiet and strange. At noon he would eat his lunch fast and go out to the street. After school he changed his clothes quickly and, even as he changed them, no matter how quick he was, the house was frightening and cold. But when she was in it, it was warm and friendly and familiar.

There was a kid in school who had to stay home five days with a toothache. He could say he had a toothache. But he wasn't sure how quickly they came on, and he wouldn't want her to know the instant she heard him mention it that he was making it up. Or a growing pain might be better — lots of the kids at school had growing pains. He was trying to decide where the growing pain would be when she came back into the room. She walked over to the hall and clicked the light on.

Then she was bending over to kiss him and he smelt the faint sweet smell of her and he hugged her with both arms and all his strength, thinking if only she would stay just long enough for him to go to sleep. It would be just a little while because he would go to sleep quickly, knowing that she was close by.

He relaxed his arms and lay down, afraid that she

might be angry if he clung to her like that, for he remembered how angry she was this morning about her blouse being wrinkled and he might wrinkle this one she had on by squeezing her so tightly. She reached toward the light by the bed and he touched her coat in a light, caressing gesture.

'Good-bye, hon,' she said and turned the light out.

Instantly the living room was plunged into darkness. He opened his eyes wide in an effort to see something other than this swift blackness. The corners of the room were there, he knew, but he couldn't see them. They were wiped out in the dark. It made him feel as though he were left hanging in space and that he couldn't know how much space there was other than that his body occupied.

The overstuffed chair near the couch had become a bulge of darkness so that it no longer looked like a chair. It was a strange, frightening object along with the card table in front of the window and the bookcase. It was as though quick, darting hands had substituted something else in place of them just as the light went off. His eyes slowly became accustomed to the darkness and he saw that the dim light in the hall reached a little way into the living room, leaving a faint yellow square of light on the blue congoleum rug. Even that was disturbing, for he couldn't quite make out the familiar plaid pattern in the rug.

'You won't let anyone in, will you?' Lutie asked.

He had forgotten she was still in the room and he looked in the direction of her voice, grateful to hear the sound of it. 'No, ma'am.'

There was a strained, breathless quality in his voice,

and Lutie turned toward him. 'Are you all right, hon?' she asked.

'Sure.' He had hoped she would notice there was something wrong with him. Then, when she did, he suddenly didn't want her to know he was a coward about the dark and about staying alone. He thought of the hard-riding cowboys, the swaggering, brave detectives in the movies, and the big tough boys in six B in school, and he said, 'Sure, I'm all right.'

Lutie walked toward the square of light and he saw her clearly for a moment — the shine of the hair on top of her head, the long, soft-flowing black skirt, the short, wide coat.

'Good-bye,' she said again, and turned toward him smiling.

''Bye, Mom,' he answered. Then the light in the hall went off. She was still there, though, because he heard her open the door and for an instant the dim light from the outside hall came into the room. He leaned toward it because it left pools of black shadows in the corners of the room, even in the small foyer. Then she closed the door.

The whole apartment was swallowed up in darkness. He listened to the sound of her key turning in the lock. Her high heels clicked as she walked down the hall. He sat up straight in order to hear better. She was going down the stairs. Her footsteps grew fainter and fainter until strain as he would he could no longer hear them.

He lay down and pulled the bedcovers up to his chin and firmly closed his eyes. They wouldn't stay closed. He kept opening them because even with his eyes shut he was aware of the dark all around him.

It had a heavy, syrupy quality — soft and thick like molasses, only black.

It was worse with his eyes open, because he couldn't see anything and he kept imagining that the whole room was changing and shifting about him. He peered into the dark, trying to see what was going on. He sat up and then he lay down again and pulled the covers over his head. There was an even stranger quality to the black under the covers. He shut his eyes and then opened them immediately afterward, not knowing what he expected to find nestling beside him under the sheets, but afraid to look and afraid not to look.

Heavy footsteps came up the stairs and he threw the covers back and sat up listening. Maybe it's Supe, he thought. The steps went past the door, on down the hall, and he lay down again disappointed. The stairs outside creaked. A light, persistent sound started in the walls, a scuttering, scampering noise that set him shivering and cowering under the covers, for he remembered the vivid stories Lil had told him about the rats and mice that ate people up.

There was a fight in the apartment next door. At first he welcomed the sound of the loud, angry voices because it shut out the sound of the rats in the walls. There was a crash of china. Something heavy landed against the wall and then plaster dropped down. He could hear it trickle down and down. The voices grew more violent and the woman screamed.

He put his fingers in his ears. The covers slipped down from his head with the movement of his arms and instantly the darkness in the room enveloped and enfolded him. He gripped the covers tight over his head and the horrid sound of the voices and the screaming came clearly through the blanket and the sheets.

'You black bitch, I oughtta killed you long ago.'

'Don't you come near me. Don't you come near me,' the woman panted.

Someone threw a bottle out of a window on the fourth floor and it landed in the yard below with a tinkling sound that echoed and echoed. There was silence for a moment. A dog commenced to bark and the voices next door started again.

The woman sobbed, and as Bub listened to the sound he became more and more frightened. It was such a lonesome sound and the room quivered with it until he seemed almost to see the sound running through the dark. There was nothing around him that was familiar or that he had ever seen before. His face tightened. He was here alone, lost in the dark, lost in a strange place filled with terrifying things.

He reached up, fumbled for the light, found the switch, and turned it on. Instantly the room lay all around him — familiar, safe, just as he had always known it. He examined it with care. All of the things that he knew so well were right where they belonged — the big chair, the card table, the radio, the congoleum rug. None of it had changed. Yet in the dark these things vanished and were replaced by strange, unknown shapes.

The sobbing of the woman next door died away. From somewhere downstairs there came the sound of laughter, the clink of glasses. He lay down relaxed, no longer frightened. Mom would be mad when she came home and found him asleep with the light on, but he couldn't turn it off again.

It occurred to him that she wouldn't mind the light being on if he could figure out some way of earning money so that he could help pay the electric bill. He frowned. She hadn't liked the shoeshine box. But there must be some other way he could make money, some way she would approve of. Finally he dropped off to sleep, still trying to think of something he could do to earn money.

At about the same time Bub was falling asleep, Lutie entered the lobby of the Casino where the smell of floor wax and dust and liquor and perfume hung heavy in the air.

At this hour the big dance hall was deserted and lifeless. The bold-eyed girls in the checkroom talked idly to each other. Their eyes constantly shifted to the thick white china plates on the shelves in front of them, as though they were fascinated by the prospect of the change that would be added to the solitary quarter and dime they had placed on the plates earlier in the evening. The rows and rows of empty coat hangers in back of them emphasized the silent, waiting look of the place.

As Lutie pushed her coat toward one of the checkroom girls, she was wondering if Bub was afraid to stay by himself and ashamed to admit it, for she remembered the sudden, frightened look on his face when she woke him up by opening the door last night.

She mechanically accepted a round white disk from the girl and put it in her pocketbook. There was something inexpressibly dreary about the Casino when it was empty, she thought. You could see all of it for what it was worth, and it was never good to see anything like that. The red carpet on the lobby floor was worn. There were dark places on it where cigarettes had been snuffed out. The artificial palms that stood at the entrance in big brass pots were gray with dust. Even the great staircase which led to the dance floor above was badly in need of a coat of paint.

The long black skirt flowed around her feet as she mounted the stairs. She was surprised to discover that she wasn't nervous or excited about singing with Boots Smith's band. Now that she was about to do it, she had regained her old feeling of self-confidence, and she walked swiftly, holding her head high, humming as she walked.

The shiny, polished dance floor looked enormous. Though it would be another hour before people arrived to dance, the colored lights were already focused on it — pale blue, delicate pink and yellow — rainbow colors that shifted and changed until the wide, smooth floor was bathed in the soft, moving bands of light.

As Lutie walked across the floor toward the bandstand where the orchestra was playing softly, she noticed that the Casino's bouncers were already on hand, standing in a small group off to one side. Their tuxedos couldn't conceal their long arms and brutal shoulders. They had ex-prize-fighter written all over them, from their scarred faces and terrible ears to the way in which their heads drew back into their shoulders as though they were dodging punches.

Boots jumped down from the bandstand when he saw her. He met her midway. 'You know,' he said, 'I began to get the feelin' that you wasn't coming. Don't know why.' His eyes traveled slowly from the curls piled high on top of her head to the red sandals on her feet. 'You sure look good, baby,' he said softly.

He linked his arm through hers and walked with her toward the men in the band. 'Boys, meet Lutie Johnson,' he said. 'She's singin' with us tonight. What do you want to start with?' he asked, turning to her

'Oh, I don't know.' She hesitated, trying to think. I guess "Darlin'"' would be best.' It was the song he had heard her sing in the Junto and had liked.

She avoided the eyes of the men in the orchestra because what they were thinking was plain on their faces. The fat pianist grinned. One of the trumpet players winked at the drummer. The others nudged each other and nodded knowingly. One of the saxophonists was raising his instrument in mock salute to Boots. It was quite obvious that they were saying to themselves and to each other, Yeah, Boots has got himself a new chick and this singing business is the old come-on.

Boots ignored them. He patted out the rhythm with his foot and the music started. She walked over to the microphone and stood there waiting for the melody to repeat itself. She touched the mike and then held onto it with both hands, for the silvery metal was cold and her hands were suddenly hot. As she held the mike, she felt as though her voice was draining away down through the slender metal rod, and the idea frightened her.

The music swelled in back of her and she began to sing, faintly at first and then her voice grew stronger, clearer, for she gradually forgot the men in the orchestra, forgot even that she was there in the Casino and why she was there.

Though she sang the words of the song, it was of something entirely different that she was thinking and putting into the music: she was leaving the street with its dark hallways, its mean, shabby rooms; she was taking Bub away with her to a place where there were no Mrs. Hedges, no resigned and disillusioned little girls, no half-human creatures like the Super. She and Bub were getting out and away, and they would never be back.

The last low strains of the melody died away and she stood holding onto the mike, not moving. There was complete silence behind her, and she turned toward the band, filled with sudden doubt and wishing that she had kept her mind on what she was doing, on the words of the song, instead of floating off into a day-dream.

The men in the orchestra stood up. They were bowing to her. It was an exaggerated gesture, for they bowed so far from the waist that for a moment all she could see were their backs — rounded and curved as they bent over. She was filled with triumph at the sight, for she knew that this absurd, preposterous bowing was their way of telling her they were accepting her on merit as a singer, not because she was Boots' newest girl friend.

'I ——' she turned to Boots.

'The job's yours, baby,' he said. 'All yours. Wrapped up and tied up for as long as you want it.'

The Street

After he said that, she couldn't remember much of anything. She knew that she sang other songs — new ones and old ones — and that each time she sang, the smile of satisfaction on Boots' face increased. But it was something that she was aware of through a blur and a mist of happiness and contentment because she had found the means of getting away from the street.

As the hands of the big clock on the wall moved toward eleven-thirty, the big smooth floor filled with dancing couples. They arrived in groups of nine and ten. The boxes at the edges of the dance floor spilled over with people — young girls, soldiers, sailors, middle-aged men and women. The tuxedoed bouncers moved warily through the crowd, forever encircling it, mingling with it. The long bar at the side of the dance floor was almost obscured by the people crowding around it. The bartenders moved quickly, pouring drinks, substituting full glasses for empty ones.

The soft rainbow-colored lights played over the dancers. There were women in evening gowns, girls in short tight skirts and sweaters that clung slickly to their young breasts. Boys in pants cut tight and close at the ankle went through violent dance routines with the young girls. Some of the dancing couples jitter-bugged, did the rhumba, invented intricate new steps of their own. The ever-moving, ever-changing lights picked faces and figures out of the crowd; added a sense of excitement and strangely the quality of laughter to the dancers. People in the boxes drank out of little paper cups, ate fried chicken and cake and thick ham sandwiches.

Lutie sang at frequent intervals. There was violent applause each time, but even while she was singing, she could hear the babble of voices under the music. White-coated waiters scurried back and forth to the boxes carrying trays heavy with buckets of ice, tall bottles of soda, and big mugs foaming with beer. And all the time the dancers moved in front of her, rocking and swaying. Some of them even sang with her.

The air grew heavy with the heat from the people's bodies, with the smell of beer and whiskey and the cigarette smoke that hung over the big room like a gray-blue cloud. And she thought, It doesn't make much difference who sings or whether they sing badly or well, because nobody really listens. They're making love or quarreling or drinking or dancing.

During the intermission Boots said to her, 'How about a drink, baby?'

'Sure,' she said. For the first time she realized how tired she was. She had come home from work and shopped for food in crowded stores, cooked dinner for herself and Bub, washed and ironed shirts for him and a blouse for herself. The excitement of coming here, of singing, of knowing that she would get this job that meant so much to her had completely blotted out any feeling of fatigue. Now that it was over, she was limp, exhausted.

'I'd love to have a drink,' she said gratefully.

He gave the bartender the order and led her to one of the small tables at the edge of the dance floor. A white-coated waiter slid a small glass across the table to Boots Then he opened the bottle of beer on his tray, poured it into a thick mug and placed the mug so squarely in front of Lutie that she wondered if he had measured the distance.

Boots filled his glass from a flask that he took from his pocket. Then he slid the glass back and forth on the table, holding it delicately between his thumb and forefinger. He looked at her and smiled. The long, narrow scar on his cheek moved up toward his eye as he smiled.

'You know, baby, I could fall in love with you easy,' he said. And, he thought, it's true. And that if he couldn't get her any other way, he just might marry her, and he laughed because the thought of being married amused him. He pushed the glass back and forth and smiled at her again.

'Really?' she said. It was beginning rather quickly. But it didn't matter because the job was hers and that was the important thing. She searched her mind for an answer that wouldn't entirely rebuff him and yet would hold him off. 'I was in love once, and I guess once you've put all you've got into it there isn't much left over for anyone else,' she said carefully.

'You mean your husband?'

'Yes. It wasn't his fault it didn't work out. And I guess it really wasn't mine either. We were too poor. And we were too young to stand being poor.'

They're all alike, he thought. Money's what gets 'em, even this one with that soft, young look on her face. And he almost purred, thinking not even marriage would be necessary. It would take a little time, just a little time, and that was all. He leaned across the table to say, 'You don't have to be poor any more. Not after tonight. I'll see to that. All you got to do from now is just be nice to me, baby.'

The Street

He had thought she would give some indication that being nice to him was going to be easy for her. Instead, she got up from the table. There was a little frown between her eyes. The thick mug in front of her was more than half full of beer.

'Hey, you ain't finished your beer,' he protested.

'I know' — she waved her hand toward the bandstand where the men were filing in. 'The boys are ready to start,' she said.

It was three o'clock when the rainbow-colored lights stopped moving over the dance floor. There was a final blast from the trumpets and the orchestra men began stowing music into the cases that held their instruments. The people filed out of the big hall slowly, reluctantly. The ornate staircase was choked with them, for they walked close to each other as though still joined together by the memory of the music and the dancing.

The hat-check girls smiled as they peeled coats off hangers, reached up on shelves for hats. Coins clinked in the thick white saucers. The men crowded around the mirrors adjusting bright-colored scarves around their necks, buttoning coats, patting their hats into becoming shapes, and adjusting the hats on their heads with infinite care.

Boots turned to Lutie. 'Can I give you a ride home, baby?'

'That would be swell,' she said promptly. Perhaps he would tell her how much the salary was that went with the job. Perhaps, too — and the thought was unpleasant — he would make the first tentative advances toward the next step — the business of being nice to him. At the moment she felt so strong and so

confident that she was certain she could put him off
deftly, neatly, and continue to do it until she signed
a contract for the job.

When they reached the lobby, there were only a
handful of stragglers left. Even these were putting
on hats and coats, the men ogling themselves in the
mirror, the women posing on the circular bench in the
center of the lobby. The women pressed their feet
deep into the red carpet, enjoying the feel of it under
their shoes, admiring the glimpses they caught of
their own reflections in the mirrors on the wall.

At the foot of the stairs one of the biggest of the
Casino's bouncers laid a hamlike hand on Boots' arm.
Lutie stared at him, for at close range the battered
flesh of his face, the queer out-of-shape formation of
his ears, and the enormous bulge of his shoulders
under the smooth cloth of the tuxedo jacket were
awe-inspiring.

'Hey, Boots,' he said. 'Go by Junto's. He wanta
see you.' The words came out of the side of his
mouth. His lips barely moved.

'He phoned?'

'Yeah. 'Bout an hour ago. Said you was to stop
when you got through here.'

'Okay, pal.'

Boots obtained Lutie's coat from the checkroom,
held it for her, pushed the big doors of the Casino
open, then helped her into his car, not really thinking
about her, but wondering what Old Man Junto
wanted that was so important it wouldn't keep until
daylight.

He drove down Seventh Avenue in silence, con-
jecturing about it. When he finally remembered that

The Street

Lutie was there in the car with him, he had reached
125th Street. 'Where'll I let you out?' he asked absently.

'At the corner of 116th Street and Seventh.'

He stopped the car at the corner of 116th Street,
reached across her to open the door. 'See you tomorrow night, baby?' he asked. 'Same time so we
can rehearse some?'

'Absolutely,' she said, and felt a faint astonishment
because his hands had gone back to the steering wheel
and stayed there. He was looking up the street, his
mind obviously far away, not even remotely concerned with her.

She watched his car until it disappeared up the
street, trying to figure out what it was that had dis-
tracted and disturbed him so that he had put her
completely out of his thoughts.

The wind lifted the full folds of her skirt, blew the
short, full coat away from her body. She shrugged
her shoulders. It was too cold to stand on this corner
puzzling about what was on Boots Smith's mind.

As she walked toward the apartment house where
she lived, she passed only a few people. They were
moving briskly. Otherwise the street was dead quiet.
Most of the houses were dark.

The cold couldn't reach through to her, even with
this thin coat on, she thought. Because the fact that
she wouldn't have to live on this street much longer
served as a barrier against the cold. It was more ef-
fective than the thickest, warmest coat. She toyed
with figures. Perhaps she would get forty, fifty,
sixty, seventy dollars a week. They all sounded
fantastically high. She decided whatever the sum

proved to be, it would be like sudden, great wealth compared to her present salary.

A man came suddenly out of a hallway just ahead of her — a furtive, darting figure that disappeared rapidly in the darkness of the street. As she reached the doorway from which he had emerged, a woman lurched out, screaming, 'Got my pocketbook! The bastard's got my pocketbook!'

Windows were flung open all up and down the street. Heads appeared at the windows — silent, watching heads that formed dark blobs against the dark spaces that were the windows. The woman remained in the middle of the street, bellowing at the top of her voice.

Lutie got a good look at her as she went past her. She had a man's felt hat pulled down almost over her eyes and men's shoes on her feet. Her coat was fastened together with safety pins. She was shaking her fists as she shouted curses after the man who had long since vanished up the street.

Ribald advice issued from the windows:

'Aw, shut up! Folks got to sleep.'

'What the hell'd you have in it, your rent money?'

'Go on home, old woman, 'fore I throw somp'n special down on your rusty head.'

As the woman's voice died away to a mumble and a mutter, the heads withdrew and the windows were slammed shut. The street was quiet again. And Lutie thought, No one could live on a street like this and stay decent. It would get them sooner or later, for it sucked the humanity out of people — slowly, surely, inevitably.

She glanced up at the gloomy apartments where the

heads had been. There were row after row of narrow windows — floor after floor packed tight with people. She looked at the street itself. It was bordered by garbage cans. Half-starved cats prowled through the cans — rustling paper, gnawing on bones. Again she thought that it wasn't just this one block, this particular street. It was like this all over Harlem wherever the rents were low.

But she and Bub were leaving streets like this. And the thought that she had been able to accomplish this alone, without help from anyone, made her open the street door of the apartment house with a vigorous push. It made her stand inside the door for a moment, not seeing the dimly lit hallway, but instead seeing herself and Bub living together in a big roomy place and Bub growing up fine and strong.

The air from the street set her skirt to billowing around her long legs and, as she stood there smiling, her face and body glowing with triumph, she looked almost as though she were dancing.

Chapter 10

AFTER MIN hung the cross over the bed, Jones took to sleeping in the living room. He could no longer see the cross, but he knew it was there and it made him restless, uneasy.

Finally it seemed to him that he met it at every turn. Wherever he looked, he saw a suggestion of its outline. His eyes added a horizontal line to the long cord that hung from the ceiling light and instantly the cross was dangling in front of him. He sought and found the shape of a cross in the window panes, in chairs, in the bars on the canary's cage. When he looked at Min, he could see its outline as sharply as though it had been superimposed on her shapeless, flabby body.

He drew an imaginary line from her head to her

feet and added another crosswise line, and thus, whenever he glanced in her direction, he saw the cross
again. When she spoke to him, he no longer looked
at her for fear he would see, not her, but the great
golden cross she had hung over the bed.

He turned and twisted on the sofa thinking about
it. Finally he sat up. Min was snoring in the bedroom. He could almost see her lower lip quiver with
the blowing-out of her breath through her opened
mouth. The room was filled with the sound. The
dog's heavy breathing formed an accompaniment.

It annoyed him that Min and the dog should be
comfortably lost in their dreams while he was wide
awake — painfully awake. He thought of Lutie's
apartment on the top floor. It was like a magnet
whose pull reached down to him and drew him toward it steadily, irresistibly. He dressed quickly in
the dark. He had to go up and see if she was home.
Perhaps he could get another look at her.

He went steadily up the stairs, his thoughts running ahead of him. This time he would tell her that
he had come to see her. She would invite him in and
they would really get to know each other. The
stairs creaked under his weight.

There was no light under the door of her apartment.
He hesitated, not knowing what to do. It hadn't
occurred to him that she might not be home. He
stared blankly at the door and then went past it,
down the hall, and climbed the short flight of stairs
to the roof. He stood looking down at the dark
street, studying the silhouette of the buildings
against the sky.

Gradually he began to discern the outline of a

whole series of crosses in the buildings. And he crept silently down the stairs and into his apartment. He didn't undress. He took his shoes off and lay down listening to the sound of Min's snoring, and the dog's heavy breathing, and hating it.

He couldn't go to sleep. His mind was filled with a vast and awful confusion in which images of Lutie warred with images of Min. His love and desire for Lutie mixed and mingled with his hatred and aversion for Min. He was stuck with Min. He hadn't been able to put her out. Yet as long as she stayed he was certain he could never induce Lutie to come and live with him. He dwelt on her figure, etching it again and again in the darkness. She wasn't the kind of girl who would have anything to do with a man who had a wreck of a woman attached to him.

There ought to be some way he could rid himself of the fear of that cross Min had put over the bed. But though he thought about it at length, he knew he could never touch it long enough to throw it out of the house. And as long as it remained, Min would be here with him.

The living room had a cold, menacing feel. He kicked the patchwork quilt onto the floor and reached for his heavy work shoes, not turning on the light in his desire to hurry and get out of the room and go down to the cellar where there was warmth from the fire in the furnace. The glow from its open door would keep him company and finally lull him off to sleep as it had so many times when he stayed in furnace rooms.

One of the shoes slid out of his hands and landed on the floor with a loud clump. Min stopped snoring.

He heard the bedsprings creak as she turned over. He turned on the light and bent over to lace his shoes up, not caring whether she knew that he was going out. He thought of her with contempt. She was probably sitting bolt upright in bed, her head cocked on one side just like the dog's, trying to figure out what the noise was that had awakened her.

Outside in the hall he opened the cellar door and then paused with his hand on the knob when the street door opened. He turned to see which of the tenants was coming in so late and he saw Lutie standing in the doorway, her long skirt blowing around her. She seemed to fill the whole hall with light. There was a faint smile playing around her mouth and he thought she was smiling at the sight of him and bending and swaying toward him.

His hand left the door in a slow, wide gesture and he started toward her, thinking that he would have her now, tonight, and trembling with the thought. His long gaunt body seemed taller than ever in the dim light. His eyes were wide open, staring. He was breathing so quick and fast in his excitement, he made a panting sound that could be clearly heard.

Lutie saw the motion of his hand leaving the door, saw his figure moving toward her. She couldn't see who or what it was that moved, for the cellar door was in deep shadow and she couldn't separate the shadow and the movement. Then she saw that it was the Super. He was either going down into the cellar or just coming out of it. At first she couldn't tell which he was doing because his lank figure was barely recognizable in the dim light.

He was walking toward her. She decided he was

going into his apartment. When she started up the stairs, she would have to pass close by him and the thought filled her with dread. She saw again the tight, hard wrinkles in her blouse and thought of how he must have squeezed it between his hands. For a moment she was unable to move. Her throat went dry and tight with fear.

She forced herself to walk toward the stairs, aware as she moved that her gait was stiff and unnatural almost as though her muscles were rebelling against any motion. He wasn't going into his apartment. He had stopped moving. He was standing motionless in front of her. Somehow she had to pass him, get past him without looking at him, get past him now, quickly, before she thought about it too long.

He side-stepped and blocked her passage to the stairs. He put his hand on her arm. 'You're so sweet. You're so sweet. You little thing. You young little thing.'

She could barely understand the words, for he was so excited that his voice came out thick and hoarse. But she caught the word 'sweet' and she moved away from him. 'Don't,' she said sharply.' The street door was in back of her. If she moved fast enough, she could get out into the street.

Instantly his arm went around her waist. He was pulling her back, turning her around so that she faced him. He was dragging her toward the cellar door.

She grabbed the balustrade. His fingers pried her hands loose. She writhed and twisted in his arms, bracing her feet, clawing at his face with her nails. He ignored her frantic effort to get away from him and pulled her nearer and nearer to the cellar door.

She kicked at him and the long skirt twisted about her legs so that she stumbled closer to him.

She tried to scream, and when she opened her mouth no sound came out; and she thought this was worse than any nightmare, for there was no sound anywhere in this. There was only his face close to hers — a frightening, contorted face, the eyes gleaming, the mouth open — and his straining, sweating body kept forcing her ever nearer the partly open cellar door.

And suddenly she found her voice. Someone in his apartment must have opened the door or else it was open all the time. For the dog was loose. He came bounding toward them down the length of the dark hall, growling. She felt him leap on her back. The horror of it was not to be borne, for the man was trembling with his desire for her as he dragged her toward the cellar, and the dark hall was filled with the stench of the dog and the weight of his great body landing on her back.

She screamed until she could hear her own voice insanely shrieking up the stairs, pausing on the landings, turning the corners, going down the halls, gaining in volume as it started again to climb the stairs. And then her screams rushed back down the stair well until the whole building echoed and re-echoed with the frantic, desperate sound.

A pair of powerful hands gripped her by the shoulders, wrenched her violently out of the Super's arms, flung her back against the wall. She stood there shuddering, her mouth still open, still screaming, unable to stop the sounds that were coming from her throat. The same powerful hands shot out and thrust the Super hard against the cellar door.

'Shut up,' Mrs. Hedges ordered. 'You want the whole place woke up?'

Lutie's mouth closed. She had never seen Mrs. Hedges outside of her apartment and looked at closely she was awe-inspiring. She was almost as tall as the Super, but where he was thin, gaunt, she was all hard, firm flesh — a mountain of a woman.

She was wearing a long-sleeved, high-necked flannelette nightgown. It was so snowy white that her skin showed up intensely black by contrast. She was barefooted. Her hands, her feet, and what could be seen of her legs were a mass of scars — terrible scars. The flesh was drawn and shiny where it had apparently tightened in the process of healing.

The big white nightgown was so amply cut that, despite the bulk of her body, it had a balloon-like quality, for it billowed about her as she stood panting slightly from her exertion, her hands on her hips, her hard, baleful eyes fixed on the Super. The gaudy bandanna was even now tied around her head in firm, tight knots so that no vestige of hair showed. And watching the wide, full nightgown as it moved gently from the draft in the hall, Lutie thought Mrs. Hedges had the appearance of a creature that had strayed from some other planet.

Her rich, pleasant voice filled the hallway, and at the sound of it the dog slunk away, his tail between his legs. 'You done lived in basements so long you ain't human no more. You got mould growin' on you,' she said to Jones.

Lutie walked away from them, intent on getting up the stairs as quickly as possible. Her legs refused to carry her and she sat down suddenly on the bottom step. The long taffeta skirt dragged on the tiled floor. Bits of tobacco, the fine grit from the street, puffed out from under it. She made no effort to pick it up. She put her head on her knees, wondering how she was going to get the strength to climb the stairs.

'Ever you even look at that girl again, I'll have you locked up. You oughtta be locked up, anyway,' Mrs. Hedges said.

She scowled at him ferociously and turned away to touch Lutie on the shoulder and help her to her feet. 'You come sit in my apartment for a while till you get yourself back together again, dearie.'

She thrust the door of her apartment open with a powerful hand, put Lutie in a chair in the kitchen. 'I'll be right back. You just set here and I'll make you a cup of tea. You'll feel better.'

The Super was about to go into his apartment when Mrs. Hedges returned to the hall. 'I just wanted to tell you for your own good, dearie, that it's Mr. Junto who's interested in Mis' Johnson. And I ain't goin' to tell you again to keep your hands off,' she said.

'Ah, shit!' he said vehemently.

Her eyes narrowed. 'You'd look awful nice cut down to a shorter size, dearie. And there's folks that's willin' to take on the job when anybody crosses up they plans.'

She stalked away from him and went into her own apartment, where she closed the door firmly behind her. In the kitchen she put a copper teakettle on the stove, placed cups and saucers on the table, and then carefully measured tea into a large brown teapot.

Lutie, watching her as she walked barefooted across the bright-colored linoleum, thought that instead of tea she should have been concocting some witch's brew.

The tea was scalding hot and fragrant. As Lutie sipped it, she could feel some of the shuddering fear go out of her.

'You want another cup, dearie?'

'Yes, thank you.'

Lutie was well on the way to finishing the second cup before she became aware of how intently Mrs. Hedges was studying her, staring at the long evening skirt, the short coat. Again and again Mrs. Hedges' eyes would stray to the curls on top of Lutie's head. She should feel grateful to Mrs. Hedges. And she did. But her eyes were like stones that had been polished. There was no emotion, no feeling in them, nothing visible but shiny, smooth surface. It would never be possible to develop any real liking for her.

'You been to a dance, dearie?'

'Yes. At the Casino.'

Mrs. Hedges put her teacup down gently. 'Young folks has to dance,' she said. 'Listen, dearie,' she went on. 'About tonight' — she indicated the hall outside with a backward motion of her head. 'You don't have to worry none about the Super bothering you no more. He ain't even going to look at you again.'

'How do you know?'

'Because I scared him so he's going to jump from his own shadow from now on.' Her voice had a purring quality.

Lutie thought, You're right, he won't bother me

any more. Because tomorrow night she was going to find out from Boots what her salary would be and then she would move out of this house.

'He ain't really responsible,' Mrs. Hedges continued. 'He's lived in cellars so long he's kind of cellar crazy.'

'Other people have lived in cellars and it didn't set them crazy.'

'Folks differs, dearie. They differs a lot. Some can stand things that others can't. There's never no way of knowin' how much they can stand.'

Lutie put the teacup down on the table. Her legs felt stronger and she stood up. She could get up the stairs all right now. She put her hand on Mrs. Hedges' shoulder. The flesh under the flannel of the gown was hard. The muscles bulged. And she took her hand away, repelled by the contact.

'Thanks for the tea,' she said. 'And I don't know what I would have done if you hadn't come out in the hall ——' Her voice faltered at the thought of being pulled down the cellar stairs, down to the furnace room ——

'It's all right, dearie.' Mrs. Hedges stared at her, her eyes unwinking. 'Don't forget what I told you about the white gentleman. Any time you want to earn a little extra money.'

Lutie turned away. 'Good night,' she said. She climbed the stairs slowly, holding on to the railing. Once she stopped and leaned against the wall, filled with a sick loathing of herself, wondering if there was something about her that subtly suggested to the Super that she would welcome his love-making, wondering if the same thing had led Mrs. Hedges to

believe that she would leap at the opportunity to
make money sleeping with white men, remembering
the women at the Chandlers' who had looked at her
and assumed she wanted their husbands. It took
her a long time to reach the top floor.

Mrs. Hedges remained seated at her kitchen table,
staring at the scars on her hands and thinking about
Lutie Johnson. It had been a long time since she
thought about the fire. But tonight, being so close
to that girl for so long, studying her as she drank the
hot tea and seeing the way her hair went softly up
from her forehead, looking at her smooth, unscarred
skin, and then watching her walk out through the
door with the long skirt gently flowing in back of
her, had made her think about it again — the smoke,
the flame, the heat.

Her mind jerked away from the memory as though
it were a sharp, sudden pain. She began thinking
about the period in her life when she had haunted
employment agencies seeking work. When she
walked in them, there was an uncontrollable revulsion in the faces of the white people who looked at
her. They stared amazed at her enormous size, at
the blackness of her skin. They glanced at each
other, tried in vain to control their faces or didn't
bother to try at all, simply let her see what a monstrosity they thought she was.

Those were the years when she slept on a cot in
the hall of the apartment belonging to some friends
of hers from Georgia. She couldn't get on relief because she hadn't lived in the city long enough. Her
big body had been filled with a gnawing, insatiable
hunger that sent her prowling the streets at night,

lifting the heavy metal covers of garbage cans, foraging through them for food.

She wore discarded men's shoes on her feet. The leather was broken and cracked. The shoes were too small so that she limped slightly. Her clothing was thin, ragged. She got so she knew night better than day because she could no longer bring herself to go out in the daytime. And she frequently wished that she had never left the small town in Georgia where she was born. But she was so huge that the people there never really got used to the sight of her. She had thought that in a big city she would be inconspicuous and had hoped that she would find a man who would fall in love with her.

It was a cold, raw night when she first saw Junto. The cold had emptied the street. She was leaning over the garbage cans lined up in front of a row of silent, gloomy brownstone houses. She had found a chicken bone and she was gnawing the meat from it, wolfing it down, chewing even the bone, when she looked up to see a squat, short man staring at her — a white man.

'What you lookin' at, white man?'

'You,' he said coolly.

She was surprised at the calm way he looked at her, showing no fear.

'You're on my beat,' he said. 'You got here ahead of me.' He pointed toward a pushcart at the curb. It was piled high with broken bottles, discarded bits of clothing, newspapers tied into neat bundles.

'I got as much right here as you,' she said truculently.

'Didn't say you haven't.' He went on examining

her, the chicken bone in her hand, the ragged coat tied around her, the men's shoes on her feet. 'Seein's you're going through this stuff ahead of me, I was thinking you might as well make some money at it.'

'Money?' she said suspiciously.

'Sure. Pick out the bottles and the pieces of metal. I'll pay you for them. It won't be much. But I can cover more ground if somebody helps me.'

Thus, Mrs. Hedges and Junto started out in business together. It was she who suggested that he branch out, get other pushcarts and other men to work for him. When he bought his first piece of real estate, he gave her the job of janitor and collector of rents.

It was a frame building five stories high, filled with roomers. Not many people knew that Junto owned it. They thought he came around to buy junk — scrap iron and old newspapers and rags. When he obtained a second building, he urged her to move, but she refused. Instead, she suggested that he divide the rooms in this building in half and thus he could get a larger income from it. And of course she made more money, too, because she got a commission on the rent she collected. She was careful to spend very little because she had convinced herself that if she had enough money she could pick out a man for herself and he would be glad to have her.

The fire had started late at night. She was asleep in the basement and she woke to hear a fierce crackling — a licking, running sound that increased in volume as she listened. There was heat and smoke along with the sound. By the time she got to the door, the hall was a red, angry mass of flame. She slammed the door shut and went over to the basement window.

It was a narrow aperture not really big enough for the bulk of her body. She felt her flesh tear and actually give way as she struggled to get out, forcing and squeezing her body through the small space. Fire was blazing in the room in back of her. Hot embers from the roof were falling in front of her. She tried to keep her face covered with her hands, so that she wouldn't see what she was heading into, so that she could keep some of the smoke and flame away from her face.

Even as she struggled, she kept thinking that all she needed to do was to get badly burned, and never as long as she lived would any man look at her and want her. No matter how much money she acquired, they still wouldn't want her. No sum of money would be big enough to make them pretend to want her.

There was nothing but smoke and red flame all around her, and she wondered why she kept on fighting to escape. She could smell her hair burning, smell her flesh burning, and still she struggled, determined that she would force her body through the narrow window, that she would make the very stones of the foundation give until the window opening would in turn give way.

She was a bundle of flame when she finally rolled free on the ground. The firemen who found her stared at her in awe. She was unconscious when they picked her up, and she was the only survivor left from that house full of people.

It was all of three weeks before Junto was permitted to see her at the hospital. 'You're a brave woman, Mrs. Hedges,' he said.

She stared at him from under the mass of bandages that covered her head and part of her face.

'Getting out of that window was wonderful. Simply wonderful.' He looked curiously at the tent-like formation that held the hospital blankets away from the great bulk of her body — a bulk increased by dressings and bandages — marveling at the indomitable urge to live, the absolutely incredible will to live, that had made her force her body through so small a space.

'You'll be all right, you know,' he said.

'The doctor told me' — her voice was flat, uninterested. 'I ain't going to have any hair left.'

'You can wear a wig. Nobody'll ever know the difference.' He hesitated, wanting to tell her how amazing he thought she was and that he would have done the same thing, but that there were few people in the world that he had come across who had that kind of will power. He touched one of her bandaged hands gently, wanting to tell her and not knowing quite how to say it. 'Mrs. Hedges,' he said slowly, 'you and me are the same kind of folks. We got to stay together after this. Close together. We can go a long way.'

She had thought about her scalp — how scarred and terrible looking it would be. The hair would never grow back. She looked steadily at Junto, her eyes unwinking. He would probably be the only man who would ever admire her. He was squat. His shoulders were too big for his body. His neck was set on them like a turtle's neck. His skin was as gray

in color as his eyes. And he was white. She shifted
her eyes so that she could no longer see him.

'You're a wonderful woman,' he was saying
softly.

And even he would never want her as a woman.
He had the kind of forthright admiration for her that
he would have for another man — a man he regarded
as his equal. Scarred like this, hair burned off her
head like this, she would never have any man's love.
She never would have had it, anyway, she thought
realistically. But she could have bought it. This
way she couldn't even buy it.

She folded her lips into a thin, straight line. 'Yes.
We can go a long way.'

Lutie Johnson made her remember a great many
things. She could still hear the soft, silken whisper
of Lutie's skirt, see the shining hair piled high on her
head and the flawless dark brown of her skin. She
thought of her own scarred body with distaste.

When Junto returned to the hospital after his first
visit, he had looked at her for a long time.

'There's plastic surgery,' he suggested delicately.

She shook her head. 'I don't want no more stays
in hospitals. It wouldn't be worth it to me.'

'I'll pay for it.'

'No. I couldn't stay in the hospital long enough
for 'em to do nothing like that.'

She would die if she did. As it was, it had been
hard enough, and to prolong it was something that
would be unendurable. When the nurses and doctors
bent over her to change the dressings, she watched
them with hard, baleful eyes, waiting for the moment when they would expose all the ugliness of her

burnt, bruised body. They couldn't conceal the expressions on their faces. Sometimes it was only a flicker of dismay, and then again it was sheer horror, plain for anyone to see — undisguised, uncontrollable.

'Thanks just the same. But I been here too long as it is.'

She stayed in the hospital for weeks during which the determination never to expose herself to the prying, curious eyes of the world grew and crystallized. When she finally left it, she moved into the house that Junto owned on 116th Street.

'There's a nice first-floor apartment I've saved for you, Mrs. Hedges,' he explained. 'I've even put the furniture in.'

Before she left the hospital, she decided that she would have to have someone living with her to do her shopping, to run errands for her. So the first few days in the new apartment she sat at the window seeking a likely-looking girl. One girl passed by several times, a thin, dispirited young thing who never lifted her eyes from the sidewalk.

'Come here, dearie,' she called to her. Seen close to, the girl's hair was thick and wiry and with a little care it would look very nice.

'Yes'm' — the girl scarcely lifted her head.

'Where you live?'

'Down the street' — she pointed toward Eighth Avenue.

'You got a job?'

'No'm' — the girl looked up at Mrs. Hedges. 'I had one, but my husband left me. I couldn't seem to keep my mind on what I was doing after that, so the lady fired me about two weeks ago.'

'Whyn't you come here and live with me, dearie? I got this place all to myself.'

'I can't pay the rent where I am now. There ain't much point in my coming here.'

'If you'll do my shopping for me, you ain't got to worry about no rent.'

So Mary came to live with her and she gradually lost her dejected look. She laughed and talked and cleaned the apartment and cooked. Mrs. Hedges began to take a kind of pride in the way Mary blossomed out.

One night a tall young man walked past the window, headed toward the house.

'Who you lookin' for, dearie?' she had asked.

'I come to see Mary Jackson,' he said. He glanced at Mrs. Hedges once and then looked away.

'She's gone out to buy something at the store. She lives here with me. You want to come in and set awhile?'

She had looked him over carefully after he uneasily selected a seat in her living room. The big-brimmed, light gray, almost white, hat, the tight-legged breeches, the wide shoulders of his coat built up with padding, the pointed-toed bright yellow shoes, all added up to the kind that rarely got married, and when they did, they didn't stay put. She stared at him until he shifted his feet and moved the light gray hat between his hands, balancing it and inspecting it as though he were judging its merits with an eye to purchasing it.

The street was full of men like him. She stopped her slow examination of him long enough to wonder if a creature like this was the result of electric light instead of hot, strong sunlight; the result of breathing soot-filled air instead of air filled with the smell of warm earth and green growing plants and pulling elevators and sweeping floors instead of doing jobs that would develop the big muscles in shoulders and thighs.

'What you do for a living?' she asked abruptly.

'Ma'am?'

'I said what you do for a living?'

'Well, I ——' He balanced the hat on one finger. 'I ain't exactly working right now at the moment,' he hedged.

'What'd you when you was working?'

'I was in a restaurant for a while. Dishwasher. Before that I was a porter in a bar.' He put the hat down on a table near the chair. 'They wasn't much as jobs go. I got tired of cleaning up after white folks' leavings, so I quit.' There was a hard, resentful, slightly fierce quality in his voice when he said the words 'white folks.'

'How you live now?' And when he didn't answer, she said pointedly, 'How you manage to eat?'

'Well, I mostly works for the fellow that runs the poolroom a couple of blocks over. He's got a game going in the back. I kind of help around.'

Yes, she thought, and you saw Mary, and you think you're going to get yourself some free loving. Only he wasn't. He was going to have to pay for it. Mary would earn money, and she, Mrs. Hedges, would earn money from Mary's earnings. The more she thought about it, the more pleased she became with the idea, for making money and saving it had become a habit with her.

The street would provide plenty of customers. For there were so many men just like him who knew vaguely that they hadn't got anything out of life and knew clearly that they never would get it, even though they didn't know what it was they wanted; men who hated white folks sometimes without even knowing why; men who had to find escape from their hopes and fears, even if it was for just a little while. She would provide them with a means of escape in exchange for a few dollar bills.

Staring at him with her hard, unwinking gaze, she could see the whole detail of a prosperous, efficient enterprise. She would get several more girls. They would be like Mary — girls that had been married and whose men had deserted them. The street was full of girls like that.

'They's one or two things you and me got to settle before Mary comes back,' she said.

'Yes'm?' His face had turned sullen.

'How much can you afford to pay when you comes here to see Mary?'

'Huh?' he asked, startled.

'Mary and me don't live here on air,' she said coldly. 'If'n you want to sleep with her, it's going to cost you.'

That was how it started. As simply and as easily as that. She explained her plan to Junto, so that he would speak to the people at the precinct and they wouldn't bother her.

'But this ain't for white men,' she warned. 'You can have them in them Sugar Hill joints you run. But they can't come here.'

He laughed out loud, something he rarely did.

'Mrs. Hedges, I believe you're prejudiced. I didn't know you were that human.'

'I ain't prejudiced,' she said firmly. 'I just ain't got no use for white folks. I don't want 'em anywhere near me. I don't even wanta have to look at 'em. I put up with you because you don't ever stop to think whether folks are white or black and you don't really care. That sort of takes you out of the white folks class.'

'You're a wonderful woman, Mrs. Hedges,' he said softly. 'A wonderful woman.'

Yes. She and Mr. Junto had gone a long way. A long, long way. Sometimes she had surprised him and surprised herself at the things she had suggested to him. It came from looking at the street all day. There were so many people passing by, so many people with burdens too heavy for them, young ones who were lost, old ones who had given up all hope, middle-aged ones broken and lost like the young ones, and she learned a lot just from looking at them.

She told Junto people had to dance and drink and make love in order to forget their troubles and that bars and dance halls and whorehouses were the best possible investments. Slowly and cautiously Mr. Junto had become the owner of all three, though he still controlled quite a bit of real estate.

It amused her to watch the brawling, teeming, lusty life that roared past her window. She knew so much about this particular block that she came to regard it as slightly different from any other place. When she referred to it as 'the street,' her lips seemed to linger over the words as though her mind paused at the sound to write capital letters and then enclosed the words in quotation marks — thus setting it off and separating it from any other street in the city, giving it an identity, unmistakable and apart.

Looking out of the window was good for her business, too. There were always lonesome, sad-looking girls just up from the South, or little girls who were tired of going to high school, and who had seen too many movies and didn't have the money to buy all the things they wanted.

She could pick them out easily as they walked past. They wore bright-colored, short-skirted dresses and gold hoop earrings in their ears. Their mouths were a brilliant scarlet against the brown of their faces. They wobbled a little on the exaggerated high-heeled shoes they wore. They wore their hair combed in high, slick pompadours.

And there were the other little girls who were only slightly older who had been married and woke up one morning to discover that their husbands had moved out. With no warning. Suddenly. The shock of it stayed on their faces.

'Dearie,' she would say, and her eyes somehow always lingered on the hair piled high above their small, pointed faces, 'I been seein' you go by. And I was wonderin' if you wouldn't like to earn a little extra money sometime.'

She and Mr. Junto had made plenty of money. Only none of it had made her hair grow back. None of it had erased those awful, livid scars on her body.

Off and on during the years he had made timid, tentative gestures toward transforming their relationship into something more personal — gestures which she had steadfastly ignored. For she never intended to reveal the extent of her disfigurement to anyone — least of all to Junto who knew her so well.

Apparently he still wasn't discouraged, because just the other night when he came to see her he brought a wig with him. He tossed it in her lap. The hair was black, long, silky. It was soft under her fingers, curling and clinging and attaching itself to her hands almost as though it were alive. It was the kind of hair that a man's hands would instinctively want to touch. She pushed it away violently, thinking how the hard, black flesh of her face, the forward thrust of her jaws, the scars on her neck, would look under that silken, curling hair.

'Take it away. I don't want it.'

'But ——' He started to protest.

'There's some things that are personal' — she touched the coarse red bandanna with her hand and glared at him fiercely.

'I'm sorry,' he said. He picked the wig up and put it back in the box it had been wrapped in. 'I thought you'd like to have it.' He groped for words. 'We've been friends a long time, Mrs. Hedges. And I guess I thought that between friends anything would be understood. If I did any harm bringing this here, I did it with good intentions. But I understand why you don't want it. I understand better than you think.'

That same night was the only time she was ever really mean to Mary. She couldn't get the memory of that soft, fine, clinging hair out of her mind. She kept remembering how Junto said he understood why she didn't want it. And Mary's hair was combed high over her small, pointed face. It was heavy with grease from the hairdresser's. There was a white rose in the center of her pompadour — the rose seemed to nestle there.

'Mrs. Hedges, Tige's got to go back to his ship tonight,' Mary had said.

She had been staring out at the street, thinking about the wig. 'Who's Tige, dearie?' she asked absently.

'The sailor boy who was here last night.'

She remembered him then. He was so young that he swaggered when he walked past her window in his tight-fitting, dark blue sailor pants. So young that his eyes were alive with laughter; his sailor's hat was perched so far back on his head and at such a precarious angle, it looked as though any sudden movement would pitch it off. His hands were thrust deep into the pockets of his short jacket and the bulky wool of the jacket couldn't conceal how flat and lean his waist was and how it tapered up to his wide shoulders in a taut, slanting line. Very, very young.

'Yes?' she said.

Mary patted a stray hair in place, and her eyes had followed the movement of Mary's hand and stayed there on the high curve of the pompadour, on the white rose that seemed to nest in the thickness of the hair.

'He spent all his money last night,' Mary went on. 'And I want to know can he come in again tonight? He says he'll mail the money back to you.' She hesitated, and added shyly, 'I like him.'

'Of course not,' she had said sourly. 'You think I'm in business for my health?' She couldn't seem to stop looking at the girl's hair. 'You can take him out in the park. Cold night like this will cool you both off.'

She turned her head away from the sight of Mary's face. All the life had gone out of it, leaving it suddenly old, drawn, flat. There were deep lines around the mouth. The little fool must be in love with him, she thought.

The boy came out of the house about an hour later. He was dragging his feet. He looked cold, miserable. They been standing up there in that hall, she thought. He had to go back to his ship tonight. Go back to fighting the white folks' war for them.

'Sailor!' she said sharply, just as he reached her window.

'What do you want?'

'Where you and Mary been?'

'We been standing in the hall talking. Where you think we been?'

'How much more time you got?'

'About two hours.'

'Listen, dearie, you go ring the bell and tell Mary I said it was all right.'

He moved so quickly she had to yell to catch him before he opened the street door.

'Listen, sailor, you send that money back prompt on the first of the month.'

'Yes, ma'am. Yes, indeed, ma'am.' He paused in the doorway to execute a dance step. And then he bowed to her, taking his flat sailor's hat off in a gesture that made her think again, He's so young — so crazy young.

Her thoughts returned to Lutie Johnson. With

that thick, soft hair, Lutie offered great possibilities for making money. Mr. Junto would be willing to pay very high for her. Very, very high, because when he got tired of her himself he could put her in one of those places he ran on Sugar Hill. With hair like that — her face twitched, and she got up from the kitchen table and went into the living room where she sat down by the window.

The window was half open and the air blowing in was cold. The street was silent, empty. As she looked, the wind lifted scraps of paper, bits of rubbish, and set them to swirling along the curb as though an invisible hand with a broom had reached down into the street and was sweeping the paper along before it.

The wind puffed the white nightgown out around her feet. She moved a little closer to the window. She had never felt really cool since the time she was in the fire.

Chapter 11

DESPITE the lateness of the hour, groups of men were still standing in front of the Junto Bar and Grill, for the brilliant light streaming from its windows formed a barrier against the cold and the darkness in the rest of the street. Whenever the doors opened and closed, the light on the sidewalk was intensified. And because the men moved slightly, laughing and talking a little louder with each sudden increase in light, they had the appearance of moths fluttering about a gigantic candle flame.

Boots Smith, who had parked his car at the corner, watched the men without really seeing them. Something must have scared the living daylights out of Old Man Junto to make him send for him at this hour, he thought. He hated to be taken by surprise, and he was still trying to figure out what it was that had upset Junto.

Finally he shrugged his shoulders, started out of the car, and then paused with his hand on the door. It could be only one thing. Somewhere along the line there had been a leak about how he had stayed out of the army. His hand left the door. Okay, he thought. He wasn't going to play soldier now any more than he was that day he got the notice to report to his draft board for a physical examination. He took the notice to Junto early in the afternoon and he had been so angered by it that he had talked fluently, easily, quickly — something he rarely did.

'Fix this thing, Junto.' He had slapped the post-card down on the table in front of Junto.

'What is it?' Junto peered at it, his turtle neck completely disappearing between his shoulders.

'Notice to report for a physical. First step on the way to the army.'

'You don't want to fight?'

'Why should I?'

'I don't know. I'm asking you.'

He had pulled a chair out and sat down across from Junto. 'Listen, Junto,' he said. 'They can wave flags. They can tell me the Germans cut off baby's behinds and rape women and turn black men into slaves. They can tell me any damn thing. None of it means nothing.'

'Why?'

'Because, no matter how scared they are of Germans, they're still more scared of me. I'm black, see? And they hate Germans, but they hate me worse. If that wasn't so they wouldn't have a separate army for black men. That's one for the book. Sending a black army to Europe to fight Germans. Mostly with brooms and shovels.'

Junto looked at him thoughtfully and then down at the postcard.

'Are you sure that's it?' he asked. 'Are you sure that you're not afraid to fight?'

'What would I be afraid of? I been fighting all my life. The Germans ain't got no way of making a man die twice in succession. No way of bringing a man alive and making him die two or three times. Naw, I'm not scared to fight.'

'Suppose there wasn't a separate army. Suppose it was all one army. Would you feel differently?'

'Hell, no. Look, Junto' — he remembered how he had leaned toward him across the table talking swiftly and with an energy and passion that sent the words flooding out of his throat. 'For me to go leaping and running to that draft board a lot of things would have to be different. Them white guys in the army are fighting for something. I ain't got anything to fight for. If I wasn't working for you, I'd be changing sheets on Pullman berths. And learning fresh all over again every day that I didn't belong anywhere. Not even here in this country where I was born. And saying "yes sir," "no sir," until my throat was raw with it. Until I felt like I was dirt. I've got a hate for white folks here' — he indicated his chest — 'so bad and so deep that I wouldn't lift a finger to help 'em stop Germans or nobody else.'

'What makes you think life would be better if the Germans ran this country?'

'I don't think it would. I ain't never said I thought so.'

'Then I don't see ——'

'Of course you don't,' he interrupted. 'You never will because you ain't never known what it's like to live somewhere where you ain't wanted and every white son-of-a-bitch that sees you goes out of his way to let you know you ain't wanted. Christ, there ain't even so much as a cheap stinking diner in this town that I don't think twice before I walk into it to buy a cup of lousy coffee, because any white bastard in there will let me know one way or another that niggers belong in Harlem. Don't talk to me about Germans. They're only doing the same thing in Europe that's been done in this country since the time it started.'

'But ——'

'Lissen' — he stopped Junto with a wave of his hand. 'One of the boys in the band come back in uniform the other night. You know what he's doing?'

Junto shook his head.

'He's playing loading and unloading ship in some god-damn port company. That boy can make a fiddle talk. Make it say uncle. Make it laugh. Make it cry. So they figured they'd ruin his hands loading ships. He tried to play when he come by the other night.' He had picked the postcard notice up, flicked the edge of it with his thumbnail. 'Jesus! He broke down and cried like a baby.' It was a long time before he said anything after that.

Then finally he had said slowly: 'I've done all the crawling a man can do in one lifetime. I don't figure to do no more. Ever. Not for nobody. I don't figure to go to Europe on my belly with a broom and a shovel in each hand.' He shoved the postcard across the table. 'What you going to do about this thing?'

Junto had sent him to a doctor who performed a slight, delicate, dangerous operation on his ear.

'You'll be all right in a month or so,' said the doctor. 'In the meantime mail this letter to your draft board.' The letter stated that Boots Smith was ill and unable to report for a physical examination. And, of course, when he was finally examined, he was rejected.

Yeah, he thought. That's what it is. He tried to decide just what would happen to him and to Junto and the doctor. And couldn't. He opened the car door, stepped out on the sidewalk. Well, at least he knew what it was that Junto wanted.

When he pushed the Junto's doors open, his face gave no indication of the fact that he was worried. He glanced at the long bar where men and women were standing packed three deep, observing that the hum of their conversation, the sound of their laughter, almost but not quite drowned out the music of the juke-box.

It was getting near closing time. The white-coated bartenders were hastily pouring drinks and making change. Waiters darted about balancing heavy trays filled with the last drinks that would be served before the wide doors closed for the night.

He paused in the doorway for a moment, admiring the way the excited movement around the bar and the movement of the people at the tables and in the booths was reflected and multiplied in the sparkling mirrors. Then he waved at the bartenders, sought and found Junto sitting at a table near the back, and sat down beside him without saying anything.

'Want a drink?' Junto asked.

'Sure.'

Junto beckoned a passing waiter. 'Bourbon for him. Soda for me.'

The waiter deposited the glasses on the table and moved off to fill the orders from a near-by table of boisterous, clamoring customers who called out to him to hurry before the bar closed.

Junto picked up his glass, sipped the soda slowly. He rolled it around in his mouth before he swallowed it as though it were a taste sensation he was anxious to retain as long as possible. Boots watched him in silence, waiting to learn how he was going to introduce the business about the army.

'That girl,' Junto said. He didn't look at Boots as he talked; his eyes stayed on the noisy crowd at the bar. 'That girl — Lutie Johnson ——'

'Yeah?' Boots leaned toward him across the table.

'You're to keep your hands off her. I've got other plans for her.'

So it wasn't the army. It was Lutie Johnson. Boots started sliding the glass of bourbon back and forth on the table, wondering if he had managed to conceal his amazement. Then, as the full meaning of Junto's words dawned on him, he frowned. He had had all kinds of girls: tall, short, wide-fannied, big-breasted, flat-breasted, straight-haired, kinky-haired, dark, light — all kinds.

But this one — this Lutie Johnson — was the first

one he'd seen in a long time that he really wanted. He had even thought that if he couldn't get her any other way, he'd marry her. He watched Junto roll the soda around on his tongue and was surprised to discover that the thought of Lutie, with her long legs, straight back, smooth brown skin, and smiling eyes, sleeping with Old Man Junto wasn't a pleasant one.

And it wasn't because Junto was white. He didn't feel the same toward him as he did toward most white men. There was never anything in Junto's manner, no intonation in his voice, no expression that crept into his eyes, and never had been during the whole time he had known him, nothing that he had ever said or done that indicated he was aware that Boots was a black man.

He had watched him warily, unbelieving, suspicious. Junto was always the same, and he treated the white men who worked for him exactly the same way he treated the black ones. No, it wasn't because Junto was white that he didn't relish the thought of him sleeping with Lutie Johnson.

It was simply that he didn't like the idea of anyone possessing her, except of course himself. Was he in love with her? He examined his feeling about her with care. No. He just wanted her. He was intrigued by her. There was a challenge in the way she walked with her head up, in the deft way she had avoided his attempts to make love to her. It was more a matter of itching to lay his hands on her than anything else.

'Suppose I want to lay her myself?' he said.

Junto looked directly at him for the first time. 'I

made you. If I were you, I wouldn't overlook the fact that whoever makes a man can also break him.'

Boots made no reply. He studied the bubbles that were forming on the side of Junto's glass.

'Well?' Junto said.

'I ain't made up my mind yet. I'm thinking.'

He fingered the long scar on his cheek. Junto could break him all right. It would be easy. There weren't many places a colored band could play and Junto could fix it so he couldn't find a spot from here to the coast. He had other bands sewed up, and all he had to do was refuse to send an outfit to places stupid enough to hire Boots' band. Junto could put a squeeze on a place so easy it wasn't funny. And he thought, Pullman porter to Junto's right-hand man. A long jump. A long hard way to get where he was now.

Yeah, he thought, Pullmans. The train roaring into the night. Coaches rocking and swaying. A bell that rang and rang and rang, and refused to stop ringing. A bell that stabbed into your sleep at midnight, at one, at two, at three, at four in the morning. Because slack-faced white women wanted another blanket, because gross white men with skins the red of boiled lobster couldn't sleep because of the snoring of someone across the aisle.

Porter! Porter this and Porter that. Boy. George. Nameless. He got a handful of silver at the end of each run, and a mountain of silver couldn't pay a man to stay nameless like that. No Name, black my shoes. No Name, hold my coat. No Name, brush me off. No Name, take my bags. No Name. No Name.

Niggers steal. Lock your bag. Niggers lie.

Where's my pocketbook? Call the conductor. That porter —— Niggers rape. Cover yourself up. Didn't you see that nigger looking at you? God damn it! Where's that porter? Por-ter! Por-ter!

Balance Lutie Johnson. Weigh Lutie Johnson. Long legs and warm mouth. Soft skin and pointed breasts. Straight slim back and small waist. Mouth that curves over white, white teeth. Not enough. She didn't weigh enough when she was balanced against a life of saying 'yes sir' to every white bastard who had the price of a Pullman ticket. Lutie Johnson at the end of a Pullman run. Not enough. One hundred Lutie Johnsons didn't weigh enough.

He tried to regret the fact that she didn't weigh enough, even tried to work up a feeling of contempt for himself. You'd sell your old grandmother if you had one, he told himself. Yes. I'd sell anything I've got without stopping to think about it twice, because I don't intend to learn how to crawl again. Not for anybody.

Because before the Pullmans there was Harlem during the depression. And he was an out-of-work piano-player shivering on street corners in a thin overcoat. The hunger hole in his stomach had gaped as wide as the entrance to the subways. Cold nights he used to stand in doorways out of the wind, and sooner or later a white cop would come up and snarl, 'Move on, you!'

He had known the shuddering, shocking pain of a nightstick landing on the soles of his feet when he slept on park benches. 'Get the hell outta here, yah bum!'

Yeah. He was a piano-player out of work, living

on hunger and hate and getting occasional jobs in stinking, smoky, lousy joints where they thought he was coked up all the time. And he was. But it was hunger and hate that was the matter with him, not coke.

He would get a meal for playing in the joint and the hard-faced white man who owned it would toss a couple of dollars at him when he left, saying, 'Here, you!' He wanted to throw it back, but he had to live, and so he took it, but he couldn't always keep the hate out of his eyes.

He had played in dives and honkey-tonks and whorehouses, at rent parties and reefer parties. The smell of cigarette smoke and rotgut liquor and greasy food stayed in his nose.

He got so he hated the sight of the drunks and dopesters who frequented the places where he played. They never heard the music that came from the piano, for they were past caring about anything or listening to anything. But he had to eat, so he went on playing.

More frequently than he cared to remember some drunken white couple would sway toward the piano, mumbling, 'Get the nigger to sing,' or, 'Get the nigger to dance.' And he would despise himself for not lunging at them, but the fact that the paltry pay he would get at the end of the night's work was his only means of assuaging his constant hunger held him rigid on the piano bench.

White cops raided the joints at regular intervals, smashing up furniture, breaking windows with vicious efficiency. When they found white women lolling about inside, they would start swinging their nightsticks with carefree abandon.

He learned to watch the doors with a wary eye, and the instant he entered a place he located a handy exit before he settled down to play.

When he got the job on the Pullman, he vowed that never again, so help him God, would he touch a piano. And in place of the stinking, rotten joints there were miles of 'Here boy,' 'You boy,' 'Go boy,' Run boy,' 'Stop boy,' 'Come boy.' Train rocking and roaring through the night. No longer hunger. Just hate. 'Come boy,' 'Go boy.' 'Yes, sir.' 'No, sir.' 'Of course, sir.'

Naw, Lutie Johnson didn't weigh that much. Even if she did, he had no way of knowing that he wouldn't come home some night to find a room full of arrested motion. Even now he never saw the wind moving a curtain back and forth in front of a window without remembering that curious, sick sensation he had when he walked into his own apartment and found the one room alive with motion that had stopped just the moment before he entered it.

Everything in the room still except for the sheer, thin curtains blowing in the breeze. Everything frozen, motionless; even Jubilee, stiff still in the big chair, her house coat slipping around her body. Only the curtains in motion, but the rest of the room full of the ghost of motion, and he couldn't move his eyes from the curtains.

It was a warm night in the spring — a soft, warm night that lay along the train like a woman's arms as it roared toward New York. It was a bland, enticing kind of night, and he kept thinking about Jubilee waiting for him at the end of the run. He couldn't wait to get to her. Going uptown on the subway, he thought the train kept slowing down, sitting motionless on the track, waiting at stations, doing every damn thing it could to keep him from getting to her in a hurry.

The street had that same soft, clinging warmth. It seemed to be everywhere around him. He tore up the stairs and put his key in the door. It stuck in the lock and he cursed it for delaying him. The instant he got the door open, he knew there was something wrong. The room was full of hurried, not quite quickly enough arrested movement. He stood in the doorway looking at the room, seeking whatever it was that was wrong.

Jubilee was sitting in the big upholstered chair. She had a funny kind of smile on her face. He could have sworn that she had got into the chair when she heard his key click in the lock.

The thin, sheer curtains were blowing in the breeze that came through the opened windows. Swaying gently back and forth at the front windows, at the fire-escape window. But the fire-escape window was always closed. Jubilee kept it shut because she said it wasn't safe to sit in a room in Harlem with a fire-escape window open. That was how people got robbed. Even in hot, sweltering weather it was closed. They had argued about it the summer before:

'Christ, baby! Open the window!'

'I won't. It isn't safe.'

'But we'll sweat to death in here.'

'That's better than being robbed ——'

He crossed the room quickly, pushed the curtains aside, and looked down. A man was going swiftly down the fire escape. Not looking up, climbing steadily down, down. He had his suit jacket over his arm. Every time the man passed a lighted window, Boots could see him quite clearly. Finally the man looked up. He had his necktie in his hand. And he was white. Unmistakably — white.

When he turned back into the room, he was so blind with fury he couldn't see anything for a moment. Then he saw her sitting in the chair, frozen with fear.

'You double-crossing bitch!' he said, and pulled her out of the chair and slammed her against the wall.

He pulled her toward him and slapped her. Then threw her back against the wall. Pulled her toward him and slapped her and threw her back against the wall. Again and again. Her face grew puffed and swollen under his hand. He heard her scream, and it pleased him to know that she was afraid of him because he was going to kill her, and he wanted her to know it beforehand and be afraid. He was going to take a long time doing it, so that she would be very afraid before she finally died.

But she fooled him. She ducked under his arm and got away from him. He took his time turning around, because there wasn't any place for her to go. She couldn't get all the way away from him, and it was going to be fun to play cat and mouse with her in this none too big room.

When he turned, she had a knife in her hand. He went for her again and she slashed him across the face.

He backed away from her. Blood oozed slowly down his cheek. It felt warm. And it shocked him to his senses. She wasn't worth going to the clink for. She was a raggle-tag slut, and he was well rid of her because she wasn't worth a good god damn.

He took the knife away from her. She cringed as though she expected him to cut her. He threw it on the floor and laughed.

'You ain't worth cutting, baby,' he said. 'You ain't worth going to jail for. You ain't worth nothing.' He laughed again. 'Tell your white boy friend he can move in any time he wants to. I'm through, baby.'

The sound of Jubilee's sobbing followed him down the hall. As he went past the silent doors that lined the hallway, he thought, It's funny with all that noise and screaming no one had tried to find out what was going on. He could have killed her easy and no one would even have rapped on the door, and he wondered what went on inside these other apartments to make their occupants so incurious.

He wanted to laugh at himself and at Jubilee. Him riding Pullman trains day in and day out and hoarding those handfuls of silver, so he could keep her here in this apartment, so he could buy her clothes. Bowing and scraping because the thought of her waiting at the end of a run kept him from choking on those 'Yes sirs' and 'No sirs' that he said week in and week out. He paused on the stairs thinking that he ought to go back up and finish the job, because leaving it like this left him less than a half man, because he didn't even have a woman of his own, because he not only had to say 'Yes sir,' he had to stand by and take it while some white man grabbed off what belonged to him.

Killing her wouldn't change the thing any. But if he'd had a gun, he would have shot that bastard on the fire escape. He went on down the stairs slowly. He never realized before what a thin line you had to cross to do a murder. A thin, small, narrow line. It was less than a pencil mark to get across. A man rides a Pullman and the woman fools around, and the man can't swallow it because he's had too much crawling to do, and the man spends the rest of his life behind bars. No. He gives up his life on a hot seat, or did they hang in this state? He didn't know, because fortunately the woman cut the hell out of him.

He concealed the slash with his handkerchief, thinking that there was a colored drugstore somewhere around and the guy would fix him up.

The druggist eyed the blood on his face. 'Get cut?' he asked matter-of-factly.

'Yeah. Put somep'n on it, will you?'

The druggist applied a styptic pencil. 'You oughtta see a doctor,' he said. 'You're going to have a bad scar.' And he thought must have been a woman who cut him. Guys built like this one don't let other guys get close enough to them to carve them with a knife. Probably ran out on the woman and she couldn't take it.

'A scar don't mean nothing,' Boots said.

'What was it — a fight?'

'Naw. A dame. I beat her up and she gave me this for a souvenir.'

There had been a lot of other women since Jubilee. He didn't remember any of them except that he had kicked most of them around a bit. Perhaps as vengeance now that he came to think about it. He only thought about Jubilee when he happened to see a pair of curtains blowing in a breeze. The scar on his face had become a thin, narrow line. Most of the time he forgot it was there, though somehow he had got into the habit of touching it when he was thinking very hard.

He looked across at Junto patiently waiting for an answer. He wasn't quite ready to answer him. Let him stew in his own juice for a while. There wasn't any question in his mind about Lutie Johnson being worth the price he would have to pay for her, nor worth the doubts that he would always have about her.

Riding back and forth between New York and Chicago he used to look forward to dropping into Junto's place. He was perfectly comfortable, wholly at ease when he was there. The white men behind the bar obviously didn't care about the color of a man's skin. They were polite and friendly — not too friendly but just right. It made him feel good to go there. Nobody bothered to mix a little contempt with the drinks because the only thing that mattered was whether you had the money to pay for them.

One time when he stopped in for a drink, he was filled up to overflowing with hate. So he had two drinks. Three drinks. Four drinks. Five drinks. To get the taste of 'you boy' out of his mouth, to shake it out of his ears, to wash it off his skin. Six drinks, and he was feeling good.

There was a battered red piano in the corner. The same piano that was there right now. And he was feeling so good that he forgot that he had vowed he'd never play a piano again as long as he lived. He sat down and started playing and kept on until he forgot there were such things as Pullmans and rumpled

sheets and wadded-up blankets to be handled. Forgot
there was a world that was full of white voices saying:
'Hustle 'em up, boy'; 'Step on it, boy'; Hey, boy, I
saw a hot-looking colored gal a couple of coaches
back — fix it up for me, boy.' He forgot about bells
that were a shrill command to 'come a-running, boy.'

Someone touched him on the shoulder. He looked
up frowning.

'What do you do for a living?'

The man was squat, turtle-necked. White.

'What's it to you?' He stopped playing and
turned on the piano bench, ready to send his fist
smashing into the man's face.

'You play well. I wanted to offer you a job.'

'Doing what?' And then, angered because he had
answered the man at all, he said, 'Sweeping the
joint out?' And further angered and wanting to fight
and wanting to show that he wanted to fight, he
added, 'With my tongue, mebbe?'

Junto shook his head. 'No. I've never offered
anyone a job like that,' saying it with a seriousness
that was somehow impressive. 'There are some
things men shouldn't have to do' — a note of regret
in his voice. 'I thought perhaps you might be willing
to play the piano here.'

He stared at Junto letting all the hate in him show,
all the fight, all the meanness. Junto stared back.
And he found himself liking him against his will.
'How much?'

'Start at forty dollars.'

He had turned back to the piano. 'I'm working at
the job right now.'

It had been a pleasure to work for Junto. There

hadn't been any of that you're-black-and-I'm-white
business involved. It had been okay from the night
he had started playing the piano. He had built the
orchestra slowly, and Junto had been pleased and
revealed his pleasure by paying him a salary that had
now grown to the point where he could afford to buy
anything in the world he wanted. No. Lutie
Johnson wasn't that important to him. He wasn't in
love with her, and even if he had been she didn't
weigh enough to balance the things he would lose.

'Okay,' he said finally. 'It doesn't make that
much difference to me.'

Junto's eyes went back to an examination of the bar.
There was nothing in his face to indicate whether
this was the answer he had expected or whether he
was surprised by it. 'Don't pay her for singing with
the band. Give her presents from time to time.' He
took his wallet out, extracted a handful of bills, gave
them to Boots. 'All women like presents. This will
make it easier for you to arrange for me to see her.
And please remember' — his voice was precise, careful, almost as though he were discussing the details
of a not too important business deal — 'leave her
alone. I want her myself.'

Boots pocketed the money and stood up. 'Don't
worry,' he said. 'That babe will be as safe with me
as though she was in her mother's arms.'

Junto sipped his soda. 'Do you think it will take
very long?' he asked.

'I dunno. Some women are' — he fished for a
word, shrugged his shoulders and went on — 'funny
about having anything to do with white men.' He
thought of the curtains blowing back from the fire-

escape window and the white man going swiftly down, down, down. Not all women. Just some women.

'Money cures most things like that.'

'Sometimes it does.' He tried to decide whether it would with Lutie Johnson. Yes. She had practically said so herself. Yet there was something — well, he wasn't sure a man would have an easy time with her. She had a streak of hell cat in her or he didn't know women, and he felt a momentary and fleeting regret at having lost the chance to conquer and subdue her.

He looked down at Junto seated at the table and swallowed an impulse to laugh. For Junto's squat-bodied figure was all gray — gray suit, gray hair, gray skin, so that he melted into the room. He could sit forever at that table and nobody would look at him twice. All those people guzzling drinks at the bar never glanced in his direction. The ones standing outside on the street and the ones walking back and forth were dumb, blind, deaf to Junto's existence. Yet he had them coming and going. If they wanted to sleep, they paid him; if they wanted to drink, they paid him; if they wanted to dance, they paid him, and never even knew it.

It would be funny if Junto who owned so much couldn't get to first base with Lutie. He wasn't even sure why Junto wanted to lay her. He couldn't quite figure it out. Junto was kind of nuts about that black woman on 116th Street, talked about her all the time. He had never forgotten the shock he got when he first saw Mrs. Hedges. He hadn't really known what to expect the night he went there with Junto, but he was totally unprepared for that hulk of a woman. He could have sworn from the way Junto looked at her that he was in love with her and that he had never been able to get past some obstacle that prevented him from sleeping with her — some obstacle the woman erected.

'How was the crowd tonight?' Junto asked.

'Packed house. Hanging from the ceiling.'

'No trouble?'

'Naw. There's never any trouble. Them bruisers see to that.'

'Good.'

'That girl sings very well,' he said. He watched Junto's face to see if he could get some clue from his expression as to what it was about Lutie Johnson that had made him want her. Because there had been all kinds of girls in and out of Junto's joints and he had never been known to look twice at any of them.

'Yes, I know. I heard her.' And Junto's eyes blinked, and Boots knew instantly that Junto wanted her for the same reason that he had — because she was young and extraordinarily good-looking and any man with a spark of life left in him would go for her.

'You heard her tonight?' Boots asked, incredulous.

'Yes. I was at the Casino for a few minutes.'

Boots shook his head. The old man surely had it bad. He had a sudden desire to see his face go soft and queer. 'How's Mrs. Hedges?' he asked.

'Fine.' Junto's face melted into a smile. 'She's a wonderful woman. A wonderful woman.'

'Yeah.' He thought of the red bandanna tied in hard, ugly knots around her head. 'She sure is.'

He turned away from the table. 'I gotta go, Junto. I'll be seein' you.' He walked out of the bar, cat-footed, his face as expressionless as when he came in.

Chapter 12

JONES, THE SUPER, closed the door of his apartment behind him. He was clenching and unclenching his fists in a slow, pulsating movement that corresponded with the ebb and flow of the rage that was sweeping through him.

At first it was rage toward Mrs. Hedges and her barging into the hall, shoving her hard hands against his chest, ordering him about, threatening him. If she hadn't been so enormous and so venomous, he would have knocked her down.

He frowned. How had the dog got out? Min must have let him out. Min must have stood right there where he was standing now, just inside the door, looking out into the hall, and seen what was going on and let the dog loose. A fresh wave of anger directed at Min flooded through him. If she hadn't let the dog out, he would have had Lutie Johnson. The dog scared Lutie so she screamed and that brought that old sow with that rag tied around her head out into the hall.

He could feel Lutie being dragged out of his arms, could see Mrs. Hedges glaring at him with her baleful eyes rammed practically into his face, could see the bulk of her big, hard body under the white flannel nightgown, and could feel all over again the threat and menace in her hands as she slammed him against the cellar door.

All of it was Min's fault. He ought to go drag her out of bed and beat her until she was senseless and then toss her out into the street. He walked toward the bedroom and stopped outside the door, remember-ing the cross over the bed and unable to get over the threshold despite his urge to lay violent hands on her. He couldn't tell by the light, rhythmic sound of her breathing whether she was asleep or just pretending. She must have scuttled back to bed the minute she saw him start toward the apartment door.

His thoughts jumped back to Mrs. Hedges. So that was why he couldn't have her locked up that time he went to the police station. He remembered the police lieutenant, 'What's her name?' and his eyes staring at the paper where it was already written down. Junto was the reason he couldn't have her arrested that time. Sometimes during the summer he had gone to the Bar and Grill for a glass of beer and he had seen him sitting in the back — a squat, short-bodied white man whose eyes never apparently left the crowd drinking at the bar. The thought of him set Jones to trembling.

He moved away from the bedroom door and walked aimlessly around the living room. Finally he sat down on the sofa. He ought to go to bed, but he'd never be able to sleep with his mind swirling full of thoughts like this. Lutie's body had felt soft under his hands, her waist had just fitted into the space between his two hands. It was small, yielding, pliant.

His face smarted where she had scratched him. He ought to put something on it — get something from the medicine cabinet, but he didn't move. The reason she had scratched him like that was because she hadn't understood that he wasn't going to hurt her, that he wouldn't hurt her for anything. He must have frightened her coming at her so suddenly.

He could feel his thoughts gather themselves together on Lutie, concentrate on her, stay put on her. Those scratches on his face were long, deep. She hadn't been frightened that bad. It wasn't just fright. It must have been something else. She had fought him like a wildcat; as though she hated him, kicking, biting, scratching, and that awful wild screaming. But she screamed because of the dog, he told himself. But even after Mrs. Hedges came out and the dog left, even after Mrs. Hedges had pulled her out of his arms, she had gone on screaming. He could hear the despairing, desperate sound of her screams all over again, and he listened to them, thinking that they sounded as though she had found his touching her unbearable, as though she despised him. No. It wasn't just fright.

The full significance of what Mrs. Hedges had said to him came over him. That was why Lutie had

fought like that and screamed and couldn't stop
She was in love with the white man, Junto, and she
couldn't bear to have a black man touch her.

His mind rebelled against the idea, thrust it away.
It wasn't true. He refused to admit it was remotely
possible. He tried to rid himself of the thought and
it crept back again quietly establishing itself. He
quivered with rage at the thought of Junto's squat
white body intimately entwined with Lutie's tall
brown body. He saw Junto's pale skin beside Lutie's
brown skin. He created situations and placed them
together — eating, talking, drinking, even dancing.

He tortured himself with the picture of them lying
naked in bed together, possibly talking about him,
laughing at him. He attempted to put words into
their mouths.

'Can you imagine, Mr. Junto, that Jones making
love to me?'

He couldn't get any further than that because his
mind refused to stay still. It seemed to have become a
livid, molten, continually moving, fluid substance in
his brain that spewed up fragments of thought until
his head ached with the effort to follow the motion,
to analyze the thoughts. He no sooner started to
pursue one of the fragments than something else took
its place, some new idea that disappeared just as he
began to explore it.

Mrs. Hedges and Min. They were the ones that had
frustrated him. Just at the moment when he had
Lutie in his arms they had fixed it so she was snatched
away from him. If only he could have got her down
into the cellar, everything would have been all right.
She would have calmed down right away.

Now he would have to begin all over again. He didn't know where to start. Maybe a little present would make her feel better toward him. He must have frightened her a lot. He was certain she had been smiling at him when she stood there in the doorway, holding the door in her hand, the long skirt blowing back around her legs as she looked toward the cellar door.

What ought he to give her? Earrings, stockings, nightgowns, blouses — he tried to remember some of the things he had seen in the stores on Eighth Avenue. It ought to be something special — perhaps a handbag, one of those big shiny black ones.

Junto probably gave her presents. His mind stood still for a moment. What present could he give her that could compare with the things Junto could give her? Junto could give her fur coats and —— He got up from the couch wildly furious, so agitated by his anger that his body trembled with it.

She was in love with Junto. Of course. That was why she had fought him off like a she-cat, clawing at him with her nails, kicking at him, filling the hall with that howl that still rang in his ears. She was in love with Junto, the white man.

Black men weren't good enough for her. He had seen women like that before. He had had women like that before. Just off the ship, hungry for a woman, dying for a woman, seeking and finding one he had known before. A door opened a narrow crack, 'No. You can't come in.' The door slammed tight shut in his face. He had waited and waited outside and seen some replete, satiated white tramp of a sailor emerge from the same room hours later.

Yes. He'd seen that kind before. No use for men their own color. Well, he'd fix her. He'd fix her good. He searched his mind for a way to do it and was surprised to find that his thinking had grown cool, quiet, orderly. Her fighting against him as though he was so dirty she couldn't bear to have him touch her, her never looking at him when she went in and out of the building, her being frightened that night when she came to look at the apartment and they were up there together — all of it proved that she didn't like black men, had no use for them.

So she belonged to a white man. Well, he would get back at both of them. Yes. He'd fix them good.

He strained his eyes in the dark of the room as though by looking hard enough in front of him he would be able to see the means by which he would destroy her. He walked up and down thinking, thinking, thinking. There wasn't anything he could think of, no way he could reach her.

But there was the kid. He paused in the middle of the room, nodding his head. He could get at the kid. He could fix the kid and none of them could stop him. They would never know who was responsible. He finally went to sleep, still not knowing what it was he would do, but comforted by the knowledge that he could hurt her through the kid. Yes. The kid.

When he woke up the next morning, Min was standing by the couch looking down at him with a curious expression on her face.

'What you looking at?' he asked gruffly, wondering what she had been able to read on his face while he lay there asleep, unaware of anyone watching him, perhaps unconsciously revealing the things he had been thinking about just before he went to sleep. How long you been there?'

'I just come,' she said. 'Breakfast is ready'; and then she added hastily: 'I ate mine already. You can have the kitchen to yourself.'

'How come you ain't gone to work yet?'

'I overslept myself. I'm gettin' ready to go now.'

She went into the bedroom. The worn felt slippers made a slapping, scuffing sound as she walked. It was a hateful sound and his anger of the night before returned so swiftly that he decided it must have stayed on the couch with him waiting for him to awaken. He thought of Lutie's high heels clicking on the stairs, of her long legs, and immediately he began puzzling over a way of fixing the kid.

In the kitchen he ate hungrily. Min had made rolls for breakfast. They were light and fluffy. He ate several of them, drank two cups of coffee and was starting on a third cup when his eyes fell on a slender glass vial almost full of a brilliant scarlet liquid. It was lying flat between the bottle of ketchup and a tin of evaporated milk right near the edge of the shelf over the kitchen table.

He stood up for a better look at it, uncorked it, and sniffed the contents. It had a sharp, acrid odor. There was a medicine dropper lying beside it.

He had never seen either of them before. And for no reason at all he thought of the candles that Min burned every night, of the sudden unexpected appearance of the cross over the bed, of her never explained absence one evening.

He picked up his coffee cup, suddenly suspicious. There seemed to be traces of the same acrid odor, fainter, to be sure, but still there in the cup. He smelt the contents of the big enameled coffee pot that was sitting on the stove and put it down, frowning. He still couldn't be sure, but there seemed to be traces of the same odor, diluted down, much fainter, but definitely there. It might be his imagination, and on the other hand it might have been only that his nose was full of the sharp smell of the red liquid and so he thought he found it again in his coffee cup and in the big pot.

She wouldn't dare put anything in his coffee. She wouldn't dare. How did he know? The candles and the cross returned sharply to his mind. For all he knew she had been working some kind of conjure on him all along, trying to bring him bad luck.

He picked up the slender vial and the medicine dropper and went toward the bedroom. He didn't go all the way into the room. He stood in the doorway.

Min was tying a triangular, faded wool scarf over her head. She had her coat on and her movements were slow, clumsy, awkward. Her galoshes were fastened tightly around her feet and he thought nobody but a half-wit would get dressed backward like that. She saw him in the door and she put one hand into her coat pocket, leaving the ends of the scarf dangling loose.

'What's this for?' — he held the bottle and medicine dropper out toward her. 'You been putting this in my coffee? You been trying to mess with me?'

'It's my heart medicine,' she said calmly.

He stared at her, not believing her and not knowing why he didn't believe her. She didn't shrink away from him, she stared back giving him look for look, and with her hand in her coat pocket she had a slightly jaunty air that made him want to strike her.

'What's the matter with your heart?'

'I don't know. Doctor gave me that for it.'

'What do you do with it?'

'Put it in my coffee.'

'Why ain't there no doctor's label on it?' he asked suspiciously.

'He said it don't need one. Couldn't mix that bottle up with no other one.'

He still wasn't satisfied. 'When'd you see him?'

'The night I went out.'

He didn't believe her. She was lying. She looked like she was lying. She didn't have nothing the matter with her heart. If it wasn't for that cross — he located it out of the corner of his eye. Yes. It was still there over the bed, and he turned his eyes away from it quickly, sorry that he had looked at it, for he would be seeing the damn thing before him everywhere he looked the rest of the day.

'Well, keep it in here,' he said hastily. He entered the room, laid the bottle and the medicine dropper down on the bureau and walked away quickly. 'Don't have it out there in the kitchen. I don't want to look at it. Or smell it.' He said the words over his shoulder.

When she emerged from the bedroom a few minutes later, the scarf tied tightly under her chin, her house dress wrapped up in a brown-paper bag that she carried under one arm, he refused to glance in her direction.

'Well, good-bye,' she said hesitantly.

He grunted by way of answer, thinking that he had been so confused at the sight of the cross he hadn't asked her what the candles were for. They didn't have anything to do with her heart. He hadn't planned to ask her about the cross, because he couldn't have brought himself to question her about it; mentioning it aloud would have given it importance. It would never do for her to know what it had done to him.

He went outside to bring in the garbage cans. He stood against the building looking up and down the street. It had snowed during the night — a light, feathery coating that clung to the brick all up and down the street, gently obscuring the dirt, covering the sidewalk with a delicate film of white. He eyed it, thinking that it wouldn't call for any shoveling. A couple of hours and it would be gone just from folks walking on it.

The Sanitation Department trucks rumbled up to the curb. The street was filled with the rattle and bang of garbage cans, the churning sound of the mechanism inside the trucks as it sucked up the refuse and rubbish from the big metal cans.

There was a steadily increasing stream of women passing through the street. They were going to work. Most of them, like Min, carried small brown bundles under their arms — bundles that contained the shapeless house dresses they would put on when they reached their jobs. Some of them scurried toward the subway entrance, hurrying faster and faster because they were late. Others plodded past slowly with their heads down as though already tired because the burden of the day's work had settled about

their shoulders, weighing them down before they had
even begun it.

Jones rolled his empty garbage cans into the areaway and returned to stand in front of the building.
In the mornings like this he was usually inside working, shaking the furnace, firing it, taking out ashes.
The street had a pleasant, lively look this morning.
The sun had come out, and what with the light coating of snow he felt a faint stirring of pleasure as he
stood there. Just this one day he ought not to do a
lick of work in the house, let the fire go out, leave
the halls full of rubbish while he stayed outside and
enjoyed himself.

As he watched the street, he saw that there were
young, brisk-walking women among the plodding,
older women. Some of them had well-shaped legs
that quivered where the flesh curved to form the calf.
His eyes lingered on one of them as she moved toward
the corner at a smart pace that set her flesh to jiggling
pleasantly.

'Right nice legs, ain't she, dearie?' Mrs. Hedges
inquired from the window.

He gave her one quick look of hate and then turned
his head away. Even early in the morning she was
there in that window like she'd been glued to it.
She was drinking a cup of coffee, and he wished that
while he was standing there she would suddenly gag
on it, choke, and die before his very eyes. So that he
could stand over her and laugh. He couldn't remain
out here with her looking at him. His pleasure in
the morning and in the street faded, died as though
it had never been.

There was nothing for him to do but go inside. He

wanted to get some more air and look around a bit. He wasn't ready to go in yet. He wasn't going to let her drive him away. He was going to stand there until he got good and ready to go. He was uncomfortably aware of her unwinking gaze and he shifted his feet, thinking he couldn't bear it. He would have to go back in the house to get away from it.

His eye caught the postman's slow progress up the street. His gray uniform disappeared in and out of the doorways. Each time he appeared, Jones noticed how the heavy mail sack slung over his shoulder pulled him over on one side, weighing him down. Watching him, Jones decided he would stay right there until the postman reached this building. That way the old sow wouldn't know she had chased him inside.

Post-office trucks backed into the street, turned and moved off with a grinding of gears. Children scampering to school were added to the stream of people passing by. The movement in the street increased with each passing moment, and he cursed Mrs. Hedges because he wanted to enjoy it and couldn't with her sitting there in the window watching him.

The superintendent next door came out to sweep the sidewalk in front of his building. Jones saw him with relief. He walked over to talk to him, welcoming the opportunity to put even a short distance between himself and Mrs. Hedges. This way she couldn't possibly think she had driven him off.

'Kind of late this morning, ain't you?' the man asked.

'Overslept myself.'

'Sure glad this wasn't a heavy snow.'

'Yeah. Don't know whether snow or coal is worse.' Jones was enjoying this brief chat. It proved to Mrs. Hedges that he was completely indifferent to her presence in the window. He searched for something humorous to say so that they could laugh and the laughter would further show how unconcerned he was. He elaborated on the theme of snow and coal, 'Got to shovel both of 'em. One time when white is just as evil as black. Snow and coal. Both bad. One white and the other black.'

The sound of the other man's laughter was infectious. The people passing by paused and smiled when they heard it. The man clapped Jones on the back and roared. And Jones discovered with regret that the hate and the anger that still burned inside him was so great that he couldn't even smile with the man, let alone join in his laughter. And the laughter died in the other man's throat when he looked at Jones' sullen face.

The man went back to sweeping the sidewalk and Jones waited for the approach of the postman. He was next door. In a minute he'd turn into this house. Yes. He was coming out now.

'Well, I gotta go.'

'See you later.'

He followed the postman into the hall, feeling triumphant. It was quite obvious to Mrs. Hedges that he had simply come inside to get his mail, not because of her looking at him. Then he felt chagrined because knowing everything like she did she probably knew, too, that he never got any mail.

The postman opened all the letter boxes at once, using a key that he had suspended on a long, stout chain. The sagging leather pouch that was swung over his shoulder bulged with mail. He thrust letters into the open boxes, used the key again to lock them and was gone.

Jones made no effort to open his box. There wasn't any point, for the postman hadn't put anything in it. He stood transfixed by the wonder of what he was thinking. Because he had found what he wanted. This was the way to get the kid. Not even Junto with all his money could get the kid out of it. The more he thought about it, the more excited he became. If the kid should steal letters out of mail boxes, nobody, not even Junto, could get him loose from a rap like that. Because it was the Government.

The thought occupied him for the rest of the morning. It was foremost in his mind while he shook down the furnace, carried out ashes, even while he put a washer in a faucet on the second floor and cleaned out a clogged drain pipe on the third floor.

During the afternoon he studied the mail box keys in his possession, taking them out of the box where he kept them and strewing them over the top of his desk. These were duplicates of the keys that the tenants had. He pondered over them. He had to figure out a master key — make the pattern for a master key. He didn't have to make the key himself, the key man up the street could turn it out in no time at all, there wasn't anything complicated about a mail-box key.

He went next door to see his friend, the super, in response to a sudden inspiration.

'Lissen,' he said craftily. 'Let me borrow one of your mail-box keys for a minute. Damn woman in

my house has lost two keys in two days. None of
my other keys will work in her box. I thought one
of yours might work. She's having a fit out there in
the hall wanting to get her mail.'

'Sure,' the man said. 'Come on downstairs. I'll
get one for you.'

Jones tried the key in the boxes in the hall. With
just a little forcing it worked. He looked at it in
surprise. Perhaps it would work anywhere on the
street. He would have liked to ask the man if it was
a master key, but he didn't dare.

He spent the rest of the afternoon drawing careful
outlines of the keys. Then he evolved one that
seemed to embody all the curves and twists of the
others. It was slow work, for his hands were clumsy,
sometimes the pencil slipped in his haste. Once his
hands trembled so that he had to stop and put the
pencil down until the trembling ceased.

The final pattern pleased him inordinately. He
held it up and studied it, surprised. This last, final
drawing wasn't really a copy. It was his own crea-
tion. He was reluctant to put it down, to let it go
out of his hands. He picked it up again and again to
admire it.

'I shoulda took up drawing,' he said, aloud.

He held it away from him, turned it around, until
finally, half-closing his eyes and staring at it, he
thought he saw a horizontal line across the length of
the drawing. He threw it down on the desk in dis-
gust, his pleasure in it destroyed.

Was he going through life seeking the outline of a
cross in everything about him? Min had done this
to him. There were other things she had done to

him which he probably didn't even begin to suspect. He thought of her standing in front of the bureau whispering, 'It's for my heart,' strangely unafraid, almost as though she had some kind of protection that she knew would prevent him from doing violence to her.

She had changed lately, now that he thought about it. She dominated the apartment. She cleaned it tirelessly, filled with some unknown source of strength that surged through her and showed up in numberless, subtle ways. She was always scrubbing and cleaning the apartment just as though it were hers, and then beaming approval at the result of her effort, so that her toothless gums showed as she smiled at her own handiwork.

Suddenly he laughed out loud. The dog pricked up his ears, scrambled to his feet, and came to where Jones was sitting at the desk and thrust his muzzle into his hand. Jones patted the dog's head in a rare gesture of affection.

Because he was going to fix Min, too. Min was going to take the drawing to the key man and get the master key made. There would be nothing, no scrap of evidence, no tiny detail to connect him with this thing. Even if the kid should say that he, Jones, had showed him how to open the boxes, had given him the key, all he had to do was deny it. He had been Super on this street for years, collecting rents and scrupulously turning them over to the white agents. That alone was proof of his honesty. No one would believe the story of a thieving little kid — a little kid whose mother was no better than she should be, whose mother openly lived with white men.

No. They'd never be able to pin anything on him It would be the kid. And if things worked out right, it would be Min, too.

When Min came home from work that night, he greeted her cordially but not too cordially, because he didn't want her to wonder what had made him change his attitude toward her.

'Your heart bother you today?' he asked.

'No,' she said. She looked at him distrustfully. 'Not much anyway,' she added hastily.

'I was wondering about it.' He hoped she would think that this concern about her heart accounted for his cordiality because he had been going out of the house almost as soon as she came home from work, not saying anything, deliberately waiting until she entered the living room and then brushing past her in order to show his distaste for her, thus making it obvious that he was hastening to get away from the sight of her.

She took off her coat and hung it up in the bedroom, shaking it carefully after it was on the hanger. When she unfastened the scarf around her head, she looked at herself in the mirror and automatically she sought the reflection of the cross hanging over the bed.

'Supper'll be ready in a minute,' she said cautiously.

'Okay.' He stood up, yawned, went through an elaborate, exaggerated stretching. 'I'm good and hungry.' He was beginning to enjoy himself.

He went to stand in the kitchen door while she set the table, talking to her companionably as she moved from table to stove. Gradually the faint suspicion, the slow caution in her face and in her eyes lessened, and then disappeared entirely. It was replaced by a quiet pleasure that grew until her face was alive with it. She talked and talked and talked. Words welled up in her, overflowed, filled the kitchen.

He ate in silence, wondering if he would ever be able to get the sound of her flat, sing-song voice out of his ears. It went on and on. He lost all sense of what she was saying, though in sheer self-defense he made the effort to catch it. It was like trying to follow the course of a tortuously winding path that continually turned back on itself, disappeared in impenetrable thickets, to emerge farther on at a sharp angle having no apparent relation to its original starting point.

'Mis' Crane's got three of the smallest kittens. Just born a month ago and the canned milk don't agree with them. So when we got to the rug on the living room we hadn't any of the soap chips. The man at the store said that kind is gone over to the war. And I got bacon there. A whole half pound. Mis' Crane was surprised because Mr. Crane has it for breakfast every morning. The drippings make the greens have a nice taste, don't they? Them Eighth Avenue stores is the only place that's got ones that have a strong taste. And the collards was fresh in this afternoon so I got it for tomorrow ——'

Finally he gave up the effort to follow the train of her thought. She wouldn't know whether he really listened or not. He nodded his head occasionally which satisfied her.

After supper he wiped the dishes, and the fact that he was standing near her, staying there to help her, increased the flow of her words until it was like a river in full flood.

He lay down on the sofa in the living room while she went through such elaborate and long-drawn-out, totally unnecessary cleaning that he couldn't control his impatience as he listened to and identified her movements. She was scrubbing the kitchen floor, washing out the oven, scouring the jets of the gas stove.

Finally she came to sit in the big chair in the living room, her eyes blinking with pleasure as she looked at the canary and talked to him. She was breathless from her scouring of the kitchen and she talked in gasps and spurts. 'Cheek! Cheek! Dickie-boy. You going to sing, Dickie-boy? Cluk! Cluk! Dickie-boy!'

'Min,' he said, and stopped because that wasn't the right tone of voice. It was too charged with urgency, too solemn, too emphasized. He had to keep his voice casual; make what he was saying sound unimportant and yet important enough for her to get dressed and go out again.

Her head turned toward him as though it were on a swivel. There was a slight rigidity in her posture as she waited for him to continue.

Jones sat up and put his hand on his head. 'I got a awful headache,' he said. 'And I got to have a mailbox key made for one of them damn fools on the third floor. She done lost two keys in two days and I ain't got another one. I was wondering if you'd take the pattern around to the key man and wait while he made it.'

'Why, sure,' she said. 'I'd be glad to. A breath of air would be real nice. Sometimes it seems awful close and shut up inside here. especially after Mis

Crane's having so much room around her and —— '

After she got her things on, he gave her the draw-ing, handing it to her carelessly. When he saw how slackly she held it, he couldn't help saying, 'Don't lose it.'

'Oh, no,' she said. 'I don't ever lose nothing. Only today I was thinking that I never lose nothing. Everything I've ever got I been able to keep —— '

She had to talk awhile longer and he listened, biting his lips in impatience as she rambled on and on. Finally she left, limping slightly because she hadn't had a chance to soak her bunions. But her face was warm with the pleasure of being able to do something for him.

The key was such a slender little thing, he thought, when Min returned with it and handed it to him; it was so small and yet so powerful.

Min soaked her feet and talked and talked and talked. She undressed and came out of the bedroom to stand near the couch where he was sitting, fondling the key.

'You ain't sleeping in the bedroom tonight?' she asked.

'No,' he said absently. He glanced briefly at her shapeless, hesitant figure. This was her way of in-viting him to sleep with her again. I think I fixed you, too, with this little key, he thought. And I hope I fixed you good. 'No,' he repeated. 'My headache's too bad.

The next afternoon Jones stood outside the building and waited for Bub. The street was swarming with children who laughed and talked and moved with gusto because school was out.

The Street

When Bub ran in from the street, he was moving so swiftly that Jones almost didn't see him. All of him was alive with the joy of movement — his arms, his legs, even his head. Kicking up his heels like a young goat, Jones thought, watching him. A little more and he'd jump right out of his skin.

'Hi, Bub,' he said.

'Hi, Supe' — he was panting, chest heaving, eyes dancing. 'Hi, Mrs. Hedges' — he waved toward the window.

'Hello, dearie,' she replied. 'You sure was going fast when you turned that corner. Thought you couldn't put your brakes on there for a minute.'

He laughed and the sound of his own laughter pleased him so that he laughed louder and harder in order to enjoy it more. 'I can go even faster sometimes,' he said finally.

'How about you and me building something in the basement this afternoon?' Jones asked.

'Sure. What'll it be, Supe?'

'I dunno. We can talk it over.'

They went into the hall and Jones opened the door of his apartment.

'Thought you said we were going into the basement.'

'We gotta talk something over first.'

Jones sat down on the sofa with the boy beside him. The boy sat so far back that his legs dangled.

'How'd you like to earn some money?' Jones began.

'Sure. You want me to go some place for you?'

'Not this time. This is different. This is some detective work catching crooks.'

'Where, Supe? Where?' Bub scrambled off the

298

sofa to stand in front of Jones, ready to run in any direction, already seeing himself in action. 'How'm I going to do it? Can I start now?'

'Wait a minute. Wait a minute: Don't go so fast,' he cautioned. This was the easiest thing he'd ever done in his life, he thought with satisfaction. He paused briefly to admire his own cleverness. 'There's these crooks and the police need help to catch them. They're using the mail and it ain't easy to get them. You gotta be careful nobody sees you or they'll know you're working for the police.'

'Go on, Supe. Tell me some more. What do I have to do?' Bub implored.

'Now what you have to do is open mail boxes and bring the letters to me. Some of them will be the right ones and some won't. But you bring all of them here to me. You gotta make sure nobody sees you give them to me. So you bring them down in the basement. I'll be down there waiting for you every afternoon.'

He took the slender key out of his pocket. 'Come on out in the hall and I'll show you how she works.'

The key was stiff in the lock. It turned slowly. He had to force it a little, but it worked. He had the boy try it again and again until he began to get the feel of it and then they returned to his apartment.

'Don't never open none of them boxes in this house,' he warned. He put one of his heavy hands on the boy's shoulder to give emphasis to his words. 'This ain't the place where the crooks are work-ing.'

He hesitated for a moment, disturbed and uneasy because Bub had been silent for so long. 'Here,' he

said finally and extended the key toward the boy.
'You got the whole street to work in.'

Bub backed away from his outstretched hand. 'I
don't think I want to do it.'

'Why not?' he demanded angrily. Was the little
bastard going to spoil the whole thing by refusing?

'I don't know' — Bub wrinkled his forehead. 'I
thought it was something different. This ain't even
exciting.'

'You can earn a lot of money.' He tried to erase
the anger from his voice, tried to make it persuasive.
'Mebbe three, four dollars a week.' The letters
would yield at least that much. Yes. He was safe in
saying it. The boy didn't answer. 'Mebbe five
dollars a week.'

'I don't think Mom ——'

'Your ma won't know nothing about it. You're
not to tell her anyhow,' he said savagely. He made a
superhuman effort to control the rage that burst in
him. He must say something quickly so that the
boy wouldn't tell her anything about it. 'This is a
secret between you and me and the police.'

'No,' the boy repeated. 'I don't want to do it.
Thanks just the same, Supe.'

And before Jones realized his intention, Bub had
run out of the apartment, slamming the door behind
him. He was left standing in the middle of the room
still holding the key in his outstretched hand and
with the knowledge that the kid could ruin him by
telling Lutie what he, Jones, had suggested.

He cursed with such vehemence that the dog
walked over to him, thrust his muzzle into his hand.
He kicked the dog away. The dog howled. It was a

sharp, shrill outcry that filled the apartment, reached to the street outside.

Mrs. Hedges nodded her head at the sound. 'Cellar crazy,' she said softly. 'No doubt about it. Cellar crazy.'

Chapter 13

I T WAS TIME for intermission at the Casino. The men in the bandstand got up from their chairs, shoved the music racks in front of them aside, yawned and stretched. Some of them searched through the crowd, seeking the young girls who had eyed them from the dance floor, intent on getting better acquainted with them, even at the risk of incurring the displeasure of their escorts. Others headed straight for the bar like homing pigeons winging toward their roosts.

The pianist and one of the trumpeters stayed in the bandstand. The trumpeter was experimenting with a tune that had been playing in his head for days. The pianist turned sideways on the piano bench listening to him.

The Street

'Ever hear it before?' he asked finally.

'Nope,' replied the pianist.

'Just wanted to make sure. Sometimes tunes play tricks in your head and turn out to be somep'n you heard a long while ago and all the time you think it's one you made up.'

The pianist groped for appropriate chords as the man with the trumpet played the tune over softly. Together they produced a faint melody, barely a shred, a tatter of music that drifted through the big ballroom. Conversation and the clink of glasses and roars of laughter almost drowned it out, but it persisted — a slight, ghostly sound running through the room.

The soft rainbow-colored lights shifted as they slanted over the smooth surface of the dance floor, softening the faces of the couples strolling by arm in arm; making gentle the faces of the Casino's bruisers as they mingled with the crowd. The moving lights and the half-heard tones of the piano and the trumpet created the illusion that the people were still dancing.

Lutie Johnson and Boots Smith were sitting at one of the small tables near the edge of the dance floor. They had been silent ever since they sat down.

'When will my salary start? And how much will it be?' she asked finally. She had to know now, tonight. She couldn't wait any longer for him to broach the subject. The intermission was half over and he was still staring at the small glass of bourbon in front of him on the table.

'Salary?' he asked blankly.

'For singing with the band.' He knew what she meant and yet he was pretending that he didn't.

She looked at him anxiously, conscious of a growing
sense of dismay. She waited for his answer, leaning
toward him, straining to hear it and hearing instead
the faint, drifting sound of music. It disturbed her
because at first she thought it wasn't real, that she
was imagining the sound. She turned toward the
bandstand and saw that two of the boys were practic-
ing. Boots started speaking when her head was
turned so that she didn't see the expression on his
face.

'Baby, this is just experience,' he said. 'Be months
before you can earn money at it.'

Afterwards she tried to remember the tone of his
voice and couldn't. She could only remember the
thin, ghostly, haunting music. But he had told her
she could earn her living by singing. He had said the
job was hers — tied up and sewed up for as long as
she wanted it.

'What happened?' she asked sharply.

'Nothing happened, baby. What makes you think
something happened?'

'You said I could earn my living singing. Just
last night you said the job was mine for as long as I
wanted it.'

'Sure, baby, and I meant it,' he said easily. 'It's
true. But I don't have all the say-so. The guy who
owns the Casino — guy named Junto — says you
ain't ready yet.'

'What has he got to do with it?'

'I just told you,' patiently. 'Christ, he owns the
joint.'

'Is he the same man that owns the Bar and Grill?'

'Yeah.'

The music faded away, returned, was lost again. She remembered Junto's squat figure reflected in the mirror behind the bar. A figure in a mirror lifted a finger, shook his head, and she was right back where she started. No, not quite; for this still, sick feeling inside of her was something she hadn't had before. This was worse than being back where she started because she hadn't been able to prevent the growth of a bright optimism that had pictured a shining future. She had seen herself moving away from the street, giving Bub a room of his own, being home when he returned from school. Those things had become real to her and they were gone.

She had to go on living on the street, in that house. And she could feel the Super pulling her steadily toward the stairway, could feel herself swaying and twisting and turning to get away from him, away from the cellar door. Once again she was aware of the steps stretching down into the darkness of the basement below, could feel the dog leaping on her back and Mrs. Hedges' insinuating voice was saying, 'Earn extra money, dearie.'

'No!' she said sharply.

'What's the matter, baby? Did it mean so much to you?'

She looked at him, thinking, He would like to know that it meant everything in the world to me. There was nothing in his expression to indicate that the knowledge that she was bitterly disappointed would concern him or that he was even faintly interested. But she knew by the eager way he was bending toward her across the table, by the intentness with which he was studying her, that he was seeking to discover the degree of her disappointment.

'I suppose it did,' she said quietly.

She got up from the table. 'Well,' she said, 'thanks for the chance anyway.'

'Yeah,' he said vaguely. He was fingering the scar on his cheek. 'Hey, wait a minute, where you goin'?'

'I'm going home. Where did you think I was going?'

'But you ain't going to stop singing with the band, are you?'

'What would be the point? I work all day. I'm not going to sing half the night for the fun of it.'

'But the experience ——'

'I'm not interested,' she said flatly.

He put his hand on her arm. 'Wait and I'll drive you home. I want to talk to you, baby. You can't walk out on me like this.'

'I'm not walking out on you,' she said impatiently. 'I'm tired and I want to go home.'

'Okay' — he withdrew his hand. 'Junto sent you this ——' He pulled a small white box out of his vest pocket and handed it to her.

The cover stuck and she pulled it off with a jerk that set the rhinestone earrings inside to glinting as the rainbow-colored lights touched them. They were so alive with fiery color that they seemed to move inside the small box.

'Thanks,' she said, and her voice sounded hard, brassy to her own ears. 'I can't imagine anything I needed more than these.'

She turned away from him abruptly, hurried across the dance floor, down the long, massive staircase to the cloakroom. She took her coat from the hat-check girl, put a quarter on the thick white saucer on the shelf. As she went out the door, she thought, I should have left the earrings with the girl, she probably needs them as badly as I do.

The Casino's doorman, resplendent in his dark red uniform, paused with his hand on a taxi-door and looked after her as she walked toward Seventh Avenue. He thought the long black skirt made an angry sound as she moved swiftly toward the corner.

She was holding the earring box so tightly that she could feel the cardboard give a little, and she squeezed it harder. She tried not to think, to keep the deep anger that boiled up in her under control. There wasn't any reason for her to be angry with Boots Smith and Junto. She was to blame.

Yet she could feel a hard, tight knot of anger and hate forming within her as she walked along. She decided to walk home, hoping that the anger would evaporate on the way. She moved in long, swift strides. There was a hard sound to her heels clicking against the sidewalk and she tried to make it louder. Hard, hard, hard. That was the only way to be — so hard that nothing, the street, the house, the people — nothing would ever be able to touch her.

Down one block and then the next — 135th, 134th, 133d, 132d, 131st. Slowly she began to reach for some conclusion, some philosophy with which to rebuild her shattered hopes. The world hadn't collapsed about her. She hadn't been buried under brick and rubble, falling plaster and caved-in sidewalks. Yet that was how she had felt listening to Boots.

The trouble was with her. She had built up a fantastic structure made from the soft, nebulous, cloudy stuff of dreams. There hadn't been a solid, practical brick in it, not even a foundation. She had built it up of air and vapor and moved right in. So of course it had collapsed. It had never existed anywhere but in her own mind.

She might as well face the fact that she would have to go on living in that same street. She didn't have enough money to pay a month's rent in advance on another apartment and hire a moving-man. Even if she had the necessary funds, any apartment she moved into would be equally as undesirable as the one she moved out of. Except, of course, at a new address she wouldn't find Mrs. Hedges and the Super. No, but there would be other people who wouldn't differ too greatly from them. This was as good a time and place as any other for her to get accustomed to the idea of remaining there.

She hoped what Mrs. Hedges had said about Jones not bothering her any more was true, for she knew she couldn't force herself to register a complaint against him. The thought of telling some indifferent desk sergeant about the details of his attack on her was one she didn't relish.

But that's what she should do. Then she thought, Suppose they locked him up for thirty days or sixty days or ninety days, or whatever the sentence was for such things. Then what? He couldn't be kept in jail indefinitely. He was the kind of man who would carry a grudge against her as long as he lived and once out of jail she was certain he would make an effort to strike back at her.

Harlem wasn't a very big place and if he was dead

set on revenge he wouldn't have any difficulty in finding her. Besides, there was Bub to be considered, for instead of harming her he might seek to avenge himself on Bub.

No. She wouldn't go to the police about him. She paused for a stop light. Have you got used to the idea of staying there? she asked herself.

From now on they would have to live so carefully, so frugally, so miserly that each pay-check would yield a small sum to be put in the bank. After a while they would be able to move. It would be hard. She might as well get used to that, too.

They would have to live so close to a narrow margin that it wouldn't really be like living; never going anywhere, never buying the smallest item that wasn't absolutely essential, even examining essential ones and eliminating them whenever possible. It was the only way they could hope to move. She thought with regret of the quarter she had so lavishly given the hat-check girl. She ought to go back and tell the girl it was a mistake, that she was angry when she gave it to her, and she tried to picture how the girl's face would look — startled, incredulous at first, and then sullen, outraged.

Nights at home she would start studying in order to get a higher civil service rating. Perhaps by the time the next exam came up, she would be able to pass it. The job at the Casino that had looked like such an easy, pat, just-right thing was out of the question and her common sense should have told her that in the beginning. Yet she found she was thinking of it with regret and of all the things it would have meant — those things that seemed to be right within reach last night when Boots said, 'The job is yours, baby.'

And she began thinking about him. 'All you gotta do is be nice to me, baby.' She hadn't done or said anything that would indicate that she had no intention of being 'nice' to him. It must have been something else that had made him lose interest in her so quickly.

She tried to remember all the things he had said to her to find some clue that would explain his indifference. For he had been indifferent, she decided. He had sat there at the table tonight, making no effort to talk, absorbed in his own thoughts, and even when he had talked to her he had looked at her impersonally as though she were a stranger in whom he didn't have even a passing interest.

'I could fall in love with you easy, baby.' He had said that just last night. And that first night she had met him, 'The only thing I'm interested in is you.'

When he drove her home last night, he had scarcely spoken. He had made no effort to touch her. She sought a reason and remembered that he had fallen silent after the bouncer at the Casino told him Junto wanted to see him.

She walked a little faster. If Junto owned the Casino, then Boots worked for him. Even so, what could Junto have said to him that would make him lose his obvious desire for her so abruptly? It must have been something else that disturbed him, she decided. Perhaps it had something to do with his not being in the army, for she remembered how he couldn't conceal his annoyance when she persisted in asking him why he hadn't been drafted.

It didn't matter anyway. Perhaps it was just as
well the thing had ended like this. At least she no
longer had to duck and dodge away from his brutal
hands. Even if she had been hired at a fat weekly
salary, his complete lack of scruple might have been
something she couldn't have coped with.

She pushed open the door of the apartment house
where she lived. The hall was quiet. There was no
movement in the pool of shadow that almost obliterated the cellar door. And she wondered if every
time she entered the hall, she would inevitably seek
to locate the tall, gaunt figure of the Super.

The cracked tile of the floor was grimy. The snow
that had been tracked in from the street during the
morning had melted and mixed with the soot and
dust on the floor. She looked at the dark brown
varnish on the doors, the dim light that came from
the streaked light fixture overhead, the tarnished mail
boxes, the thin, worn stair treads. And she thought
time had a way of transforming things.

Only a few hours had elapsed since she stood in
this same doorway, completely unaware of the dim
light, the faded, dreary paint, the filth on the floor.
She had looked down the length of this hall and seen
Bub growing up in some airy, sunny house and herself free from worry about money. She had been
able to picture him coming home from school to
snacks of cookies and milk and bringing other kids
with him; and then playing somewhere near-by, and
all she had to do was look out of the window and see
him because she was home every day when he arrived.
And time and Boots Smith and Junto had pushed her
right back in here, deftly removing that obscuring

cloud of dreams, so that now tonight she could see this hall in reality.

She started up the stairs. They went up and up ahead of her. They were steeper than she remembered them. And she thought vaguely of all the feet that had passed over them in order to wear the treads down like this — young feet and old feet; feet tired from work; feet that skipped up them because some dream made them less than nothing to climb; feet that moved reluctantly because some tragedy slowed them up.

Her legs were too tired to move quickly, so that her own feet refused to move at their usual swift pace. She became uneasily conscious of the closeness of the walls. The hall was only a narrow passageway between them. The walls were very thin, too, for she could hear the conversations going on behind the closed doors on each floor.

Radios were playing on the third and fourth floors. She tried to walk faster to get away from the medley of sound, but her legs refused to respond to her urging. 'Buy Shirley Soap and Keep Beautiful' was blared out by an announcer's voice. The sounds were confusing. Someone had tuned in the station that played swing records all night, and she heard, 'Now we have the master of the trumpet in Rock, Raleigh, Rock.'

That mingled with the sounds of a revival church which was broadcasting a service designed to redeem lost souls: 'This is the way, sisters and brothers. This is the answer. Come all of you now before it's too late. This is the way.' As she walked along, she heard the congregation roar, 'Preach it, brother, preach it.' Suddenly a woman cried loud above the other sounds, 'Lord Jesus is a-comin' now.'

The congregation clapped their hands in rhythm. It came in clear over the radio. And the sound mingled with the high sweetness of the trumpet playing 'Rock, Raleigh, Rock,' and the soap program joined in with the plunking of a steel guitar, 'If you wanta be beautiful use Shirley Soap.'

A fight started on the third floor. Its angry violence echoed up the stairs, mingling with the voices on the radio. The conversations that were going on behind the closed doors that lined the hall suddenly ceased. The whole house listened to the progress of the fight.

And Lutie thought, The whole house knows, just as I do, that Bill Smith, who never works, has come home drunk again and is beating up his wife. Living here is like living in a structure that has a roof, but no partitions, so that privacy is destroyed, and even the sound of one's breathing becomes a known, familiar thing to each and every tenant.

She sighed with relief when she reached the fifth floor. The stairs had seemed like a high, ever-ascending mountain because she was so tired. And then she thought, No, that wasn't quite true, because the way she felt at this moment was the way a fighter feels after he's been knocked down hard twice in succession, given no time to recover from the first smashing blow before the second one slams him back down again.

And the second blow makes him feel as though he were dying. His wind is gone. His heart hurts when it beats, and it goes too fast, so that a pain stays in his chest. The air going in and out of his lungs adds to the pain. Blood pounds in his head, so that it feels dull, heavy. All he wants to do is crawl out of sight and lie down, not moving, not thinking. She knew how he would feel, because that about summed up what had happened to her, except that she had received, not two blows, but a whole series of them.

Then she saw with surprise that there was a light under her door and she stopped thinking about how she felt. 'Why isn't he asleep?' she said, aloud.

But Bub was asleep, so sound asleep that he didn't stir when she entered the room. He is afraid here alone, she thought, looking down at him. He was sprawled in the center of the studio couch, his legs and arms flung wide apart. The lamp on the table was shining directly in his face.

Each time she had come home from the Casino, he had been sleeping with the light on. Yes, he was definitely afraid. Well, she wouldn't be going out any more at night, leaving him alone. She switched the light off, thinking that it would be years now before he had a bedroom of his own. It was highly doubtful that he would ever have one, and there was still the problem of his having no place to go after school.

After she undressed and got into bed, she lay staring up at the ceiling for a long time. She thought of Junto, who could so casually, so lightly, perhaps at a mere whim, and not even aware of what he was doing, thrust her back into this place, and of Boots Smith, who might or might not have been telling the truth, who might for purposes of his own have decided that she wasn't to be paid for singing. And

a bitter, angry feeling spread all through her, harden-
ing and congealing.

She was stuck here on this street, in this dark,
dirty house. It was going to take a long time to get
out. She thought of the Chandlers and their friends
in Lyme. They were right about people being able to
make money, but it took hard, grinding work to do
it — hard work and self-sacrifice. She was capable
of both, she concluded. Furthermore, she would
never permit herself to become resigned to living here.
She had a sudden vivid recollection of the tragic, resigned faces of the young girls and the old man she
had seen in the spring. No. She would never become like that.

Her thoughts returned to Junto, and the bitterness
and the hardness increased. In every direction, anywhere one turned, there was always the implacable
figure of a white man blocking the way, so that it
was impossible to escape. If she needed anything to
spur her on, she thought, this fierce hatred, this deep
contempt, for white people would do it. She would
never forget Junto. She would keep her hatred of him
alive. She would feed it as though it were a fire.

Bub woke up before she did. He had put the water
for the oatmeal on to boil when she came into the
kitchen.

She kissed him lightly. 'You go get dressed while
I fix breakfast.'

'Okay.'

And then she remembered the light shining on his
face while he was asleep. 'Bub,' she said sternly,
'you've got to stop going to sleep with the light on.'

He looked sheepish. 'I fell asleep and forgot it.'

'That's not true,' she said sharply. 'I turned it out when I left. If you're scared of the dark, you'll just have to go to sleep while I'm here, so you won't be afraid, because this way the bill will be so big I'll never be able to pay it. Furthermore, I don't like lies. I've told you that over and over again.'

'Yes, Mom,' he said meekly. He started to tell her just what it was like to be alone in the dark. But her face was shut tight with anger and her voice was so hard and cold that he decided he'd better wait until some other time.

It seemed to him that all that week she talked to him about money. She was impatient, she rarely smiled, and she only half-heard him when he talked to her. Every night after dinner she bent over a pile of books placed on the card table and stayed there silent, intent, writing down queer curves and hooks over and over until she went to bed. He decided he must have done something to displease her and he asked her about it.

'Mom, you mad at me?'

They were eating supper. Lutie was startled by his question. 'Why, of course not. What made you think I was?'

'You sort of acted like it.'

'No, I'm not mad at you. I couldn't be.'

'What's the matter, Mom?'

She framed her answer carefully, trying not to let the hard, cold anger in her color her reply. She frowned, because her only explanation would have to be that they needed to save more than they were doing. 'I've been worried about us,' she said. 'We seem to spend so much money. I'm not able to save very much. And we have to save, Bub,' she said earnestly, 'so that we won't always have to live here.'

During the next week she made a conscious effort to stop talking to Bub about money. Yet some reference to it inevitably crept into her conversation. If she found two lights burning in the living room, she found herself turning one of them out, saying, 'We've got to watch the bill.'

When she was mending his socks, she caught herself delivering a lecture about being careful and watching out for nails and splinters that might snag them. 'They have to last a long time and new ones cost money.'

If he left a cake of soap soaking in the bowl in the bathroom, she pointed out how it wasted the soap and that little careless things ate into their meager budget. When she went to bed, she scolded herself roundly because it wasn't right to be always harping on the cost of living to Bub. On the other hand, if they didn't manage to save faster than she had been able to do so far, it would be months before they could move and moving was uppermost in her thoughts. So the next day she explained to him why it was necessary to move, and that they had to be careful with money if they were going to do it soon.

Her days were spent in working and at night she cooked dinner, washed and ironed clothes, studied. She found that, in spite of her resolve never again to dream about some easier and more remunerative way of earning a living, and in spite of her determination to put all thought of singing out of her mind, she couldn't control a faint regret that assailed her when she least expected it.

The Street

Coming home on the subway one night, she picked up a Negro newspaper that had been discarded by a more affluent passenger. And because of her reluctance to give up the idea of singing, it seemed to her that an advertisement leaped at her from the theatrical pages: 'Singers Needed Now for Broadway Shows. Nightclub Engagements. Let Us Train You for High-Paying Jobs.'

She tore it out and put it in her pocketbook, thinking cautiously that it was at least worth investigating, but not permitting herself to build any hopes on it.

The next night after work she went to the Crosse School for Singers. It was on the tenth floor of a Forty-Second Street office building. Going up in the elevator, she somehow couldn't prevent the faint stirring of hope, the beginnings of expectancy.

A brassy haired blonde was the sole occupant of the small waiting room. She looked up from the book she was reading when Lutie opened the door.

Lutie produced the advertisement from her purse. 'I came for an audition.'

'Have a seat. Mr. Crosse will see you in a minute.'

A buzzer sounded, and the girl stopped reading to say, 'Mr. Crosse'll see you now. It's that door to the left. Just walk right in.'

Lutie opened the door. The walls of the room inside were covered with glossy photographs of smiling men and women clad in evening clothes. A hasty glance revealed that all the pictures were warmly inscribed to 'dear Mr. Crosse.'

She walked toward a desk at the end of the room. It was a large flat-topped desk and Mr. Crosse had his feet on top of it. As she drew closer to him, she saw that the desk was littered with newspaper clippings, photographs, old magazines, even piles of phonograph records, and two scrapbooks whose contents made the covers bulge. A box of cigars, an ash tray that hadn't been emptied for weeks from the accumulation of soggy cigar butts in it, and an old-fashioned inkwell, its sides well splashed with ink, were right near his feet. A row of dark green filing cabinets stood against the wall behind the desk.

She was quite close to the desk before she was able to see what the man sitting behind it looked like, for his feet obstructed her view. He was so fat that he appeared to be bursting out of his clothes. His vest gaped with the strain of the rolls of fat on his abdomen. Other rolls of fat completely obliterated his jaw line. He was chewing an unlit cigar, and he rolled it to one side of his mouth. 'Hello,' he said, not moving his feet.

'I came for an audition,' Lutie explained.

'Sure. Sure. What kind of singing you do?' He took the cigar out of his mouth.

'Nightclub,' she said briefly, not liking him, not liking the fact that the end of the cigar he was holding in his hand had been chewed until it was a soggy, shredding mass of tobacco, and that the room was filled with the rank smell of it.

'Okay. Okay. We'll try you out. Come on in here.' One of the doors of his office led to a slightly larger room. She stood in front of a microphone on a raised platform facing the door. A bored, too thin man accompanied her at the piano. He smoked while he played, moving his head occasionally to get the smoke out of his eyes. His hands were limp and flat as they touched the keys. Mr. Crosse sat in the back of the room and apparently went to sleep.

At the end of her first song, he opened his eyes. 'Okay, okay;' he said. 'We'll go back to the office now.'

He lowered his bulk into the swivel chair behind his desk, put his feet up. 'Sit down,' he said, indicating a chair near the desk. 'You've got a good voice. Very good voice,' he said. 'I can practically guarantee you a job. About seventy-five dollars a week.'

'What's the catch in it?' she asked.

'There's no catch,' he said defensively. 'Been in business here for twenty years. Absolutely no catch. Matter of fact, I don't usually listen to the singers myself. But just from looking at you I thought, That girl is good. Got a good voice. So I decided to audition you myself.' He put the cigar in his mouth and chewed it vigorously.

'When do I start working at this seventy-five dollar a week job?' she asked sarcastically.

'About six weeks. You need some training. Things like timing and how to put a song over. Called showmanship. We teach you that. Then we find you a job and act as your agent. We get ten per cent of what you make. Regular agents' fee.'

'What does the training cost?'

'Hundred and twenty-five dollars.'

She got up from the chair. One hundred and twenty-five dollars. She wanted to laugh. It might as well be one thousand and twenty-five dollars. One was just as easy to get as the other.

'I'm sorry to have taken your time. It's out of the question.'

'They all say that,' he said. 'All of 'em. It sounds out of the question because most people really don't have what it takes to be singers. They don't want it bad enough. They see somebody earning hundreds a week and they never stop to think that person made a lot of sacrifices to get there.'

'I know all that. In my case it's impossible.'

'You don't have to pay it all at once. We arrange for down payments and so much a week in special cases. Makes it easier that way.'

'You don't understand. I just don't have the money,' she turned away, started past his desk.

'Wait a minute.' He put his feet on the floor, got up from the swivel chair and laid a fat hand on her arm.

She looked down at his hand. The skin was the color of the underside of a fish — a grayish white. There were long black hairs on the back of it — even on the fingers. It was a boneless hand, thick-covered with fat. She drew her arm away. He was so saturated with the smell of tobacco that it seeped from his skin, his clothing. The cigar in his flabby fingers was rank, strong. Seen close to, the sodden mass of tobacco where he had chewed the end of it sent a quiver of revulsion through her.

'You know a good-looking girl like you shouldn't have to worry about money,' he said softly. She didn't say anything and he continued, 'In fact, if you and me can get together a coupla nights a week in Harlem, those lessons won't cost you a cent. No sir, not a cent.'

Yes, she thought, if you were born black and not too ugly, this is what you get, this is what you find.

The Street

It was a pity he hadn't lived back in the days of slavery, so he could have raided the slave quarters for a likely wench any hour of the day or night. This is the superior race, she said to herself, take a good long look at him: black, oily hair; slack, gross body; grease spots on his vest; wrinkled shirt collar; cigar ashes on his suit; small pig eyes engulfed in the fat of his face.

She remembered the inkwell on the desk in back of him. She picked it up in a motion so swift that he had no time to guess her intent. She hurled it full force in his face. The ink paused for a moment at the obstruction of his eyebrows, then dripped down over the fat jowls, over the wrinkled collar, the grease-stained vest; trickled over his mouth.

She slammed the door of the office behind her. The girl in the reception room looked up, startled at the sound.

'Through so quick?' she asked.

'Yes.' She walked past the girl. Hurry, she told herself. Hurry, hurry, hurry!

'Didya fill out a application?' the girl called after her.

'I won't need one' — she said the words over her shoulder.

She boarded a Sixth Avenue train at Forty-Second Street. It was crowded with passengers. She closed her eyes to shut them out, gripping the overhead strap tightly. She welcomed the roar of the train as it sped toward Fifty-Ninth Street, welcomed its lurching, swaying motion. She wished that it would go faster, make more noise, rock more wildly, because the tumultuous anger in her could only be quelled by violence.

She sought release from the urgency of her rage by deliberately picturing the train plunging suddenly off the track in a fury of sound — the metal coaches rushing headlong on top of each other in a whole series of thunderous explosions.

The burst of anger died away slowly and she began to think of herself drearily. She was running around a small circle, around and around like a squirrel in a cage. All this business of saving money in order to move added up to less than nothing, because she had forgotten or blithely overlooked the fact that she couldn't find any better place to live, not for the amount of rent she could pay.

She thought of Mr. Crosse with a sudden access of hate that made her bite her lips; and then of Junto, who had prevented her from getting the job at the Casino. She remembered the friends of the Chandlers who had thought of her as a nigger wench; only, of course, they were too well-bred to use the word 'nigger.' And the hate in her increased.

The train stopped at Fifty-Ninth Street, took on more passengers, then gathered speed for the long run to 125th Street.

Streets like the one she lived on were no accident. They were the North's lynch mobs, she thought bitterly; the method the big cities used to keep Negroes in their place. And she began thinking of Pop unable to get a job; of Jim slowly disintegrating because he, too, couldn't get a job, and of the subsequent wreck of their marriage; of Bub left to his own devices after school. From the time she was born, she had been hemmed into an ever-narrowing space, until now she was very nearly walled in and the wall had been built up brick by brick by eager white hands.

When she got off the local at 116th Street, she didn't remember having changed trains at 125th Street. She was surprised to find that Bub was waiting for her at the subway entrance. He didn't see her, and she paused for a moment, noting the anxious way he watched the people pouring into the street, twisting his neck in his effort to make certain he didn't miss her. She was so late getting home that he had evidently been worried about her; and she tried to imagine what it would be like for him if something had happened to her and she hadn't come.

At this hour there were countless children with doorkeys tied around their necks, hovering at the corner. They were seeking their mothers in the homecoming throng surging up from the subway. They're too young to be familiar with worry, she thought, for their expressions were exactly like Bub's — apprehensive, a little frightened. They're behind the same wall already. She walked over to Bub.

'Hello, hon,' she said gently. She put her arm around his shoulders as they walked toward home.

He was silent for a while, and then he said, 'Mom, are you sure you're not mad at me?'

She tightened her grip on his shoulder. 'Of course not,' she said. She was neatly caged here on this street and tonight's experience had increased the growing frustration and hatred in her. It probably shows in my face, she thought, dismayed, and Bub can see it.

'I'm not mad at you all. I couldn't be' — she caressed his cheek. 'I've been worried about something.'

She thought of the animals at the Zoo. She and Bub had gone there one Sunday afternoon. They arrived in time to see the lions and tigers being fed. There was a moment, before the great hunks of red meat were thrust into the cages, when the big cats prowled back and forth, desperate, raging, ravening. They walked in a space even smaller than the confines of the cages made necessary, moving in an area just barely the length of their bodies. A few steps up and turn. A few steps down and turn. They were weaving back and forth, growling, roaring, raging at the bars that kept them from the meat, until the entire building was filled with the sound, until the people watching drew back from the cages, feeling insecure, frightened at the sight and the sound of such uncontrolled savagery. She was becoming something like that.

'I'm not mad at you, hon,' she repeated. 'I guess I was mad at myself.'

Because she was late getting home and she knew that Bub was hungry, she tried to hurry the preparation of dinner. And when she tried to light the gas stove, there was a sudden, flaring burst of flame that seared the flesh of her hand and set it to smarting and burning. Bub was leaning out of the kitchen window intently watching the dogs in the yard below.

'Damn it,' she said. She covered her hand with a dishtowel, holding the towel tightly to keep the air away from the burn. It wasn't a bad burn, she thought; it was a mere scorching of surface skin.

Yet she couldn't check the rage that welled up in her. 'Damn being poor!' she shouted. 'God damn it!'

She set the table with a slam-bang of plates and a furious rattling of knives and forks. She put the glasses down hard, so that they smacked against the table's surface, dragged the chairs across the floor until the room was filled with noise, with confusion, with swift, angry movement.

The next afternoon after school, Bub rang the Super's bell.

'I changed my mind, Supe,' he said. 'I'll be glad to help you.'

Chapter 14

IT WAS ONLY TWO–THIRTY in the afternoon. Miss Rinner looked at the wriggling, twisting children seated in front of her and frowned. There was a whole half-hour, thirty long unpleasant minutes to be got through before she would be free from the unpleasant sight of these ever-moving, brown young faces.

The pale winter sunlight streaming through the dusty windows and the steam hissing faintly in the big radiators intensified the smells in the room. All the classrooms she had ever taught in were permeated with the same mixture of odors: the dusty smell of chalk, the heavy, suffocating smell of the pine oil used to lay the grime and disinfect the worn old floors, and the smell of the children themselves. But she had long since forgotten what the forty-year-old buildings in other parts of the city smelt like, and with the passing of the years had easily convinced herself that this Harlem school contained a peculiarly offensive odor.

At first she had thought of the odors that clung to the children's clothing as 'that fried smell' — identifying it as the rancid grease that had been used to cook pancakes, fish, pork chops.

As the years slipped by — years of facing a room swarming with restless children — she came to think of the accumulation of scents in her classroom with hate as 'the colored people's smell,' and then finally as the smell of Harlem itself — bold, strong, lusty, frightening.

She was never wholly rid of the odor. It assailed her while she ate her lunch in the corner drugstore, when she walked through the street; it lurked in the subway station where she waited for a train. She brooded about it at home until finally she convinced herself the same rank, fetid smell pervaded her small apartment.

When she unlocked the door of her classroom on Monday mornings, the smell had gained in strength as though it were a living thing that had spawned over the week-end and in reproducing itself had now grown so powerful it could be seen as well as smelt.

She had to pause in the doorway to nerve herself for her entry; then, pressing a handkerchief saturated with eau de Cologne tight against her nose, she would cross the room at a trot and fling the windows open. The stench quickly conquered the fresh cold air; besides, the children insisted on wearing their coats because they said they were cold sitting under open windows. Then the odors that clung to their awful coats filled the room, mingling with the choking pine odor, the dusty smell of chalk.

The sight of them sitting in their coats always forced her to close the windows, for the coats were shabby, ragged, with gaping holes in the elbows. None of them fit properly. They were either much too big or much too small. Bits of shedding cat fur formed the collars of the little girls' coats; the hems were coming out. The instant she looked at them, she felt as though she were suffocating, because any contact with their rubbishy garments was unbearable.

So in spite of the need for fresh air she would say, 'Close windows. Hang up coats.' And for the rest of the day she would avoid the clothes closet in the back of the room where the coats were hung.

Thus drearily she would start another day. It always seemed as if by Monday she should have been refreshed and better able to face the children, but the fact that the smell lingered in her nostrils over the week-end prevented her from completely relaxing. And when the class assembled, the sight of their dark skins, the sound of the soft blurred speech that came from their throats, filled her with the hysterical desire to scream. As the week wore along, the desire increased, until by Fridays she was shaking, quivering inside.

On Saturdays and Sundays she dreamed of the day when she would be transferred to a school where the children were blond, blue-eyed little girls who arrived on time in the morning filled with orange juice, cereal and cream, properly cooked eggs, and tall glasses of milk. They would sit perfectly still until school was out; they would wear starched pink dresses and smell faintly of lavender soap; and they would look at her with adoration.

These children were impudent. They were ill-clad, dirty. They wriggled about like worms, moving their arms and legs in endless, intricate patterns, and they frightened her. Their parents and Harlem itself frightened her.

Having taught ten years in Harlem, she had learned that a sharp pinch administered to the soft flesh of the upper arm, a sudden twist of the wrist, a violent shove in the back, would keep these eight- and nine-year-olds under control, but she was still afraid of them. There was a sudden, reckless violence about them and about their parents that terrified her.

She regarded teaching them anything as a hopeless task, so she devoted most of the day to maintaining order and devising ingenious ways of keeping them occupied. She sent them on errands. They brought back supplies: paper, pencils, chalk, rulers; they trotted back and forth with notes to the nurse, to the principal, to other teachers. The building was old and vast, and a trip to another section of it used up a good half-hour or more; and if the child lingered going and coming, it took even longer.

Because the school was in Harlem she knew she wasn't expected to do any more than this. Each year she promoted the entire class, with few exceptions. The exceptions were, she stated, unmanageable and were placed in opportunity classes. Thus each fall she started with a fresh crop of youngsters.

At frequent intervals the children would bring

penknives into the classroom. Her mind immediately transformed them into long, viciously curving blades. The first time it happened, she attempted to get a transfer to another district. Ten years had gone by and she was still here, and the fear in her had now reached the point where even the walk to the subway from the school was a terrifying ordeal.

For the people on the street either examined her dispassionately, as though she were a monstrosity, or else they looked past her, looked through her as though she didn't exist. Some of them stared at her with unconcealed hate in their eyes or equally unconcealed and jeering laughter. Each reaction set her to walking faster and faster.

She thought of every person she passed as a threat to her safety — the women sitting on the stoops or leaning out of the windows, the men lounging against the buildings. By the time she dropped her nickel into the turnstile, she was panting, out of breath, from the cumulative effect of the people she had met. It was as though she had run a gantlet.

Waiting for the train was a further trial. She searched the platform for some other white persons and then stood close to them, taking refuge in their nearness — refuge from the terror of these black people.

Once she had been so tired that she sat down on one of the benches in the station. A black man in overalls came and sat next to her. His presence sent such a rush of sheer terror through her that she got up from the bench and walked to the far end of the platform. She kept looking back at him, trying to decide what she should do if he followed her.

The Street

Despite the fact that he remained quietly seated on the bench, not even glancing in her direction, she didn't feel really safe until she boarded the train and the train began to pull away from Harlem. After that, no matter how tired she was, she never sat down on one of the benches.

Her thoughts returned to the street she had to walk through in order to reach the subway. It was as terrifying in cold weather as it was in warm weather. On balmy days people swarmed through it, sitting in the doorways, standing in the middle of the sidewalk so that she had to walk around them, filling the length of the block with the sound of their ribald laughter. Half-grown boys and girls made passionate love on the very doorsteps. Discarded furniture — overstuffed chairs thick with grease, couches with broken springs — stood in front of the buildings; and children and grown-ups lounged on them as informally as though they were in their own living rooms.

When it was cold, the snow stayed on the ground, growing blacker and grimier with each day that passed. She walked as far away from the curb where it was piled as she could, so that even her galoshes wouldn't come in contact with it, for she was certain it was teeming with germs. Lean cats prowled through the frozen garbage that lay along the edge of the sidewalk.

The few people on the street in cold weather had a desperate, hungry look, and she shuddered at the sight of them, thinking they were probably diseased as well; for these blacks were a people without restraint, without decency, with no moral code. She

refused to tell even her closest friends that she worked
in a school in Harlem, for she regarded it as a stigma;
when she referred to the school, she said vaguely that
it was uptown near the Bronx.

And now, as she watched the continual motion of
the young bodies behind the battered old desks in
front of her, she thought, They're like animals —
sullen-tempered one moment, full of noisy laughter
the next. Even at eight and nine they knew the foul-
est words, the most disgusting language. Working
in this school was like being in a jungle. It was filled
with the smell of the jungle, she thought: tainted
food, rank, unwashed bodies. The small tight
braids on the little girls' heads were probably an Afri-
can custom. The bright red ribbons revealed their
love for gaudy colors.

Young as they were, it was quite obvious that they
hated her. They showed it in a closed, sullen look
that came over their faces at the slightest provoca-
tion. It was a look that never failed to infuriate her
at the same time that it frightened her.

Every day when the classes poured out of the building at three o'clock, she hastened toward the subway,
and as she went she heard them chanting a ghastly
rhyme behind her:

> Ol' Miss Rinner
> Is a Awful Sinner.

When she turned to glare at them, they would be
clustered on the sidewalk, standing motionless, silent,
innocent. The rest of the rhyme followed her as she
went down the street:

The Street

She sins all day
She sins all night.
Won't get a man
Just for spite.

She glanced at her wrist watch and saw with relief
that it was now quarter of three. She would have
them put their books away and that would occupy
them until they got their frowzy hats and coats on.

The order, 'Put your books away!' was on the tip
of her tongue when Bub Johnson's hand shot up in
the air. The sight of it annoyed her, because she
didn't want even so much as a second's delay in getting out of the building.

'Well?' she said.

'Bathroom. Got to go to the bathroom,' he an-
nounced baldly.

'Well, you can't. You can wait until you get out
of school,' she snapped. All of them said it like that
— frantically, running the words together and managing to evoke the whole process before her reluctant
eyes.

Bub got out of his seat and stood in the aisle, jiggling up and down, first on one foot and then on the
other. All the children did this when she refused
them permission to leave the room. It was a performance that never failed to embarrass her, because
she couldn't determine whether they were acting or
whether their desperate twisting and turning was the
result of a real and urgent need. If one of them should
have an accident — and she felt a blush run over her
body — it would be horrible. The thought of having
to witness one of the many and varied functions of

the human body revolted her, and with boys — she looked away from Bub determinedly.

'No,' she said sternly. It happened every day with some one of the children and every day she weakened and let them go. Somehow they had cunningly figured out this dangerously soft spot of hers. 'No,' she repeated.

Then, in spite of herself, her eyes crept back toward him. He was still standing there beside his desk. He had stopped twisting and turning. His face was contorted with that look she feared — that look of sullen, stubborn, resentful hate.

'Go ahead,' she said. She filled her voice with authority, made it cross, waspish, in the hope that the sound would so overawe the class they wouldn't realize that she had lost again. 'Take your books and your coat with you and wait for us downstairs.' He would be gone long before the class got down, but it was just as well. It made one less of them to herd down the stairs. She saw that he had left his books on his desk, but she didn't call him back to get them.

Thus, Bub Johnson got out of school early and was able to beat all the other kids to the candy store across the street from the school.

He peered into the smoke-hazy showcases, trying to find something pretty to buy for his mother — something shiny and pretty. And as he looked, he murmured, 'Ol' Miss Rinner Is a Awful Sinner.'

Last week he had earned three dollars working with Supe — three whole dollar bills that he had put under the radio on the living-room table. Before he left for school in the morning, he put one of them in

his pants pocket because he was going to buy Mom
a present — today.

He passed by the smooth, fat chocolates; the bright-
colored hard candy, the green packages of gum, and
came to a dead stop in front of the case that spilled
over with costume jewelry: shiny beads and brace-
lets and earrings and lapel pins.

'You want something?' the short, thin woman who
ran the store asked.

'Yup,' he said. Her nose was sharpened to a point.
Even her glasses had a sharp, pointed look. Her
mouth was a thin, straight line. He looked at her
hard, remembering what Mom had said about white
people wanting colored people to shine shoes. He
would have liked to stick his tongue out at her to
show her he wasn't going to be hurried.

'What is it you want?'

'I don't know yet. I got to look around.'

Each time he moved to look at something in the
case she moved, too. Then the store filled up with
kids and she walked away from him. By the time
she reached the front of the store, he had made up his
mind.

'Hey,' he called. 'I want these.' He pointed to a
pair of shiny, hoop earrings. They were gold-
colored, and they ought to look good on Mom. They
were fifty-nine cents. She counted the change into
his hand, put the earrings in a small paper bag. The
change made a pleasant clinking.

'Hey, look, that kid's got money.'

Bub stole a cautious glance at the front of the store.
It was Gray Cap, one of the big six-B boys who had
spoken. He had five other big boys with him. They

could easily take his change and his earrings, too.
He edged near the door.

Gray Cap got up from the counter. Bub was sure
they wouldn't take his money away from him here in
the store. If he was quick — he darted out of the
door, running fleetly up the street, heart pounding as
he heard the hue and cry in back of him.

He fled toward the corner, plunging into the thick
of the crowd crossing the street — slipping, twisting,
turning in the midst of it, bumping into people, and
going on. He ignored the exclamations of anger, of
surprise, of chagrin, that followed in his wake.
'You knocked my groceries!' 'Eggs in here ——'
'Boy, watch where you're going!' 'If I get my hands
on you, you little black devil ——' 'Ouch! My foot!'

His pursuers ran head-on into the confusion he left
behind him. He turned to look — a large lady had
Gray Cap by the ear, was indignantly pointing at the
groceries spilling out of a brown-paper bag on the
sidewalk. Bub chuckled at the sight and kept running.

Two blocks away, he slowed his pace and looked
back. The boys were nowhere in sight. He had
thrown them off completely. He walked on, not
thinking, merely trying to catch his breath. His
heart was thudding so hard, he thought it was just
as though it had been running, too. He smiled at the
idea. It had been running right alongside of him, so
that it had to go faster and faster to keep up with him.
He could almost see it — red like a Valentine heart
with short legs kicking up in back of it as it ran.

He wondered if he ought to start working in this
block. Supe hadn't said not to go in other streets,

and this one was quite unfamiliar. The sun added a shine and a polish to the buildings; it sparkled on the small muddy streams at the crossings where the snow had melted. Yes, he would try working here where the strangeness of his surroundings offered a kind of challenge, like exploring a new and unknown country. In fact, he would start in that house right across the street — the one where two men were sitting on the steps talking. He felt a quiver of excitement at his own daring.

There was a vast and lakelike expanse of water in the middle of the street. Bub paused to wade through the exact center of it and then ducked out of the way as a passing car sent a shooting spray of water splashing to the curb.

He walked quietly up the steps, past the two men, and paused in the doorway. They weren't paying any attention to him. They were talking about the war, and they were so engrossed he knew they would soon forget he was there behind them. Water dripped down from the roof, gurgled into the gutters.

'Sure, sure, I know,' the man in overalls said impatiently. 'I been in a war. I know what I'm talking about. There'll be trouble when them colored boys come back. They ain't going to put up with all this stuff' — he waved toward the street. His hand made a wide, all-inclusive gesture that took in the buildings, the garbage cans, the pools of water, even the people passing by.

'What they going to do about it?' said the other man.

'They're going to change it. You watch what I tell you. They're going to change it.'

'Been like this all these years, ain't nothing a bunch of hungry soldiers can do about it.'

'Don't tell me, man. I know. I was in the last war.'

'What's that got to do with it? What did you change when you come back? They're going to come back with their bellies full of gas and starve just like they done before ——'

'They ain't using gas in this war. That's where you're wrong. They ain't using gas ——'

Bub opened the door of the hall and slipped inside. The hall was quiet and dark. He listened for footsteps. There was no sound at all. He made no effort to open the mail boxes, but peered inside them. The first three were empty. The next two contained letters — he could see the slim edges showing up white in the dark interior of the boxes.

Slow footsteps started on the stairs and he examined the hall with care. There was no place to hide. He didn't want to appear suddenly on the steps outside, for the two men would notice him and wonder what he had been doing.

He sat down on the bottom step of the stairs and bent over, pretending to tie his shoelace. Then he untied it, waited until he heard the footsteps reach the landing above him and started shoving the lacers through the eyelets of his shoe.

The footsteps came closer and he bent over further He looked toward the sound. A skirt was going past him — an old lady's skirt because it was long; there were black stockings below the skirt and shapeless, flat-heeled shoes.

'Having trouble with your shoelace, son?'

'Yes'm.' He refused to look up, thinking that she would go away if he kept his head down.

'You want me to tie it?'

'No'm.' He lifted his head and smiled at her. She was a nice old lady with white hair and soft, dark brown skin.

'You live in this house, son?'

'Yes'm.' Her old eyes were sharp, keen. He hoped she couldn't tell by looking at him that he was doing something not quite right. It wasn't really wrong because he was helping the police, but he hadn't yet been able to get over the feeling that the letters that weren't the right ones ought to be put back in the boxes. He would talk to Supe about it when he went home. Meantime, he grinned up at her because he liked her.

'You're a nice boy,' she said. 'What's your name?'

'Bub Johnson.'

'Johnson. Johnson. Which floor you live on, son?'

'The top one.'

'Why, you must be Mis' Johnson's grandson. You sure are a nice boy, son,' she said.

She went out the door, murmuring, 'Mis' Johnson's grandson. Now that's real nice he's here with her.'

Bub remained on the bottom step. He had told two lies in succession. They came out so easily he was appalled, for he hadn't even hesitated when he said he lived here in this house and then that he lived on the top floor. That made two separate, distinct ones. What would Mom think of him? Perhaps he oughtn't to do this for Supe any more. He was certain Mom would object.

But he earned three whole dollars last week. Three whole dollars all at one time, and Mom ought to be pleased by that. When he had a lot more, he'd tell her about it, and they would laugh and joke and have a good time together the way they used to before she changed so. He tried to think of a word that would describe the way she had been lately — mad, he guessed. Well, anyway, different because she was so worried about their not having any money.

He opened three mail boxes in succession. The key stuck a little, but by easing it he made it work. He stuffed the letters in the big pockets of his short wool jacket.

The street door opened smoothly. He slipped quietly outside to the stoop. The men were still talking. They didn't turn their heads. He stood motionless in back of them.

'The trouble with colored folks is they ain't got no gumption. They ought to let white folks know they ain't going to keep on putting up with their nonsense.'

'How they going to do that? You keep saying that, and I keep telling you you don't know what you're talking about. A man can't have no gumption when he ain't got nothing to have it with. Why, don't you know they could clean this whole place out easy if colored folks started to acting up. What else they going to do but ——'

Bub walked past them, hands in his pockets; paused for a moment right in front of them to look up and down the street as though deciding in an aimless kind of fashion which way he'd go and how he'd spend the afternoon.

And standing there with people going past him,

the two men behind him arguing interminably, aimlessly, a sudden, hot excitement stirred in him. It was a pleasant tingling similar to the feeling he got at gangster movies. These men behind him, these people passing by, didn't know who he was or what he was doing. It could be they were the very men he was trying to catch; it could be the evidence to trap them was at that very moment reposing in the pockets of his jacket.

This was more wonderful, more thrilling, than anything he had ever done, any experience he had ever known. It wasn't make-believe like the movies. It was real, and he was playing the most important part.

He walked slowly down the street, his hands in his pockets, savoring his own importance. He paused in the middle of the block where he lived to watch a crap game that was going on. A big man leaning against an automobile pulled into the curb, held the stakes in his hands — fistfuls of money, Bub thought, looking at the ends of the dollar bills. Boy, but he's big all over — big arms, big shoulders, big hands, big feet. The other men formed a small circle around him, squatting down when they rolled the dice, standing up to watch whoever was shooting.

A thin, tall boy breathed softly on the dice cupped tight in his hand. 'Work for poppa. Come for poppa. Act right for poppa. Hear what poppa say.' His body rocked back and forth as he talked to the dice, oblivious of everything, the street, the big man, the impatient little circle around him.

'Come on, roll 'em! What the hell!'

'Christ, you going to kiss them dice all day?'

'Roll 'em, boy! Roll 'em!'

The boy ignored them, went on talking softly, sweetly to the dice. 'Do it for poppa. Show your love for poppa. Come for poppa.'

The big man kept turning his head, taking quick looks first up and then down the street. Bub looked, too, to see what it was he was seeking. A mounted cop turned into the block from Seventh Avenue. The horse picked up his feet delicately, gaily, as he came side-stepping and cavorting toward them. The sun glinted on the bits of metal on his harness, enriched the chestnut brown of his hide. Bub stared at the approaching pair completely entranced, for the street stretched away and away in back of them and the horse and the man glowed in the sunlight.

'Blow it,' the big man said out of the side of his mouth.

Bub didn't move. He edged closer to the thin boy and stared at the boy's hand closed so tightly over the dice as he waited to hear again the rhythm of the boy's soft talking.

'Scram, kid,' the big man said.

Bub moved a little nearer to the thin boy in the hope that if he stayed long enough he might be able to get his hands on the dice and talk to them himself.

'Get the hell out of here,' the man growled, pushing him violently away.

Bub trotted off down the street. The big palooka, who does he think he is? The big palooka! He liked the sound of the words, and he said them over and over to himself as he walked along — the big palooka, the big palooka.

The key in his pants pocket made a pleasant jingling

as he walked, because it clinked against his doorkey.
He skipped along to make it louder. Then he ran a
little way, but the sound seemed to disappear, so he
slowed down, and began to imitate the dancing, cavorting horse that he had seen picking his way along
the street with the sun shining on him.

'The big palooka,' he said softly. He stopped
trotting like the horse and the key jingled in his
pocket. The sound reminded him that he hadn't
done any work in his own street that afternoon.

Before he headed for home, he had stopped in three
apartment houses. The letters he obtained formed
lumps in his pockets. Going in and out of the doorways, pausing to listen for footsteps in the halls,
walking stealthily up to the mail boxes, sitting
down on a bottom step to tie his shoe whenever
someone came in or went out, tiptoeing out of the
buildings, quickened the excitement in him. People
in the houses were completely and stupidly unaware
of his presence; their voices coming from behind the
closed doors of the apartments added to his sense of
daring.

He wished he could share the wonder of it with
someone. Supe was too matter-of-fact and never took
any interest in the details. His excitement and his
pleasure in this thing he was doing enchanted him
so that he walked straight into the middle of the
gang of boys who had chased him earlier in the afternoon.

They were standing under Mrs. Hedges' window,
talking.

'Aw, you can't go down there. Them white cops
are mean as hell ——'

'You're afraid of 'em,' Gray Cap said. There was a sneer on his lean, black face. The light-colored gray cap that gave him his name was far back on his head; the front turned toward the back so that his face was framed against the pale fuzzy wool.

'Who's afraid of 'em?'

'You are.'

'I ain't.'

'You are, too.'

It might have ended in a fight except that Gray Cap spied Bub approaching. He was coming toward them, so wrapped in thought, so unaware, so full of whatever dream was foremost in his mind, that they nudged each other with delight. They spread out a little so they could encircle him.

'You start it,' one of them whispered.

Gray Cap nodded. He was standing feet wide apart, hands on hips, dead center in Bub's path, grinning. It always worked, he thought. Start a fight and then take the kid's money and anything else he had on him. You could rob anybody that way in broad daylight. The gang simply closed in once the fight got started.

He waited, watching Bub's slow approach, savoring the moment when he would look up and see that he was trapped. Three boys had moved slowly, carefully, so that they were in back of Bub. There. They had him. Gray Cap moved forward a little, to hasten the entry of the bird into the trap. Perfect.

'Hi,' he said, and grinned.

Bub looked up, surprised. He turned his head slowly, knowing beforehand what he would find. Yes, there was one on each side of him; two, no, three, in back of him. He kept on walking, thinking that he would walk right up to Gray Cap, and then suddenly swerve past him and run for the door.

Gray Cap's hand shot out, grabbed the collar of Bub's jacket.

'Take your hands off my clothes,' Bub said feebly.

'Who's going to make?' Bub didn't answer. 'Who's going to make?' Gray Cap repeated. Bub still didn't answer. Gray Cap's eyes narrowed. 'Your mother's a whore,' he said suddenly.

Bub was startled. 'What's that?'

'He says he don't know what it is. Look at him.' Gray Cap grinned at his henchmen. 'He don't know what his mother is.'

'She is not,' Bub said defensively, impelled to deny whatever it was that had set Gray Cap to grinning and winking.

'What you mean she ain't? You just said you don't know what it is. Look at him. He don't know what it is and he says she ain't. Look at him.'

Bub didn't answer.

'His mother's a whore,' Gray Cap repeated. 'Does nasty things with men,' he elaborated.

'She don't either,' Bub said indignantly. 'And you stop talking about her.'

'Yah! Who's going to make? Your mother's a whore. Your mother's a whore.'

Bub doubled up his fist and reached for and found the boy's nose.

'Why, you ——' The boy aimed a blow at Bub — a blow that slanted off as Bub ducked. Gray Cap pushed close against him, then knocked him off balance so that he went sprawling backward on the pavement. Bub got up and the boy hit him squarely on the nose. His nose started to bleed.

The others closed in, forming a tight knot around him, their hands reaching, ready to explore his pockets. Gray Cap spied Mrs. Hedges sitting in the window imperturbably watching the proceedings. He was so delighted with the thought of this young and tender victim ready for the plucking that he yelled out, 'Yah! You're a whore, too!'

'You, Charlie Moore' — Mrs. Hedges leaned out of her window. 'Leave that boy alone.'

Their faces turned toward the window — sullen, secret, hating. Their hands were still extended toward Bub, reaching for him.

Gray Cap glared at her without replying.

None of them moved. 'You heard me, you little bastards,' she said in her rich, pleasant voice. 'You leave that boy alone. Or I'll come out there and make you.'

'Aw, nuts.' Gray Cap's hands went down to his sides. The boys backed off slowly, turned toward the street, staying close together as they went.

Gray Cap was the last to leave. He turned to Bub. 'Get other people to fight for you, huh? I'll fix you. I'll catch you coming home from school and I'll fix you good.'

'No, you won't neither, Charlie Moore. That boy come home all messed up and I'll know you done it. Don't you fool with me.'

He backed away from her hard eyes. 'Aw, his mother's a whore and so are you,' he muttered. It was a mere shred of defiance, and he didn't say it very loudly, but he had to say it because the gang was standing at the curb. Their hands were in their pockets as they stared up the street in apparent indifference, but he knew they were listening, because it showed up in every line of their lounging bodies.

'You go on outta this block, Charlie Moore.' Mrs. Hedges' rich, pleasant voice carried well beyond the curb. 'And don't you walk through here no more'n you have to.'

Mrs. Hedges remained at the window, her arms folded on the sill. She and Bub looked at each other for a long moment. They appeared to be holding a silent conversation — acknowledging their pain, commiserating with each other, and then agreeing to dismiss the incident from their minds, to forget it as though it had never occurred. The boy looked very small in contrast to the woman's enormous bulk. His nose was dripping blood — scarlet against the dark brown of his skin. He was shivering as though he was cold.

Finally their eyes shifted as though some common impulse prompted them to call a halt to this strange communion. Mrs. Hedges concentrated on the street. Bub went into the apartment house, his nose blowing bubbles of blood.

He was afraid. He examined his fear, standing in the hall. It was as though something had hold of him and refused to let go; and whatever it was set him to trembling. He decided it was because he had been lying and fighting all in one day. Yet he couldn't have avoided the fight. He couldn't let anyone talk about his mother like that.

He rapped on the cellar door under the stairs. He was still shaking with fear and excitement. The slow, heavy tread of the Super coming up the stairs sounded far away — menacing, frightening. When the Super opened the door, he followed him down the steep, old stairs to the basement in silence.

When they reached the bottom step, he began to feel better. He always delivered the letters to Supe down here. The fire was friendly, warm. The pipes that ran overhead with their accumulation of grime, the light bulbs in metal cages, the piles of coal — shiny black in the dim light — even the dusty smell of the basement, turned it into a kind of robbers' den.

It was a mysterious place and yet somehow friendly. The shadowed corners, the rows of garbage cans near the door that led to the areaway gaping wide and empty, the thick hempen ropes of the dumb-waiter, helped make it strange, secret, exciting. Those long brown ropes that held the dumb-waiter offered a way of escape if sudden flight became necessary. He could almost see himself going up, hand over hand, up and up, the stout ropes.

There was so much space down here, too. As he looked at the small dusty windows just visible in the concrete walls, at the big pillars that held the house up, he forgot about his bloody nose. The sudden sharp pain of hearing his mother talked about while the other boys laughed slowly left him. Only the memory of the horrid-sounding words that had come from Gray Cap's hard, wide mouth stayed with him.

This was real. The other was a bad dream. Going upstairs after school to a silent, empty house wasn't real either. This was the reality. This great, warm, open space was where he really belonged. Supe was captain of the detectives and he, Bub, was his most valued henchman. At the thought, the memory of Gray Cap's jeering eyes and of the hard, young bodies pressed suffocatingly close to his slipped entirely away.

He lifted his hand to his forehead in salute. 'Here you are, Captain.' He pulled the wadded-up letters from his pockets.

The Super held them lightly in his great, work-worn hands. 'I'll turn 'em over to the 'thorities tomorrow.' He looked at Bub curiously. 'You been in a fight?' he asked.

Bub wiped his nose on his jacket sleeve. 'Sure,' he said. 'But I won. The other guy was all messed up. Two black eyes. And he lost a tooth. Right in the front.'

'Good,' Jones said. And thought they oughtta killed the little bastard.

'Supe,' Bub said, 'oughtn't those letters that ain't the right ones — oughtn't those others be put back?'

'Yeah,' Jones nodded in agreement. 'The other fellows put 'em back.'

'Oh,' he said, relief in his voice. And then eagerly, 'Have they caught any of the crooks yet?'

'No. But they will. It takes a little time. But don't you worry none about it. They'll catch 'em all right.'

'I guess I'll do a little more work, Captain,' he said. Mom wouldn't be home for a long time yet. The street was better than that clammy silence up-stairs. And this time he would keep a sharp eye out for Gray Cap and his gang. He wouldn't walk right into the middle of them like he did just now.

'That's good,' Jones said. 'The more you work, the sooner the cops'll catch the crooks.'

Chapter 15

M IN came out of the apartment house with a brown-paper bag hugged tight under her arm. It contained her work clothes — a faded house dress and a pair of old shoes, the leather worn and soft and shaped to her bunions. She paused before she reached the street to look up at the sky. It was the color of lead — gray, sullen, lowering. Wind clouds of a darker gray scudded across it. She frowned. It was going to rain or snow; probably snow, because the air was cold and the wind blowing through the street smelt of snow.

The street was wrapped in silence. It was dark. The houses across the way were barely visible. Even the concrete sidewalk under her feet was recognizable as such only there where she was standing. By now she ought to be used to this early morning darkness, only she wasn't. It made her uneasy inside, and she kept turning her head, listening for sounds and peering across at the silent houses while she shifted the brown-paper bag from one arm to the other. It was the overcast sky and the threat of snow in the air that made her feel so queer.

Last winter there had been more mornings when the sky was a clear, deep blue and the sun spread a pink glow over the street. She had been filled with content then because she was free from the burden of having to pay rent and she was saving money to get her false teeth and getting little things to make Jones' apartment cozier and more homey.

She looked at the gloomy gray of the sky, at the dark bulge of the buildings, at the strip of sidewalk in front of her, and she saw the whole relentless succession of bitter days that had made this the longest, dreariest winter she had ever known. And Jones was the cause of it. She was used to going to work in the early morning dark, to coming home in the black of winter evenings; used to getting only brief and occasional glimpses of the sun when she made hurried purchases for Mis' Crane, and she had never minded it or thought very much about it until Jones changed so.

The change in him had transformed the apartment into a grim, unpleasant place. His constant anger, his sullen silence, filled the small rooms until they were like the inside of an oven — a small completely enclosed place where no light ever penetrated. It had been like that for weeks now, and she didn't think she could bear it much longer.

Things had only been nice that time he had the headache. He had talked to her all evening and come to stand close to her while she washed the dishes and he wiped them, and then later on for the first time he asked her to do something for him.

When she went to get the key made for him, a happy feeling kept bubbling up inside her. She waited impatiently while the man fiddled with the metal that would eventually come out of his machine as a key, for she had been certain that Jones would move back to the bedroom that same night, would once again sleep beside her.

That was another thing. Though the apartment had grown smaller, the bed had grown larger; night after night it increased in size while she lay in the middle of it — alone. It wasn't right for a woman to be sleeping by herself night after night like that; it wasn't natural for a bed to stretch vast and empty around all sides of her.

But when she came back with the key, he said his headache was too bad, that he'd stay outside in the living room. The next evening she had hurried home from work, looking forward to a repetition of the pleasant evening they spent together the night before, and he had acted so crazy mad that she stayed in the bedroom with the door closed, so she wouldn't see him and wouldn't hear him. But the hoarse wildness of his voice came through the closed door in a furious, awful cursing that went on and on.

The sound of his own voice seemed to increase his fury, and as the minutes dragged by, his raging grew until she thought he would explode with it. She sat down on the bed close under the cross and put her hand in the pocket where she kept the protection powder the Prophet gave her.

The Street

Maybe she should go see the Prophet again. No. He had done all he could. He kept her from being put out, and Jones still wouldn't try to put her out, but she didn't want to stay any more.

Her eyes blinked at the thought. Her mind backed away from it and then approached it again — slowly. Yes, that was right. She didn't want to stay with him any more. Strange as it seemed, it was true. And it just went to show how a good-looking woman could upset and change the lives of people she didn't even know. Because if Jones hadn't seen that Mis' Johnson, she, Min, would have been content to stay here forever. As it was — and this time she acknowledged the thought, explored it boldly — as it was, she was going somewhere else to live.

Jones had never been the same after Mis' Johnson moved in, and he got worse after that night he tried to pull her down in the cellar; got so bad, in fact, that living with him was like being shut up with an animal — a sick, crazy animal.

Worst of all, he never looked at her any more. She could have stood his silence because she was used to it; could even perhaps have grown more or less accustomed to the rage that forever burned inside him, but his refusal ever to look in her direction stabbed at her pride and filled her with shame. It was as though he was forever telling her that she was so hideous, so ugly, that he couldn't bear to let his eyes fall upon her, so they slid past her, around her, never pausing really to see her. It was more than a body could be expected to stand.

Yes, she would move somewhere else. It wouldn't be on this street and she wasn't going to tell him that

354

she was going. She took a final look at the sky. She would try to get her things under cover in some other part of town before the snow started. Mis' Hedges would get a pushcart man for her. She glanced at the street. It wasn't somehow a very good place to live, for the women had too much trouble, almost as though the street itself bred the trouble. She went to stand under Mrs. Hedges' window.

The window was open, and though she couldn't see her, she knew she must be close by, probably drinking her morning coffee. 'Mis' Hedges,' she called.

'You on your way to work, dearie?' Mrs. Hedges' bandanna appeared at the window suddenly.

'Well, not exactly' — Min hesitated. She didn't want Mis' Hedges to know she was moving until she was all packed up and ready to go. 'I ain't feeling so well today and I thought I'd stay in and do a little work 'round the house. I was wondering if you saw a pushcart moving man go past if you'd stop him and send him in to me.'

'You movin', dearie?'

'Well, yes and no. I got some things I want moved somewhere else, but I haven't got my mind full made up yet about me actually moving.'

Mrs. Hedges nodded. ''Bout what time you want him, dearie?'

Jones had gone out of the apartment wearing his paint-splashed overalls early this morning, so he was probably painting upstairs somewhere and wouldn't come back down until around twelve o'clock or so, and the man could load her things on the cart in a few minutes. It wouldn't take her very long to get them together, so by nine o'clock she should be gone.

'Tell him 'bout eleven,' she said, and was startled because her mouth seemed to know what she should do before her mind knew. She hadn't thought about it before, but she needed to sit down in the apartment and really decide that she was going to get out, for it never paid to do things in a hurry. At the end of an hour or two, she would have her mind full made up, and she'd never regret leaving, because she would know it was the only thing she could have done under the circumstances. Queer how her mouth had known this without any prompting from her mind.

''Bout eleven,' she repeated.

'Okay, dearie.'

When she opened the door of the apartment and walked into the living room, she saw that Jones was standing by the desk. He was tearing some letters into tiny pieces. The small bits of paper were falling into the wastebasket, swiftly and quietly like snow.

He didn't hear her come in, and when he became aware of her he turned on her with such suddenness, with such a snarling 'What you doin' in here?' that she backed toward the door, one hand reaching up toward her chest in an instinctive gesture aimed to quiet the fear-sudden hurrying of her heart.

'What you doin' here?' he repeated. 'What you doin' spyin' on me?'

The fact that she moved away from him seemed to enrage him, and he started toward her. His eyes were inflamed, red. His face was contorted with hate. She thrust her hand in her coat pocket, groping for the small box of powder, reached in further, more frantically. It wasn't there. She explored the other pocket. It, too, was empty.

As he approached her, she shrank away from him, half-closing her eyes so that she shut out his face and saw only his overalls — the faded blue material splashed with thick blobs of tan-colored paint and brown varnish; the shiny buckles on the straps and the rust marks under the buckles.

He would probably kill her, she thought, and she waited for the feel of his heavy hands around her neck, for the violence of his foot, for he would kick her after he knocked her down. She knew how it would go, for her other husbands had taught her: first, the grip around the neck that pressed the windpipe out of position, so that screams were choked off and no sound could emerge from her throat; and then a whole series of blows, and after that, after falling to the ground under the weight of the blows, the most painful part would come — the heavy work shoes landing with force, sinking deep into the soft, fleshy parts of her body, her stomach, her behind.

As she waited, she wondered where she had put the powder. She'd had it only yesterday in her coat pocket and last night she'd put it in the pocket of her house dress. That's where it was now, in the pocket of the dress hanging in the closet — the dress with the purple flowers on it that she'd bought in that nice little store on the corner where the lady was so pleasant, only the dress had run when she washed it and the purple flowers had spread their color all over the white background, muddying the green of the small leaves that were attached to the flowers.

He had lifted his hand. So it would be the face first and the neck afterward. She closed her eyes, so that she wouldn't see his great, heavy hand coming at her face, and thus she shut out the overalls and the paint on them and the rusting buckles that fastened the straps.

Nothing but trouble, always trouble, when there was a woman as good-looking as that young Mis' Johnson in a house. She wondered if white women, good-looking ones, brought as much of trouble with them, and then she thought of the Prophet David with warmth and affection. He had done the best he could for her. This that was going to happen wouldn't have come about if she had followed his instructions. It was a pity she had been so careless and left the protection powder in the pocket of that other dress.

And then the big, golden cross came to her mind. Nights alone in the bedroom she had sometimes sat up and turned on the light and looked up at it hanging over her head and been comforted by it. And it wasn't just because of the protection it offered either. There was something very friendly about it and just looking at it never failed to remind her of the Prophet and the quiet way he had listened to her talk.

She took her hand out of her pocket and without opening her eyes, and only half-realizing what she was doing, she made the sign of the cross over her body — a long gesture downward and then a wide, sweeping crosswise movement.

Jones' breath came out with a sharp, hissing sound.

She was so startled that she opened her eyes, for it was the same sound that she had heard snakes make, and it sent an old and horrid fear through her. For a moment she thought she was back in Georgia in a swampy, sedgy place, standing mesmerized with fear because she had nearly stepped on a snake that was coiled in front of her and she half-expected to see its threadlike tongue licking in and out.

'You god damn conjurin' whore!' Jones said.

His voice was thick with violence and with something else — almost like a sob had risen in his throat and got mixed up with the words. She stared at him, bewildered, reassuring herself that it was he who had made the hissing sound, that she was not back in the country, but instead was facing Jones in this small, dark room.

She was surprised to see that he had backed away from her. There was half the distance of the room between them. He was over by the desk, and his hands were no longer lifted in a threatening gesture; they were flat against his face. The sight held her motionless, unable to deny or affirm his charge of conjuring.

He walked out of the room without looking at her. She ought to explain why she had come back so unexpectedly, but he had reached the foyer before she could get the words out.

'My heart was botherin' me,' she said in her whispering voice. He made no reply, and she wasn't certain whether he had heard her. The door slammed with a bang, and then he was going up the stairs — walking slowly as though he was having trouble with his legs.

She cocked her head on one side listening, because the room was filled with whispers, and it was her own voice saying over and over again, 'My heart was botherin' me,' 'My heart was botherin' me.' It had a gasping, faintly surprised quality, and she realized with dismay that she was saying the words aloud over and over again and that her heart was making a sound like thunder inside her chest.

Her legs were shaking so badly that she walked over to the sofa and sat down. This was where he slept when she was in the bedroom alone. It was a long sofa, very long, and yet tall as he was, when he was stretched out on it, his head would be about where she was sitting and his feet would have touched the arm at the other end. She wondered if he had been comfortable or had he twisted and turned unable to sleep because he didn't have room enough. She punched the seat with her fist. It didn't have much give to it.

What would he have done if she had come and lain down beside him on this sofa on one of those nights when she couldn't sleep? Only, of course, her pride wouldn't have permitted it — especially after that experience with the nightgown. She squirmed as she thought of its bright pinkness, its low cut, and of the vivid yellow lace that edged the neck and the armholes.

She had looked at it a long time in the store before she finally bought it. It was the same store where she'd got that nice flowered dress, only this time the lady wasn't there, and the white girl who waited on her got a little impatient with her, but she had a hard time making up her mind because she'd never worn anything like it before and it didn't look decent.

'But it's so beautiful, honey,' the girl urged. Her

long red fingernails had picked up a bit of the lace edging.

'I dunno,' Min had said doubtfully.

'And it's glamorous. See?' The girl held it up in front of herself, catching it in tight at her waist and holding the neck up with her other hand, so that her breasts were suddenly accentuated, seemed to be pushing right out of the bright pink material.

Min looked away, embarrassed. 'I ain't never wore one of them kind.'

'Why, honey, you've missed half of life.' The girl moved her shoulders slightly to attract Min's glance. Min's eyes stayed focused on the front of the store and the girl stretched the nightgown out on the counter, started putting it back into its crisp folds, and said impatiently, 'Well, honey?'

'I still dunno.' The shiny pink material, the yellow lace, the gathers at the bosom, were startling even spread out flat on the counter.

The girl sought desperately for some way to close the sale. 'Why — why ——' she fumbled, then, 'Why, any man who sees you in this would get all excited right away.'

Two-ninety-eight it had cost, and she remembered with a pang of regret how that night after she bought it she had put it on. It was a little too long and she had to walk carefully to keep from tripping, but she made several totally unnecessary trips back and forth through the living room, walking as close as possible to the sofa where Jones was sitting. He was so absorbed in some gloomy chain of thought that he didn't pay any attention until she stumbled over the hem and nearly fell.

'Jesus God!' he said, staring.

But after that first look, he had kept his eyes on the floor, head down, unseeing, apparently indifferent. The only indication that he wasn't wholly unconcerned showed in the way he started cracking his knuckles, pulling his fingers so that the joints made a sharp, angry sound.

No, she could never have brought herself to lie down on this couch with him, and anyway she ought to start packing. Her house dresses and the pink nightgown and the other ordinary nightgowns could go in a paper bundle along with her shoes and slippers and spring coat and what else — oh, yes, the Epsom salts for her feet. The comb and brush and hand mirror could go in the same package. That was about all except for the cross and the table and the canary cage. She wouldn't really need the medicine dropper and that red don't-love medicine the Prophet gave her, but she'd take them, because she might run across some friend with husband trouble who could use them.

Funny how she got to believe that not having to pay rent was so important, and it really wasn't. Having room to breathe in meant much more. Lately she couldn't get any air here. All the time she felt like she'd been running, running, running, and hadn't been able to stop long enough to get a nose full of air. It was because of the evilness in Jones. She could feel the weight of it like some monstrous growth crowding against her. He had made the whole apartment grow smaller and darker; living room, bedroom, kitchen — all of them shrinking, their walls tightening about her.

Like just now when he came at her with his hand upraised to strike; he had swallowed the room up until she could see nothing but him — all the detail of the overalls and none of the room, just as though he had become a giant and blotted out everything else.

These past few weeks she had become so acutely aware of his presence that his every movement made her heart jump, whether she was in the bedroom or the kitchen. Every sound he made was magnified. His muttering to himself was like thunder, and his restless walking up and down, up and down, in the living room seemed to go on inside her in a regular rhythm that set her eyes to blinking so that she couldn't stop them. When he beat the dog, it made her sick at her stomach, because as each blow fell the dog cried out sharply and her stomach would suck in against itself.

But when he had been quiet and no sound came from him, she felt impelled to locate him. The absence of sound was deeply disturbing, for there was no telling what awful thing he might be doing.

If she was in the kitchen, she would keep turning her head, listening, while she scrubbed the floor or cleaned the stove, until, unable to endure not knowing where he was or what he was doing, she would finally tiptoe to the living-room door only to find that he was sitting here on this sofa, biting his lips, glaring at her with eyes so bloodshot, so filled with hate, that she would turn and scuttle hastily back to the kitchen. Or if she was in the bedroom she would sit on the edge of the bed, watching the doorway, half-expecting to see him appear there suddenly, and then the silence from the living room would force her to get up and look at him only to find his hate-filled eyes focused straight at her.

She got up from the sofa, satisfied. She had full made up her mind now and she would never regret going, for there wasn't anything else for her to do. He was more than flesh and blood could bear.

She carefully inspected the kitchen to make certain none of her belongings were there and then entered the bathroom where she took a five-pound package of Epsom salts from under the sink. There was nothing of hers in the living room but the table and the canary's cage.

On her way into the bedroom, she glanced at the top of Jones' desk. He hadn't finished tearing up the letters and she looked at them curiously. He never got any mail that she knew of and these weren't advertising letters, they were regular ones with handwritten addresses.

She picked up two of the envelopes. The names had been partly torn off, and she traced what remained of the writing with her finger, spelling each letter out separately. None of them were for Jones. One envelope was almost intact, and she saw with surprise that it wasn't intended for this house. It belonged in a house across the street near the corner, that house where there were so many children and dogs that they overran the sidewalk and every time she went past it, whether it was morning or night, she had to pick her way along to keep from bumping into them.

But if it belonged across the street, what was it doing on Jones' desk? Perhaps the people were friends of his or maybe they were going to rent an apartment here and had dropped the letters when they came to pay a deposit or perhaps Jones had stolen them from a mail box.

And at the thought the envelopes slid out of her hands, landing on the floor. She was too frightened to pick them up. And what was it he had said when she came in and found him tearing them into little pieces? What was it — 'What you doin' spyin' on me?'

Jones was doing something crooked. He was up to something that was bad. He had been ready to kill her just now because he thought she had found him out. If there had been any part of her that felt a reluctance about leaving the security that his apartment had offered, it disappeared entirely now, for she knew she would never be safe here again.

She walked carefully around the envelopes, entered the bedroom. There was the packing to be done and she would do it swiftly, so that she could be gone. She knelt on the bed and lifted the cross down, dusting it carefully with her hand. It should be wrapped in something soft to keep it safe. The pink nightgown, of course. It was new and silky and highly suitable. And she would wrap her house dresses and underwear and shoes and the slippers in with it. She would wear her galoshes because it was going to snow.

She transferred the protection powder from the pocket of her house dress to her coat pocket and then put the comb and brush, a hand mirror, and a towel on the bed near the cross. Mis' Crane would probably be mad because she hadn't come to work today. She got mad easy. Well, she'd tell her there was sickness in the family. It was true, too. Jones was sick;

at least he certainly wasn't what you'd call well and healthy, so he must be sick.

She added her spring coat, a straw hat, and a felt hat to the pile of items on the bed. She brought newspapers from the kitchen to wrap them in. It was going to be a pretty large bundle, and she decided to make two separate packages and wrap the cross and the house dresses by themselves. She would carry that package, because these pushcart men were very careless and sometimes let things slip off the back of their carts.

The closet floor was dusty. She wiped it up with a damp rag and then scrubbed it with scouring powder until the boards had a bleached, new look that pleased her. When she straightened up, she started to wipe her hands on the sides of her dress and halted the motion abruptly. She was still wearing her coat, had the woolen scarf tied over her head.

'I musta known all along I was going,' she said, aloud. 'Never even took my hat and coat off.'

The doorbell rang with a sudden loud shrilling that stabbed through her. She jumped and gave a frightened exclamation. Immediately she thought of Jones and her breathing quickened until she was gasping. Then the fear in her died. He never rang the bell. It must be the moving man that Mis' Hedges had sent.

She went to the door. 'Who is it?' she said. He must be a heavy-handed man, a strong man from the vigorous way he'd pushed the bell.

'Pushcart man,' the voice was deep, impatient, almost a growl.

She opened the door. 'Come in,' she said, and led him toward the living room, talking to him over her shoulder. 'It's the big table, the canary cage, and a bundle. I'll go get the bundle. The little one I'll carry myself, and how much will it be?'

She brought the big bundle out and put it on top of Jones' desk.

'This all?'

'Yes,' she said, and looked him over carefully. He had wide strong shoulders, though he wasn't very tall. His skin was weather-beaten, so that the dark brown of it had a reddish cast as though he had plenty of sun on him. 'Only the table is heavy. The other things is light,' she said.

'How far they go?'

She wasn't going to live on this street or very close to it and she searched her memory of other near-by streets. A couple of blocks up near Seventh Avenue she had seen signs in the windows, 'Lady Boarder Wanted' — she'd try there first.

''Bout two blocks.'

'Three dollars,' he said. And then, as though he felt impelled to justify the price, 'That there table weighs more than most folks' furniture put together.'

'All right.'

She held the door open while he struggled through it with the big table on his back. He went very slowly, so slowly that she grew impatient and kept looking up the stairs, afraid that Jones might have finished painting and would come down them before she got moved good. Then the pushcart man got the table out to the street and came back and picked up the big bundle and the canary cage.

'I'll be right out,' she said. 'You wait, because I'll be going along with the things.'

The Street

He went out the door and she walked over to Jones' desk and laid the doorkey in the middle of it, where he couldn't possibly miss it when he sat down there. She stared at the key. She had held it in her hand when she left for work in the morning, because the last thing she did before she went out was to make sure she had it with her; and at night, too, she'd clutched it tight in her hand when she approached the door on her return. Leaving it here like this meant that she was saying good-bye to the security she had known; meant, too, that she couldn't come back, never intended coming back, no matter what the future held for her.

She ought to be going. What was it that held her here staring at this key? It was only a doorkey. She had her mind full made up to go. It wasn't safe here any more, she couldn't stand Jones any more. She looked around the room impatiently, seeking what it was that held her here while the pushcart man waited outside, while the danger of Jones coming into the apartment increased with every passing moment.

The trouble was she didn't know why she was going. Why was it? There was something that she hadn't satisfactorily figured out, some final conclusion that she hadn't reached. Ah, yes, and as this last full meaning dawned on her, she sighed. It was because if she stayed here she would die — not necessarily that Jones would kill her, not because it was no longer safe here, but because being shut up with the fury of him in this small space would eventually kill her.

'And a body's got the right to live,' she said softly. When she walked away from the desk, she didn't look back at the key. But she paused in the doorway filled with a faint regret that there wasn't anyone for her to say good-bye to, because a leave-taking somehow wasn't complete without a friend to say farewell, and in all this house she didn't know a soul well enough to say an official good-bye to them.

But there was Mis' Hedges. She walked briskly out of the door at the thought. Once outside, she verified the safety of the big varnish-shiny table. The pushcart was drawn up close to the curb and the table was slung atop of it. The ornate carved feet were up in the air. She saw with satisfaction that practically every woman who walked past paused to admire it; their eyes lingered on the carving, then they drew closer as they enviously estimated its length.

If she hadn't put a dark cover over Dickie-Boy's cage, everyone passing could have seen that, too, and their mouths would have watered. Too bad she had covered it, but if she hadn't he would have been excited by his strange surroundings and probably stopped singing for a week or more.

She turned toward Mrs. Hedges. 'I come to say good-bye,' she said.

'You goin', dearie?' Mrs. Hedges looked at the large newspaper-wrapped bundle under Min's arm.

Min nodded. 'Prophet kept me from being put out, but I don't want to stay no more.' Then her voice dropped so low that Mrs. Hedges had to strain to hear what she was saying. 'Jones really ain't bearable no more,' she said apologetically. She paused, and when she spoke again her voice was louder. 'Well, good-bye now,' she said, and smiled widely so that her toothless gums were revealed.

'Jones know you're leavin'?'

'No. I didn't see no point in telling him.'

'Well, good-bye, dearie.'

'See you,' Min said. And then loudly, clearly, very distinctly she said again, 'Well, good-bye now.'

She walked near the curb, following the table's slow progress up the street. The table was heavy and the man had to lean all his weight on the handles of the cart in order to push it. With his legs braced like that, he looked like a horse pulling a heavy load. Well, he wouldn't have far to go, just a couple of blocks or so.

As she trudged along beside the cart, her thoughts turned to Jones; maybe if he'd had more sun on him he would have been different. After that time he'd tried to pull Mis' Johnson down in the cellar, he just got worse and worse. That was a terrible night, what with Mis' Johnson screaming and that long skirt all twisted around her and so dark near the cellar door that the two of them looked like something in a bad dream the way you'd remember it the next morning when you woke up.

Actually today was the first time Jones had gone for her since she went to the Prophet, because of course with the kind of protection she had it was only natural that he wouldn't try to put his hands on her. She gripped the bundle more tightly, searching for the shape of the cross through the softness of the dresses, felt for the protection powder in her coat pocket.

She looked at the pushcart man again. A woman living alone didn't stand much chance. Now this was a strong man and about her age from the wiry gray hair near his temples; willing to work, too, for this work he was doing was hard.

No, a woman living alone really didn't stand much chance. Landlords took advantage and wouldn't fix things and landladies became demanding about the rent, waxing sarcastic if it was even so much as a day behind time. With a man around, there was a big difference in their attitude. If he was a strong man like this one, they were afraid to talk roughly.

Besides, when there were two working if one got sick the other one could carry on and there'd still be food and the rent would be paid. It was possible to have a home that way, too — an apartment instead of just one hall room and with the table her money would always be safe.

This was a very strong man. His back muscles bulged as he pushed the cart. She moved closer to him.

'Say,' she said, and there was a soft insinuation in her voice, 'you know anywhere a single lady could get a room?' Then she added hastily, 'But not on this street.'

Chapter 16

JONES laid the big calcimine brush down on top of the ladder, pulled his watch out of the pocket of his overalls. It was two-thirty, way past the time when he usually ate. He climbed slowly down the ladder, feeling for each step. He was so damn tired that even his feet hurt.

He'd gone up and down the stairs until he'd lost track of how many times it was and all because he'd been fool enough to stick a note in the bell 'Super Painting in 41,' and it looked like everybody in the house had immediately discovered something wrong that had to be fixed right away — sinks and faucets on the third floor, a stopped-up tub on the second floor. He mimicked the old woman who lived on the second floor, 'Clothes in the tub soakin', soakin', soakin', and the water ain't runnin' out, and what am I goin' to do with them wet pieces that need rinsin'?' On top of that, he'd gone down in the basement to fire the furnace.

He slammed the door of the apartment behind him, then turned and locked it. He'd better catch a breath of air before he fixed himself something to eat, because the smell of the paint was in his nose, looked like it had even got in his skin.

Min was home today. She was in the apartment right now. His steps slowed on the stairs as he remembered how he'd almost got his hands on her this morning. Had she made the sign of the cross or had he imagined it? Even now he didn't really know. There must be some way he could get over his fear of that cross just long enough to choke her good; and she'd leave so fast it wouldn't be funny. And she had to get out, because even without the cross being involved, he couldn't bear to look at her any more. Much as he hated Lutie Johnson, every time he looked at Min he thought of Lutie.

Once in the hall downstairs he walked swiftly past the door of his apartment, forcing his thoughts away from Min and Lutie, concentrating on how good the air would feel once he was out on the street.

The first thing he noticed when he got outside was that the sun had come out. He leaned against the building, breathing deeply, watching the people who walked past. He sniffed the air appreciatively. It was cold, but it smelt fresh and clean after the paint smell. Not much warmth in the sun, though, and the sky was grayish as though there was snow building up in it. Yes, it would snow tonight or tomorrow.

'Min's gone,' Mrs. Hedges said blandly.

He clenched his fists as he turned toward her window. She was always interfering with him. He had been quietly studying the sky and enjoying the clear, cold air, and then that voice of hers had to interrupt him. He took another step toward the window and stood still, remembering the white man Junto who protected her, the white man who had a drag with the police and who had taken Lutie Johnson away from him. Some day he would get so mad he would forget that she had protection and he would pull her over that window sill and big as she was, he would beat her and go on beating her until she was all pulp and screams and then —— His mind echoed her words. She had said something about Min.

He looked directly at her. 'What?' he said.

'Min's gone, dearie,' Mrs. Hedges repeated.

'Gone?' He walked closer to the window, not understanding. 'What you mean she's gone? Gone where?'

'She's moved out. Took her table and the canary and left about eleven o'clock.'

'That's fine,' he said. 'I hope she don't come back. If she tried to come back I'd — I'd ——' The words twisted in his throat and he stopped talking.

'She won't be back, dearie.' Mrs. Hedges' voice was calm, placid. 'She's gone for keeps.' She leaned toward him, established her elbows in a comfortable position on the window ledge. 'Now what was it you said you was going to do if she tried to come back?'

He turned away without answering her and went inside the house. It could be that she was lying, had made the whole thing up to see what he was going to say. It was probably a trap, some kind of trap, and the quicker he found out what it was all about the better.

The instant he opened the door, he knew that Mrs. Hedges had told the truth. Min had gone. The living room was deserted, empty. She was never home at this time of day, and he looked around him wondering what it was that made him so sharply aware that she had gone; trying to determine what the difference was in the room.

The wall in front of him was bare, blank. That was it — that long empty space was where the table used to stand. He pushed the easy-chair over against the wall and stared at it, dissatisfied. It couldn't begin to take the place of the table; instead it emphasized the absence of the gleam and shine of the table's length; made him remember how majestic the claw feet had looked down near the floor. He hadn't realized how familiar he had become with all the detail of that table until it was gone. It was only natural he should miss it, because he had stared at it for hours on end when he sat there on the sofa.

He would put his desk there instead. That's where it was before Min moved in. Immediately he began pushing and pulling the desk across the room, and while he struggled with it he wondered why he bothered, tired as he was.

The room still didn't look right. The wood of the desk was dull oak. It was grimy. It had no shine to it. He shrugged his shoulders. In a coupla hours or so he would be used to it. Meanwhile, he'd go into the bedroom and see if she took anything that didn't belong to her.

375

He was turning away when his eyes fell on the torn envelopes on top of the desk. How could he have moved the desk and not noticed them? Where had they come from? He brushed his hand across his face in an effort to clear his mind because it was as cloudy as though it were full of cobwebs. He picked the letters up and looked at them. They were the same ones he was tearing up this morning when Min came back into the house, the letters that thieving little kid had brought to him last night. He'd stuck them in his pocket and forgotten about them until this morning.

Min had seen them, seen him tearing them, probably examined them after he went out of the house. And he didn't know where she'd gone, and as long as she was alive, he wasn't safe, because she undoubtedly thought he'd stolen them and she'd tell on him.

He should have killed her this morning, only he couldn't because of that cross, and he didn't know whether she'd really made the outline of it over her body or whether his eyes had been playing tricks on him again. He ought to get out of here in a hurry, go somewhere else where the police couldn't find him.

There were parts of an envelope over near the bedroom door, too. Or was it his imagination? No, they were partly torn and they were real. Two of them. Had they fallen off the desk when he was moving it or had Min dropped them and left them there, so he would know that she had seen them?

He walked up and down the room. There must be some way he could figure this thing out. This way he was left holding the bag and the kid would go free, and Lutie Johnson would go on sleeping with that white bastard. Only he mustn't think about that, he got all confused whenever he did, got so he couldn't do anything, couldn't even move, just like he was paralyzed.

After all, it was only Min's word against his. She was the one who got the key made and there couldn't be much longer to wait before the kid got caught. All he had to do was bide his time, and if Min said anything, why, he would say that she was the one who'd done the stealing.

That was it. He could see himself now in front of the Judge. 'I tell you that woman hated me.' He'd point right at her. He could see her eyes blink and she would crouch away from him all down in a heap, so that she looked like a bag of old clothes. 'Yes, sir, she hated me. And so she moved out and tried to get me in trouble. She was the one who done the stealin' and she done it because she was dead set on gettin' even with me. All she ever caused me was trouble. Used to take my money every time I turned around. I saw them letters for the first time when she left.'

That would be his story, and it was a good one. There wasn't any point in his getting himself all worked up. He was still safe, and there wasn't a thing she could do that would really harm him, and if she actually did start any trouble, why, his story would land her behind jail bars. He'd leave those torn letters right there where they were. They would show he was innocent, because if he'd been guilty, why, the first thing he would have done would have been to burn them up.

Now that was settled, he'd look in the bedroom
and see how she left things. With a woman like her
there was no telling what she'd take that wasn't hers.

He glanced around the room, carefully avoiding
the place where the cross had hung over the bed.
The furniture was all here. He looked in the closet.
It was empty. There was nothing — no bit of dust,
no worn-out shoe or old discarded hat — nothing to
indicate that Min had ever used it. The floor boards
were scrubbed so clean and white they re-emphasized
the closet's emptiness. The coat hangers dangling
from the hooks in the back of the closet had been
dusted. They looked as though they had never been
used.

'I oughtta put some clothes on 'em,' he said, aloud.

He turned away from the closet. The dresser was
bare and clean, too. Min's worn hairbrush and
toothless piece of comb had always been on the right-
hand side; and a long-handled celluloid mirror used
to be on the opposite cover. They were gone, and
so was the towel she kept on top of the dresser. The
bare, ugly wood was exposed.

He looked at himself in the mirror and then, with
no intention, no conscious effort, his eyes went toward the bed, hunted for the cross. He gave a start.
She had left it behind.

'God damn her,' he said. 'She left it here to haunt
me.'

He looked again. No. The cross was gone, but
while it hung there the walls had darkened with
grime and dust, so when it was removed its outline
was left clear and sharp on the wall — an outline the
exact size and shape of the cross itself.

It was everywhere in the room. He saw it again and again plain before his eyes. She had conjured him with it — conjured him and the apartment and gone. He left the room hastily and slammed the door shut behind him.

He walked restlessly through the living room, the kitchen, in and out of the bathroom, listening to the empty echo of his own footsteps. He could see the cross on the floor in front of his feet; it appeared suddenly over the kitchen stove; he had to look twice before he saw that it wasn't actually suspended from the center of the ceiling in the narrow confine of the bathroom.

Min had done this to him. And if he went on like this, seeing crosses all about him and never being certain whether they were real or figments of his imagination, he would go to pieces. But he didn't have to stay here. He paused in the middle of the living room to enumerate all the reasons why he should live somewhere else. He'd be away from the constant, malicious surveillance of Mrs. Hedges. He wouldn't have to see Lutie Johnson going back and forth to work with her head up in the air, never glancing in his direction, looking straight ahead as though he were a piece of dirt that would soil her eyes.

Nobody liked him much here, either. The folks weren't friendly. Well, when the white agent came around next week, he'd tell him he was quitting. The thought of leaving made him feel free. He could still have his revenge, too. Because wherever he went he'd make it a point to keep in with Bub and eventually the little bastard would get caught.

The Street

This place was too small, anyway. He'd find a house where the super's apartment looked out on the street, a place that had a front window where he could sit down when he had any spare time and see what was going on outside.

The thought of a front window made him suddenly hungry for the sight of people, eager to watch their movements. He would go outside and stand awhile. And he'd get well out of sight of Mrs. Hedges' window, around near the front of the building where she couldn't look at him.

It was mighty cold standing outside. The people who went by moved along at a brisk pace. He picked out young women and watched them closely, thinking that now that he was free, now that Min was gone, he could get himself any one of these girls who swung past. It was too bad it was winter and they had on thick concealing coats, because it was difficult to get an accurate picture of just what they looked like.

They moved past without glancing at him or, if they did glance at him, they looked away before he could catch their eyes. He shifted his attention across the street where a group of men talked and laughed together in the thin sunlight.

If he should join them, try to get into the conversation, they would stop talking. He'd never acquired the knack of small talk and after a while his silence would weigh on them so heavily that the conversation would slow up, grow halting, and then die completely. The men would drift away. It always happened.

Maybe if he could think of a story, something to hold their attention, they would stay put. It was a

jolly little group. He could catch phrases here and
there. 'Man, you ain't heard nothin' yet,' and then
the voice of the man who spoke would grow fainter
and the little group drew closer to the one who
talked.

He started talking to himself, softly, under his
breath, rehearsing what he would say. 'Man, you
ain't heard nothin' yet,' he said.

It sounded so good that he repeated it. 'Man, you
ain't heard nothin' yet. You oughtta work in one
of them houses' — he'd gesture toward this house.
'You don't never know what a fool woman is goin'
to think of next. Why, one time one of 'em come
runnin' down the stairs, hollerin' there was a mouse
in the dumb-waiter and what was I goin' to do about
it. Well, man, I told her ——'

He was so intent on the slow unfolding of his story
that he was completely unaware of the two white
men who had stopped in front of him until the
shorter of the two spoke.

'You the Super in this building?'

'What's it to you?' He hadn't had time to look
them over and he was instantly on the defensive because they had caught him off guard.

'Post-office investigators.' The pale sunlight
glinted on a badge.

This was what he'd been waiting for. His eyes
followed the badge until it disappeared inside the
man's coat pocket. 'Yeah,' he said. His voice was
thick, not quite intelligible, because there was a
beating inside his head from the blood pounding there
and the same beating was inside his throat, blurring
his voice. 'Yeah,' he repeated, 'I'm the Super.'

'Any of the tenants complain about letters being stolen?'

'Nope.' He had to be careful what he said. He had to go slow. Take it easy. 'I'm around too much for anybody to do any stealin'.'

'That's funny. There've been complaints from almost every house in the block except this one.' They were turning away.

'Say, listen,' he said. He talked slowly as though the idea had just come to him, and he was feeling it out in his mind. 'There's a kid lives in this house' — he indicated the building in back of him with a motion of his head. 'He's always runnin' in and out of the hallways up and down the street. I seen him every afternoon after school and wondered what he was doin'. Could be him.'

The men exchanged dubious glances. 'Might as well hang around. If you see him go past, call him over to you and put your hand on his shoulder.'

'Okay.'

Jones waited impatiently as he watched the kids swarming into the street. School was out and Bub ought to be coming along. Maybe he wouldn't come. Just when everything was fixed, he probably wouldn't come, just to spite him. That was the way everything turned out.

Then Bub came running through the crowded street. His school books were swinging from a strap. He ducked and dodged through the crowd, never allowing anyone to impede his progress, never slackening his pace, twisting, turning, coming swiftly.

'Hi, Bub,' Jones called.

The boy stopped, looked around, saw the Super.

'Hi, Supe,' he said eagerly. He walked over to him.
'How come you're out on this side today?'

'Air's better over here,' Jones said. Bub grinned
appreciatively. Jones placed a heavy hand on the
boy's shoulder, kept it there. Yes. The men were
watching. They were standing a little way off, near
the curb. 'You oughtta start work right now,' he
said.

'Okay, Captain.' Bub lifted his hand in salute.

He darted across the street, lingered on the sidewalk
for a moment, and then disappeared through the doorway of an apartment house.

The white men followed him. 'Listen,' the shorter
one said. 'If we catch this kid, we got to get him in
the car fast. These streets aren't safe.'

The other man nodded. They, too, disappeared
into the building. Jones, watching from across the
street, licked his lips while he waited. A few minutes later, he saw the men come out of the house with
Bub between them. One of them held a letter in his
hand. The white envelope showed up clearly. The
boy was crying, trying to pull away from them.

There was a short, sharp struggle when they
reached the sidewalk. Bub wriggled out of their
hands and for a fraction of a second it looked as
though he would get away.

The people passing stopped to stare. The men
lounging against the side of the building straightened
up. Their faces were alert, protesting, angry.

'Hey, look. They got a colored kid with them.'

The sight of the people edging toward the car
parked at the curb set the two men to moving with
speed, with haste, with a dispatch that landed Bub

on the seat between them, closed the car door. Then the car was off up the street.

'What happened?'

'What'd he do?'

'I dunno.'

'Who were they?'

'I dunno. Two strange white men.'

The car disappeared swiftly, not pausing for the red light at the corner. The people stared after it. The men who had been leaning against the building walked back to the building slowly, but they didn't resume their lounging positions. They stood up straight, silent, motionless, looking in the direction the car had taken.

Slowly, reluctantly, the people moved off. Finally the men leaned their weight against the building; other men resumed their lounging on the stoops. And each one was left with an uneasy sense of loss, of defeat. It made them break off suddenly in the midst of a sentence to look in the direction the car had taken. Even after it was dark, they kept staring up the street, disturbed by the memory of the boy between the two white men.

Long after the car had gone, Jones stayed in front of the building. That was that. Even Junto couldn't get him out of it. They had caught him red-handed and there wasn't any way of fixing such cases. The little bastard would do time in reform school sure as he was standing there. He'd fixed her good. He'd fixed her plenty good.

He couldn't move away from here now. He had to stay and watch her and laugh at her efforts to get Bub out of it. Maybe there was some way of letting her know he had a hand in it. The more he thought about it, the more excited he became. He'd stay on here and one of these days she'd ring his bell and say, 'I come down to call on you, Mr. Jones. It's kind of lonesome upstairs with the boy gone and everything.' And he'd slam the door shut in her face, but first he'd tell her what he thought of her and how he'd had a hand in fixing her.

'You — you ——' he began, but the rest of the words, the words saying exactly what he thought of her, refused to come out. He might as well go inside. His feet were tired. He felt tired all over from the excitement, from the satisfaction of having her where he wanted her. His head ached a little, too, because of the way the blood had pounded through it.

'Bub's kind of late today, ain't he?' Mrs. Hedges hailed him as he went past her window.

'I dunno,' he said gruffly. She couldn't know anything. He'd never talked to Bub out here on the street. And just now, when he talked with the white men, he had been well out of earshot. It was impossible for her to know what he had done.

Perhaps he had been right in the beginning and she could really read his mind. The thought frightened him so that he stumbled in his haste to get inside, away from that queer speculative look in her eyes. No matter what she knew, he couldn't leave here until he saw Lutie Johnson all broken up by what had happened to her kid. He just wouldn't stand outside on the street any more. That way he'd be safe, because it was a sure thing Mrs. Hedges couldn't read his mind through the walls of the house.

The Street

Mrs. Hedges stopped Lutie as she came home from work. 'Dearie,' she said, 'they're waitin' for you.'

'Who?' Lutie said.

'Detectives. Two of 'em. Upstairs.'

'What do they want?' she asked.

'It's about Bub, dearie.'

'What about him?' she said sharply. 'What about him?'

'Seems he's been taking letters from mail boxes. They caught him at it this afternoon, dearie.'

'Oh, my God!' she said.

And then she was running up the stairs, going up flight after flight, not pausing to catch her breath, not stopping on the landings, but running, running, running, without thought, senselessly, up and up the stairs, with her heart pounding as she forced herself to go faster and faster, pounding until there was a sharp pain in her chest. She didn't think as she ran, but she kept saying, Oh, my God! Oh, my God! Oh, my God! over and over in her mind.

The two men standing outside the door of her apartment talked as they waited.

'Every time I come in one of these dumps, I can't help thinking they're not fit for pigs to live in, let alone people.'

The other shrugged. 'So what?' They were both silent, and the one who had shrugged his shoulders continued, 'Mebbe you don't know that a white man ain't safe in one of these hallways by himself.'

'What's that got to do with it?'

'I dunno.'

They were silent again. And then one of them said,

'Wonder what the mother looks like,' idly, aimlessly, passing the time.

'Probably some drunken bitch. They usually are.'

'Hope she doesn't start screaming and bring the whole joint down on our ears.' He looked uneasily at the battered wood of the closed doors that lined the hall.

When Lutie reached the top floor, she was panting so that for a moment she couldn't talk. 'Where is he?' she demanded. She looked around the hall. 'Where is he? Where is he?' she asked hysterically.

'Take it easy, lady. Take it easy,' one of them said.

'Don't get excited. He's down at the Children's Shelter. You can see him tomorrow,' said the other, as he extended a long, white paper. It crackled as he placed it in her hand.

Then they left, jostling against each other in their haste to get down the stairs.

She tried to read what it said on the paper and the print wavered and changed shape, grew larger and then smaller. The stiff paper refused to stay still because her hands were shaking. She flattened it against the wall, and looked at it until she saw that it said something about a hearing at Children's Court.

Children's Court. Court. Court. Court meant lawyer. She had to get a lawyer. She started down the stairs, walking slowly, stiffly. Her knees refused to bend, her legs refused to go fast. Her legs felt brittle. As though whatever had made them work before had suddenly disappeared, and because it was gone they would break easily, just snap in two if she forced them to go quickly.

The Street

She had thought Bub would be waiting there at the top of the stairs. But he was in the Children's Shelter. She tried to visualize what kind of place it could be and gave up the effort.

Bub would go to reform school. She stopped on the fourth-floor landing to look at the thought, to examine it, to get used to it. Bub would go to reform school. And she reached out and touched the wall with her hand, then leaned the weight of her body against it because her legs were trembling, the muscles quivering, knees buckling.

Her thoughts were like a chorus chanting inside her head. The men stood around and the women worked. The men left the women and the women went on working and the kids were left alone. The kids burned lights all night because they were alone in small, dark rooms and they were afraid. Alone. Always alone. They wouldn't stay in the house after school because they were afraid in the empty, silent, dark rooms. And they should have been playing in wide stretches of green park and instead they were in the street. And the street reached out and sucked them up.

Yes. The women work and the kids go to reform school. Why do the women work? It's such a simple, reasonable reason. And just thinking about it will make your legs stop trembling like the legs of a winded, blown, spent horse.

The women work because the white folks give them jobs — washing dishes and clothes and floors and windows. The women work because for years now the white folks haven't liked to give black men jobs that paid enough for them to support their families. And finally it gets to be too late for some of them. Even wars don't change it. The men get out of the habit of working and the houses are old and gloomy and the walls press in. And the men go off, move on, slip away, find new women. Find younger women.

And what did it add up to? She pressed closer to the wall, ignoring the gray dust, the fringes of cobwebs heavy with grime and soot. Add it up. Bub, your kid — flashing smile, strong, straight back, sturdy legs, even white teeth, young, round face, smooth skin — he ends up in reform school because the women work.

Go on, she urged. Go all the way. Finish it. And the little Henry Chandlers go to YalePrincetonHarvard and the Bub Johnsons graduate from reform school into DannemoraSingSing.

And you helped push him because you talked to him about money. All the time money. And you wanted it because you wanted to move from this street, but in the beginning it was because you heard the rich white Chandlers talk about it. 'Filthy rich.' 'Richest country in the world.' 'Make it while you're young.'

Only you forgot. You forgot you were black and you underestimated the street outside here. And it never occurred to you that Bub might find those small dark rooms just as depressing as you did. And then, of course, there wasn't any other place for you to live except in a house like this one.

Then she was shouting, leaning against the wall, beating against it with her fists, and shouting, 'Damn it! Damn it!'

She leaned further against the wall, seemed almost to sink into it, and started to cry. The hall was full of the sound. The thin walls echoed and re-echoed with it two, three floors below and one floor above.

People coming home from work heard the sound when they started up the first flight of stairs. Their footsteps on the stairs, slowed down, hesitated, came to a full stop, for they were reluctant to meet such sorrow head-on. By the time they reached the fourth floor and actually saw her, their faces were filled with dread, for she was pounding against the wall with her fists — a soft, muted, dreadful sound. Her sobbing heard close to made them catch their breaths. She held the crisp, crackling white paper in her hand. And they recognized it for what it was — a symbol of doom — for the law and bad trouble were in the long white paper. They knew, for they had seen such papers before.

They turned their faces away from the sight of her, walked faster to get away from the sound of her. They hurried to close the doors of their apartments, but her crying came through the flimsy walls, followed them through the tight-shut doors.

All through the house radios went on full blast in order to drown out this familiar, frightening, unbearable sound. But even under the radios they could hear it, for they had started crying with her when the sound first assailed their ears. And now it had become a perpetual weeping that flowed through them, carrying pain and a shrinking from pain, so that the music and the voices coming from the radios couldn't possibly shut it out, for it was inside them.

The thin walls shivered and trembled with the

music. Upstairs, downstairs, all through the house, there was music, any kind of music, tuned up full and loud — jazz, blues, swing, symphony, surged through the house.

When Lutie finally stopped crying, her eyes were bloodshot, the lids swollen, sore to the touch. She drew away from the wall. She had to get a lawyer. He would be able to tell her what to do. There was one on Seventh Avenue, not far from the corner. She remembered seeing the sign.

The lawyer was reading an evening paper when Lutie entered his office. He stared at her, trying to estimate the fee he could charge, trying to guess her reason for coming. A divorce, he decided. All good-looking women invariably wanted divorces.

He was a little chagrined when he discovered he was wrong. He listened to her attentively, and all the time he was trying to figure out how much she would be able to pay. She had such a good figure it was difficult to tell whether her clothes were cheap ones or expensive ones. And then, as the case unfolded, he began to wonder why she didn't know that she didn't need a lawyer for a case like this one. He went on scribbling notes on a pad.

'Do you think you can do anything for him?' she asked.

'Sure' — he was still writing. 'It'll be simple. I'll paint a picture of you working hard, the kid left alone. He's only eight. Too young to have any moral sense. And then, of course, the street.'

'What do you mean?' she asked. 'What street?'

'Any street' — he waved his hand toward the window in an all-inclusive gesture. 'Any place where there's slums and dirt and poverty you find crime. So if the Judge is sympathetic, the kid'll go free. Maybe get a suspended sentence and be paroled in your care.' There was sudden hope in her face. 'My fee'll be two hundred dollars.' He saw anxiety, defeat, replace the hope, and added quickly, 'I can practically guarantee getting him off.'

'When do you have to have the money?'

'Three days from now at the latest.'

He escorted her to the door, and stood watching her walk down the street. Now why in hell doesn't she know she doesn't need a lawyer? He shrugged his shoulders. It was like picking two hundred bucks up in the street.

'And who am I to leave it there kicking around?' he said, aloud. He picked up the notes he had made, inserted them in an envelope which he placed in an inside pocket, and went back to reading the paper.

Chapter 17

'TWO HUNDRED DOLLARS. Two hundred dollars. Two hundred dollars.' Lutie repeated the words softly under her breath as she left the lawyer's office.

If it were in dollar bills and stacked up neatly, it would make a high mound of green-and-white paper. A bundle that size could buy divorces, beds with good springs and mattresses, warm coats, and pair after pair of the kind of shoes that wouldn't wear out in a hurry. It could send a kid to camp for a couple of summers. And she had to find a stack of bills like that to keep Bub out of reform school.

She had never known anyone who had that much money at one time. The people that she knew got money in driblets, driblets that barely covered rent and food and shoes and subway fare, but it never added up to two hundred dollars all at once and piled up in your hand.

Pop wouldn't have it. His only assets were an apartment filled with seedy roomers and shabby furniture and the rank smell of corn liquor. The corn liquor brought in occasional limp dollar bills. None of it added up to a pile of green-and-white paper that high. He wouldn't even know where or how to get it if she should ask him for it.

Neither would Lil. She had never seen a mound of money like that, never needed it because nickels and dimes for beer took care of all her wants, and she had always been able to find someone like Pop to provide her with a place to sleep and eat and keep her supplied with too tight housecoats.

She walked toward the small open space where St. Nicholas Avenue and Seventh Avenue ran together, forming a triangle which was flanked with benches. She sat on one of the benches and watched pieces of newspaper that were being blown by the wind. The ground under the benches was packed firm and hard and the newspapers skimmed over it, twisting against the trunks of the few trees, getting entangled with the legs of the benches. A large woman waddled past with a dog on a leash. Two children banged on the sides of a garbage can with a heavy stick. Otherwise the streets on both sides of the square were deserted.

The wind made her turn her coat collar up close around her throat. Even though it was cold, she could think better out here in the open. She didn't own anything that was worth two hundred dollars. A second-hand furniture dealer might offer ten dollars for the entire contents of her apartment lumped together. But she ought to make certain. Just around the corner on 116th Street there was a group of second-hand stores; their wares edging out to the sidewalk. She could at least inquire as to the price they were asking for things.

It would be a waste of time. All of it put together — battered studio couch, rungless chairs, wobbly kitchen table, small scarred radio — wouldn't bring a cent more than ten dollars.

She thought of the girls who worked in the office with her She didn't know any of them intimately. She didn't really have time to get to know them well, because she went right home after work and there was only a forty-five-minute lunch period. She always took a sandwich along for lunch, and when the weather was good she ate it on a park bench, and when it was rainy or snowing she stayed inside, eating in the rest room and there were confused and incomplete snatches of conversation and that was all.

None of them would have two hundred dollars even if she knew them well enough to ask them. By the time the income-tax deductions and the war-bond deductions were taken out, there wasn't much left to take home. Most of them cashed the bonds as soon as they got them just like she did, because it was the only way they could manage on the small pay.

Remembering bits of the conversation she had heard in the rest room, she knew they had husbands and children and sick mothers and unemployed fathers and young sisters and brothers, so that going to an occasional movie was the only entertainment they could afford. They went home and listened to the radio and read part of a newspaper, mostly the funnies and the latest murders; and then they cleaned their apartments and washed clothes and cooked food, and then it was time to go to bed because they had to get up early the next morning.

There ought to be more than that to living, she thought, resentfully. Perhaps living in a city the size of New York wasn't good for people, because you had to spend all your time working to pay for the place where you lived and it took all the rest of the hours in the day to keep the place clean and fix food, and there was never any money left over. Certainly it wasn't a good place for children.

If she had been able to get that job singing at the Casino, this wouldn't have happened. And for the first time in weeks she thought of Boots Smith. He would have two hundred dollars or would know where to get it. She started to get up from the bench and sat back down again. She didn't have any reason to believe he would lend it to her just because she needed it. It would take her a long time to pay him back and certainly she wasn't a very good risk.

Half-angrily she decided he would lend it to her because she would make him. It didn't matter that she had neither seen nor heard from him since the night he had told her she wouldn't be paid for singing. It didn't matter at all. He was going to lend her two hundred dollars because it was the only way to keep Bub from going to reform school and he was the only person she knew who could lay hands on that much money at one time.

She went into the cigar store across the street, thumbed through the phone book, half-fearful that he wouldn't have a telephone, or if he had one that it wouldn't be listed. There it was. He lived on Edgecombe Avenue. She memorized the address, thinking that she would call him and then go up there now, tonight, because she didn't want to tell him what she wanted over the phone. It was best to go and see him and if he looked as though he were going to refuse, she could talk faster and harder.

She dialed the number and no one answered. There was only the continual insistent ringing of the phone. He had to be home. She simply would not hang up. The phone rang and rang and rang.

'Yeah?' a voice said suddenly; and for a moment she was too startled to reply.

The voice repeated, 'Yeah?' impatiently.

'This is Lutie Johnson,' she said.

'Who?' His voice was flat, indifferent, sleepy.

'Lutie Johnson,' she repeated. And his voice came alive, 'Oh, hello, baby. Christ! where you been?'

He didn't understand what she was saying and she had to begin all over again, going slowly, so slowly that she thought she sounded like a record that had got stuck on a victrola. She said she had to see him. It was very important. She had to see him right away. Because it was very important. And instantly he said, 'Sure, baby. I been wanting to talk to you. Come on up. It's apartment 3 J.'

'I'll be right there. I'll take the bus,' she said. And thought again that she sounded like a victrola, but not one that had got stuck, like one that had run down, that needed winding.

'Where are you now?'

'116th Street and Seventh Avenue.'

'Okay, baby. I'll be waitin' for you.'

It took her a few minutes to get the receiver back on the hook. She made futile, fumbling dabs at it, missing it because her hands were taut and tense and unmanageable.

She waited impatiently for the bus and when it came and she got on it, it seemed to her it crawled up Seventh Avenue; and each time it halted for a red light, she could feel her muscles tighten up. She tried to erase the hopes and fears that kept creeping into her mind and couldn't. Finally the bus turned and crossed the bridge, and she remembered that it didn't stop at Edgecombe Avenue. If she wasn't careful, she'd ride beyond it and have to walk back a long way.

But there was no mistaking the apartment house where Boots lived. It loomed high above all the other buildings and could be seen for a long distance. She pulled the stopcord hastily and got off the bus.

As she walked toward the awninged entrance, she recalled the stories she'd heard about the fabulous rents paid by the people who lived here. She remembered when Negroes had first moved into this building and how Pop had rattled the pages of the paper he was reading and muttered, 'Must have gold toilet seats to charge that much money.'

Her only reaction to the sight of the potted shrubs in the doorway and to the uniformed doorman was that if Boots could afford to live here, then lending her two hundred dollars would present no problem to him.

Inside there was a wide, high-ceilinged hall. An elevator with gleaming red doors opened into it.

The Street

The elevator boy took her up to the third floor, and in answer to her inquiry said, 'It's the fourth door down the hall,' before he closed the elevator doors.

She pressed the bell harder than she'd intended and drew her hand away quickly, expecting to hear the loud shrilling of a bell. Instead there was the soft sound of chimes and Boots opened the door. His shirt was open at the throat, the sleeves rolled up.

'Sure is good to see you, baby,' he said. 'Come on in.'

'Hello,' she said, and walked past him into a small foyer. The rug on the floor was thick. It swallowed up the sound of her footsteps.

The living room was a maze of floor lamps and overstuffed chairs. The same kind of thick, engulfing carpet covered the floor. Logs in an imitation fireplace at the far end of the room gave off an orange-red glow from a concealed electric light. The winking light from the logs was like an evil eye and she looked away from it. Ponderously carved iron candlesticks flanked the mantel.

She couldn't go on standing here, taking an inventory of the room. She had to tell him what she wanted. Now that she was here, it was difficult to get started. There was nothing encouraging about his appearance and she had forgotten how tough and unscrupulous his face was.

'Let me take your coat,' he said.

'Oh, no. I'm not going to stay that long. I can't.'

'Well, sit down anyway.' He sat on the arm of the sofa, one leg dangling, his arms folded across his chest, his face completely expressionless. 'Christ!'

he said. 'I almost forgot what a warm-looking babe you are.'

She sat down at the far end of the sofa, trying to think of a way to start.

'What's on your mind, baby?' he said.

'It's about my son — Bub ——'

'You got a kid?' he interrupted.

'Yes. He's eight years old.' She talked swiftly, afraid that if she stopped, if he interrupted her again, she wouldn't be able to finish. She didn't look at him while she told him about the letters Bub had stolen and the lawyer and the two hundred dollars.

'Go on, baby,' he said impatiently when she paused.

His face had changed while she talked to him. Ordinarily his expression was unreadable; now he looked as though he had suddenly seen something he had been waiting for, seen it spread right out in front of him, and it was something that he wanted badly. She puzzled over it while she repeated what the lawyer had said and then decided the expression on his face was due to surprise. He hadn't known about Bub. She had forgotten that she hadn't told him she had a child.

'Can you let me have it? The two hundred dollars?' she asked.

'Why, sure, baby,' he said easily. 'I haven't got that much on me right now. But if you come by here tomorrow night about this same time I'll have it for you. Make it a little later than this. About nine.'

'I can't ever thank you,' she said, standing up. 'And I'll pay you back. It'll take a little while, but you'll get every cent of it back.'

'That's all right. Glad to do it.' He stayed on

400

the arm of the sofa. 'You ain't going so soon, are you?'

'Yes. I have to.'

'How about a drink?'

'No, thanks. I've got to go.'

He walked to the door with her, held it open for her. 'See you tomorrow night, baby,' he said, and closed the door gently.

The thought that it had been very easy stayed with her all the way home. It wasn't until she opened the door of her apartment and was groping for the light in the hall that it occurred to her it had been too easy, much too easy.

She turned on all the lights in the house — the ceiling lights in the bedroom and the bathroom, the lamp in the living room. The flood of light helped thrust away the doubts that assailed her, but it did nothing to relieve the emptiness in the rooms. Because Bub wasn't sprawled in the middle of the studio couch, all the furniture had diminished in size, shrinking against the wall — the couch, the big chair, the card table.

The lights made no impression on the quiet in the apartment either and she switched on the radio. Bub usually listened to one of those interminable spy hunts or cowboy stories, and at night the living room was filled with the tumult of a chase, loud music and sudden shouts. And Bub would yell, 'Look out! He's in back of you.'

This lavish use of light is senseless, she thought. You used to lecture him about leaving lights on at night because the bill would be so big you couldn't pay it. He left them burning because he was frightened, just like you are now. And she wondered if he was afraid now in that strange place — the Children's Shelter — and hoped there were lights that burned all night, so that if he woke up he could see where he was. It was easy to picture him waking in the dark, discovering that he wasn't here where he belonged, and then feeling as though he had lost himself or that the room he knew so well had changed about him while he slept.

She sat down near the radio, tried to listen to a news broadcast, but her thoughts kept twisting and turning about Bub. What would happen to him after this was over? The lawyer had assured her he could get him paroled in her care. But he would have a police record, and if he played hookey from school two or three times and broke a window with a ball and got into a fight, he would end up in reform school, anyway.

Even his teachers at school would have a faint but unmistakable prejudice against him as a juvenile delinquent and they would refuse to overlook any slight infraction of the rules because he had established himself in their minds as a potential criminal. And in a sense they were right, because he didn't have much chance before living in this street so crowded with people and children. He had even less now.

They would have to move away from here. She would get a job cooking for a family that lived in the country. Unfortunately, the idea didn't appeal to her. She knew what it would be like. He would become 'the cook's little boy,' and expected to meet some fantastic standard of behavior. He would have to be silent when he was bursting to talk and to make noise. 'Because Mrs. Brentford or Mrs. Gaines or Mrs. Somebody Else has guests for dinner.'

She didn't want him to grow up like that — eating hurried meals at a kitchen table while he listened to 'the family' enjoying a leisurely meal in a near-by dining room; learning young the unmistakable difference between front-door and back-door and all that the words implied; being constantly pushed aside because when he came home from school running over with energy, she would be fixing salads and desserts for dinner and only have time to say, 'Get a glass of milk out of the icebox and go outside and play and be quiet.'

It was quite possible that he wouldn't have much opportunity for playing. Lil had painted a grim picture of what it could be like, based on the experience of one of her friends. 'That poor Myrtle said they counted practically every mouthful that poor boy child of hers ate. And wanted him to work, besides. Little light tasses the madam said like cleaning the car and mowing the lawn.' Lil had taken a big swallow of beer before continuing, 'And Myrtle and that poor child of hers had to sleep together because the madam said, well, of course, you all wouldn't expect me to buy another bed and he's small and don't take up much room.'

The pay would be miserable because of Bub, and the people she worked for would subtly or pointedly, depending on what kind of folks they were, demand more work from her because they would feel they were conferring a special favor by permitting his presence in their home.

Perhaps it wouldn't be like that. Even if it was, it was the best she could do for him. Somebody else's kitchen was a painfully circumscribed area for a kid to grow up in, but at least it would be safe. She would be with him all the time. He wouldn't come home to a silent, empty house.

She switched off the radio, put out all the lights except the one in the bedroom, thinking that tomorrow she wouldn't go to work. Instead, she would go to the Children's Shelter and see Bub.

While she undressed, she tried to remember if she had been afraid of the dark when she was Bub's age. No, because Granny had always been there, her rocking chair part of the shadow, part of the darkness, making it known and familiar. She was always humming. It was a faint sound, part and parcel of the darkness. Going to sleep with that warm sound clinging to your ears made fear impossible. You simply drifted off to the accompaniment of a murmured 'Sleepin', Sleepin', Sleepin' in the arms of the Lord.' And then the gentle creak of the rocking chair.

She had never been alone in the house after school. Granny was always home. No matter what time she reached the house, she knew in the back of her mind that Granny was there and it gave her a sense of security that Bub had never known.

When there was no one in a house with you, it took on a strange emptiness. This bedroom, for instance, was strangely empty. The furniture took up the same amount of room, for she bumped her knee against the corner of the bed. But the light in the ceiling reached only a little way into the living room. She stared at the shadows beyond the brief expanse of light. She knew the exact size of that room, knew the position of every piece of furniture, yet it would be easy to believe that beyond the door, just beyond that oblong of light, there stretched a vast expanse of space — unknown and therefore dangerous.

After she turned out the light and got into bed, she kept listening for sounds, waiting to hear the stir of some movement from the shadows that enveloped the bed and turning her head from side to side in an effort to make out the familiar outline of the furniture.

When people are alone, they are always afraid of the dark, she thought. They keep trying to see where they are and the blackness around them keeps them from seeing. It was like trying to look into the future. There was no way of knowing what threat lurked just beyond tomorrow or the next day, and the not knowing is what makes everyone afraid.

She woke up at seven o'clock and jumped out of bed, reaching for her dressing-gown and thinking that today they had assembly at school and she had forgotten to iron a white shirt for Bub and she would have to hurry so he wouldn't be late.

Then she remembered that Bub was at the Children's Shelter. She wasn't going to work today. She was going to see him.

It was her fault he'd got into this trouble. No matter how she looked at it, it was still her fault. It was always the mother's fault when a kid got into trouble, because it meant she'd failed the kid somewhere. She had wanted him to grow up fine and strong and she'd failed him all the way along the line.

She had been trying to get enough money so that she could have a good place for him to live, and in trying she'd put so much stress on money that he'd felt impelled to help her and started stealing letters out of mail boxes.

Lately she had been so filled with anger and resentment and hate that she had pushed him farther and farther away from her. He didn't have any business in the Children's Shelter. He didn't have any business going to court. She was the one they ought to have arrested and taken to court.

Pulling the cord of the robe tight around her waist with an angry jerk, she went into the kitchen where she put coffee into an enamel pot on the stove. While she waited for it to boil, she raised the window shade and looked out. It was a dark, grim morning. The blackness outside pressed against the panes of glass, and she drew the shade hastily.

She scrambled eggs and made toast, but once she was seated at the kitchen table she thrust the food away from her. The very sight and smell of it was unpleasant. The coffee didn't go down her throat easily; it kept sticking as though an ever-tightening band were wrapped around her neck, constricting her throat.

Getting dressed for the trip to the Center was a slow process, for she found herself pausing frequently to examine all kinds of unrelated ideas and thoughts that kept bobbing up in her mind. Pop had never got anywhere in life and certainly Lil hadn't ever achieved anything, but neither one of them had ever been in jail. Perhaps it was better to take things as they were and not try to change them. But who wouldn't

have wanted to live in a better house than this one
and who wouldn't have struggled to get out of it? —
and the only way that presented itself was to save
money. So it was a circle, and she could keep on
going around it forever and keep on ending up in the
same place, because if you were black and you lived
in New York and you could only pay so much rent,
why, you had to live in a house like this one.

And while you were out working to pay the rent
on this stinking, rotten place, why, the street outside
played nursemaid to your kid. The street did more
than that. It became both mother and father and
trained your kid for you, and it was an evil father and
a vicious mother, and, of course, you helped the
street along by talking to him about money.

The last thing she did before she left the apartment
was to put the stiff, white paper in her pocketbook.
And on the subway she was so aware of its presence
that she felt she could see its outline through the
imitation leather of the bag.

It was just nine o'clock when she got off the subway. She asked the man in the change booth which
exit was nearest the Shelter.

'You shoulda took another line,' he said. 'Walk
five blocks that way' — he pointed to the right-hand
exit. 'And then two down.'

The crosstown blocks were long. She started walking rapidly and then, tired by the effort, she slowed
down. She had never been in this section of the city
before. The streets were clean and well-swept, and
the houses and stores she passed had a shine and a
polish on them. Immediately she thought of Bub
leaning out of the kitchen window playing a game

that involved the inert dogs sleeping amidst the rubbish in the yard below.

This was, by comparison, a safe, secure, clean
world. And looking at it, she thought it must be
rather pleasant to be able to live anywhere you
wanted to, just so you could pay the rent, instead of
having to find out first whether it was a place where
colored people were permitted to live.

The Children's Shelter was housed in a tall brick
building. And as she approached it, she kept thinking, But it can't be full of children. She walked up
the steps, conscious of a hollow, empty feeling in the
pit of her stomach. A uniformed guard stopped her
just inside the door.

'I came to see my son,' she said. She drew the stiff
white paper from her pocketbook. 'He was brought
here yesterday.'

He gestured toward a waiting room just off the
hall. It was a large room filled with people, and the
instant she entered it she was assailed by the stillness
in the room.

The gray-haired woman behind a desk marked
'Information' asked for her name and address, riffled
through a thick card file.

'His case comes up Friday,' the woman said. 'If
you care to wait, you can see him for a few minutes
this morning.'

Lutie sat down near the back of the room. It was
filled with colored women, sitting in huddled-over
positions. They sat quietly, not moving. Their
patient silence filled the room, made her uneasy.
Why were all of them colored? Was it because the
mothers of white children had safe places for them to

play in, because the mothers of white children didn't have to work?

She had been wrong. There were some white mothers, too — three foreign-looking women near the door; a gray-haired woman just two seats ahead, her hair hanging in a lank curtain about the sides of her face; a tall, bony woman up near the front who kept clutching at the arms of her fur coat, a coat shiny from wear; and over on the side a young, too thin blond girl holding a small baby in her arms.

They were sitting in the same shrinking, huddled positions. Perhaps, she thought, we're all here because we're all poor. Maybe it doesn't have anything to do with color.

Lutie folded her hands in her lap. Fifteen minutes went by. Suddenly she straightened her shoulders. She had been huddled over like all these other waiting women. And she knew now why they sat like that. Because we're like animals trying to pull all the soft, quivering tissue deep inside of us away from the danger that lurks in a room like this, and the silence helps build up the threat of danger.

The room absorbed sound. She couldn't hear even a faint murmur of traffic or of voices from the street outside. As she waited in the silent room, she felt as though she were bearing the uneasy burden of the sum total of all the troubles these women had brought with them. All of us started with a little piece of trouble, she thought, and then bit by bit more was added until finally it grew so great it pushed us into this room.

When the guard finally escorted her to the small room where Bub waited, she had begun to believe the

409

silence and the troubled waiting that permeated the room had a smell — a distinct odor that filled her nose until it was difficult for her to breathe.

Bub had grown smaller. He was so little, so forlorn, so obviously frightened, that she got down on her knees and pulled him close to her.

'Darling,' she said softly. 'Oh, darling.'

'Mom, I thought you'd never come,' he said.

'You didn't think any such thing,' she said, patting the side of his face. 'You know you didn't really think that.'

'No,' he said slowly. 'I guess I really didn't. I guess I knew you'd come as soon as you could. Only it seemed like an awful long time. Can we go home now?'

'No. Not yet. You have to stay here until Friday.'

'That's so long,' he wailed.

'No, it isn't. I'll be back tomorrow. And the next day. And the next day. And then it'll be Friday.'

Then the guard was back, and she was going out of the building. She hadn't asked Bub anything about the letters or if he'd been frightened. There were so many things she hadn't said to him. Perhaps it was just as well, because the most important thing was for him to know that she loved him and that she would be coming to see him.

There was a whole day to be got through. And once she was back in the apartment, time seemed to stretch out endlessly in front of her. She scrubbed the kitchen floor and cleaned out the cupboards over the sink. While she was working, she kept thinking of all the reasons why Boots might not have the money for her tonight.

She started to wash the windows in the living room. She sat on the window sill, her long legs inside the room, the upper part of her body outside. At first she rubbed the panes briskly and then stopped.

It was so deadly quiet. She kept listening to the silence, hoping to hear some sound that would destroy it. It was the same kind of stillness that had been in the waiting room at the Shelter.

She polished one pane of glass over and over. The soft sound of the cloth did nothing to disturb the pool of silence that filled the apartment. She turned to look at the blank windows of the apartment houses that faced her windows. They revealed no sign of life. In the distance she could hear the faint, tinny sound of a radio. The sky overhead was dark gray. A damp cold wind rattled the windows, tugged at the sleeves of the cotton dress she was wearing.

Suppose that for some reason Boots didn't have the money for her tonight? Doubt grew and spread in her, alarming her so that she stopped washing the windows, went inside the room. She collected the window-washing equipment, poured the water out of the enamel pan she had been using, and stood watching it go down the sink drain. It was black and syrupy, thick with the grime and dirt from the windows. She put the window cloths to soak in the set tub.

He would either give her the money or he wouldn't. If he didn't, she would have to figure out some other way of getting it. There was no point in her worrying about it. And as long as she stayed alone in these small rooms, she would worry and wonder and the knot of tension inside her would keep growing and her throat would keep constricting like it was doing now. She swallowed hard. Her throat felt as though the opening were growing smaller all the time. It was smaller now than it had been this morning when she tried to drink the coffee.

If she went to the movies, it would take her mind away from these fears that kept closing in on her. But once inside the theater, she was abruptly dismayed. As her eyes became adjusted to the dimness, she saw that there were only a few seats occupied. She deliberately sat down near a little group of people — a protective little group in back of her and in front of her.

And the picture didn't make sense. It concerned a technicolor world of bright lights and vast beautiful rooms; a world where the only worry was whether the heroine in a sequined evening gown would eventually get the hero in a top hat and tails out of the clutches of a red-headed female spy who lolled on wide divans dressed in white velvet dinner suits.

The glitter on the screen did nothing to dispel her sense of panic. She kept thinking it had nothing to do with her, because there were no dirty little rooms, no narrow, crowded streets, no children with police records, no worries about rent and gas bills. And she had brought that awful creeping silence in here with her. It crouched along the aisles, dragged itself across the rows of empty seats. She began to think of it as something that was coming at her softly on its hands and knees, coming nearer and nearer to her aisle by aisle.

She left in the middle of the picture. Outside the theater she paused, filled with a vast uneasiness, a restlessness that made going home out of the question. There was a beauty parlor at the corner. She would get a shampoo that she couldn't afford, but she would have people around her and it would use up a lot of time.

Walking toward the shop, she tried to figure out what was the matter with her. She was afraid of something. What was it? She didn't know. It wasn't just fear of what would happen to Bub. It was something else. She was smelling out evil as Granny said. An old, old habit. Old as time itself.

It was quiet in the beauty shop except for the noise that the manicurist made. She was sitting in the front window, chewing gum, and the gum made a sharp, cracking sound. It was the only sound in the place.

The hairdresser, normally talkative, was for some reason in an uncommunicative mood. She rotated Lutie's scalp with strong fingers and said nothing. It was so quiet that the awful stillness Lutie had found in the Shelter settled in the shop. It had followed her in here from the movies and it was sitting down in the booth next to her. She shivered.

'Somep'n must have walked over your grave' — the hairdresser looked at her in the mirror as she spoke.

And even under the words Lutie heard the stillness. It was crouched down in the next booth. It was waiting for her to leave. It would walk down the street with her and into the apartment. Or it might leave the shop when she did, but not go down the street at all, but somehow seep into the apartment before she got there, so that when she opened the door it would be there. Formless. Shapeless. Waiting. Waiting.

Chapter 18

I T WAS BEGINNING TO SNOW when Lutie
left the beauty parlor. The flakes were fine,
small; barely recognizable as snow. More like
rain, she thought, except that rain didn't sting one's
face like these sharp fragments.

In a few more minutes it would be dark. The outlines of the buildings were blurred by long shadows.
Lights in the houses and at the street corners were
yellow blobs that made no impression on the ever-
lengthening shadows. The small, fine snow swirled
past the yellow lights in a never-ending rapid dancing
that was impossible to follow and the effort made
her dizzy.

The noise and confusion in the street were pleasant
after the stillness that hung about the curtained

booths of the beauty shop. Buses and trucks roared to a stop at the corners. People coming home from work jostled against her. There was the ebb and flow of talk and laughter; punctuated now and then by the sharp scream of brakes.

The children swarming past her added to the noise and the confusion. They were everywhere — rocking back and forth on the traffic stanchions in front of the post-office, stealing rides on the backs of the crosstown buses, drumming on the sides of ash cans with broomsticks, sitting in small groups in doorways, playing on the steps of the houses, writing on the sidewalk with colored chalk, bouncing balls against the sides of the buildings. They turned a deaf ear to the commands shrilling from the windows all up and down the street, 'You Tommie, Jimmie, Billie, can't you see it's snowin'? Come in out the street.'

The street was so crowded that she paused frequently in order not to collide with a group of children, and she wondered if these were the things that Bub had done after school. She tried to see the street with his eyes and couldn't because the crap game in progress in the middle of the block, the scraps of obscene talk she heard as she passed the poolroom, the tough young boys with their caps on backward who swaggered by, were things that she saw with the eyes of an adult and reacted to from an adult's point of view. It was impossible to know how this street looked to eight-year-old Bub. It may have appealed to him or it may have frightened him.

There was a desperate battle going on in front of the house where she lived. Kids were using bags of garbage from the cans lined up along the curb as ammunition. The bags had broken open, covering the sidewalk with litter, filling the air with a strong, rancid smell.

Lutie picked her way through orange skins, coffee grounds, chicken bones, fish bones, toilet paper, potato peelings, wilted kale, skins of baked sweet potatoes, pieces of newspaper, broken gin bottles, broken whiskey bottles, a man's discarded felt hat, an old pair of pants. Perhaps Bub had taken part in this kind of warfare, she thought, even as she frowned at the rubbish under her feet; possibly a battle would have appealed to some unsatisfied spirit of adventure in him, so that he would have joined these kids, over-looking the stink of the garbage in his joy in the conflict just as they were doing.

Mrs. Hedges was leaning far out of her window, urging the contestants on.

'That's right, Jimmie,' Mrs. Hedges cried. 'Hit him on the head.' And then as the bag went past its mark, 'Aw, shucks, boy, what's the matter with your aim?'

She caught sight of Lutie and knowing that she was home earlier than when she went to work, immediately deduced that she had been somewhere to see Bub or see about him. 'Did you see Bub?' she asked.

'Yes. For a little while.'

'Been to the beauty parlor, ain't you?' Mrs. Hedges studied the black curls shining under the skull cap on Lutie's head. 'Looks right nice,' she said.

She leaned a little farther out of the window.

'Bub being in trouble you probably need some money.
A friend of mine, a Mr. Junto — a very nice white
gentleman, dearie ——'

Her voice trailed off because Lutie turned away
abruptly and disappeared through the apartment
house door. Mrs. Hedges scowled after her. After
all, if you needed money you needed money and why
anyone would act like that when it was offered to
them she couldn't imagine. She shrugged her shoulders and turned her attention back to the battle going
on under her window.

As Lutie climbed the stairs, she deliberately accentuated the clicking of the heels of her shoes on the
treads because the sharp sound helped relieve the hard
resentment she felt; it gave expression to the anger
flooding through her.

At first, she merely fumed at the top of her mind
about a white gentleman wanting to sleep with a
colored girl. A nice white gentleman who's a little
cold around the edges wants to sleep with a nice warm
colored girl. All of it nice — nice gentleman, nice
girl; one's colored and the other's white, so it's a
colored girl and a white gentleman.

Then she began thinking about Junto — specifically
about Junto. Junto hadn't wanted her paid for singing. Mrs. Hedges knew Junto. Boots Smith worked
for Junto. Junto's squat-bodied figure, as she had
seen it reflected in the sparkling mirror in his Bar and
Grill, established itself in her mind; and the anger in
her grew and spread directing itself first against Junto
and Mrs. Hedges and then against the street that had
reached out and taken Bub and then against herself
for having been partly responsible for Bub's stealing.

Inside her apartment she stood motionless, assailed by the deep, uncanny silence that filled it. It was a too sharp contrast to the noise in the street. She turned on the radio and then turned it off again, because she kept listening, straining to hear something under the sound of the music.

The creeping, silent thing that she had sensed in the theater, in the beauty parlor, was here in her living room. It was sitting on the lumpy studio couch.

Before it had been formless, shapeless, a fluid moving mass — something disembodied that she couldn't see, could only sense. Now, as she stared at the couch, the thing took on form, substance. She could see what it was.

It was Junto. Gray hair, gray skin, short body, thick shoulders. He was sitting on the studio couch. The blue-glass coffee table was right in front of him. His feet were resting, squarely, firmly, on the congoleum rug.

If she wasn't careful she would scream. She would start screaming and never be able to stop, because there wasn't anyone there. Yet she could see him and when she didn't see him she could feel his presence. She looked away and then looked back again. Sometimes he was there when she looked and sometimes he wasn't.

She stared at the studio couch until she convinced herself there had never been anyone there. Her eyes were playing tricks on her because she was upset, nervous. She decided that a warm bath would make her relax.

But in the tub she started trembling so that the

water was agitated. Perhaps she ought to phone Boots and tell him that she wouldn't come tonight. Perhaps by tomorrow she would be free of this mounting, steadily increasing anger and this hysterical fear that made her see things that didn't exist, made her feel things that weren't there.

Yet less than half an hour later she was dressing, putting on the short, flared black coat; pulling on a pair of white gloves. As she thrust her hands into the gloves, she wondered when she had made the decision to go anyway; what part of her mind had already picked out the clothes she would wear, even to these white gloves, without her ever thinking about it consciously. Because, of course, if she didn't go tonight, Boots might change his mind.

When she rang the bell of Boots' apartment, he opened the door instantly as though he had been waiting for her.

'Hello, baby,' he said, grinning. 'Sure glad you got here. I got a friend I want you to meet.'

Only two of the lamps in the living room were lit. They were the tall ones on each side of the davenport. They threw a brilliant light on the squat white man sitting there. He got up when he saw Lutie and stood in front of the imitation fireplace, leaning his elbow on the mantel.

Lutie stared at him, not certain whether this was Junto in the flesh or the imaginary one that had been on the studio couch in her apartment. She closed her eyes and then opened them and he was still there, standing by the fireplace. His squat figure partly blocked out the orange-red glow from the electric logs She turned her head away and then looked toward him. He was still there, standing by the fireplace.

Boots established him as Junto in the flesh. 'Mr. Junto, meet Mrs. Johnson. Lutie Johnson.'

Lutie nodded her head. A figure in a mirror turned thumbs down and as he gestured the playground for Bub vanished, the nice new furniture disappeared along with the big airy rooms. 'A nice white gentleman.' 'Need any extra money.' She looked away from him, not saying anything.

'I want to talk to you, baby,' Boots said. 'Come on into the bedroom' — he pointed toward a door, started toward it, turned back and said, 'We'll be with you in a minute, Junto.'

Boots closed the bedroom door, sat down on the edge of the bed, leaning his head against the headboard.

'If you'll give me the money now, I'll be able to get it to the lawyer before he closes his office tonight,' she said abruptly. This room was like the living room, it had too many lamps in it, and in addition there were too many mirrors so that she saw him reflected on each of the walls — his legs stretched out, his expression completely indifferent. There was the same soft, sound-absorbing carpet on the floor.

'Take your coat off and sit down, baby,' he said lazily.

She shook her head. She didn't move any farther into the room, but stood with her back against the door, aware that there was no sound from the living room where Junto waited. She had brought that awful silence in here with her.

'I can't stay,' she said sharply. 'I only came to get the money.'

'Oh, yes — the money,' he said. He sounded as though he had just remembered it. 'You can get the money easy, baby. I figured it out.' He half-closed his eyes. 'Junto's the answer. He'll give it to you Just like that' — he snapped his fingers.

He paused for a moment as though he were waiting for her to say something, and when she made no comment he continued: 'All you got to do is be nice to him. Just be nice to him as long as he wants and the two hundred bucks is yours. And bein' nice to Junto pays off better than anything else I know.'

She heard what he said, knew exactly what he meant, and her mind skipped over his words and substituted other words. She was back in the big shabby ballroom at the Casino, straining to hear a thin thread of music that kept getting lost in the babble of voices, in the clink of glasses, in the bursts of laughter, so that she wasn't certain the music was real. Sometimes it was there and then again it was drowned out by the other sounds.

The faint, drifting melody went around and under the sound of Boots' voice and the words that he had spoken then blotted out what he had just said.

'Baby, this is just experience. Be months before you can earn money at it.'

'Nothing happened, baby. What makes you think something happened?'

'I don't have all the say-so. The guy who owns the Casino — guy named Junto — says you ain't ready yet.'

'Christ! he owns the joint.'

The guy named Junto owned the Bar and Grill, too. Evidently his decision that she wasn't to be paid for singing had been based on his desire to sleep with her; and he had concluded that, if she had to continue living in that house where his friend Mrs. Hedges lived or in one just like it, she would be a push-over.

And now the same guy, named Junto, was sitting outside on a sofa, just a few feet away from this door, and she thought, I would like to kill him. Not just because he happens to be named Junto, but because I can't even think straight about him or anybody else any more. It is as though he were a piece of that dirty street itself, tangible, close at hand, within reach.

She could still hear that floating, drifting tune. It was inside her head and she couldn't get it out. Boots was staring at her, waiting for her to say something, waiting for her answer. He and Junto thought they knew what she would say. If she hummed that fragment of melody aloud, she would get rid of it. It was the only way to make it disappear; otherwise it would keep going around and around in her head. And she thought, I must be losing my mind, wanting to hum a tune and at the same time thinking about killing that man who is sitting, waiting, outside.

Boots said, 'Junto's a good guy. You'll be surprised how much you'll take to him.'

The sound of her own voice startled her. It was hoarse, loud, furious. It contained the accumulated hate and the accumulated anger from all the years of seeing the things she wanted slip past her without her ever having touched them.

She shouted, 'Get him out of here! Get him out of here! Get him out of here quick!'

And all the time she was thinking, Junto has a brick in his hand. Just one brick. The final one needed to complete the wall that had been building up around her for years, and when that one last brick was shoved in place, she would be completely walled in.

'All right. All right. Don't get excited.' Boots got up from the bed, pushed her away from the door and went out, slamming it behind him.

'Sorry, Junto,' Boots said. 'She's mad as hell. No use your waiting.'

'I heard her,' Junto said sourly. 'And if this is something you planned, you'd better unplan it.'

'You heard her, didnya?'

'Yes. But you still could have planned it,' Junto said. He walked toward the foyer. At the door he turned to Boots. 'Well?' he said.

'Don't worry, Mack,' Boots said coldly. 'She'll come around. Come back about ten o'clock.'

He closed the door quietly behind Junto. He hadn't intended to in the beginning, but he was going to trick him and Junto would never know the difference. Sure, Lutie would sleep with Junto, but he was going to have her first. He thought of the thin curtains blowing in the wind. Yeah, he can have the leavings. After all, he's white and this time a white man can have a black man's leavings.

Junto had pushed him hard, threatened him, nagged him about Lutie Johnson. This would be his revenge. He locked the door leading to the foyer and put the key in his pocket. Then he headed toward the kitchenette in the back of the apartment. He'd fix a drink for Lutie and one for himself.

The murmur of their voices came to Lutie in the bedroom. She couldn't hear what they said and she waited standing in front of the door, listening for some indication that Junto had gone.

As soon as Junto left, she would go home. But she had to make certain he had gone, because if she walked outside there and saw him she would try to kill him. The thought frightened her. This was no time to get excited or to get angry. She had to be calm and concentrate on how to keep Bub from going to reform school.

She'd been so angry just now she had forgotten that she still had to get two hundred dollars to take to the lawyer. Pop might have some ideas. Yes, he'd have ideas. He always had them. But she was only kidding herself if she thought any of them would yield two hundred dollars.

There was the sound of a door closing, and then silence. She looked out into the living room. It was empty. She could hear the clinking sound of glasses from somewhere in the back of the apartment.

And then Boots entered the room carrying a tray. Ice tinkled in tall glasses. A bottle of soda and a bottle of whiskey teetered precariously on the tray as he walked toward her.

'Here, baby,' he said. 'Have a drink and get yourself together.'

She stood in front of the fireplace, holding the glass in her hand, not drinking it, just holding it. She could feel its coldness through her glove. She would go and talk to Pop. He'd lived three steps in front of the law for so long, he just might have a friend who was a lawyer and if Pop had ever done the friend any favors he might take Bub's case on the promise of weekly payments from her.

And she ought to go now. Why was she standing here holding this glass of liquor that she didn't want and had no intention of drinking? Because you're still angry, she thought, and you haven't anyone to vent your anger on and you're halfway hoping Boots will say something or do something that will give you an excuse to blow up in a thousand pieces.

'Whyn't you sit down?' Boots said.

'I've got to go.' And yet she didn't move. She stayed in front of the fireplace watching him as he sat on the sofa, sipping his drink.

Occasionally he glanced up at her and she saw the scar on his cheek as a long thin line that looked darker than she had remembered it. And she thought he's like these streets that trap all of us — vicious, dangerous.

Finally he said, 'Lissen, you want to get the little bastard out of jail, don't yah? What you being so fussy about?'

She put the glass down on a table. Some of the liquor slopped over, oozing down the sides of the glass, and as she looked at it, it seemed as though something had slopped over inside her head in the same fashion, was oozing through her so that she couldn't think.

'Skip it,' she said.

Her voice was loud in the room. That's right, she thought, skip it. Let's all skip together, children.

All skip together. Up the golden stairs. Skipping hand in hand up the golden stairs.

'Just skip it,' she repeated.

She had to get out of here, now, and quickly. She mustn't stand here any longer looking down at him like this, because she kept thinking that he represented everything she had fought against. Yet she couldn't take her eyes away from the ever-darkening scar that marred the side of his face; and as she stared at him, she felt she was gazing straight at the street with its rows of old houses, its piles of garbage, its swarms of children.

'Junto's rich as hell,' Boots said. 'What you got to be so particular about? There ain't a dame in town who wouldn't give everything they got for a chance at him.' And he thought, Naw, she ain't acting right. And she was all that stood between him and going back to portering or some other lousy, stinking job where he would carry his hat in his hand all day and walk on his head, saying 'Yessir, yessir, yessir.'

She moved away from the fireplace. There wasn't any point in answering him. Right now she couldn't even think straight, couldn't even see straight. She kept thinking about the street, kept seeing it.

All those years, going to grammar school, going to high school, getting married, having a baby, going to work for the Chandlers, leaving Jim because he got himself another woman — all those years she'd been heading straight as an arrow for that street or some other street just like it. Step by step she'd come, growing up, working, saving, and finally getting an apartment on a street that nobody could have beaten. Even if she hadn't talked to Bub about money all the time, he would have got into trouble sooner or later, because the street looked after him when she wasn't around.

'Aw, what the hell!' Boots muttered. He put his glass down on the table in front of the sofa, got up and by moving swiftly blocked her progress to the door.

'Let's talk it over,' he said. 'Maybe we can work out something.'

She hesitated. There wasn't anything to work out or talk over unless he meant he would lend her the money with no strings attached. And if he was willing to do that, she would be a fool not to accept it. Pop was a pretty feeble last resort.

'Come on, baby,' he said. 'Ten minutes' talk will straighten it out.' And she went back to stand in front of the fireplace.

'Ain't no point in your getting mad, baby. We can still be friends,' he said softly, and put his arm around her waist.

He was standing close to her. She smelt faintly sweet and he pulled her closer. She tried to back away from him and he forced her still closer, held her hands behind her back, pulling her ever closer and closer.

As he kissed her, he felt a hot excitement well up in him that made him forget all the logical, reasoned things he had meant to say; for her skin was soft under his mouth and warm. He fumbled with the fastenings of her coat, his hand groping toward her breasts.

'Aw, Christ, baby,' he whispered 'Junto can get his afterward.' And the rhythm of the words sank into him, seemed to correspond with the rhythm of his desire for her so that he had to say them again. 'Let him get his afterward. I'll have mine first.'

She twisted out of his arms with a sudden, violent motion that nearly sent him off balance. The anger surging through her wasn't directed solely at him. He was there at hand; he had tricked her into staying an extra few minutes in this room with him, because she thought he was going to lend her the money she so urgently needed; and she was angry with him for that and for being a procurer for Junto and for assuming that she would snatch at an opportunity to sleep with either or both of them. This quick surface anger helped to swell and became a part of the deepening stream of rage that had fed on the hate, the frustration, the resentment she had toward the pattern her life had followed.

So she couldn't stop shouting, and shouting wasn't enough. She wanted to hit out at him, to reduce him to a speechless mass of flesh, to destroy him completely, because he was there in front of her and she could get at him and in getting at him she would find violent outlet for the full sweep of her wrath.

Words tumbled from her throat. 'You no good bastard!' she shouted. 'You can tell Junto I said if he wants a whore to get one from Mrs. Hedges. And the same thing goes for you. Because I'd just as soon get in bed with a rattlesnake — I'd just as soon ——'

And he reached out and slapped her across the face. And as she stood there in front of him, trembling with anger, her face smarting, he slapped her again.

'I don't take that kind of talk from dames,' he said. 'Not even good-looking ones like you. Maybe after

I beat the hell out of you a coupla times, you'll begin to like the idea of sleeping with me and with Junto.'

The blood pounding in her head blurred her vision so that she saw not one Boots Smith but three of him; and behind these three figures the room was swaying, shifting, and changing with a wavering motion. She tried to separate the three blurred figures and it was like trying to follow the course of heat waves as they rose from a sidewalk on a hot day in August.

Despite this unstable triple vision of him, she was scarcely aware of him as an individual. His name might have been Brown or Smith or Wilson. She might never have seen him before, might have known nothing about him. He happened to be within easy range at the moment he set off the dangerous accumulation of rage that had been building in her for months.

When she remembered there was a heavy iron candlestick on the mantelpiece just behind her, her vision cleared; the room stopped revolving and Boots Smith became one person, not three. He was the person who had struck her, her face still hurt from the blow; he had threatened her with violence and with a forced relationship with Junto and with himself. These things set off her anger, but as she gripped the iron candlestick and brought it forward in a swift motion aimed at his head, she was striking, not at Boots Smith, but at a handy, anonymous figure — a figure which her angry resentment transformed into everything she had hated, everything she had fought against, everything that had served to frustrate her.

He was so close to her that she struck him on the side of the head before he saw the blow coming.

429

The Street

The first blow stunned him. And she struck him again and again, using the candlestick as though it were a club. He tried to back away from her and stumbled over the sofa and sprawled there.

A lifetime of pent-up resentment went into the blows. Even after he lay motionless, she kept striking him, not thinking about him, not even seeing him. First she was venting her rage against the dirty, crowded street. She saw the rows of dilapidated old houses; the small dark rooms; the long steep flights of stairs; the narrow dingy hallways; the little lost girls in Mrs. Hedges' apartment; the smashed homes where the women did drudgery because their men had deserted them. She saw all of these things and struck at them.

Then the limp figure on the sofa became, in turn, Jim and the slender girl she'd found him with; became the insult in the moist-eyed glances of white men on the subway; became the unconcealed hostility in the eyes of white women; became the greasy, lecherous man at the Crosse School for Singers; became the gaunt Super pulling her down, down into the basement.

Finally, and the blows were heavier, faster, now, she was striking at the white world which thrust black people into a walled enclosure from which there was no escape; and at the turn-of-events which had forced her to leave Bub alone while she was working so that he now faced reform school, now had a police record

She saw the face and head of the man on the sofa through waves of anger in which he represented all these things and she was destroying them.

She grew angrier as she struck him, because he seemed to be eluding her behind a red haze that obscured his face. Then the haze of red blocked his face out completely. She lowered her arm, peering at him, trying to locate his face through the redness that concealed it.

The room was perfectly still. There was no sound in it except her own hoarse breathing. She let the candlestick fall out of her hand. It landed on the thick rug with a soft clump and she started to shiver.

He was dead. There was no question about it. No one could live with a head battered in like that. And it wasn't a red haze that had veiled his face. It was blood.

She backed away from the sight of him, thinking that if she took one slow step at a time, just one slow step at a time, she could get out of here, walking backward, step by step. She was afraid to turn her back on that still figure on the sofa. It had become a thing. It was no longer Boots Smith, but a thing on a sofa.

She stumbled against a chair and sat down in it, shivering. She would never get out of this room. She would never, never get out of here. For the rest of her life she would be here with this awful faceless thing on the sofa. Then she forced herself to get up, to start walking backward again.

The foyer door was closed because she backed right into it. Just a few more steps and she would be out. She fumbled for the knob. The door was locked. She didn't believe it and rattled it. She felt for a key. There was none. It would, she was certain, be in Boots Smith's pocket and she felt a faint stirring of anger against him. He had deliberately locked the door because he hadn't intended to let her out of here.

The anger went as quickly as it came. She had to go back to that motionless, bloody figure on the sofa. The stillness in the room made her feel as though she was wading through water, wading waist-deep toward the couch, and the water swallowed up all sound. It tugged against her, tried to pull her back.

The key was in his pocket. In her haste she pulled all the things out of his pocket — a handkerchief, a wallet, book matches, and the key. She held on to the key, but the other things went out of her hand because as she drew away from him she thought he moved. And all the stories she had ever heard about the dead coming back to life, about the dead talking, about the dead walking, went through her mind; making her hands shake so that she couldn't control them.

As she moved hurriedly away from the couch, she almost stepped on the wallet. She picked it up and looked inside. It bulged with money. He could have given her two hundred dollars and never missed it.

The two hundred dollars she needed was right there in her hand. She could take it to the lawyer tonight. Or could she?

For the first time the full implication of what she had done swept over her. She was a murderer. And the smartest lawyer in the world couldn't do anything for Bub, not now, not when his mother had killed a man. A kid whose mother was a murderer didn't stand any chance at all. Everyone he came in contact with would believe that sooner or later he, too, would turn criminal. The Court wouldn't parole him in her care either, because she was no longer a fit person to bring him up.

She couldn't stop the quivering that started in her stomach, that set up a spasmodic contracting of her throat so that she felt as though her breath had been cut off. The only thing she could do was to go away and never come back, because the best thing that could happen to Bub would be for him never to know that his mother was a murderer. She took half the bills out of the wallet, wadded them into her purse, left the wallet on the sofa.

Getting back to the foyer door was worse this time. The four corners of the room were alive with silence — deepening pools of an ominous silence. She kept turning her head in an effort to see all of the room at once; kept fighting against a desire to scream. Hysteria mounted in her because she began to believe that at any moment the figure on the sofa might disappear into one of these pools of silence and then emerge from almost any part of the room, to bar her exit.

When she finally turned the key in the door, crossed the small foyer, and reached the outside hall, she had to lean against the wall for a long moment before she could control the shaking of her legs, but the contracting of her throat was getting worse.

She saw that the white gloves she was wearing were streaked with dust from the candlestick. There was a smear of blood on one of them. She ripped them off and put them in her coat pocket, and as she did it she thought she was acting as though murder was something with which she was familiar. She walked down the stairs instead of taking the elevator, and the thought recurred.

When she left the building, it was snowing hard. The wind blew the snow against her face, making her walk faster as she approached the entrance to the Eighth Avenue subway.

She thought confusedly of the best place for her to go. It had to be a big city. She decided that Chicago was not too far away and it was big. It would swallow her up. She would go there.

On the subway she started shivering again. Had she killed Boots by accident? The awful part of it was she hadn't even seen him when she was hitting him like that. The first blow was deliberate and provoked, but all those other blows weren't provoked. There wasn't any excuse for her. It hadn't even been self-defense. This impulse to violence had been in her for a long time, growing, feeding, until finally she had blown up in a thousand pieces. Bub must never know what she had done.

In Pennsylvania Station she bought a ticket for Chicago. 'One way?' the ticket man asked.

'One way,' she echoed. Yes, a one-way ticket, she thought. I've had one since the day I was born.

The train was on the track. People flowed and spilled through the gates like water running over a dam. She walked in the middle of the crowd.

The coaches filled up rapidly. People with bags and hatboxes and bundles and children moved hastily down the aisles, almost falling into the seats in their haste to secure a place to sit.

Lutie found a seat midway in the coach. She sat down near the window. Bub would never understand why she had disappeared. He was expecting to see her tomorrow. She had promised him she would come. He would never know why she had deserted him and he would be bewildered and lost without her.

Would he remember that she loved him? She hoped so, but she knew that for a long time he would have that half-frightened, worried look she had seen on his face the night he was waiting for her at the subway.

He would probably go to reform school. She looked out of the train window, not seeing the last-minute passengers hurrying down the ramp. The constricton of her throat increased. So he will go to reform school, she repeated. He'll be better off there. He'll be better off without you. That way he may have some kind of chance. He didn't have the ghost of a chance on that street. The best you could give him wasn't good enough.

As the train started to move, she began to trace a design on the window. It was a series of circles that flowed into each other. She remembered that when she was in grammar school the children were taught to get the proper slant to their writing, to get the feel of a pen in their hands, by making these same circles.

Once again she could hear the flat, exasperated voice of the teacher as she looked at the circles Lutie had produced. 'Really,' she said, 'I don't know why they have us bother to teach your people to write.'

Her finger moved over the glass, around and around. The circles showed up plainly on the dusty surface. The woman's statement was correct, she thought. What possible good has it done to teach people like me to write?

The train crept out of the tunnel, gathered speed as it left the city behind. Snow whispered against the windows. And as the train roared into the darkness, Lutie tried to figure out by what twists and turns of fate she had landed on this train. Her mind balked at the task. All she could think was, It was that street. It was that god-damned street.

The snow fell softly on the street. It muffled sound. It sent people scurrying homeward, so that the street was soon deserted, empty, quiet. And it could have been any street in the city, for the snow laid a delicate film over the sidewalk, over the brick of the tired, old buildings; gently obscuring the grime and the garbage and the ugliness.

THE END